The Best Short Stories 2024

The O. Henry Prize Winners

Guest Editor:
Amor Towles

Series Editor:
Jenny Minton Quigley

Vintage Books
A Division of Penguin Random House LLC
New York

In memory of Peter Matthiessen
—Amor Towles

Contents

Introduction • xi
  Amor Towles

Roy • 3
  Emma Binder, *Gulf Coast*

The Soccer Balls of Mr. Kurz • 18
  Michele Mari, translated from the Italian by Brian Robert
  Moore, *The New Yorker*

Orphans • 36
  Brad Felver, *Subtropics*

The Home Visit • 65
  Morris Collins, *Subtropics*

The Import • 85
  Jai Chakrabarti, *Ploughshares*

Didi • 101
  Amber Caron, *Electric Literature*

Serranos • 123
   Francisco González, *McSweeney's Quarterly Concern*

Hiding Spot • 143
   Caroline Kim, *New England Review*

Junior • 165
   Katherine D. Stutzman, *Harvard Review*

My Good Friend • 173
   Juliana Leite, translated from the Portuguese by Zoë Perry,
   The Paris Review

The Castle of Rose Tellin • 188
   Kate DiCamillo, *Harper's Magazine*

Rain • 201
   Colin Barrett, *Granta*

Marital Problems • 212
   Robin Romm, *The Sewanee Review*

The Last Grownup • 231
   Allegra Goodman, *The New Yorker*

The Honor of Your Presence • 245
   Dave Eggers, *One Story*

The Paper Artist • 282
   E. K. Ota, *Ploughshares*

The Room-Service Waiter • 307
   Tom Crewe, *Granta*

Seeing Through Maps • 318
   Madeline ffitch, *Harper's Magazine*

The Dark • 336
   Jess Walter, *Ploughshares*

Mobilization • 348
   Allegra Hyde, *Story*

*The O. Henry Prize Winners 2024: The Writers
   on Their Work* • 357
Publisher's Note: A Brief History of the O. Henry Prize • 375
How the Stories Are Chosen • 379
Afterword • 381
   Jenny Minton Quigley
Publications Submitted • 385
Permissions • 407

Introduction

In serving as the judge of this year's O. Henry Prize, I have been reminded of the special role that surprise can play in the reading of a short story.

For a variety of reasons, surprise is less significant in our experience of the novel. Often, when we begin to read a novel, we already know something of what it contains. After all, a description of the book is typically included right there on the dust jacket. Many reviewers, in their published critiques, rely heavily on synopsis. When friends recommend a novel or mention what they're reading in their book group, they will generally give us a sketch. And many novels we are drawn to read are already part of the cultural conversation because they are revered classics or contemporary bestsellers.

For all these reasons, when we pick up a novel and turn to the first page, before we start reading the opening sentence, we often have a sense of the journey on which we are about to embark. At minimum, we probably know whether the story takes place in the past, the present, or the future. We probably know where it is set, be that Paris or New York, the South or at sea. We may have a mental picture of the central character and a general sense of the book's themes. In all likelihood, we already have identified the novel on a categorical matrix, having gleaned from various sources that it is either uplifting or tragic, comic or romantic, a page-turner or a slog. While the reality of this pre-awareness in no way undermines the pleasure or enrichment we can have from reading a novel, it does tend to diminish the overall role that surprise is going to play.

But there is a more fundamental reason that our surprise is likely to be tempered when reading a novel, and that is because the artistic intention of the novelist tends to run counter to our experience of surprise. Practically speaking, novelists understand that a book detached from time and place, unclear in its direction, and obscure in its syntax will only be tolerated by the typical reader for so many pages. Thus, it is rarely the intention of a novelist to mystify. Rather, in preparing the opening chapters of a novel, most authors—consciously or unconsciously—are trying to *orient* their readers. They are carefully describing the setting, establishing the times, and introducing the principal characters so that readers can venture forth into the narrative proper with a sense of context and confidence.

Revisit any novel you admire, and you may be surprised to discover how much information the author imparts in the first fifteen pages in order to situate you in the world of the story to come. Here, for example, are just the first three sentences of Edith Wharton's *The House of Mirth:*

> Selden paused in surprise. In the afternoon rush of the Grand Central Station his eyes had been refreshed by the sight of Miss Lily Bart.
>
> It was a Monday in early September, and he was returning to his work from a hurried dip into the country; but what was Miss Bart doing in town at that season?

What a bounty of information we receive from this brief passage. Geographically, we are in New York City, or more specifically,

Manhattan. Temporally, we can sense the era in which the story is set from the fact that it is rush hour in a train station and yet Selden refers to the woman he observes as "Miss Lily Bart," a combination of modernism and quaintness that points to the early twentieth century. Although we don't know it yet, Wharton has just introduced us to the book's two central characters and given us critical insight into their situations. Of Selden, we know that he has a job (so he is not a man of leisure), but he has just spent the weekend "dipping into the country" (so he has the habits of the well-to-do). He appears to be single (he's traveling alone), and he is clearly attracted to the acquaintance whom he has happened upon by chance. As for Miss Bart, she is obviously unmarried and apparently of that social class that has the liberty to leave the city for the entire summer. Finally, in this brief sketch, Wharton is giving us a glimpse of two of the novel's overarching themes—the influence of class in New York society, and the life of the unmarried woman as an object of public admiration, curiosity, and opinion.

Alternatively, here are the first three sentences of Gabriel García Márquez's masterpiece *One Hundred Years of Solitude:*

> Many years later, as he faced the firing squad, Colonel Aureliano Buendía was to remember that distant afternoon when his father took him to discover ice. At that time Macondo was a village of twenty adobe houses, built on the bank of a river of clear water that ran along a bed of polished stones, which were white and enormous, like prehistoric eggs. The world was so recent that many things lacked names, and in order to indicate them it was necessary to point.

Given the colonel's name and the fact that Macondo was once made up of adobe houses, we can guess from Márquez's opening sentence that we are somewhere in Latin America. In the sentence, the author also alerts us that we are about to enter a saga that will span from "that distant afternoon" when the colonel was a boy, Macondo a village, and ice a novelty; through a period when the unnamed country has modernized enough to have a standing army; to "many years later," a point at which political upheaval has led to firing squads. Tonally, Márquez introduces us to the magical realist style for which he is famous by fancifully referring to the colonel's childhood as a time when "many things lacked names." And thematically, he reveals that the book we are about to read will be a tug-of-war between the traditional and the modern, between the individual and the state, and between memory and the historical record.

But as in most novels, Wharton and Márquez do not rely on the first three sentences to orient their reader. They spend pages establishing our sense of the landscape and times. They give detailed descriptions of architectural spaces, the appearances and personalities of key characters, the interrelationships of families, prevailing socioeconomic factors, and events from the past that have bearing on the present. And much of this is laid out before anything of significance happens.

The author's interest in orientation does not end with the first few chapters. Many of the aesthetic tools with which the novelist constructs meaning rely upon the reader's cumulative familiarity with characters, events, and images. To appreciate a story's narrative arc, the evolution of its protagonists, the layering of its interlinked events, and the resonance of its repeated motifs, readers must not only remember what they've read but be constantly updating their sense of where they are in the tale.

A final aspect of the novel that runs counter to the experience of surprise is the thematic power of inevitability. In the culminating chapters of a well-crafted novel, when the unexpected suddenly occurs, our initial surprise is usually followed quite quickly by a sense of the event's inevitability. Upon reflection, we realize that everything the author has laid out in the preceding pages— the family histories, the characters' personalities, the course of events—has led to the dénouement inescapably. This prefiguring is the very essence of Shakespearean tragedy. The murder of Desdemona by Othello, the death of Hamlet at the hand of Laertes, the misguided suicides of Romeo and Juliet—these wrenching events are unavoidable outcomes. That is what separates them from instances of deus ex machina, when a problem intrinsic to a story is resolved, unsatisfyingly, through a sudden intervention, an unlikely occurrence, or the revelation of a new piece of information.

Suffice it to say that inasmuch as surprise plays a role in the novel, it is a subservient one, diminished in its power thanks to reader pre-awareness, authorial orientation, and the dictates of narrative inevitability.

What I have said above in regard to the novel cannot so easily be said of the short story.

First, it is quite unusual for us to begin a short story with a sense of what it is about. Whether we read the story in a periodical, an anthology, or an author's collection, we will not find a synopsis of it on the dust jacket. Most stories we encounter haven't been summarized in a review or sketched out for us by a recommending friend. Even when we consider the stories of the most revered practitioners, very few have entered the popular consciousness. And for those that have (Edgar Allan Poe's "The Tell-Tale Heart," Shirley Jackson's "The Lottery," Ernest Hemingway's "Hills Like White Elephants"), it is generally because they were taught to us in school.

So, when we read the opening sentence of most short stories, we are delightfully in the dark. Without the pre-awareness that accompanies novels, we don't know where or when the story is taking place. We don't know what sort of person will be at its center, whether male or female, old or young, black or white, Asian or Latino. We don't know if the narrator is omniscient, an interested observer, or the principal player. We don't know if the tone is going to be cynical or wistful, compassionate or angry, unnerving or hilarious. Which is all to the better. For our discovery of each of these elements as we read the story will provide its own little jolt of surprise.

And it's sure to require some discovery on our part, because a short story writer will not orient us in the manner of a novelist. By definition, a short story must have a greater economy of expression. It can't dedicate the first fifteen pages to introductory information with which to establish familiarity and context through detailed descriptions of settings or personal histories. The whole story may well be *over* in fifteen pages!

Given a short story's brevity, its author cannot make use of many of the aesthetic tools with which the novelist generally constructs meaning. All of those elements of craft must be either curtailed, abbreviated, or abandoned. Instead of describing a narrative arc in its entirety, the short story writer provides us with a closely observed moment. Instead of revealing the evolution of a character through time, we get a glimpse of a personality. Instead of a series of interlinked events, we are likely to witness a single encounter or occurrence. And instead of an accumulation of harmonious poetic elements, we are presented with images that are striking and haunting, but often in isolation.

Another way of putting this is that we experience surprise differently in the novel than we do in the short story because of textual dilution. As we read a narrative, we can experience the pleasure of surprise in relation to almost any element of craft: we can be surprised by a turn of events; by something a character says; by an allusion, an image, a word. But a novel is made up of a plethora of actions, hundreds of images, and tens of thousands of words. So, in the context of a novel, the power of any one of these individual surprises tends to be watered down.

In the context of a short story, however, the exact same surprise—whether it's a turn of events, an image, or a word—is sure to have more potency. It will stand out more prominently, linger in our consciousness more durably, and play a more powerful role in our formulation of thematic meaning.

By way of example, let's consider Raymond Carver's "Cathedral." Only fifteen pages long, the story focuses on just a few hours in the lives of three people spent in two adjacent rooms. The narrator begins by telling us that his wife has invited her old boss—a recently widowed blind man whom she hasn't seen for ten years—to visit. When she brings the blind man home from the train station, they all have a few drinks, eat dinner, and then return to the living room, where they drink some more, smoke some dope, and converse late into the night with the television on in the background.

In crafting this story, Carver makes little effort to orient us. Neither the narrator nor his wife is ever named. We never learn their ages, their appearances, or their professions. We don't learn how they met or how long they've been together. We don't know where they live, other than that it is reachable from New York City by the Hudson River line. We do learn that the narrator doesn't like his work, has no plans to quit, and smokes marijuana every night. More generally, we sense that he and his wife are part of the vast American population of hardworking men and women with jobs, rather than careers, living in modest houses with no clear ambitions for the future.

While the narrator does not physically describe himself or his wife, he describes the blind man in vivid detail. This is in part because the visitor, when he arrives, upends the narrator's expectations of how a blind man would appear. He doesn't carry a cane, for instance, or wear dark glasses. He is heavyset and balding with a full beard. He has a booming voice and chain-smokes.

Earlier, the narrator has shared with us two details about his wife's relationship with her old boss: first, that on her last day working with him, the blind man asked to touch her face, feeling her every feature with his fingers; and second, that the two of them have maintained a close friendship by sending cassette tapes back and forth on which they describe their lives. Both of these details seem to unnerve the narrator a little, and he is openly ambivalent about the blind man's visit.

But late that night, while the narrator's wife has nodded off, a documentary about cathedrals comes on the television. At the blind man's request, the narrator tries to describe a cathedral, but he can't seem to do the structure justice. So, the blind man suggests they draw one together. The narrator finds a pen and grabs a shopping bag after shaking out some old onion skins. He spreads the bag out on the coffee table. The two men sit side by side on the carpet. Then the blind man closes his hand over the narrator's hand, and the narrator begins to draw.

In reading Carver's story, we have no pre-awareness of its contents. He provides us little in the way of orientation. There is no time for a narrative arc or character development. There is not an elaborate cumulation of images, allusions, and metaphors. There is no prefiguring of how it will all end. Instead, we are invited to witness a brief encounter in which there are a number of wonderful little surprises—a series of unanticipated elements, each standing out in sharp relief against the sparseness of the tale.

Among these I would include the very notion of a blind man coming to visit; the image of the blind man touching the narrator's wife's face on their last day of work; the fact that they have maintained a relationship all these years by cassette tape; the blind man's request that the narrator draw a cathedral with him; the narrator's use of a shopping bag as drawing paper; and his discovery of the onion skins at the bottom of the bag, a strange little detail that all of us can visualize. But most surprising is the culminating image of this unnamed narrator in his nondescript home with his nondescript job finding himself seated on the carpet with a blind man's hand closed over his own as he attempts to draw a cathedral for the first time in his life. It is an image that startled me and moved me when I first read the story forty years ago, and it has stayed with me ever since.

By definition, a surprise can't be announced, anticipated, or prefigured, which is to say, it must come out of the blue. But the power of surprise can also be diminished in its aftermath through explanation and elaboration. In other words, the most powerful surprises come without preamble or epilogue. And that is why the short story is so well suited to delivering them.

As the editor of this edition, I am envious of you for all the delightful surprises you have yet to experience in the pages ahead.

Amor Towles
New York City
October 2023

The Best Short Stories 2024

Emma Binder

Roy

IN THE SUMMER between seventh and eighth grade, my dad's brother, Uncle Roy, came to watch my sister Missy and me while our parents saw our grandma Lori die. Lori lived in an aluminum shack down in Nebraska; she was our mom's mother, but our mom couldn't travel two states southward alone, couldn't be trusted to drive herself. That summer, she was trapped in her brain's dark aquarium, prone to sobbing while drying dishes or seeing something bloody on TV. Over breakfast, she once glimpsed a prop plane flicker through the window in the sky, wandered out there in bare feet to look at it, and didn't return until the next morning. She needed our dad to chaperone.

Missy and I had never met Uncle Roy, but we'd seen a single photo: in it, he stood on a dirt road outside his slouch-roofed ranch house in the Upper Peninsula, wearing denim overalls and no shoes, head globed in wiry red hair. He looked nothing like our dad. To embroider the scene, Roy held a scrawny raccoon aloft in his hands like it was Simba in *The Lion King*. He and our dad only talked once a year, on Christmas, but he was the only person they could find to watch us on short notice.

We'd also heard stories: Roy drank too much, ate skinned snakes and possums. Roy, at ten years old, tried to train-hop from

Iron Mountain to the Catskills to live in a hollowed-out tree. Roy had once hosted a poker game where a man got shot, but when the police arrived, they found no gun and a room full of men who claimed the bullet came through the window.

"If he starts drinking, call us," our dad said to me the day before Roy arrived. "If he brings anyone over, call us. He promised not to bring a gun, but if he does, what do you do?"

"Call you," I said.

On the day they left, Roy careened too fast into our neat gravel driveway in the North Woods, driving an old Ford Ranchero with blisters of rust on its matte black hood. It was mid-July. I could hear aluminum cans and loose tools sliding around his truck bed. By the time he pulled up, our mom was already in the car with her purse and suitcase, lying fully prostrate in the back seat.

Before our dad left the house, he bent to kiss my and Missy's foreheads. "If there was anything I could do, I'd do it," he said.

From our bedroom, Missy and I heard Roy and our dad exchange muffled words in the kitchen. Then the kitchen door slammed, and we heard our dad backing his car down the driveway. Missy and I crept out of our room. We found Roy drinking a carton of apple juice in the kitchen. He looked like he did in his photo but older: his coarse orange hair wild but tinseled silver, his clothes faded as if leached of their color by rain. A violet scar stretched from his temple to his chin, cleaving his face like a crack in a vase. He looked at us and grinned. A tooth was missing from either side of his mouth.

"My nieces," he said. "In living color. You two look just like your mom."

He put down the juice and started pulling drawers in the kitchen and pantry. He rummaged through the fridge and freezer, opening jars of vinegar and bacon grease to smell what was inside. Then he started on the living room, opening desk drawers, slipping spare quarters and matchbooks into his pockets. Missy and I waited in the kitchen, listening to him scrounge through all the rooms of our house, until we finally heard him make his way to our bedroom.

I marched into the hallway and found him standing in our doorway.

"That's our room," I said, standing before him with my arms crossed. Missy stood behind me, watching. He turned around.

"I get it," Roy said, slowly looking from Missy to me. "She's the princess, and you're the tough guy."

Missy and I both blushed with pleasure.

That night, Roy told us he was off to find a drink, and peeled down the driveway in his Ranchero. Two hours later, he marched into the kitchen with a twelve-pack of Miller, three scratch tickets, and a rifle wedged under his armpit.

As soon as Missy saw the gun, she started to cry.

"Don't worry," Roy said. "I'll show you how to hold it."

"We need to eat dinner," I said.

"Sure," Roy said. "I know that."

Roy cracked a beer and got cooking: Hamburger Helper from the pantry, fried in Crisco and Kraft steak sauce. The room bloomed with steam and the smell of fat. Missy, at eight years old, hung in the kitchen doorway, while I sat at the kitchen table, watching Roy drink two, three, four beers in the span of a half hour.

"Is it true you eat snakes?" Missy said shyly, half-hiding behind the doorway.

"I've been known to eat a snake or two," he said. "But that's not the craziest thing I've ate."

He'd eaten cow tongues, he told us, shoe tongues, cattails, prison food. He'd eaten hundred-year-old pickled eggs from behind a bar shelf in Houghton. You're lying, we said, and he shrugged, then set two bowls before us of Hamburger Helper that turned my stomach before I even tasted it. Roy himself didn't eat it, just headed to the screened-in porch with a beer in his front overalls pocket and a pouch of tobacco. Smoke wafted through the kitchen window and mingled with the overhead lamplight, at which point I realized that smoke was still curling from the stove. I got up to shut off the burner, and when I turned around, I found Missy dramatically scraping her meal into the garbage.

"When are Mom and Dad coming back?" she said, eyes glassed over with tears.

"Not until Lori dies," I said. I squeezed her shoulder. "Come on. It's not like Mom does much better."

Roy wobbled back inside, garbed in cigarette smoke, and handed us each a scratch ticket. He showed us how to rub off its coating with a penny. Missy gave a yelp: she'd won twenty dollars.

"Lucky girl," he said. "I'll redeem that for you." Missy handed him the ticket and he slid it into his pocket, never to be seen again.

That summer, I'd just become friends with two girls from school named Natalie Golding and Lauren Shipley. I already knew that our friendship wasn't going to last, but I felt lucky to have friends at all. I'd been eating lunch by myself for years. They treated me like a project they'd undertaken with burdened hearts: they somberly taught me how to braid my hair at sleepovers, told me what music to listen to, sternly chided me when I said something odd. One night they dressed me up in Natalie's clothes, since she and I were supposedly the same size: flare jeans, a tight pink shirt, and a dust-blue patent leather belt. I stood in front of them in Natalie's room while they stared, heads cocked.

"I don't know what it is," Natalie said. "It's like it doesn't fit." She circled me once.

"Can you stand up straighter?" Lauren said. I pulled my broad shoulders back.

"I guess that's better," Natalie said. "Sort of."

I was already expending huge amounts of energy to look and act more like a girl: tweezing the fledgling hairs between my eyebrows, shaving my legs and armpits, wearing my mom's drugstore lipstick at school. That year, I'd finally quit wearing the loose-fitting boy's clothes that I'd liked since I could remember. None of it felt natural, but what did? Becoming friends with Natalie and Lauren seemed like a fluke, a lucky accident that the universe would soon correct. In the meantime, I tried to learn, copying the way Natalie's sentences curled at their ends, or how Lauren, who took year-round ballet and gymnastics lessons, walked as if led by a firm kite string.

I rode my bike to Natalie's house a few days after Roy showed up. Just that afternoon, he'd taken me and Missy into the back-yard, rifle in hand, and set up a line of beer cans on a stump. It was time we learned how to shoot, he told us. My dad's instructions rang in my ears—*What do you do?*—but Roy was unlike anyone I'd ever met, and something told me that if I didn't learn everything he had to teach me, I would never get another chance.

When I got to Natalie's, I told her and Lauren about Roy and the gun. The bone-splitting sound of it. The way I sent bullets into the crowns of trees, and all Roy did was whoop, like I'd done something great. I pulled the front of my shirt down and showed them where a violet-blue bruise was already growing on my collarbone from the rifle's kickback.

"That sounds dangerous," Natalie said, glancing at Lauren.

"It totally was," I said. I felt exhilarated and strange. I plopped down on the floor of Natalie's room. "What do you guys wanna do?"

"We were going to ride bikes to the ice cream shop," Natalie said. "You can come. Unless you want to shoot people with your uncle."

I rolled my eyes and stood up. "Let's go," I said.

I bounded down the stairs and pulled on my white high-tops from the Salvation Army, then walked outside with Natalie and

Lauren close behind me. Natalie's mom, Mrs. Golding, was in the yard in a visor and sunglasses, hosing the hedges. "You girls ride safe," she said, waving as we biked down the drive.

On our way into town, Natalie and Lauren pulled ahead of me, talking in tones that I couldn't hear. Sometimes their friendship with each other seemed coded and secretive, characterized by a barrier I couldn't pass. I pedaled faster, replaying Mrs. Golding's words: *You girls, you girls, you girls.* I always winced when I heard those words, as if bitten.

Behind them on the road, I tried to pedal faster, focusing only on the crunch of my tires against gravel and the steady pulse of my heart. Ahead of me, Natalie and Lauren erupted in laughter, like two roses blooming at the same time.

Most days Roy slept until noon or one o' clock, so Missy and I spent our mornings watching PBS in the hot living room with the windows open. Dust from the sofa seats wafted through sunlight like flour. When we got bored, we did handstands in the yard in bare feet or wandered in the woods that bordered our backyard, where a skinny creek unspooled like a piece of yarn off Torch River. These mornings, I felt like I was only waiting for Roy to get up and make my life interesting.

Then we would hear the slam of the refrigerator door, heavy boot-steps on the floorboards: Roy had sprung alive and started drinking.

First thing, he started making phone calls. He called a guy in Manistique who owed him money, then another guy who he claimed was his friend but never picked up the phone. Then he left a rambling voicemail on the machine of a woman named Daisy in the Upper Peninsula, who, we gathered, had recently left him for another man. He told Daisy's machine that he was getting his act together. When he got back to Houghton, he would light candles for her, reel in the stars, buy her gold hubcaps, whatever.

"I'm at my brother's place," he rambled into the phone. "These girls need me, honey. But I'll be back as soon as I can, my flower, my love."

Missy and I listened to him from the living room with the TV on mute. Then he readied his tackle box and went fishing in the backwoods creek. Missy and I trailed behind him through the woods, asking him questions.

"Do you have a job?" I asked.

"I'm a purveyor of what other, lesser men call trash," he said.

"Why do you drink so much?" Missy said.

"To ease the pain of my memories."

"What's your worst memory?"

"Wouldn't you like to know!"

Downstream from Roy, we waded in the creek while he fished for brown trout. We listened to him curse and mumble and sing out-of-tune Hank Williams. I watched him thread worms on a hook with his broad, coarse hands graven in dirt. When the sun started angling slantwise through the pines and mosquitoes came out in droves, the three of us made our way back to the house, at which point Roy started drinking with a real sense of purpose.

Nights, he took off in his truck for the Blue Dog, a gravel-lot bar a few miles down the road with flickering neon in the windows. Depending on if he lost or won money playing pool, he came back in either a grand or a foul mood. One late night, he brought a woman home. Tense in our side-by-side twin beds, Missy and I heard her voice through our bedroom door, shining through the dark like an axe blade.

"Who is that?" Missy said, her voice small.

"How should I know?" I said.

Missy started to cry softly into her pillow. "I don't like him," she said.

"Shh," I said.

Music came on from the kitchen radio and the woman laughed. Glasses clinked, Roy let out a hoot, the music turned up. After not too long, we heard them stumbling into our parents' room, where through the thin walls we could hear them breathe and moan. Missy put a pillow over her head but I went on listening, trying to imagine what the woman looked like.

The sounds didn't last long. My throat was dry, heart pounding. I felt the way I did when I bought candy from the cashier named Willa at the Rhinelander Sunoco, a high school senior who had long brown hair with streaks of red, ears laddered with silver rings. I always tried not to look at her face, but instead watched her hands as she counted change. They were small and deft. I fell asleep thinking of coins slipping between her fingers, clattering to the counter. Her narrow hands reaching to pick them up again.

My dad phoned one night from the hospital in Nebraska where our grandmother was dying.

"How's everything up there?" he said. "Is Roy drinking?"

I thumbed a bottle of Old Crow on the counter. "No. Everything's good."

"He's not acting strange? He's feeding you?"

"Yep."

"What did you eat last night?"

I thought back to the last dinner I'd had at Natalie's house. "Casserole. And a salad with croutons."

"That doesn't sound like Roy," my dad said. "But I'll take it."

"How's Grandma?"

"Like we expected," he said. A steady beeping noise pulsed in the background. "Your mom's fine. Don't worry about her. We'll be back as soon as we can, okay?"

"Okay," I said.

"Sit tight," he said. "And look after your sister."

Roy shot and cooked a possum living under our porch steps. He rustled between couch cushions for change. He came home one evening with a burst vessel in his eye, blood stitching the cracks in his teeth, from a pool game gone sour. Some nights he stumbled inside after a night at the Blue Dog and wept into Daisy's voice-mail machine.

"I'm hurting," he cried. "I've got nobody. I'm in this strange town, and these girls need me, honey, but I'm here all alone . . ."

The night after his pool fight, I found Roy on the screened-in porch, looking contemplative. He'd decided to stay home, he said, while his eye and his pride healed. The broken blood vessel made his right eye look livid and evil. I sank into the chair beside him and asked him to tell me about the time he ran away to the Catskills.

"You ever read that book *My Side of the Mountain*?" he said. "No? I don't know what happens in schools anymore." He sank into his chair and took a long pull from his bottle of Old Crow. "I packed some bread and clothes and my dad's Swiss Army knife. It was easier than you might think. Early in the morning, I took off for the trainyard, and made it across state lines before the police caught me and took me home."

"Why did you do it?"

He drank again and looked out the screened window. The porch light came ablaze in his red and silver hair, dousing him in what looked like a halo. "I just didn't fit in," he said. "Not like your dad always did. I wanted to live in a different way, getting dirt in my teeth." When he looked at me, his eyes were shining. "You're a little rougher than some. You understand."

I nodded. I did, I did.

One evening, Roy drank more than usual and had an idea: we would all go to the casino together.

"You girls play slots before?" he said.

We shook our heads. Before Roy had mentioned it, I didn't even know there was a casino in Rhinelander.

"Let's go," he said. He tucked a half-empty fifth of Jim Beam into the front pocket of his overalls and pulled his boots on, then stumbled out the kitchen door without tying his laces. We followed him and climbed into his truck. As he backed down the driveway, he veered to the left and drove into a lilac bush.

"Goddamn," he said, and pulled forward. "Fuckin' trees everywhere." On the second try, he made it onto the road. All the way to the casino, he drifted onto the shoulder and braked too hard at stop signs. I thought I was going to be sick. Missy burrowed her head in my armpit. But we eventually pulled into the parking lot of a huge building, as big as a hotel.

"Like riding a limousine to heaven," Roy mumbled.

We followed Roy inside, where we found a brave new world of light and sound and smoke. Slot machines made sounds like coins dropping into bright tin cans. Missy latched herself to my hip, gripping my hand so tightly I had to shake her off. Patrons sat wreathed in cigarette smoke, fixed on machines or broad green tables with cards and dice. Roy gave us each two dollars and told us he was going to play blackjack.

"Win big," he said, and wandered off.

Missy and I lingered for a few minutes behind a man playing slots, her head burrowed in my hip, while I studied what he did. It seemed simple enough. We sat down behind a slot machine and had just fed it all four of our dollars when a uniformed woman walked up to us.

"Hey," she said, squinting at us. "How old are you two?"

"I'm thirteen," I said. "She's eight."

"That's not good," the woman said. "You here with your parents?"

"Our uncle."

"Where's he?"

We pointed him out. Roy sat slouched forward at the blackjack table with one overalls strap falling off his shoulder.

"Let's get this sorted out," she said. The three of us walked over to Roy. She tapped him on the shoulder. "Did you bring these kids in here?" she said.

Roy looked at us. "They're my lucky stars," he said.

"This is no place for little girls," she said.

"Did you say little girls?" Roy stood up and stumbled. I could see the black cap of his Jim Beam poking out of the top of his overalls pocket. "This one here," he said, pointing at me, "is the toughest guy I know."

"All right," she said. "Time to go."

"Let me finish this game."

"Not a chance," she said. "Get out or I'll call the police."

Roy raised his hands. "Hey. We're on our way." He pulled the Jim Beam from his overalls pocket and took a sip. "We're on our way."

The woman scowled. We followed Roy out of the casino, the uniformed woman walking close behind us. People stared at us, but I walked with my chest puffed out, proud as hell: *the toughest guy I know.*

Roy seemed clearer and calmer as we drove home, as if the bright lights of the casino had shocked him into sobriety. He turned the radio on and sang along softly. Back on the dark road leading back to our parents' house, we saw a grouse dart through his headlights. To our surprise, Roy swerved into the right shoulder, hitting it with his right front tire, eliciting a bright shriek from Missy.

Roy pulled over to the right and asked for his work gloves from the glove box. I handed them to him.

"Why did you do that?" I asked.

"Don't worry," he said. "Just a little North Woods hunting."

On the bench seat between us, Missy began to cry. "It's dead," she said.

"That's right!" Roy said cheerfully. He got out of the truck. In the glare of his headlights, we watched him kneel at the front tire and stand up, holding the bloodied bird in his gloved hand. He held it by its broken neck and waggled it for us in front of the windshield. Missy let out a sob. He circled to the back of the truck, threw the grouse in the bed, and got back behind the wheel.

"It's an ancient rivalry, girls," he said to us. "Bird versus truck. Bird never wins."

The next night, after helping Roy dress and quarter his grouse, I went to Natalie's house for dinner. It had only been a week since I'd last seen Natalie and Lauren, but it could have been years; I felt older from spending time with Roy, steely and changed. When Natalie opened the door, I felt her looking long at my clothes and face before letting me inside. I followed her to the kitchen, where Lauren was sitting at the table and Natalie's mom stood over the sink, washing pans. She looked at me and paused.

"Sophie," her mom said, looking at my jeans. "Is that blood?"

I thumbed a rusty spot on my thigh. "Me and my uncle went hunting."

"You need to change clothes, sweetie," she said, furrowing her brow. "I'll go get some of Natalie's from the dryer."

She left the kitchen and I stood there, suddenly afraid to touch anything or sit down. Natalie and Lauren stayed sitting at the kitchen table, staring at me. They had chicken and green beans on their plates, paper towels folded into halves.

"You have a feather in your hair," Lauren said flatly.

I rustled around and found it: a single mottled grouse feather, which I plucked from my hair and laid on the tablecloth. All three of us stared at the small brown feather. I should have felt ashamed, but I felt giddy and proud.

"I think I'm gonna go," I said after a long beat of silence. "I have to help my uncle with something."

I turned and walked out of Natalie's house, knowing that it was all over, just like I knew it would be.

That night, I found Roy on the screened-in porch, drinking alone and rolling a cigarette. Shiny dried grouse blood stained the front of his overalls.

"Back so soon?" he said.

"Yeah," I said, sinking into the chair beside him. "What are we doing tomorrow?"

Roy clumsily lit his cigarette. "What do you want to hang around with an old man for?" he said. "You don't have any other friends?"

My face flushed. I suddenly felt burning mad at Roy. I got up to leave the porch and he waved me back down.

"Sit," he said. "Just teasing you."

We watched bugs circle the overhead porch light for a while.

"You looking forward to your mom and dad coming home?" he said.

"Not really," I said, thumbing the coin of blood on my jeans.

"Is that so."

"My mom cries all the time. She just sits around all day."

"Well, she's an odd woman," Roy said. "I never thought she was right for your dad."

In the dark, a howl gleamed from the woods. Roy got up, opened the screen door. The porch light seemed trapped inside his nest of hair, which he threw back at the sky as he hollered back into the dark. I could see the moon wobbling over the pines, brimful and gibbous, as if about to spill.

"You know your mom and I once made love," Roy said, wheeling back around. He let the screen door slam behind him. "She's a wild horse. I've got a porch around my heart for that woman, to this day."

I sat quietly for a moment, absorbing the idea. "Does my dad know?" I said.

"Maybe," he said, easing back into his chair. "Or maybe he's willed himself not to." He looked at me and shook his finger. "You can't help who you love, Sophie. It's your fate."

"What about Daisy?"

"Daisy?" he said, as if surprised that I knew the name. "Well, sure. A person needs company."

As I was getting ready for bed that night, Roy's words circled around my head: *it's your fate, it's your fate*. I thought about Willa at the Sunoco, her long fingers, the little shells of her ears. My fate.

I stood for a long time in the bathroom after brushing my teeth, staring at myself. In the two weeks that Roy had been at our house, I'd forgotten to shower more than once or shave my legs. My unbrushed hair had grown matted and thick. I looked wild. A thumbprint of dirt smeared my cheek. I felt different, full of strength and hot blood, like I would never again go back to school, wear someone else's clothes, or pretend to be what I wasn't.

A few days later, the phone rang. It was our dad. Lori had finally died, he told me, and now he and our mom were on the road back from Nebraska. They would be back late that night, or early the next morning.

"Let me talk to Roy," he said.

I peered through the kitchen window. Roy's truck was gone, I told him.

"Well, tell him we'll be there soon," he said. He sounded worn thin.

I lay awake all night, buzzing with dread. At three in the morning, I heard the distinctive sound of Roy's Ranchero pulling into the driveway, then the slam of the kitchen door, and his heavy boots stamping through the living room. Several hours later came another car and the muffled sounds of our parents talking through the window. Dawn crept forward, dousing my bedsheets in pink and white.

I crawled out of bed and shook Missy awake. We met our parents as they were walking into the kitchen, where Roy's gun sat propped against the wall, and beer cans cluttered the table and counter. My mom looked older than she had when I last saw her, her face scribbled with pain, hair listless and greasy. Her arms felt thin as she hugged me. Then we heard a groan, and in came Roy from the living room, wearing the rumpled clothes he fell asleep in, boots still on his feet.

His face changed when he saw our mother. They stood still for a moment, apprehending each other. What passed between them was silent and electric. She stepped forward to try to slip past him on her way to her bedroom, but Roy reached to take her hand. She pushed him away.

"Don't," she said.

Our dad, meanwhile, seemed not to see their exchange. He was too busy staring at the state of the kitchen: the gun, the beer cans and bottles, cards and cigarettes littering the table.

"Roy," he said, his voice quavering. "What is all this?"

Missy and I went back to our bedroom before too long. But we heard their whole fight unspooling through our window: Our dad cursing out Roy, Roy howling with laughter, our dad throwing beer cans at his truck until he drove away. Cans rattling in Roy's Ranchero bed as he sped down the driveway and onto the road. His bright, unruly hair shining almost audibly through the rear truck window.

Eventually, our dad came into our room and knelt between my and Missy's beds, where we sat with our knees pulled up to our chins. He told us that he was sorry, he should have known better; everything would go back to normal now. But I knew that it wouldn't, even if I never saw Roy again. I didn't want it to. The room was thick with light. There was a spark growing inside me, calling me into a different future, like a train hurtling fast into the wilderness.

Michele Mari

Translated from the Italian by
Brian Robert Moore

The Soccer Balls of Mr. Kurz

F OR BRAGONZI, the only beautiful thing in the sad life of the
boarding school in Quarto dei Mille was the soccer matches.
And yet even that beauty was anguished. He realized it as early
as the first match, when he saw that, once the moment came to
shoot, even the best, even the oldest players, suffered a kind of
muscular contraction, as if forcing themselves to hold back; and,
in fact, what emerged was a weak, uncertain shot, which the goalie
blocked with ease. And to think that a second earlier that same
forward had seemed full of confident vigor, impetuously swooping down onto the ball, defending it, rushing with long strides
toward the goal area—but then . . . but then that feeble shot.

Only at the third match did he make up his mind to ask, after
he'd happened to give a hard kick and the ball, flying upward,
just barely missed going over to the other side, beyond the wall
that constituted the end of the schoolyard: "Aaaah . . . ," all the
little boys groaned in chorus, covering their eyes with their hands,
and when the ball fell back down into the schoolyard, rather than
rejoicing, they rebuked Bragonzi bitterly. "But why? What did I
do wrong?" he asked Paltonieri as they went back inside for snack
time. "And even if the ball did go over, why make such a big deal
about it?"

And so Paltonieri explained. He said that on the other side of the wall lived a Mr. Kurz, whom no one had ever seen but who must have hated all the boarding-school children, because whenever the ball ended up on his side he never gave it back (as is civil and urbane custom: you've sent it hurtling over there and now you anxiously wait, speculating by the wall, and, lo, by silent miracle it returns, tracing its trajectory in the sky, returning, returning—and with your heart overflowing with gratitude you give resounding thanks: "Thank you!" you say, you don't know to whom, but you say it. Or else the miracle is delayed, and you walk away uncertainly, saddened by the game's forced end; but when you come back the following morning the ball is there in the yard, for how long you don't know, and so your "thank you" is all the more heartfelt, because you only think it, addressing it to the past). Not only that, but vain would have been any attempt to get the ball back; at least this was what was claimed by the young instructresses, who, a long time ago, caving to universal insistence, had gone over to speak to Mr. Kurz. "Mr. Kurz is well within his rights," they apparently relayed with an air of annoyance, "and can keep whatever makes its way into his yard." Such a response, noted Paltonieri, who had heard the story from Morchiolini, sent the message that the instructresses hadn't put much of an effort into their mission: if only the boys could have gone themselves, just once, to speak to that man, maybe they would have convinced him, maybe he would have yelled at them a little, sure, but in the end he would have given back all the balls confiscated that year and, who knows, even in previous years. But nothing could be done, the rules barred the boys from leaving the school, and, besides, what would be the point? Mr. Kurz had said no to them, and they were schoolmistresses—never mind a bunch of snot-nosed kids! For that matter, the instructresses had added, from that day forward they would not be going back to see that man. They had a sense of dignity, they did, and they weren't interested in being humiliated by someone who—they stressed with a hint of sadism—happened to be correct!

Of course, Paltonieri continued, if the school had been endowed with an ample supply of soccer balls, there would be nothing to get upset about in all this; if they lost one they could requisition another, and Mr. Kurz could do as he pleased. But the reality was that the endowment of balls not only wasn't ample but wasn't even provided for, and the boys had to make do with the odd privately owned ball. "Do you understand what this means?" Paltonieri pressed Bragonzi, now thoroughly worked up. "It means having to keep tabs on the new kids, the ones who've just arrived with a suitcase full of toys, and hope that they have a ball, and, if they do, persuade them to lend it to us, giving them gifts, which is already enough to make them suspicious, maybe the ball is new and so they guard it jealously, and if you try to take it away from them they squeal and then the instructresses come running, understand? And when you've finally convinced them—you've given them heaps of trading cards and comics, promised them they'll also get to play, even if they're so little they don't have a clue what a soccer match is—when finally it's all worked out and the game begins, *pow!*, some idiot kicks the ball over the wall, and we're ruined. And it's not even possible to get our parents to buy balls when they come to see us and take us to Genoa, because visiting days are on Sunday and everything's closed . . . You know today's ball, the one you almost sent over to the other side? It's Randazzo's, and to get it he had to write to his dad a month ago, telling him to bring it last Friday, and his dad lives in Messina and only comes twice a year, understand?"

Bragonzi understood, and he understood, too, that theirs would never be real matches but monstrosities, unnerving endeavors in which, more than the struggle between the two teams, what counted was the unspoken battle being played between all of them and that cruel man lying in wait. As months passed, this image grew and grew in Bragonzi's mind, and he became accustomed to thinking of Mr. Kurz as an enormous black spider, motionless in the middle of his yard but lightning fast when pouncing on the balls that fell like fat insects into his web; then, seizing them with his foul legs, horrifically he sucked till there was naught left but the floppy remains . . . This rapacity was the scariest thing of all, because it enveloped the soccer ball even before it went over the wall, beckoning it and infecting it with a bluish leprosy, so that playing with it was a bit like contracting that disease, or like conversing with a man condemned to death; at other times, it seemed to him that the ball was a beautiful woman promised in marriage to a jealous tyrant, and that terrible torments awaited the reckless fool who dared so much as to graze her.

It was but little consolation that he now played on a permanent basis for the Weenies. Dividing all the boys into Champs and Weenies had been thought up by Saniosi, whose intellect, faced with the impossibility of resolving the problem of Mr. Kurz, had at least conceived of a way to transform that nightmarish presence from a paralyzing element into an active part of the game. What he proposed was simple, and founded on the eradication of switching sides at halftime: the Weenies would always shoot at the goal chalked on the dormitory wall, the Champs at the one on the wall separating the schoolyard from Mr. Kurz; that way, Saniosi thought, the fear of losing the ball would hinder the Champs, weakening their abilities and thus leveling the playing field. And so it was—but for the fact that they all wanted to be welcomed into the ranks of the Weenies, and to this end deliberately tripped themselves up, displayed profound shortcomings in technique never previously revealed, spread their legs wide open so as to garner the supreme humiliation of the nutmeg. It became necessary to form a tribunal of memory keepers, who by punctiliously citing past dribbling and counterattacks, crosses and headed goals, forced the Champs to face, with no chance of appeal, their own talent.

So Bragonzi was a Weenie, but this didn't prevent him from

noticing during the games—almost absorbing it from the uncertain looks in the eyes of the Champs—a general sense of distress. This feeling only worsened after the episode with Lamorchia.

It happened as follows: For an agonizingly long week, the boys were left without a ball, to rave, bored, in the emptiness. Then, on Sunday, Tabidini's dad took his son to Genoa. Seeing him heave a sigh in front of the lowered shutter of a toy store, he questioned the boy and, finding out the truth, gave a good long laugh; then, without another word, he took his son by the hand and pulled him along until they reached the nearest park, where several gangs of children were playing ball. "Which would you like?" he asked, encompassing in a single wave of his hand that entire swarm.

"What do you mean, 'which'?" gulped Tabidini, who had understood perfectly.

"Don't you worry about it. There must be a ball here that tickles your fancy more than the others, no?"

Tabidini observed: over here, the children were gratifying themselves with an unsizable rubber sphere, colorful and flabby, the kind for little kids; another group, right behind them, was scrambling around a ball that was more serious but also deflated— you could tell from the noise it made and from its pitiful bounce. Tabidini looked beyond the drinking fountain: over there was the biggest showdown, with at least ten players per side, and the ball was sound, but lightweight, too, made of taut plastic, one of those balls that shoot up bizarrely, almost taking flight of their own volition, no, no, too dangerous, a real shame, though; to their left, in a completely grassless area, enshrouded in an earthy cloud, six desperately lanky dawdlers were playing with a dirt-colored ball of an indecipherable nature; he looked at them more closely— they didn't have "the goods" and were playing in loafers, their long socks pulled up to their knees, a scraping of soles, a slip-sliding amid expletives. Tabidini waited for the ball to emerge for an instant from the dust cloud to observe it more carefully: huh, it was leather, one of those prehistoric hand-stitched balls, with a wide valve like a ten-lira coin and that nutty color that had been vanquished long ago by black-and-white, weighty and lumpy and somewhat pear shaped, of a mineral substance that had been chemically enriched over the years with mud and emotions . . . Headaches and blackened nails lay in store for the imprudent soul who opted for that ball, no thank you, better take a look at that other group in the field all the way at the far end; he asked his father for permission to go, then walked through the park until he was close enough to taste this new match—a match into which fathers and sisters had been frivolously mixed, a match that was revolving, alas, around an exceedingly light beach ball, literally lighter than a feather, a complimentary item included with the purchase of sunscreen for the sportily benighted. Disheartened, Tabidini went back to his dad, with one last glance at some other pilgrims who were blissfully delighting—poor fools!—in a felt tennis ball.

"Well, then?"

Tabidini was about to reply that he wasn't exactly spoiled for choice when he was distracted by the simultaneous arrival of four cars, then of two more right after. Out of them came twenty or so older adolescents in tracksuits, loaded with gym bags and duffel bags. It was enough for one of them to tweak his hamstring muscles, tenderizing them a bit, for Tabidini, melting with emotion, to understand: yes, he didn't need to see over it to know what was behind the park's high gray wall, the group's clear destination. A real soccer field! A real match! he thought, now liquefied, just as one of the last adolescents, having rested his duffel on the ground, pulled out a plastic bag, which he opened and then put back down, laying bare its contents: shimmering in the morning light of the sun, so new and untouched as to appear enameled, flawlessly round, soft and taut at once, planet of glory, the most beautiful soccer ball Tabidini had ever seen. Propelled by an irrepressible impulse, he slipped his chubby hand out of his father's and started to run toward the player, who had remained behind his companions and was now meticulously closing his duffel bag. As soon as he was close enough to make out the words, Tabidini stopped, and he read, "World Cup." Oh! His heart skipped a beat. And then, right below, in a different pentagon, "Official Soccer Ball—Patented—Licensed—Tested," and slightly lower still, "No. 3." But what made Tabidini's eyes bulge out of his head was the signature, the uttering signature stamped along the length of two other pentagons (at first glance he didn't want to believe it, looked more closely at the squiggle—but, yes, it was true, beyond a shadow of a doubt): "George Best." Best! Best's soccer ball! The greatest player of them all! The legend who was invoked after every intoxicating mazy run! At school, they'd only ever had one ball with a name on it: "Totonno Juliano," it was called, it even bore Juliano's picture, though the product was made of plastic, brought back from Naples by Fiorillo—a good ball, but nothing more, and, in any event, after just a few days it became the prey of Mr. Kurz. But this one! And Best's, to boot! Desperately he turned toward his father, who started to walk over. Meanwhile, the adolescent, giving a shout to his companions, sent the ball their way, essentially inviting them to have a taste. Tabidini was no stranger to that weakness, that yielding to the temptation to try out a new ball while still off the field and out in the street, despite knowing full well that the rough concrete would leave a mark on its luster—as if the owner, unable to bear so much perfection, wanted to artificially dirty and age the ball in order to finally recognize it as his own.

Mr. Tabidini knew his son. Without saying a word, he trotted over to the youngsters, whom he reached right at the little iron gateway in the wall. At a distance, his son watched them talk: his father on one side, the others curved around him in a semicircle, their bags placed on the ground. They were shaking their heads, gesticulating nervously. Then his father took his wallet out of his jacket and started sliding out bills. The players shook their heads some more; then, seeing that he was still pulling out bills, they started to discuss the matter among themselves. One of them moved off, gesturing as if to tell another to go to hell, though he soon came back. Now Tabidini's dad was standing there in silence; one guy came right up to him, shaking his fists, but three others grabbed him and shoved him out of the group. The discussion continued until Tabidini's father finally stuck his fingers back into his wallet. When Tabidini saw one of the players pick the ball up and hand it to his father, he thought he was dreaming. Kissed by the sun as he walked back (the adolescents, behind him, went on gesticulating and arguing), Tabidini's father looked like a paladin returning with the Grail.

That evening, in a jubilant riot of oohs and ahs, Tabidini was greeted as a hero by the entire boarding school, and every boy, before falling asleep, fantasized in his bed about the match announced for the following day. So radiant was the image of George Best that, for one night, there was no room in their heads for Mr. Kurz.

What followed was something horrific, and each boy found himself suddenly older. Bragonzi was left with the special sorrow of having failed to touch the ball even once. It was only a minute into the game, and the Champs were on the attack, when the ball rebounded and went soaring into the air like a sublime bird: in everyone's consciousness it came back down in slow motion, while below a roaring, elbowing melee raged. In the general confusion, no one noticed Lamorchia—only Bragonzi saw him getting ready to kick a volley: "No! No!" he shouted, or maybe he merely thought it, while the ball descended with unreal slowness, and already that kid was slanting, twisting his upper body and rearing back his right leg, already he was bending his knee as he lifted his shoe off the ground, "No! No!" not like this, not in the air, let it bounce, but Lamorchia couldn't hear him, it was as though he were being drawn heavenward, ankle first, every sensory faculty now transferred to that ascending ankle, into that outward thrust that is called an instep. Abandoning the man he was marking, Bragonzi dived into the melee toward Lamorchia, imploring him all the while, sending him messages, and then, in a flash, everyone realized, and froze as if turned to stone, limbs caught and tangled, and, unable to give voice, each one thought inside himself, Don't do it, don't do it, no one daring to look at Lamorchia's ankle, looking only at his swooning eye, captivated by his bliss and at the same time horrified . . . *Pow!* went the ball as it was struck from too low and from the side, rising once again, though no longer vertically, rather in an excruciating, mournful trajectory: Best's soccer ball fell precisely on the flat top of the wall, taking everyone's breath away, and then, after an imperceptible stasis, it plunged down definitively on the other side, and became the property of Mr. Kurz.

No one did Lamorchia any harm, because the harm was locked in their hearts. Lamorchia himself, for that matter, was never the same after that day, nor did he ever again wish to play soccer: he could be seen off at the edge of the field, sitting like a pensioner warming himself in the afternoon sun, and when the ball wound up in his vicinity, and shouts of "Ball!" were directed at him from the field, he would pick it up, but, not having the courage to kick or throw it, he would carry it all the way to the center of the field, squeezing it to his chest, and, once there, set it down with care.

Six months had passed since that day, during which at least twelve balls had made their way to Mr. Kurz. Then, tired of so much heartache, the boys ceased to play except with balls of knotted rags, which had the advantage of never leaving the ground: monstrous turbans that kept up the fiction of sphericality for no more than half an hour before starting to unravel, coarse comets dragging a tail of dusty tatters. After four months of this punishing humiliation, Bragonzi stopped one fine fall day in the middle of a rightward attack, and amid general protest grabbed that simulacrum of a ball in his hands.

"Companions, friends," he would have said if he had been an ancient tribune, "consider who we are, who we have been, and, gazing upon yourselves in this ignominious rag as in a mirror, may you hence derive sufficient shame to spur you to redeem a life perhaps not yet lost to the cause of Soccer. Think of those who, scorning danger, preceded us on this selfsame field, and let it conjure within you those Greats in whose shadow all of us, in regrettably distant days of yore, sought to shape ourselves: Tumburus, Fogli, Mora, Pascutti, Bobby Charlton, Chinesinho, del Sol. They are watching us—and do we not shudder? And yet we hesitate?"

His words were not these, naturally, but this was the spirit, and the result—judging by the gritting of teeth—was no different from the one such a speech would have inspired. And so war was declared, but for the moment, needing also to fight on the internal front with the instructresses, and not knowing what they would find on the other side of the wall, they limited their actions to the launching of a reconnaissance mission. In the insanity of the hour, everyone volunteered, but it was unanimously decided that if there was one among their number to whom the honor of that mission was rightfully owed, it was Bragonzi. To decide who would join him, they proceeded to draw lots, from which emerged the names of Tabidini and Sieroni.

At two o'clock that night, Bragonzi slid out from under his covers and, feeling his way along the walls in the dark, came to the end of the hallway, where their instructress's bedroom lay. He knocked three times, and when she opened the door, disheveled and furious and searching in the shadows for whoever the pest was, he said in one breath, "Quick, come, Tabidini is unwell!" While she ran to the afflicted, though not before covering her shoulders with a shawl, Bragonzi infiltrated her room and rummaged through everything (resisting the distraction of stockings and lace) until he found the coveted bunch of keys. Then, after hiding them in a carefully selected spot in the bathroom, he went back into the dormitory, giving the agreed-upon signal to Tabi-dini, who promptly ceased his stertorous gurgling.

An hour later, when silence reigned anew, Bragonzi and Sieroni got dressed and slipped like thieves to the bathroom, and, with the keys retrieved, were now masters of the boarding school. First, they opened the janitor's closet, grabbing a flashlight and a hand-some collection of screwdrivers; then, after unlocking two other doors, they exited onto the field, and suddenly (or was it only a shiver from the freezing air?) it was as though Mr. Kurz could see them. One last door, to the gardener's shed, and they came into possession of a long ladder. Bragonzi tried his best not to think about what he was doing, and, actually, thanks to a hint of fever, he was aware of it all as though he were already remember-ing it, as though it were a thing of the past: the ladder, which was slightly shorter than the wall; the struggle to stand it upright like an Egyptian obelisk; Sieroni hesitating, owing to an onset of second thoughts, which resulted in a necessary rebuke; his own frightening ascent, rung after rung, with the terror of spotting over the top of the wall the first of the eight hairy legs; his precari-ous balancing act up at the top followed by the work of lifting the ladder and lowering it on the other side, first pushed from below by Sieroni, then held solely with his own strength; the cold air on his face and the impossibility of seeing anything whatever on Mr. Kurz's side; Sieroni's whimpering invitation to turn back; and, at last, his descent into the darkness below.

After landing in Kurz's yard, Bragonzi stood a long while in silence, until, all being quiet, he finally turned on the flashlight. The yard was small, much smaller than the school's, and not paved. Here, then, on this earth, was where the balls fell. In front of him, a low house, two stories, its windows shut: Kurz's house. The yard was bordered on the sides by two walls that were as tall as the one he had just climbed, but along the left wall ran a strange, glimmering structure. Bragonzi approached it and saw that it was made of glass, with leaded panes: Kurz's greenhouse. He tried to look inside, but the glass offered back only the flashlight's glow. The perfect place to hide the ladder, he thought, for if Kurz sees it I'm a goner. His next thought was that the screwdrivers would now come in handy, but there was no need for them: the little door to the greenhouse was closed by a latch with no padlock, and that things could be so easy immediately brought back to mind the ghastly mouth of the spider.

Having flung the door wide, Bragonzi dragged and then pushed the ladder inside, making sure to erase the grooves left on the ground: he had seen this done in movies by American Indian women to the tracks of their shining warriors. Now that he was shut inside the greenhouse, he turned the flashlight back on to better conceal the ladder, and he saw them. He saw all of them, all at once, and with them the generations, the jerseys, the hopes, the dashes and dives.

The greenhouse was filled with three long shelving units, two units on the sides and one in the center, like a kind of backbone, resulting in two parallel corridors; each had seven rows of shelves, each row a continuous line of flowerpots, each pot holding a soccer ball. Slightly larger in diameter than the pots, the balls protruded by three-fourths, touching one another at the sides like the segments of a monstrous caterpillar. Stunned, unsure whether to be horrified or to rejoice, his heart rioting in his chest, Bragonzi moved closer and focused the beam of light on the first ball on the shelf to his left. It was an incredibly old ball, more gray than brown, completely peeled and with several unstitched seams. He touched it: the coarsest thing he had ever felt. There was something written on the pot in black block letters, faded with time: "May 8, 1933." Bragonzi was trembling. He shone the light on the next ball: this one looked worn out like an old sweater, and, busted, dented, and covered in tarlike stains, it had sunk deeper than the others into its pot; here, too, the pot bore a faded inscription: "November 13, 1933." It's a dream, Bragonzi thought, refusing to understand. He slowly went down the corridor, moving the beam of light: February 4, 1934; April 28, 1934; May 16, 1934; June 2, 1934; June 18, 1934; August 3, 1934; September 3, 1934 . . . then eight balls from 1935, six from 1936, ten from 1937, seven from 1938, five from 1939, none from 1940 to 1945, twelve from 1946, sixteen from 1947 . . . Could it be? He turned from the shelves on the left, and, pointing the light at the central unit, immediately read, "July 21, 1956." This one was a double shelf, each pot corresponding to a pot facing the opposite side; here he ran breathlessly, and read at random, "March 7, 1960," "August 11, 1961." And, finally, the shelves on the right, full of orbs from 1963, from '64, from '65, from '66 . . . Overcome, he sped up his pace as he moved down the aisle, toward the back, where he knew what he would find . . . He would find Fermenti's soccer ball, the very first one he had seen go flying over to the other—to this—side, and Randazzo's ball, there they were! and the "Totonno Juliano" (there! "March 9, 1967," yes, that was the day it had happened), and his own, his red-and-black beloved, it was there, too (he was about to take it but withdrew his hand), and all the others up to Best's, there it was! shining more brightly than the rest in the glow of the flashlight, still unblemished and new smelling, and then all the lost balls up to the day of the conversion to rags, not one was missing, oh, dearest soccer balls! But what sent a shudder running through his entire body was what he saw after the last ball, even if he could have imagined it beforehand: a line of empty pots, ready to welcome new arrivals . . .

He contemplated at length the emptiness of those pots, successively lighting up their interiors, and he wondered where, in that precise moment, the balls destined to fill them were, in what storeroom or window display, and wondered, too, when they would rain down like ripe fruits from over the wall, on what date, a sixteenth of October or a twentieth of March—impossible to say. For now, the boys played with balls made of rags, but someday things would go back to normal, it was inevitable, and on that day Mr. Kurz would be happy once more. What did he think of the temporary suspension of soccer balls? Maybe from the more muffled sound of their kicks he had figured out the truth and was awaiting his hour, as he had since 1933.

Bragonzi returned to the front of the greenhouse and stood before that first ball: looking at it, and thinking that those who had played with it must have been older than his father by now, he considered how the balls with which an individual plays in his life get lost in thousands of ways, rolling down countless streets, landing in rivers and on rooftops, torn apart by the teeth of dogs or boiled by the sun, deflating like shriveled prunes or exploding on the spikes of gates, or simply disappearing, you thought you had them and you look all over but they're nowhere to be found, who knows how much time has passed since you lost them or since someone swiped them at the park; he considered how all of the balls touched by those children had thus dissipated, and if he were in their presence and asked them, "Where are all your soccer balls?" they would shrug, unable to account for the fate of a single one. That ball alone had been snatched from the clutches of destruction; only that ball, from May 8, 1933, went on being a ball. Oh, he knew all too well how things had unfolded, for how many times had he witnessed the same scene! The ball had shot upward, and even before it went over the wall everyone thought, It's lost—goodbye, ball. But no, only in that moment was it saved. And many years later, when all those children went down into their graves, that ball would be more alive than them, the last memory of the matches of yesteryear.

Bragonzi passed one more time through the entire collection, observing more closely some spheres that he hadn't noticed before: a hard and clumpy one resembling a truffle, a still-pristine one on which was written "From Grandma, to her sweet pea," a rubber one with the faces of the players who had died in the Superga air disaster, one with Hamrin's signature forged by an uncertain juvenile hand. And he noticed something else, which brought a lump to his throat: Mr. Kurz had arranged each ball in its pot so as to look its best, the least dented or unstitched part forward, the part with the faces or signatures, as though he loved those soccer balls.

The glow of the flashlight kept growing dimmer, and so Bragonzi decided to turn it off for a little while. In the darkness, after a few seconds had passed, the silhouettes of the soccer balls began to appear like fluorescent specters, first the whiter ones, then slowly but surely the rest, and it seemed to Bragonzi that they were quivering, and that they wanted to say something. Concentrated in that luminescence was the first glimmer of morning, as yet imperceptible in the sky. Before long it would be dawn (had he been in the greenhouse for that long?), and Bragonzi didn't know what to do, whether to turn the flashlight back on and keep looking around, or get out of there, or scope out other areas of the yard. Instead he carried on as before, wandering slowly up and down those two corridors, one moment laying his hands on an orb whose pentagons looked like black fish in a pitcher of water, the next on a globe of gaseous yellow.

The first light of sunrise took him by surprise and convinced him that he should go back. He dragged the ladder to the foot of the wall after being assailed by a gust of freezing air upon leaving the greenhouse. Then, just as he was about to climb the ladder, he noticed something in the middle of the yard, something that had been hidden before in the dark. He moved closer: it was a wooden chair with a wicker seat, turned to face the boarding school. Oh, it didn't take much to understand what the person who sat in it waited for, and Bragonzi shivered at the thought of him sitting there, motionless, patient, day after day from morning till night, saddened by the fruitless days, weeks, months . . . He immediately walked away from the chair, then he went back; he wanted to try to sit in it, and he did. Opposite, one saw only the wall, and, above, the sky, nothing more. He tried to imagine a match taking place behind that wall, Secerni's attacks, Saniosi's feints, Piva's fouls, Fognin's drives. He saw the sweaty faces, the dust clouds, the scraped and scabbed knees, he saw the arguments over offsides and the rock-paper-scissors to decide the teams, he saw the rage and he saw the joy. And he saw a ball spring up from the top of the wall like a black moon from the sea, saw it rise, tracing its arc in the sky, and falling to earth on this side, bouncing a few meters from the chair, then stopping meekly in the dust. Hello, ball, he said, tenderly contemplating it in the light of the dawn.

When he reached the top of the wall, he realized that Sieroni had fallen asleep on the ground, right there below him; he woke him by dropping a shoe on his back. He then pulled up the ladder and climbed back down into the schoolyard. At the first occasion they had to talk about it, his throng of classmates made only a collective impression upon him while—unable to bring any one face or name into focus, surrounded by their disappointed eyes—he told of locked doors and darkness.

It rained the following days, and the schoolyard remained deserted. That Sunday, their instructress told Bragonzi that there was a surprise in store for him, his dad had come from Milan to see him, he was to run and get dressed, chop-chop! His dad took him to a restaurant and then to the movies to see a Lemmy Caution film, after which they strolled around the port looking at the ships. Toward evening they got in a taxi, but instead of giving the school's address his father said, "To the train station." Bragonzi didn't ask any questions, and he kept silent even in the baggage room, where his father reclaimed a big black bag. They returned to the school in another taxi, and only when they were in front of the gate, with the taxi driver waiting to head back to the station, did his father crouch down and open it. The first thing to emerge was an issue of *Soldino,* but already Bragonzi had started to tremble; then came a stick of modeling clay and a little puzzle, and meanwhile the rustling of cellophane could be heard underneath; then there was a balsa-wood model-airplane kit; and then, finally, that transparent bag, which his father gave to him after making him wait longer than for the other presents, as he smiled back in silence and hoped that his tremors weren't visible. "Thank you," he said, and he wanted to add something else, but while he was thinking about what this should be his dad had already gotten back in the taxi. And so Bragonzi hid everything under his raincoat and ran to the dormitory. It was past the hour when boys needed to come back from any outings "already fed," for the rules barred these temporary escapees from joining the others in the refectory during meals (his father didn't know this, since Bragonzi had never been brave enough to tell him), and so there was no one around. After putting the other presents in his closet, Bragonzi sat on the bed with the see-through bag on his knees. It was closed with a thin red drawstring and, in addition to the ball, contained the pump and the needle for inflating it, as well as a little box of wax and a small felt cloth with zigzag edges for polishing: once opened, the bag released a delightful leathery aroma, which reminded Bragonzi of the smell of his nicest pair of shoes. The pump was icy cold, the ball less so. He stuck the needle into its valve and began to inflate it with care: Some of the air in this room, he thought, is going to end up inside there, and it will never come out again. When every last pentagon had popped out convexly, he removed the needle. He spread his thighs slightly apart to better hold the ball, not wanting it to touch the floor. It was magnificent, a Derbystar "Deliciae Platearum," even more beautiful than Best's "World Cup" ball; he couldn't imagine how hard his father must have had to look before finding it, or how much he had paid for it, its white just slightly pearlier than the rest, with iridescent reflections, and black pentagons framed by a subtle red outline, and a little yellow star right underneath its brand name, a ball even Rivera would kick cautiously, truly like nothing he had ever seen before . . . He fondled it awhile with his fingertips and slid it against his cheeks to take in its smoothness, decided to give it a few more pumps, then went back to caressing it. He looked at the clock: before long, the other boys would all be coming back upstairs, he had to be quick. He put the pump and the bag in the closet, and went down to the atrium with the Deliciae Platearum under his arm. From there, he passed through the television lounge before skirting the refectory, crouching down beneath the windows so as not to be spotted by the diners; at the end of the hallway, the door to the schoolyard was open—the instructresses liked to take a stroll right after dinnertime.

It was not yet completely dark in the schoolyard, and from the sky, now that the rain had stopped and the clouds had been torn asunder, Bragonzi could tell that the next day would be a beautiful one. He avoided the puddles as he moved to the center of the soccer field, which was marked with faded white paint. He looked at the ball in his hands, even more beautiful in the moonlight. He checked that the top of his right shoe wasn't muddy, looked at the wall in front of him and then above the wall, too, took a deep breath, looked once more at the ball, threw it into the air, waited for it to come back down, and kicked it with his instep when it was roughly thirty centimeters from the ground, and he knew from the sound it made that he had kicked it well, saw it rise quickly into the air, first darkly silhouetted against a cloud whitened by the moonlight, then brightly against the night sky, and it seemed to rest there, suspended in midair, until it descended, and disappeared behind the black horizon of the wall.

Now he could go back, and bury himself in his bed.

Brad Felver

Orphans

WHEN GUS TOOK ON AN APPRENTICE, a kid eager as a chipmunk, he didn't expect it to last. The shop teacher at the high school had sent the occasional wayward teenager his way over the years, kids who seemed to hang on the precipice of this life or that life. Gus always did what he could, welcoming them out to the farm, walking them through the workshop, his approach to dovetail layout, how to keep the grain downhill while milling lumber. But it was months before he let them touch any tool except the palm sander. He always started them on sanding, and sanding always broke them. They probably thought it was some hazing ritual, but it wasn't that at all. It was a kindness. Sanding exposed temperaments: either you had the right sensibilities for this work or you didn't. Better to find out straightaway.

You could just see the impatience in these kids, visible as a tumor. No, the apprenticeships never lasted. A brief spike of companionship before Gus returned to the long quiet.

But the kid sanded without complaint. Seemed to relish the tedium of it, methodically moving up grits, had a knack for hitting the tightest corners without going cross-grain.

"But how do you know when you're done sanding, sir?" he'd asked his second week. Everything else had a clear end point, but sanding was different. You chose when to be done.

"Sand until this feels like a Siberian labor camp," Gus said. "That's your halfway point."

The shop teacher had warned Macon about the old man. Well, not so much warned as primed. The old man wasn't dangerous, nothing like that, but he was eccentric. A recluse. No one in town knew what to make of him, and mostly they didn't make anything. But rumors still spread like viruses. Sloppy in their cruelty. The hermetic old man on his farm on the edge of town. Rumors left to circulate eventually become true.

One story claimed that he'd been a Catholic priest but then was excommunicated, and another that he'd been a Green Beret in Vietnam. Terrible PTSD, unpredictable and dangerous outbursts. One boy said that the old man sat in his barnyard at twilight, shooting bats with a twelve-gauge just to watch them tumble out of the sky. Rotting bats strewn across the barnyard.

All of these assumed, as rumors do, that the old man had secrets. But it only took about twenty minutes with him to see how wrong they all were. No outbursts or violent impulses. No bat carcasses. A kind, soft-spoken nature. And patience—the old man was like the god of patience, like he had some extra organ. Never rushed, never raised his voice. Never made mistakes, but also never seemed to mind when Macon made them. Plenty of extra lumber, he'd say, and plenty of time to set things right.

No, the rumors got the old man all wrong. Macon still didn't know exactly who the old man was, but he knew who he wasn't. He'd been most struck by how *ordinary* the old man was. Wasn't even eccentric. He was just quiet and sad.

. . .

That spring, Ruth retired from her teaching position at the community college. Her colleagues bought her an ice-cream cake and said good luck as if they would see her again on Monday. She thought it would feel like a new grace, so many free hours, time become expansive, generous. She would take long walks, long baths, would read long books. And she did all of those things. But she hadn't foreseen the loneliness. Not the loneliness of body, of missing another human presence, but the loneliness of obsolescence. The world was a great choir, she stood there nestled in its rows, but now she did not sing.

Harold Gutman, her partner of the past twenty years, still worked long hours and always would. Left before seven and walked down Charles Street to the hospital. She couldn't remember the last time he'd kissed her goodbye.

Her mind turned inward, of course. Tumbled backward into memory. Her life seemed to have changed directions. Somehow, it was memory that now lay before her.

Gus and Annabelle and a backyard full of wet leaves. Annabelle running and jumping and skinning her knees. Ornery as a badger one minute, innocent and cherubic the next. Building dioramas and sledding before sunrise. Fending off requests for a puppy, and then a kitten, and then a gerbil. Sometimes Ruth even laughed. The absurdities of parenthood: single socks scattered around the house like shrapnel, grape juice crusted into Annabelle's nose hair, diapers full of colors that didn't exist anywhere else in nature. And each night, collapsing into bed with Gus, the feeling of exhaustion earned, as if they'd just donated blood.

Dear Gus. A marriage like defiance of destiny. It was worth any catastrophe, in its way. She'd never told him that and wished she could. They'd crashed into each other like asteroids. A wild intensity to that sort of love, an entire lifetime crammed into a dozen years. Life packed so densely it needed an atomic number. But then Annabelle died, and everything ruptured.

Then the Lost Years. A swift divorce. Two decades of silence, an impenetrable barricade, which they erected and defended together. Annabelle's ghost perpetually sat between them, staring, unblinking. They were like escaped convicts who were shackled together. She moved back to Boston, Gus back to the family farm. She settled in with Harold Gutman. It was companionship, not entirely without love. But Gus had the courage to remain alone. He would later admit that there were entire years when he hadn't spoken a word aloud.

And then they'd crashed into each other again. Life had eroded so much of them, and this had neutralized something. They could bear the weight of the past for short stretches. Now they talked on the phone every Sunday. Hearing his voice through the receiver left Ruth feeling like Moses hearing the voice of God.

They talked as people do, about taxes and bad drivers and cholesterol medication. But mostly, they talked about Annabelle, remembered stories aloud, conjuring her bodily, each reminding the other one of the memories. Each had to ensure that someone else was safeguarding them. Because if one of them died, and the other one wasn't clutching that memory, well, then it would just be gone.

The kid still called Gus *sir,* like Gus was some colonel. More than a year now of *yes sir*s and *no sir*s, and it drove Gus crazy. He'd told the kid to just call him Gus, but the kid couldn't manage it, not even now. It was the one direction he hadn't obeyed.

There was a sadness to the kid. Gus recognized it straightaway. He'd devoted the second half of his life to grief. Grieving people have everything in common, and they have nothing in common.

But now the kid was hardly a kid anymore, would be old enough to vote soon. Rounding into a fine woodworker, methodical as an orthopedist. Gus sometimes watched the kid as he set his featherboard or positioned his cauls for a glue-up, and the kid's breathing changed. Got quicker but softer. His concentration was absolute. Like watching an artist work, one who was just a little bit crazy. Van Gogh or Pollock. Ten thousand board-feet run through the table saw, and the work still thrilled the kid, all of it. Still thrilled Gus, too, though his body hurt all the time now. His lungs sagged from sixty years of sawdust. He saw the finish line, and maybe that's what he'd had in mind when he took the kid on.

"All we do," the old man said, "is *remove* wood. You can't add, only remove, and once it's gone, you can't put it back."

He spoke of woodworking as the art of shadow-making. Shadow lines as design features on desks and tables; shadow angles to consider from lamps on desks; inlays on tabletops designed to mimic the shadows. They made sawdust, which was just the shadow of wood.

The old man had strong opinions, like all of the lonely artists. Art required loneliness. But he tried to hold his views close and seemed regretful when he divulged them. Apologized for slipping into sermon. He didn't want to be that sort of man. He even asked what Macon thought. Did he have it all wrong? Shadow-making? He'd been doing this work all his life, and that could be its own sort of burden.

He preferred fixed tenons to loose. Preferred dovetails cut by hand, no jigs, no machines. Preferred his old German marking gauges to mechanical pencils. He designed tables and desks to sit on three legs, not four. A fourth leg was like a malignant growth. It was like saying an obvious thing at a party. His hands were gnarled and bent like an old boxer's. Knuckles with open gashes, though he never seemed to notice.

But wouldn't jigs be easier? Macon asked. And what about those loose-tenon joiners he'd seen? Wouldn't that speed things up?

"Do you not like the work anymore?"

Macon said of course he did. He liked it more than anything.

The old man just nodded, said nothing else, but Macon could see the silhouette of what he hadn't said. *If you like the work, why invent ways to rush through it?*

The furniture they built existed as a sculpture of the old man's mind. He was brilliant, there was no ignoring that, but he was so quiet about it. Maybe even ashamed. Brilliant the way an oak tree is brilliant.

Each day the kid walked out to the farm from town, almost two miles, and the last fifty yards or so, he sometimes ran. Sprinted across the barnyard. Gus had seen him do it, the kid running to the workshop, like a lost child running to his mother.

The first month of his apprenticeship, the kid had shown up at three thirty, directly after school, and hadn't left until after supper time. It didn't take long for Gus to leave him alone in the workshop, and not much longer until he pointed out that the door didn't lock. Didn't even latch, actually. The doorknob had broken years earlier, pulled clean off, and he just leaned a length of bur oak against it. A farmer's dead bolt.

Sometimes the kid forgot to reset the farmer's dead bolt, and the workshop door would catch in the wind, flap back and forth like a sail. If the sun was just right, it would throw shadows across the barnyard. Long, lean shadows, shadows sharp as blades, arcing in wide parabolas. The first time Gus saw them, it pulled him up short. Shadows that seemed to remake the barnyard physically. He stared as a little boy seeing fireworks for the first time.

Gus offered to drive the kid home each evening, but the kid always declined, said, No sir, it was fine, he liked the walk. And if it was okay, maybe he'd stay a little later some nights? Until nine or even ten?

Gus wanted to tell the kid to pace himself. This kind of work accumulated. He'd feel old long before he actually was. But he worried this would sound like an admonishment. Mentors were a lot like dictators. You had to be judicious with that sort of power. Everything you said, or didn't say, would stick.

The kid was an orphan in a town that didn't have orphans. Had no room for them, as no town has room for them. Their only charge is to remain unseen. They are too sad to look at. They look different than other children, can be spotted like weeds in the grass, though no one can say what is so different. People could tell that Gus wasn't the kid's father. Knew instinctively that something was missing from him.

Could you still say that? *Orphan?* Gus wasn't sure, and he wanted to get it right, but how did you figure it out? When nomenclature changed, it seemed like you were supposed to just *know,* and if you didn't, it was probably evidence of some deeply embedded prejudice, and maybe it was. Maybe it really was. He'd never wondered until now, and that had to mean something.

No, Gus hadn't given much thought to the kid's parents, but then the shop teacher called and asked after the kid. This was maybe two months into the apprenticeship. Had Gus seen the kid lately? Apparently he'd dropped out of school and was staying in the basement of the Presbyterian church, which was the town's unofficial homeless shelter.

"What about his folks?"

The shop teacher drew in a breath that felt like a rebuke. "He's an orphan, is all I know."

When Gus brought it up, the church basement, the kid got sheepish as a bird dog. Apologized again and again, seemed afraid that Gus might send him packing.

"I'm just trying to understand," Gus said.

"I can't go back to one of those homes," the kid said. He looked down at his boots.

Gus could feel him coiling up, like a snake that was afraid it might need to strike. He wanted to reassure the kid, tell him that he'd never send him packing. Not ever. He felt bonded to the kid, and he wasn't the sort of man who felt bonded to other people.

"So, your parents . . . ?"

The kid shook his head. He wouldn't say any more about his parents, not right now. There was some terrible story lurking, and it would come out at some point. The kid was awfully young to be so full of scar tissue.

Then the kid started talking, almost like a way to evade questions about his parents, and once he'd started, he couldn't stop. Spoke more words in three minutes than he had in two months. "It's just all I want to do," he said. "Working with wood. Shadow-making. It's just—is this how people feel when they go skydiving? So many little things, like the way you chamfer the edges of your stop blocks or running the bench plane's iron over the diamond plate, the way the sound changes. You can actually *hear* when it's sharp. And the smell. Bur oak all smells like bur oak, that moldy vanilla sort of smell, but every board smells different from the others. Probably because it used to be alive, which you just forget sometimes."

Truth was, Gus admired the kid, even more now. Maybe that was misguided, but he did. In some ways, the kid was stunted. The world had refused him entry. Had no room for him. In other ways, he was an old soul. Already wise, but he didn't know it. Wise people never thought of themselves as wise. God—he was going to be such a remarkable man. Already he knew that no one could understand the intricacies of your heart, not really, and mostly no one cared. And yet he politely declined to be beaten down by any of this. Met the cruelty with industriousness. It was a quiet, daily sort of courage that no one would ever notice. The world offered no one dignity, but the kid would make his own.

Gus remembered youth, barely. He'd spent the first half of his life exploring the world and the second half retreating from what he'd discovered. But the kid was still an explorer. Gus himself felt incapable of that sort of hopefulness now. He felt old, and his body felt heavy, little more than a repository for so much grief accumulated along the way, which was just what happened to people who managed to live long enough.

"Sometimes," the kid said, "it feels like we're giving those trees a whole second life."

Gus nodded but said nothing. He just wanted to keep listening to the kid.

"The way you make furniture, the way you're teaching me, it'll last forever, just absolutely forever, so we're almost making the trees immortal."

"Right," Gus said.

"Just thinking about the workshop makes me homesick," the kid said. "Ever love something like that?"

Gus wanted to hug the kid. He hadn't hugged another person in years, not since his own daughter. Thirty years earlier, when she was a toddler. And then she'd died, and Gus had lived an impenetrable silence ever since. Until this remarkable kid showed up like God's own apology.

The old man set Macon up in the back bedroom, the one with low dormers. It was like a time capsule. A Crosby, Stills & Nash poster on the wall and an old baseball glove with cracked leather hanging from a nail.

Get some new posters if you want, the old man said. Move the furniture around, leave it messy. It was Macon's room now, he said, and he'd never enter uninvited. Did he like bacon or sausage better for breakfast?

Macon lay in bed that first night and listened to the old house groan under a driving westerly wind. He closed his eyes and felt like he was on a ship's prow. The wind beating against the house, the walls trembling. It should have made him feel exposed, but it didn't. The house had endured that wind for two hundred years.

"What about rent?" Macon asked. He had no money at all, nor any way of making any.

"This is an old family place," the old man said. "Can't charge you rent on something I got just by existing."

Macon didn't yet understand about the furniture they were making, had no clue that it had all sold long before it was finished, most pieces for as much as a used Hyundai.

If anyone in town found the arrangement strange, they only whispered it. More likely, no one noticed. Theirs were shadows cast by walking toward the light. Shadows unseen. But the farm, the workshop, its soft halogen lamps spilling onto the barnyard late into the night, that was their world. A population of two, but when they were out there, working together like some precision crankshaft, it felt so much fuller. It felt like intimacy.

Sunday evenings, the phone would ring, and the old man would dash off to his bedroom like he'd heard the smoke detector. It was the only time he hurried. Macon could hear him talking late into the night, that low rumble, and sometimes he even heard laughter. The next day, the old man didn't say anything, but he seemed lighter, like he'd been out dancing.

Sometimes Macon stood in his doorway and listened. He couldn't make out the words, and didn't want to, but he could hear that rumble. Even the old man had someone beyond the boundaries of the farm. No one called Macon, and probably no one ever would. He didn't have an old family house where he could retreat. It made him wonder—would the old man have kept him on if he hadn't taken to sanding like that?

Macon knew he wasn't supposed to ask about the phone calls. The boundary line around their relationship was as sturdy as a split-rail fence, and that made him curious. It was a real predicament: he had a feeling that the old man wanted to talk about the calls, wanted to talk about so many things, but he didn't know how, not really. And Macon wanted that, too, but it was the first step—how did people take that first step? How did people ever dare fall in love? He understood the idea of *being* in love, intimacy, being devoted to someone more than yourself. That made a good, clean sort of sense, and he'd always thought he'd be good at that. He was loyal. But how did that happen? How did you enter that room? Was there some sort of door that everyone else saw but that was invisible to him?

Something of the phone calls summoned memories of his parents. He thought he remembered them, or maybe he just wanted to. Memory was hard to trust. Probably, they were just memories of old pictures. The rest was invention. His father's deep baritone. The colorful ties he wore: saxophones in a swirl of musical notes, stilt-legged pelicans, old penny-farthing bicycles. His mother's calm smile, no teeth. The way she would squint and pinch her mouth shut when she was concentrating.

They were inventions in which he chose to believe. Or maybe they were genuine. Who could say for sure? It seemed possible: memories passed from one generation to the next, like hair color or gait.

Every time the phone rang, he thought it might be his mother or father. It was the briefest reflex, hope like a lightning strike. You could know something and not, all at once.

For Ruth, Sunday evenings were the great exhalation. All week she held her breath without meaning to. Then Sunday came like discovering a new religion. Sundays, when Harold Gutman walked over to the hospital for a few hours. There was nothing improper about her conversations with Gus, but still. It was easier this way.

She strolled Boston as they talked, cell phone pushed to her ear. Beacon Hill, Back Bay, sometimes the North End or Charlestown. She walked and talked and felt like some young dancer. Nimble. Graceful. Youth thrust upon her, briefly. And health. She felt healthy, which she hadn't been for years.

It was lymphoma. She could feel it accumulating. Her variety killed you so slowly that it hardly felt different than old age. That's what Harold Gutman had said. That felt right. She hadn't told Gus, not yet. She couldn't tell him and had to tell him. It was a poison that worked slowly. There was time.

Macon wanted to feel at home in the old farmhouse, and he admired the old man, he really did. He just *knew* everything, and not just about woodworking. Knew why they got an infestation of ladybugs when the neighbors harvested soybeans, or why a carbureted engine smelled diffcrent than fuel injection. Sometimes they sat on the front porch and watched scud clouds form on the horizon, and the old man had a knack for predicting which direction they'd go.

Evenings, they would sit together on the back porch. It grew dark slower out in the country. Land so flat, so clean, you could hear the shadows as they encroached.

The old man paged through stacks of *Fine Woodworking*, and Macon read old comics he'd found in the closet. There was a computer in the den, and sometimes Macon watched old cartoons. Sometimes the old man drank a High Life, and he didn't mind if Macon had one too.

But Macon still felt like an interloper. It wasn't anything the old man had done, but there was no ignoring the weight of history. Generations of his people had lived on that farm, long enough that the family pictures lining the walls seemed to conjure ancient myths. They all seemed like decent people, modest like the old man, but they weren't Macon's people.

More than a year in the old house, and Macon still held his pee in the middle of the night because of the creaky floors.

Gus cooked breakfasts that covered the kitchen table: sausage, eggs, English muffins, oatmeal, frozen hash browns. They ate big in the morning so they wouldn't have to stop working until supper. The kid learned to drink coffee, and to drink it black. As with everything, he didn't complain, like he'd never been taught how.

Gus had hoped that big, slow-moving breakfasts would make the kid feel welcome, might puncture that membrane between them. Something about a big meal was disarming, naturally social. But the kid stayed drawn taut as a clothesline.

He'd never asked the kid to do the dishes or to vacuum. The kid just did those sorts of things instinctively. He wasn't sure how to feel about that. He liked having a clean house, admired the kid's sense of decorum, but he didn't want the kid feeling like a tenant. Beholden. Like the kid was perpetually seeking penance for some awful crime he wouldn't talk about.

One evening Macon answered the phone, something he normally avoided. But the old man was in the shower, and it rang, and there was no escaping it.

It was a woman's voice, and she was expecting the old man. "Oh, well, hello there."

"Yes, ma'am, hello." He paused, unsure of what to say next. "He's just over in the shower right now."

"And you must be Macon." Macon got the impression that the old man had mentioned him to the woman, the apprenticeship, but maybe he hadn't told her everything? For instance, that Macon had been staying there?

"Yes, ma'am. Macon."

She cleared her throat and then coughed sidelong without covering the receiver. "Well, excuse me," she said. "It's lovely to meet you. Hear you, I guess. I'm Ruth."

Macon didn't know what to say to that. He'd never talked much on the telephone. "Yes, ma'am," he said again.

"And how old are you now, Macon?"

"Seventeen. Eighteen in a couple weeks."

"Eighteen. The big one. Do you two have anything special planned?"

"Oh, well, no, ma'am. I guess not. That's a Thursday, and Thursdays we usually do catfish and potatoes."

The woman laughed at that, and it was such a genuine laugh, a high hoot, and she surrendered to it. An enchanting laugh, so easy, and it made him laugh, too, like the laugh needed to escape his body. He couldn't remember the last time he'd laughed.

"Oh, dear, Macon. That's a riot. Catfish for your birthday."

"Yes, ma'am," Macon said. He was still chuckling.

"When was the last time he fed you something green?"

"I guess we had some radishes in June."

"Gus is just a sturdy old goat. I never had any luck reforming him either."

An ex-wife then. But she still adored the old man. Loved him, even now. You could just hear it. Everything about him was still in the present tense for her. That was so like the old man, incapable of making enemies of anyone, even ex-wives.

She fell silent, and Macon got the feeling that she was trying to picture it all. Their daily routines. Ruth had a quiet confidence. She ruled the silence, not in an unkind way, but it still pulled Macon off balance. She was older, wealthy, educated, and Macon was none of those things.

"Well, what would you want?" she asked finally.

"Ma'am?"

"For a birthday present, what would you choose?"

"A go-kart," he said, almost automatically. He hadn't even known he'd been thinking it.

"A go-kart." She laughed again, as if Macon had told a joke. "Most kids your age want a car."

"Yes, ma'am."

That was when the old man emerged from the bathroom. He was shirtless and wiping the backs of his ears with the towel. When he saw Macon standing there, holding the phone, he pulled up.

Macon froze. It felt like he'd been caught shoplifting, though he'd never stolen anything in his life. The old man just stared at him, as if two distinct worlds had just collided, two continent-sized icebergs.

Macon handed the old man the phone without saying goodbye to Ruth and scuttled away.

For a moment, Gus watched the doorway, like he might still see the kid's imprint. He held the phone up to his ear, and before he could speak, Ruth said, "Nice kid," like she could feel his presence on the line.

"He really is."

But then Ruth didn't follow up with more questions, and Gus didn't offer any explanations, and the kid's presence hung over them like rainclouds. They talked about the Red Sox and the upcoming presidential election. Ruth talked about going out to the Cape for a couple weeks, and Gus talked about the dining table they were working on. Then they talked about Annabelle, settling into memories like an embrace.

They were just getting ready to hang up when Gus spoke of the kid again.

"You ever worry that you're prejudiced?" he asked.

"Prejudiced? No, not really, I guess. But now I will."

"Sorry. It's just, I don't know. I can't get the kid to open up. He's just so clenched, and I have a feeling it's something I've done or something I'm doing or, I don't know. Something awful I don't even know I'm doing?"

"Prejudiced in what way?"

"He was homeless for a while, I don't know how long. He's an orphan."

"And you're afraid . . . ?"

"I don't know. I think the world has trained him to be invisible. And I don't know how you undo that sort of thing."

"Sure."

"He must feel so alone."

"You've thought about this a lot."

"All the time."

"Oh, Gus," she said.

They lapsed into silence. Not at all uncomfortable. They were both considering. Each listened to the other breathing. They were better at that now, letting the silence just *be*. Silence was a skill that had emerged with age. They could veer in and out of old conversations now. They had memorized each other, like painters who could recall making each brushstroke.

"I'll think on it some more," she said.

"Thanks. Sorry."

"You paying the kid a fair rate?"

"Well, it's more of an apprenticeship, I guess."

"Gus. Jesus Christ."

"It's not that—"

"You're working a young homeless kid sixty hours a week and not paying him? And you're asking me if I think *I* might be prejudiced?"

"Okay."

"And you wonder why he's timid? Jesus, Gus. Pay the kid."

Gus hadn't meant to be stingy. It just hadn't occurred to him, not even when it was clear the kid had no money. He used to wonder after Ruth's ancestral wealth. *Mayflower* money, they called it in New England. Money just wasn't something she'd ever thought about. Gus had grown up poor, his people had been poor for two hundred years, but now he had plenty of money, so much that he wasn't even sure how much he had. But he didn't want much of anything, and so he never thought about it either.

They drove to New York to deliver work. The old man rented a box truck, and they filled it up quickly, desks and dining tables and a heap of chairs. A season's worth of work. Macon stood at the back and just stared at the haul, mesmerized.

"It's like everything, the lines, they're so tidy, it's almost like camouflage," he said.

"Our job is to make furniture that you hardly notice."

That sounded right to Macon, too. Furniture that left something unsaid. They drove in silence for the first couple hours. Macon stared out the window as they crossed Pennsylvania, and he wondered when hills became mountains. Who decided? Those low-slung valleys with ambling streams. They summited the peaks, the lumbering box truck grunting under its own weight. His ears felt like they had wool in them, and he could only clear it away by swallowing. When they got closer to the city, the skyline rose in the distance like mountains, and Macon didn't even realize he was leaning forward until his neck started to ache.

"Something else, isn't it?" the old man said.

They unloaded the truck at a store in the East Village. Macon was careful to be the one walking backward down the ramp, to set his end down last. A salesman stood off to the side and watched them. He had the upright posture of a sapling and wore a suit that cleaved to his body.

"Macon made half of this haul," the old man said.

The salesman smiled awkwardly. "It's a pleasure, young man," he said. He turned back to the old man and handed him an envelope, and they shook hands. Then he and Gus were off, back onto the street, which thrummed like an anthill.

"Should we grab a hotel for the night? Go get a nice steak dinner?"

"Maybe we could," Macon said. "Or maybe we could just head home?"

The old man smiled and nodded, and they heaved themselves up into the truck.

When they'd finally escaped the city, the old man handed Macon the envelope.

"Sir?"

"Back pay," he said.

Macon pulled the flap back and peered inside. The check was made out to the old man in the amount of $87,000.

"That's only the front half," the old man said. "Every vendor is a little different. But you'll get the back half when we make the next delivery."

"Sir," Macon said, but then he didn't know what else to say. He hadn't much thought about money until this trip. Felt like the old man was already giving him something sturdier than money. He checked the envelope again and looked at the old man and then looked back out the window like it might offer some refuge.

The go-karts arrived later that week. One was red, and the other was blue. Both had high roll cages and good-sized Briggs & Stratton motors.

The old man looked over at Macon and then back at the go-karts.

"I might have said something about a go-kart," Macon admitted. "For my birthday. I didn't mean anything by it. I thought, I don't know, I thought we were just talking."

"To Ruth," the old man said, realizing. He turned toward Macon and grinned like a toddler.

They drove the go-karts all morning, drove until they'd worn an oblong path through the barnyard. It was the first time they hadn't spent the morning out in the shop, and neither of them seemed to notice. The old man was the better driver, but Macon was more aggressive, almost reckless—that fun sort of reckless you could be with a go-kart. He learned how to drift around the corners, gliding but still under control. There was a depression in the middle of the yard, maybe from an old tree that had gone down, and if Macon timed it just right, he could ramp it. Race after race, they circled the barnyard, their backs going sweaty against the seats. The old man yelled at Macon as he cornered and tried to pass him on the inside, and Macon just grinned back at him.

. . .

The old man put Ruth's phone number on the fridge. He didn't say anything else, but Macon understood. He loved the way the old man did that, said things without saying them. Macon wanted to be like that someday.

Macon sat in his bedroom and dialed the number. The old house groaned like it always did at night. All that chatter had unnerved him at first, but it was just the humidity. That's what the old man had told him, anyway. Everything about the house was wood. Took on moisture like a sponge. Two or three gallons of water coming and going with the humidity, joints expanding and contracting. Like the old house was alive, and it was talking.

When Ruth came on the line, Macon thanked her before even saying hello.

"Oh, goodness, Macon. Of course. I'm so glad you like them. I thought you could use them more now, before winter comes."

"Yes, ma'am. We drove them all morning."

"Gus, too?"

"He was like a race driver, ma'am."

"His knees must have been up to his ears."

"Yes, ma'am. Like a clown. You should have seen it."

She hesitated, and Macon felt the weight of history, like he'd stumbled onto an old battlefield. "Oh, Macon. I'd love to see it," she said.

"Oh, yes, ma'am, you should. You really should. You could come for my birthday."

Ruth went quiet on the other end of the line. It was only a few moments, but it felt much longer. Maybe it was age, or maybe it was the class divide. Highborn and lowborn, New England and Midwest. There was nothing unkind about her lapses into silence. In fact, there was a comfort to them, a chance for them to sort out their thoughts. He liked talking to Ruth. She seemed to know what he meant even when it wasn't exactly what he'd said.

Before she spoke again, she drew in a deep breath. Sharp. She'd been crying. He'd somehow caused it. But she steeled herself. "Macon," she said, "I'd love to come for your birthday."

And that was it, like a contract they'd both signed. "We'd love that," he said. "We both would, I know it."

"Catfish and potatoes."

"Yes, ma'am. And some radishes."

The memory of this moment would hum through Macon for the rest of his life, swelling and elongating through time. Sometimes it was dread that overcame him, the feeling that he'd inserted himself into some generational tension he wasn't old enough to understand. Other times he was convinced that it was only Ruth's sense of decorum that had made her agree. To decline his invitation would have been tantamount to admitting that he was a mere tenant. No, she *had* to come.

It wasn't until years later, when the old man lay dying in hospice, that the old man thanked Macon. Reached out for him. Tremors ran through his hands. Their fingertips touched. *You were the child,* he said, *who appears in the doorway when his parents are fighting.*

They opened the kid a bank account. Gus slid the check over to the bank manager and she said, "Two names on the account, then," and Gus said, "No, no. Only the young man."

The kid kept his ATM card and cash in his pocket because he didn't have a wallet. For the next month, Gus would catch him logging on to the bank website and staring at the balance as if he were marveling at a new winter coat.

That weekend the kid walked into town. Said he might buy some Red Wing boots. He was gone a couple of hours, and Gus paced the barnyard like an old dog waiting on its owner. When the kid finally appeared in the distance, he was carrying a little plastic bag, too small for boots. Afternoon had eased into evening. Long shadows from the telephone poles stretched down the gravel lane.

"Do you know how much Red Wing boots cost?" he said.

Gus smiled, but he understood. There was shame in poverty, but there was shame in escaping it, too.

"I need to tell you something," the kid said. He looked at Gus and then away. He handed Gus the bag but still wouldn't meet his eyes. "I think I messed up."

Gus stared at the kid and then opened the bag. Inside was a new doorknob for the workshop.

Ruth booked her flight and rental car as if in a fever dream. She packed her suitcase a week in advance and then stared at it every time she walked into the bedroom.

"A birthday party?" Harold Gutman asked.

"A birthday," she said. "Not really a party."

"For a kid you've never met."

It was too hard to explain, and she didn't really want to anyway.

"Where will you stay?"

She stared at him. Tension vibrated off his body, but Ruth hardly cared. She'd spent most of her life behaving, doing what needed to be done. Her ancestors were Puritans. She could see their scowling faces.

"I'll be home on Saturday," she said. "Maybe Sunday."

He glared at her suitcase like it was the real culprit. He was talking, his voice rising and falling in anger, but Ruth didn't hear his words. She'd slipped off into memory. The memory of Gus, the last time she'd seen him. Ten years ago now, though the reunion still murmured through her body, advancing and retreating like the tides. Nothing so present as the past. They'd sat together at a little café in the Back Bay and drunk tea and tried to talk as if they had carried on without each other, but they both knew better. Gus wasn't angry or resentful as some men might have been. He was just sad. Mostly she talked and he listened like he always had. Quiet as an oak tree, all his energy reserved for listening.

They'd sat there for, what, two, three hours? When they'd finally willed themselves to leave, he stared at his boots and said goodbye, and she tugged at his forearm, and they embraced. She held on to him as if gripping a cliff face, and he let her. He let her. And then he was gone. She watched him amble away, meandering through the bustle of Newbury Street, hands clasped behind his back as if to make his body narrower.

She turned and went back to their table. She sat and collected herself. Cups of tea long gone cold. There was a coaster picturing a little seahorse with angular shadows, just a cardboard thing. Disposable. But she pocketed it. It sat on her nightstand now, the fibers of the cardboard pulling loose.

On the morning of Macon's birthday, the old man seemed off. Moody, like a dog sensing a storm. Forgot to even say happy birthday until midmorning.

The old man didn't reprimand him for inviting Ruth, which almost made it worse. In fact, he didn't say much of anything. Went quiet as an owl. Just held the doorknob in both hands and stared down at it like it was the most precious thing he'd ever owned. Like he was holding the eucharist.

Macon hid in his bedroom that night. He hadn't been so mortified for years. Not since that foster home, the third one, where the woman had caught him hiding chicken nuggets in his pocket. She hadn't been angry, not exactly, but she just hadn't understood. Once you'd felt real hunger, it never left you. You never trusted tomorrow again.

Ruth was set to arrive at four thirty, but the old man moved out to the front porch at three. Macon could sense the tension. He felt for the old man, but there was also envy. Who had ever fretted about his own arrival or noticed his absence?

But the old man. God—he was just besieged. It pained Macon to see. There was an intensity to his existence right then, pain and joy in equal measure. He watched the old man from the window, and eventually he joined him on the porch.

For a while, they sat quietly. They rocked back and forth in their chairs and stared down the long lane as if it were a telescope. The old man sat flat-footed, hands on his thighs, but his breathing was too fast. A vein in his temple pulsed.

"When my folks died," Macon said, and then stopped as if repositioning his grip. He realized he'd been telling the old man this story for a long time in his head, but he'd never spoken the words aloud. "They died years back. I was a baby."

The old man was staring at him fixedly.

"Bad car accident." Normally, this was when Macon would offer a few sparse details followed by his appraisal that he'd been lucky, all things considered. He was a baby, couldn't remember it.

"Tell me about them," the old man said.

No one had ever asked that. Other people had always seemed eager to push past this part, maybe for Macon's sake, but probably for their own.

"My father wore these colorful ties. Purple and green mixed together. Pictures of trumpets and kangaroos on them." The old man leaned back and smiled. "My mother, I guess she had the smartest voice you've ever heard. Like somebody on *Jeopardy!* She studied insects. She was working at Oberlin, which is how we ended up here. Up north like a Yankee."

The old man smiled again. He knew what Macon was doing, but he let the enchantment spread over him anyway.

"Insects," the old man said, like he was holding the word in his hands and inspecting it.

"That's all secondhand," Macon said. "I was too little. But I have some pictures."

"Yeah."

"Now here I am," he said.

The old man was studying him again. Sad eyes. It wasn't pity. There was more to it than that. The old man knew plenty about that sort of thing. How people cast longer shadows in death than they had in life. How this was something you couldn't understand until it happened to you. And now their griefs had intersected, and did that soothe the pain or amplify it? That was a tougher business. But there was some goodness, maybe, in two people grieving next to each other.

"I used to work twenty, thirty hours straight," the old man said. "Back when I was younger and sorting through things. Death. But I found that no matter how tired you are, there's always enough energy left for the pain."

He'd been staring off, but now he turned toward Macon. "Why is that?"

Macon didn't answer, and the old man didn't want him to. What he'd said—it felt true as gravity, and just as inexplicable. He was an old man, but he was also a little boy, asking why things died, which might be the only question worth asking.

When the car finally appeared at the end of the lane, the old man stood and retucked his shirt, and Macon went inside. Reunions were inelegant things. They didn't need an audience.

Ruth was smaller than he remembered. She walked with a slight limp, bad hips, but if there was pain, she ignored it. She had an easy elegance, as if she'd never much thought of it. She seemed like the kind of woman who was used to hard winters. When she hugged Macon, she sighed. It felt like they'd known each other for years.

They spent the afternoon wandering around the farm, through the barn, through the workshop. Macon talked about their latest projects. Ruth gazed around as if at a museum, and Macon understood that she'd wandered back in time. She traced her hands across half-sanded tabletops. She held a bench plane under the light and studied it like a jeweler. Beautiful lines, lithe lines. Macon said it was his favorite, a Stanley Bailey #4.

Ruth watched Macon as he talked. Whatever clench had once existed in him had loosened. This was his home, Gus was his father. They told stories jointly. One would start, and the other would finish. They had melded together, held memories mutually like an old married couple. They were everything together that she had hoped and feared.

After dinner, they lingered in the kitchen, drinking coffee. Macon put the glasses away while the old man scrubbed the fish smell out of the broiler pan. As he worked, Macon stole glances at Ruth, the way her eyes traveled the house.

"Thirty years," she said. "But you're still using the same tea towels."

The old man stopped scrubbing. "Did you know we have tea towels, Macon?"

Macon imagined the old man and Ruth when they were younger. They would have been the kind of parents who slow-danced in front of their kids.

Gus and Ruth took turns racing Macon around the barnyard. A rough dirt track worn in the grass, oblong and winding. Macon won every race and never grew tired of winning. Eventually, Ruth and Gus begged off. Too tired, they said. Too old. But Macon kept driving on his own, carving tracks in the barnyard through the dimness of dusk.

Ruth and Gus moved to the back porch. Gus had a beer, and Ruth sipped on a gin. They watched Macon and didn't even feel their faces curl into smiles as he drove past and waved.

Gus looked upward. Clouds twisted together like dancers.

"Do you ever feel," he asked, "like your life is really just preparation for another life that you'll never quite have?"

She didn't respond straightaway, and he didn't expect her to. Eventually, she said, "You don't have to stay unhappy forever."

He seemed to think about this prospect as if for the first time. The last of the shadows leaned from the barnyard to the back porch, stretching like pulled taffy. Macon kept circling and waving, lap after lap.

"I mean it, Gus. You don't have to stay unhappy."

He stared out at the field of corn. He squinted at something that wasn't there.

"Well, I guess I've come this far."

. Later, Macon came and sat next to them. He was breathing hard, disturbing their calm. He could feel it. The old man poured him a glass of water, and he drank it down without tasting it. The adrenaline had taken hold of him, and he couldn't sit still. Ruth and the old man weren't talking, but they had been. You could feel the echoes of their words. It was like that hollow in the barnyard from an old tree. There and not there. He didn't want to interrupt anything, so wandered out toward the workshop.

Ruth and Gus sat and listened and spoke intermittently. Dusk's silent advance. Gusts of wind rustling the corn.

"I think he holds his pee in the middle of the night."

"Your father would have liked him."

They sat with that thought for a while.

"You need to start introducing him to your vendors. It'll make it easier when he takes over."

"That's true."

"He'll want it?"

Gus tried to picture the kid with gray hair, a labored bearing. "The problem is that I want more for him. More than this."

"I'm not sure you realize how much this is."

A metallic grating sound came from the workshop. Gus leaned forward as if he might see it through the darkness. Macon. He was putting on the new doorknob.

"When I'm gone," he said, "I'll know I could have done better. Could have done more with my life. More good, I mean. Could have added more to the world."

"Gus."

He shrugged. Resigned, if not at peace. His life hadn't gone the way he'd hoped. He'd never quite become the man he'd wanted to be. It was such an ordinary regret. He'd come closest back when he was a father. The man he was and the man he wanted to be, they'd nearly aligned then. Nearly eclipsed each other. If only he'd had a bit more time.

"But the kid." He gestured vaguely toward the workshop. "He's pure as dew. He's just . . ." His voice failed him.

"That's because of you partly. That kindness."

He shook his head. "This isn't kindness. You can't call it that. It's just basic courtesy. No one else ever bothered, but that doesn't make it kindness. Sharing water with a stranger in the desert. It's hardly anything at all, really."

"It's something, Gus."

"And look at him. Over there, changing out that doorknob."

They both looked toward the workshop. They couldn't see Macon out there in the shadows, but they could hear him working. He was humming to himself.

"Do you remember when she fell from that door and skinned her elbow?" Ruth asked, and Gus was already nodding. He remembered, of course he did.

Annabelle had been swinging on the door, back and forth. She was waiting for Gus to finish work for the day. Begging him to come and play. And Gus had said, "Soon, soon," though he hadn't really meant it. A father's refrain. She'd started swinging on the door, like a carnival ride, and Gus yelled at her to stop it, she was going to hurt herself, but she ignored him. Or maybe she didn't hear. She was laughing like a little sprite. But then the doorknob pulled clean off and she tumbled to the ground and cried, and Gus couldn't remember what happened after that.

"You never fixed it," Ruth said, but Gus didn't answer. He was afraid of disrupting the spell she had cast.

Then she was looking right at him, her face next to his. "Do you ever feel like a father again?"

Gus couldn't hold the tears this time. They came for him, and he let them. She let him cry, didn't try to fix him. She turned back toward the kid, kept trying to see him through the shadows. Finally, she stood and walked across the barnyard until she disappeared, too. He could hear them talking but couldn't untangle the words.

A few minutes later, she emerged from the shadows as a ship through fog. She looked at him, not unkindly, never unkindly, but she wanted an answer, she wanted to torture herself, which Gus did understand.

"Yes," he said. "Sometimes." It felt like an admission of guilt before a judge.

"Gus?" she said.

"Hmm?"

"Look at me, dear."

He did. She was staring into him. He felt her eyes like a second sun.

"You're allowed to love him," she said.

It felt so quiet, just the breeze and the kid out there humming some tune. He'd led such a lonely life. But it had never felt quiet, not like this. There was always memory, and memory was loud. The past was always trying to overwhelm the present.

Ruth leaned her head on his shoulder. He held his body rigid as a totem. He hadn't been so terrified in years. They sat like that and stared out at the workshop.

"Not everything has to be grief," she said.

"That's a thought."

"You don't think so?"

The kid was out there, humming louder now as he worked. Gus couldn't place the tune, but it didn't matter. Ruth adjusted her head, seeking out that soft tissue in the well of his shoulder. She breathed in and out rhythmically.

"I never found the thing that comes after grief," he said.

They sat for a few moments, and then she said, "I don't know about that."

They went quiet again. Night had come on like a sigh. They couldn't see Macon, but they watched the space where he was. It felt like they were sitting inside of a silence they'd made themselves.

High green corn on all sides like a palisade. Who would have ever noticed them, and who would have cared? A farm that looked like farms do. A bleak, forgettable place. Three quiet people, not even related. People ordinary as dandelions. Who would have even paused to stare?

Gus would have stayed there forever, the three of them. Motionless, but not. Together but not, as every family is. But they were the rare family that understood this.

Gus closed his eyes. Ruth breathed evenly onto his neck. The kid sneezed and said "Pardon me" to no one. It seemed like he was closer than he really was. Within arm's reach. Gus felt Ruth, too, that beguiling radiation of another human being. They didn't talk, but it felt like they did. There was no music, but it felt like there was. There was the sea of corn trembling under the breeze. And there was the kid, across the barnyard, putting a new doorknob on the workshop door. He was humming. It felt like the world had just taken a breath. It felt like they were dancing.

Morris Collins

The Home Visit

IT WAS TIME to adopt a cat. After months of his decrepitude and vomit and wild shitting, of screaming in confusion at the ceiling, and then settling down to purr in the bathtub or behind the toilet or headfirst like a doltish sphinx against the bare wall, in places that would have been funny if they weren't a sign of some kind of feline dementia, we acknowledged that our old friend, the glue—"Don't say glue," my wife wept—that held our marriage together, was failing. So we went to the shelter that was attached to the animal hospital where we had recently spent a lot of time and basically all of our disposable income—fifteen years earlier, at twenty-two, we had not considered pet insurance, or anything else—to find his replacement. There was only one cat available.

"Slim pickings in the cat department," said the woman who helped us.

It's important to make a good impression during the rescue process. I remembered that from the last time, and from the horror stories of friends. "It was harder to adopt my poodle than my fucking kid," Stacy, a friend of ours, had said recently when, over drinks, we admitted that we were beginning, in the most hypothetical of ways, to discuss our *next* cat. For ages Stacy had been the last of our friends without children. But then: her adopted infant Rebecca. "It's crazy," she said, "but I think she's beginning to look like me." A moment passed; we all stared into the infant's blank and baffled, sticky face; we all smiled, though she didn't smile back. Then I said, "On that note, we have to get home to give the cat his meds." Stacy downed her wine. "You left him alone when he's sick?" she said. "The shelter people wouldn't like that. They're very judgmental. They get off on, like, the power."

The woman before us—Sarah, according to her name tag—wore a nose ring and big circular glasses and did look kind of judgmental. And a little older than usual for the shelter staff. Like, not twenty-four. Not our age either, but closer to it.

"We've had a run on cats recently," she said. "Cats, cats, cats. Everybody wants cats."

"Why do you think that is?" I asked.

"Loneliness," Sarah said. Beneath her glasses her eyes were wide and unblinking as a lemur's. "These are very lonely times. Actually," she said, "it's something I have to be on the lookout for. A lonely home is no home for a cat."

"No worries there," I said, and put my arm around Alex, pulling her in kind of chummily, like a coach. "We've got each other."

Alex tried to smile. She hated making impressions of any kind. "Yeah," she added. "We're married." It was a slightly weird thing to say, but we don't wear rings and Alex, whose idea that was, felt uncomfortable about it in official situations.

"Sometimes that can be worse," Sarah said.

We met the one unclaimed cat. It was not exactly a kitten, or not as much of a kitten as we had hoped, but certainly much more of a kitten than our old guy, who, when we'd got him, was so small we brought him home in a shoebox. That very first night he crawled into our bed, a futon that doubled as our couch, and nestled between us. It was summer and we had the mattress directly under the open window, deep enough against the wall so that the streetlight was not in our faces but shone through the fire escape onto our stomachs and legs in a lattice of shadow and greenish light. A few nights before, we'd made love facing the other direction, so that the luminescent bands, crosshatched across our faces and arms, seemed to be binding us together, and because sex makes everything literal, I'd believed for the first time that our lives were interwoven, converging in a way I had not, at twenty-two, expected, and I felt suddenly adult and real, and the next morning, in celebration or in search of some ceremony of permanence, I suggested that we get a cat. The night we did, when he crawled into bed with us, Alex sat up a little, into the light that softened her face, glazing it with the kind of awe you imagine on people who are just about to be abducted by aliens. "Come here, baby," she said, and the kitten trotted into her arms. Sometime later I woke and saw them sleeping with their foreheads touching, and it was beautiful, a vision of the future I knew for sure I wanted, a new family I was both outside of and more in than ever before, and I lay like that for an hour, just beyond their shared affection, afraid to enter or ruin it by moving.

After we finished meeting the new cat, Sarah took us into a little office to ask us some questions. Primarily the office contained a lamp and a corkboard full of pictures of Sarah—wide-eyed, staring directly into the camera—posing with animals. There was no desk, but there was one chair facing two chairs, so we sat in the two chairs.

Sarah slumped into the other one. She put her head in her hands and then looked up, at us, and made a big show of sighing.

"Is everything okay?" Alex said. Again, she did not like feeling judged, especially unfairly, and seemed, I felt anyway, about two seconds from breaking her chair across Sarah's face.

"It's sad to see them go," Sarah said.

"You must get attached," I said.

"They get attached to me," she said. "Very attached. It can be hard for them. Some families ask me to visit." She pointed her thumb back over her shoulder at the pictures of her in what, I now realized, were other people's homes with their pets.

"I bet they do," I said.

"It can be a burden. At times," she said, "I have had to arbitrate."

"Arbitrate?" Alex said.

"During divorces. Just me and the lawyers. Cats aren't babies, I tell them. It's not like King Solomon. You can't cut them in half."

"You definitely cannot cut a cat in half," I said.

Sarah was sitting up much straighter, her chin actually raised a little, her head tilted back and to the side, like those pictures of Napoleon surveying something that must not have been the Russian winter, and her eyes, convexed in her round glasses, wobbled with what I could only assume was pride. I thought to myself: *Alex, don't.*

"Solomon didn't cut the baby in half," Alex said.

"She was just making a point," I said.

"But that *is* the point," Alex said.

Sarah said, "I think I'll have to make a home visit."

At home, furious as usual, Alex said, "This shit would never happen in Pennsylvania." Alex was from rural Pennsylvania, but not so rural that her town wasn't filled with unused train tracks or meth. She was petting our old guy while she talked, sort of dropping her palm on his forehead, pushing down, and then pulling back along his bony spine so that he splayed and flattened against the floor like a bearskin rug.

"Don't pet him when you're mad," I said. "He knows you're mad, but doesn't know why." I often felt the same way.

"He's fine," she said, and we both looked at him where he lay, bony and pancaked, under her palm.

"In Pennsylvania," she said, "they would have just given us the fucking cat. They would have been like, 'How many cats do you want? You want cats? Here's five cats. This one's a fisher cat, which is a giant carnivorous weasel, but take it too. It's great with kids as long as they're not pussies.'"

I wasn't sure that this was a better system, but then again I wasn't in any way certain that I even wanted a new cat, or a new anything. What I wanted was the past, or a life that, like a dubious uncle, pretended to be in some way related to the past, that appeared to derive from the past other than by way of slow loss or grotesque diminishment. A new cat seemed to be giving up on the cat I had, though to be fair, the cat I had—flat, bad smelling, in several ways oozing—was at present doing a really accurate impression of roadkill.

Outside the shelter there had been a guy shouting about how animals would not be allowed into the Kingdom of Heaven. He held up a sign on which he had painted: HEY MILLENNIALS: JESUS NOT PUSS PUSS. I think his point was that instead of getting pets, people should be fruitful and multiply.

"What about that guy at the shelter?" I said. "Should he get a cat?"

I don't know why I said this. Or what point I was trying to make other than that what upset Alex wasn't the right thing to be upset by, even though I was upset by it too. I mean, I might not have wanted a new cat but I knew I was deserving of one. Although the last decade had revealed my limitations in ways that were shocking to us both, ways that made me sometimes seize up with a feeling of incomprehensible disappointment only to—as I had in youth—lurch toward my wife for reassurance and find that she wasn't expecting to have to arrange her face at the speed of my longing. Instead, I'd see her own surprise at what I'd become echoed there, as if she were the heroine in some German nightmare who realized that she had married her beloved's evil doppelgänger if that doppelgänger wasn't so much evil as anxious, a klutzy, indecisive doppelgänger, a vaguely weepy, know-it-all doppelgänger whose ability at twenty-three to make a perfect Manhattan had appeared like a token of possibility, but was in fact an end point, not a sign of the future but the future itself, its full expression and limit, with the one exception, surprising to us both, that I took really good care of our cat.

"Don't worry," Sarah said. "This is customary." She was standing in the doorway to our apartment, holding what looked like a medical bag in both hands against her chest.

"Is it?" I said.

"Not really. But it happens." She stepped inside. "I was expecting a house. Or at least something house-ish."

She sat in the middle of the floor, in our living room, next to the coffee table, on our Persian rug. Moving very slowly, as in yoga, she shifted onto her hands and knees and arched her back. She started, quietly, under her breath and to herself, to meow. "Pretend I'm not here," she said.

We were still in the doorway, Alex and I, in collapsing postures of welcome, and one of us would have to say something.

"We have chairs," Alex said, pointing at all the chairs—two armchairs, both leather and both with ottomans, and the couch. In truth we had more available seating than was, or had been recently, entirely necessary, since most of our friends now owned homes and children and Alex had gotten us kicked out of our book club.

"Getting a cat's-eye vantage," Sarah said, "can be very instructive."

"Our cat likes to sit in chairs," I said.

Sarah stood abruptly and mashed her glasses back on her face. "Are there other cats in this home?"

"No," Alex said.

"Yes," I said.

"Sort of," she said. "For now."

"This is Derek," I said, and pointed at Derek where he sat in the corner, only a few steps from the door, beneath the hat rack, facing the wall. "He didn't used to do that," I said.

"What is that?" Sarah asked.

"That's Derek," I said. "He's just kind of flat right now."

"No," Sarah said, "the thing he's under."

"It's a hat rack," Alex said.

"Oh, I thought it was like, art."

"It is *like* art," I said. "Because we don't have any hats."

Alex used to have many hats, so many hats that she bought a vintage teak hat rack to hold them. Fedoras, borsalinos, fishermen's caps, two berets. At one point hats were Alex's look. And then she started getting rid of things that reminded her of herself. But we kept the hat rack. A lot of our apartment was haunted like that.

Sarah said slowly, "Derek?"

We finally managed to encourage her into an armchair. From her medical bag she produced an oxblood leather journal—"This is Moroccan," she said—and a pencil. "So I can change my mind."

On his own, Derek made his way out from beneath the hat rack. "Good boy," I said, at which he looked up at the three of us, trotted forward into the room, stood in the middle of the rug, and began to vomit. This was not unusual in terms of frequency, but there are some events, like orgasms, that never lose their ability to command the senses, that in their occurrence compress all consciousness into a monomania of sensation, awe, or queasy witness, and Derek's projectile vomiting was such a marvel, as he erupted with a startling ferocity, the power of each expulsion heaving him around like he was an automated lawn sprinkler on a swivel.

Alex was up and singing "Motherfucker motherfucker motherfucker" as she ran to the kitchen to grab our reserve of paper towels, sponges, and carpet cleaner. She returned arms full and got down onto her hands and knees.

I wanted to say that she should let it dry first but remembered, just, that suggesting this to my wife, wrist-deep in barf, let alone with Sarah watching, would be socially unacceptable. Meanwhile though, because there's no truly functional implement for lifting wet cat vomit from a deep-pile Persian rug other than your hands gloved by quickly disintegrating paper towels, Alex was having a really bad time—especially since she had just tried to scrub one portion of the circle's arc with her right hand while plopping her left hand in another.

"So, why do you want a new cat?" Sarah said.

Finally settled again, after a longish interval of silence while Alex recovered and began to drink (I expected) in the kitchen, we were all back as we had been.

"Will you name the new cat Derek as well?" Sarah asked.

"Why would we do that?"

"It happens more often than you'd think."

"We are not trying to replace Derek," Alex said.

"Derek," I said, "is irreplaceable."

"We are simply preparing for eventualities."

"The Buddhists have a saying about that," Sarah said.

We waited.

"It was something about flowers." She began writing at speed in her notebook.

"You control what you can control," I said.

"Which is why you might call him Derek."

Alex seized her armrest. We all watched her pretend that she hadn't. "We did that because of his paws."

Sarah looked up and squinted. "His paws?"

"The way they're white."

"Isn't it just fur?"

"While the rest of him is black. That's why we named him Derek."

Sarah opened her mouth and then closed it again.

"Like a domino," Alex said. "Derek and the Dominos."

"I opted for Eric," I said. "Eric Catton."

Alex hated puns and took classic rock very seriously and she mimed tugging at her leg and then pretended to throw up into what must have been a boot. She had definitely been hitting the vodka in the kitchen.

"Overruled," I explained.

Sarah flushed and she was gripping her pencil sort of like a dagger. "I don't understand anything that you are saying to me," she said.

In life so much is inscrutable. But not everything: the house visit, barely begun, was not going well.

"Would you like a drink?" Alex asked. She was always asking people if they wanted a drink at inappropriate times, which also certainly affected how things went down with the book club, but she was already standing and leaning toward the kitchen, she had already clearly made the decision for herself, and it was too late to undo it, and there I was, scrambling to find a way to make a joke of my wife's suggestion, to clean up another social situation, to correct, if I could, what had already occurred, which was both impossible and what a lot of my life felt like.

"Yes, please," Sarah said.

"The problem is loneliness," Sarah said over her second martini.

"The cat won't be lonely," I said.

"The cat won't be lonely," Alex added, "because my husband"—she pointed at me with a cocktail stick—"works from home."

We all heard the way she said *works*.

"I do not mean the cat," Sarah said. "I mean in the home. Loneliness about the home. A general loneliness."

"When I enter my apartment," Alex said, "I sense alternately good taste and clutter. There's really no fucking room for loneliness."

"Loneliness is an internal state," I said.

"If we lived in a house and had space to ourselves, perhaps I could get in touch with my internal states," Alex said.

"I was expecting a house," Sarah said. She had gulped the first martini in two or three quick pulls, but Alex had made a pitcher.

"Home is a feeling," I said. "Love is a feeling. A family, when you get right down to it, is a feeling."

"A cat makes a family," Sarah said.

"We agree," I said.

"Bullshit," Alex said. "A family makes a cat. It's all in the name—a pet. What's a cat without people to pet it? Nothing good."

"Actually," Sarah said, "there are many theories that it's humans who have been domesticated by cats, not the other way around."

Alex shouts when she drinks. And swears. "Have you ever fucking seen a barn cat? I grew up with them. Yowling. Pissing everywhere. Killing constantly."

"You grew up with barn cats?"

"In Pennsylvania," I said.

"It was just killing," Alex said. "Twenty-four/seven killing."

I had always wondered what to do when things start to get bad. Against uncertainty Alex had made an entire pitcher of martinis. But how often do our efforts to protect ourselves become the next problem? And what now? After all, it had been this kind of thing that had gotten us kicked out of our book club, which I whispered to Alex, as best I could, from across the room, but Alex did not like being whispered at in public. I knew this.

"I got us kicked out? All you did was drink whiskey and say, 'It's best not to theorize.'"

It's true. I had felt, at the time, that, faced with the lives of others, who could know anything? And yet, some things are discernible, some things allow precision, as in: we got kicked out of book club because Alex gulped her wine, looked across the string cheese at our host, and called her a dumb cunt.

"You looked straight across the string cheese and called Marlee a dumb cunt," I said.

"Well, she was a dumb cunt." Alex glared up from her drink. "Was she not a dumb cunt?"

Marlee always frowned before she spoke, as if her own opinions displeased her, which they should have. The book we were discussing was *Portnoy's Complaint*. An odd choice in many ways. Marlee had frowned and said, "I was expecting some Jews, but not so many. Maybe I would have liked it more if there had been fewer Jews."

"Wow," Alex had said. "You're a dumb cunt."

The room gaping, aghast. Between us all, tension and string cheese. Everyone's gaze, oddly, on me. The group expected me to stand up for, or discipline, or explain, my wife.

"It's best not to theorize," I said at this, the last of our social functions.

At some point, maybe halfway into the second pitcher, Derek wandered back into the room. As a kitten he was friendly with all guests, anyone who might pet or feed him; then, as he got older, he was friendly with no one except us and began to hide at the sight of strangers, which was a philosophical position for him, considering that some of these people he had been cajoled out from under the bed to meet—while they pretended to care—upwards of thirty times. Consequently, his emotional life, like our own, seemed to wane, until eventually, also like us, he stopped seeing other people altogether. But now, in his enfeebled dotage, he had become friendly again, gentle and calm—when he wasn't emitting fluid or lost or yowling—and he sat before us, upright on his hind legs, with his head cocked to the side, staring at Sarah, sweetly befuddled.

"There he is," I said, as if reminding us all, including Derek, that Derek was still here. At the vet—despite his frantic panting, his shedding and nervous farting—he was widely acknowledged as "handsome." Maybe it's what they say about all male cats, but I still took a weird pride in the way that the vet techs, after donning protective sweatshirts and rubber gloves and looking at us recriminatorily, as if on past occasions we hadn't adequately explained to Derek how to behave at the vet, they'd lift his sweaty bulk from the cat carrier and croon, always, "What a handsome boy!"

Sarah put one hand over one eye and leaned forward. "Not much time left for him," she said.

For a few years when Derek was still a kitten, Alex and I lived in a three-story house in Baltimore. It belonged to her aunt, who had married and moved to Virginia, but the market was not right to sell, and so she'd let us rent it for almost nothing, and it was one of those big old houses, surrounded by wisteria and creepers, that remind you that Baltimore is a Southern city. The houses in our neighborhood all sagged with a kind of stately disrepair, listing verandahs looking down over patios strewn with pinecones and windfall leaves, flower beds dug through otherwise unkempt yards pocked by stagnant frog ponds and divided by azaleas. Though our place was smaller than many around, we had a bench beneath a cherry tree in the front, under which we often read, and a kitchen that opened onto a back garden walled in by hedges and live oaks where Alex used to put Derek in a harness and leash and take him on weekend afternoons. That he resisted this, that he writhed against any limits on his movement, was both frustrating to her and deeply relatable. "He's like me," she said. "He doesn't want to be controlled," she said. "He's my cat," she said, as a joke but always in the same context, watching his squirming anxiety, and speaking to me as if I couldn't quite understand the peculiarities of their discontent, as if our household were divided into two teams, she and the cat and I and the leash, which was unfair to me but not to her because she did find herself frustrating and frustrated, always twisting against a harness she could never quite identify but suspected might be the limited ways I knew how to live, and though Derek loved the backyard, its smells and insects and the grass he was determined to chew, and didn't actually want to wander, was content to stay by our side like a tennis spectator, looking left and right as sparrows swooped overhead, it was almost as if he wished he wanted to do more exciting things and blamed the leash, still slack, for his timidity and turned on it, this thing he was always at first so excited to see, and from which we'd soon have to untangle him and carry him back inside before he strangled himself. Then we'd return to our books and sit there, feeling young, and drinking fantastic amounts of Pikesville Rye out of the plastic handle, or blearily inventing cocktails that Alex named after authors she liked, all of which we topped with cheap prosecco, or listening to crickets, or smoking cigars with friends around the fire pit, while Derek remained inside, at the back door on his hind legs, pounding against the glass, desperate to join us again. And now, sitting here in our living room, a participant in and observer of our diminishment, I understood that he'd be leaving soon, half of a team that didn't include me, and wondered if, when that happened, alone and sideless, Alex would go too.

"How do you know when it's time?" I asked.

"It's time," Sarah said.

"Don't say that," Alex said.

"When they are no longer themselves," Sarah said.

Suddenly it was dusk and the dusk had become melancholy. Martinis can do that. They start as a silver benediction, glimmering and fresh and absolutely healthy tasting, and end with nostalgia and doom, and we were together on their wavelength now where we didn't have to verify our subjects. Or we were just boozy enough to say the obvious.

"Maybe that's right," Alex said.

"It's terrible not to be yourself. Or not to be able to be yourself."

"Exactly," Alex whispered.

"I'm not sure," I said. "Everybody changes."

"But not to that."

Alex was thinking what I was thinking—which was of Derek panting at the ceiling, or howling with his eyes closed in the corner, or falling asleep in his litter box and then not knowing where he was when he woke.

"He's so afraid of the vet, though," she said. "It terrifies him. It terrifies him and there's nothing we can say to make it better, to explain or give him comfort. I don't want his last moments to be like that."

"We can do it here," Sarah said.

"You guys do house calls?"

"No," Sarah said. "Of course not. But I carry the serum in my bag. Just in case."

"Just in case what?"

"Roadkill. It's a magnetism thing. Animals are attracted to me. Look at yours, staring. And it gives my life meaning. Profound meaning. But it's a liability on the road. They actually run at my car. Afterward, I always stop and often they're not dead. Have you ever tried to put down a baby possum with an ice scraper?"

Sarah like some kind of murderous mix of Saint Francis of Assisi and Dr. Kevorkian, dispatching roadkill along the interstate—this was not an image for the fourth martini. She rummaged around and pulled out two glass medicine bottles and two syringes. "The first puts him to sleep. The second does the other thing. Over in the blink of the eye. Super humane. We can do it right now."

One of my problems, Alex often said, was that I never wanted to make any decisions about the future. My fixation on the past was a kind of pathology that kept me—kept us—from moving forward. But my sense was always: forward to what? The future was not a destination to be enthusiastically anticipated. And even if a new cat was something we could look forward to, murdering our old cat was not the same as getting a new one. Which

Alex knew, of course, but for Alex the trick was to tear the Band-Aid off, no matter what it was holding on. Once she was anxious about something, it became all she could think about, and she began to nod and encourage Sarah, to ask questions about the process, how to do it, how painless it would be, the many ways it mimicked mercy.

"But I don't want to just throw him out," Alex said.

Sarah agreed that we couldn't throw the cat away. Not, she suggested, in an apartment with shared trash bins.

I was watching Derek, who was watching the wall as if the wall were watching him.

But there was a beautiful place, Sarah was saying, a place she knew, a clearing in the forest, dotted by wildflowers, near a creek, shady, sunny, dappled, fragrant, secluded but easy to find, not far away. It would be the perfect spot to bury him. We could go there now.

And then she was standing and on the phone. "We need a ride," she said to someone abruptly, then hung up. A few moments later, a beep from downstairs.

"Maybe bring the cat," Sarah said, and Alex scooped him up and threw him over her shoulder as she'd done when he was kitten, a position he liked, half-climbing on her back, looking behind her as she walked, and we were on our way, as easy as that, or maybe it was just the drunken compression of time, but we were in the apartment talking and then we were together, all of us, in a Jeep driven by a woman with pale pigtails who didn't turn around when we got in. From the front seat Sarah said, "This is my coworker, Jennifer."

"I brought the shovel," Jennifer said.

I can only say, to explain how I let any of this happen, that it felt like a dream I had once: driving down a country road in the dark, Alex and I with Derek, sleepy and curious between us, heading somewhere quietly, without upset, but with a growing sense of loss, a sense that I was in fact alone, which is a feeling I often have

in dreams and must be how Derek felt when he awoke in his lit-
terbox. But the streets were empty, the sky was muddy with clouds
and ambient light from somewhere else, and Alex was rubbing the
bridge of Derek's nose while he closed his eyes and purred. Soon we
were veering left off the highway onto a gravel road. I knew there
was a ski resort near here, about twenty minutes outside of the city,
but it wasn't popular because these weren't really mountains, just a
seam of hills where people biked or four-wheeled in the summer.
But Jennifer turned the beams on high and we rolled down a lane
of deserted ski cabins: uniform black triangles shaded against the
spruce forest behind them, the branches closed and shimmering
under the headlights like the wings of a sleeping bird.

The road ended at the last cabin. Jennifer parked and reached
over and touched the inside of Sarah's arm, briefly, and they got
out without looking back at us and we followed them and left
Derek in the Jeep.

"This is the place," Sarah said.

The cabin was like all the others: a tin A-frame roof sagged over
small rectangular windows and a mossy porch. Sarah and Jennifer set off, walking around the side to the back, where, amid the
patches of mud and grass, wooden stakes like the kind you'd tie
saplings to stood in geometric rows, so that the place looked less
like the lovely clearing in the forest that Sarah had described than
the ruins of a tree nursery.

"Just listen," Sarah said. "Can you hear the creek?"

From beyond the treeline came a moist sort of seeping sound,
as if the forest were leaking.

"I think I can," said Alex.

"It's just so fucking beautiful," said Jennifer.

"Whose place is this?" I asked.

"Nobody's," Sarah said.

Sensor lights had illuminated the front porch when we drove
up. The wall of the night dissolved into moths and midges scrambling in their glow and I thought, *I don't want to bury my cat
around all these bugs.*

"It's clearly somebody's," I said.

"Technically my father-in-law owns it," Sarah said.

"Ex-father-in-law," Jennifer said.

"He lets me use it," Sarah said. "He has to. It was part of the deal."

A door slammed. "Sarah, is that you again?"

A man stood on the back deck with a child, maybe eight years old. They were both wearing tank tops and porkpie hats.

Sarah did not turn around. "Go back inside, Gene."

"We want to watch," he said.

"Who is the kid?" I asked.

"If you watch," Sarah said, "you have to be solemn."

Alex and I had been hanging back and the man turned to us. "Cat or dog?" he asked.

"What?" I said.

"You don't look like horse people."

"Centaurs," said the kid in the matching hat.

"Take it easy," the man said.

"Go back inside," Sarah said.

I was trying to find a way to tell Alex that *all those stakes in the yard were people's pets,* but did not know how to do so without making it sound exactly like it was.

Alex said nothing. She was concentrating. She was probably still listening for the creek, like if she could hear it, everything would be okay, and I remembered the day she brought home the hat rack. Though she wouldn't say it like this, Alex believed that she was enchanted, trapped in a spell, but that the right moment, if curated or recognized, the right piece of furniture or clothing, the right painting seen at the right time, even the right person, could free her, let her discover herself again as she wanted to be: awake and unsnared in the world. There were years when she thought that I was the charm and clung to me with the desperation of a pilgrim who expects, just by touching, to be saved, and I—happy to be sacred and happy to be touched—believed I could be a piece of magic furniture, a mirror in which, when she looked, she'd see herself as I did: brilliant, beautiful, still becoming, but whole—and we had both watched with disappointment when that wasn't the case. By the time she turned to hats neither of us was expecting it to work and in fact, as with each of her attempts to rediscover herself, the failure of the remedy started to feed the problem: soon hats were everywhere, they accumulated in piles, odd shaped, absurd, disorderly, and her mission to reveal her life's contours again devolved into a simple domestic task—the struggle to neatly manage what was fragile and strange. She tried everything, uniform boxes she bought on the web, stackable shelving, nails in the wall all along the ceiling so that, with the little stepladder required to access them, our bedroom looked like an antiquarian library for haberdashers. And then one day she found the vintage hat rack: tall, teak, enormous. "It's perfect," she said. She was relieved and happy, she took my hand and pulled me into the bedroom to gather and sort hats on the bed before it all began again, and now, watching her, I saw she was pushing herself toward the same edge, listening for that creek as if hearing it would protect us from whatever we were losing, and I realized that I would not save her, I would let her live this way because I wanted her to think that we were not what was wrong, that the charm was out there, the solution to how to live, and maybe that meant I had to let them do this thing to our cat.

"We're staying," the man said. "It's my land and I get to watch."

"Go get him," Sarah said.

Alex wiped her face and took a step back toward the car and I reached out and caught her wrist. She turned sleepily to me. "Let's not do this," I said.

She nodded, but started to pull away.

"We'll call a cab," I said.

"A cab won't let you bring a cat," Sarah said.

"Cabbies have rigorous standards," the man said.

"I'm not sure if that's true," said Sarah.

"When it comes to cats."

"I have a ferret," the kid on the porch said. He was making fists and the man reached down and tapped the brim of his hat.

"Enough of that," he said. He looked over at us and shook his head. "He does not have a ferret."

This will be something we look back on, I thought. Look back on with wonder. Remember that night, in that hard middle season of our marriage, when we got blitzed and almost killed Derek and buried him in an enthusiast's pet cemetery? We'd laugh and shake our heads, finding ourselves still together on the far side of this moment. It'd be a story we told to friends over drinks in our apartment or someplace else, all the chairs filled.

"I'll get him," Jennifer said, and trudged off toward the Jeep with her shovel over her shoulder.

I imagined Derek sleeping in the back seat. For some reason, when we left him, he wasn't afraid. He wouldn't know what was happening. But when do we ever? A week ago Alex and I had had a terrible fight. We actually hadn't talked to each other much since and, though we never used to go to bed mad, that night she had stormed off and passed out. When I went to check on her she was asleep on top of the covers and my anger was gone. I couldn't remember what we'd fought about or why it had seemed to matter, or how under the speed of our lives our tenderness washed away from us and everything became brittle and precarious and I wanted to walk in and touch her cheek and wake her up and take her in my arms. I was like her in this way, I guess, to think that there was always a fix, that if I could cut through the tangle of thorns to where she slept and cradle her back into our first days, then this, just this, our touch, would be enough to save us. By now I knew it wouldn't work, that she'd still be mad when she woke, but still I lifted the sheets and covered her and stood in the room, waiting, with a little bit of moonlight falling through the window, cooler and paler than that light outside our apartment in New York all those years ago, hoping she could—even in her sleep, a little warmer now, a little more protected—feel my love. And then the cat started crying.

I found him lost, facing the wall, behind the hat rack. He was upset, the hair on his back was up in hackles and his ears were flat. He was staring straight ahead and yowling at the plaster. I said his name—once, twice. He heard me, even recognized my voice, and cried out. Alex groaned in her sleep. I said his name again. He quieted and listened. All he had to do was turn around. Simple enough, but no one can do it.

Jai Chakrabarti
The Import

RIGHT AWAY, Raj could tell Rupa apart from the other passengers. Even though he'd encouraged his mother to send her in American travel gear, she'd arrived in a homespun sari that looked like a hand-me-down, beleaguered and wrinkled as it was from the long journey. She clasped her hands together in greeting and tried to touch his feet, which alarmed Bethany.

"Oh, no, that's all right," said his wife. Like Rupa, she wore a nose ring, a little gem that once upon a time had set her apart.

Rupa blinked in response. The question of how well she understood English was a hotly debated topic. Raj's mother had claimed that she had enough education to be a barista, though any claim made by Raj's mother was inevitably questioned by Bethany, who still believed that Rupa knew little English and even less of the ways of the world. He had tried his best to stay out of the fray. They'd made a decision, and for the next six months they'd have to abide.

Raj located Rupa's luggage; when Bethany was out of earshot, he spoke to her in Bengali. "It's all right," he said. "Don't mind Bethany-didi."

When she smiled at him, he could see a winsome gap between her two front teeth, slight enough to at once be memorable and charming. They'd left Shay at home with his temporary babysitter, also a college-age girl, but one who spent more time on her phone than watching Shay's antics, which, as he'd turned three, had grown increasingly complicated, the turns of his imagination both rousing and enervating. Shay ran to the door as soon as he saw them, though when Rupa entered, dragging her one large duffel bag, he retreated behind the cover of Raj's legs.

"Who's that one?" shrieked Shay.

"This is your new babysitter," Bethany said. "Her name is Rupa, and Rupa is going to be staying with us."

"Oh. Why is she wearing that?" asked Shay.

"Ask her yourself," Raj said.

"No, I won't," said Shay, but he came out from Raj's legs and tugged at Rupa's sari.

She held the fabric tight against her body. "Hello, friend," she said in staccato English.

"You're not my friend," Shay said.

"That's not how we treat our guests," Bethany said.

Raj thought he heard a pleased note in her voice. When he'd first revealed the plan, she'd laughed, thinking it a joke, then, on realizing how committed he was to the notion, had argued at every turn. One of her fears, he believed, though she'd never said it outright, was that of being usurped, but here was their little boy showing his loyalties.

That night, he put Shay down as Rupa looked on. He demonstrated how much milk to pour, which books to read for bedtime, what songs to sing. At Bethany's insistence, they'd installed a nanny cam in Shay's room, so they watched from their bedroom as Rupa lay next to his crib, stroked his forehead. Once or twice, Shay called for his parents, but the day had been long, and he had little fight left. Rupa sang her own song when Shay cried. Raj recognized the tune, thinking at first that it was one of those film numbers, until he heard the song for what it was—a harbinger of rain, of harvest.

"Let's go on a date," he said.

"You're crazy," Bethany whispered, though Rupa was out of earshot. "We barely know her."

"We've got the baby monitor," he said. "Don't worry so much." He was forever lampooning her child-rearing anxieties, though, truth be told, Bethany had loosened up. Anyway, it made sense, given all the trips to the fertility clinic, resulting in two miscarriages in quick succession. When Shay finally came, those early months, each crawl, step, and then dash had felt like a disaster in waiting. There was only so much babyproofing one could do. Shay had survived, seemingly no worse for a few falls.

"Okay, but I'm keeping the monitor open the whole time," Bethany said.

They ended up having two cocktails apiece at their favorite local bar, which was just two doors down and close enough, perhaps, to even hear Shay crying if it came to that.

"He asked me where the moon comes from," Raj told Bethany. He knew dates were meant to exclude talk of Shay, but he couldn't help but reminisce about all that his son was saying.

She smiled as if confronted with a fading beauty, which meant that she wasn't listening to him. Maybe she was thinking about work or the roses he'd once ordered her from Kyoto. Time was passing her by. She was on business trips a quarter of the year, which meant she missed Shay more than he did. Time was passing him by, though he couldn't account for the reason. He chugged his cocktail and asked, "Now do you think it's a good plan?"

"Darling," she said, coming back to him, "your mother is always right."

It was, in fact, his mother's plan. Rupa was part of an entourage of servants that hung around their old colonial home in Kolkata. He didn't know her from Adam but trusted his mother's judgment. She'd suggested that live-in help would restore domestic bliss and offered up Rupa, for whom the six-month salary was equal to several years' wages. Not only that, but she'd offered to arrange for Rupa's visa, her flight costs, and even her salary. Inch by inch, Bethany had caved in.

"We can actually go out again. We can go out on the town and be who we were," he said.

"Trust me. We can't be who we were, this village girl or no."

"Just you wait," he said. "Just you wait and see."

He had visions of reliving his early New York life, only this time with Bethany in tow. They'd met eleven years ago speed dating at a speakeasy. He won her favor by holding her gaze. Now they were parents, living through the weather. Ever since Shay had been born, they'd tried to leave the city, but something held them there. Some vital force prevented egress, and even though they'd had their fill of dazzle and moonshot, even though their bank accounts said nothing for their time toiling away, they remained as they were.

"What does *the Import* eat?" Bethany asked. Two cocktails in, she'd found a nickname for Rupa that tickled them both.

"Mac and cheese?" he asked. "Cocoa Puffs with chocolate milk?"

That first week, he stayed home to help Rupa acclimate. Their house in India knew little of modernity's offerings, so Rupa marveled at the many settings of the dishwasher and the washing machine. Mostly, she admired the wide variety of snacks that were available to Shay at any time. Looking through her eyes, he could see how it might feel overwhelming for his little boy, as he was posed with choices at every hour—organic strawberries or cheese sticks or veggie straws or Goldfish. Perhaps it was like that for Rupa now.

"Goldfish is not really fish. It's more like a cracker," he explained.

"GOLDFISH IS NOT FISH," said Shay, who was already lording over his new babysitter. He was off preschool for the summer, which had expedited the need for childcare.

That first morning, they went to Prospect Park. Rupa bonded with Shay as he ran around a playground with a statue of a dragon, whose mouth spewed water instead of fire. Up the stairs she walked, and down the slide she came. He could tell that Shay loved the singularity of the attention. She was speaking Bengali to him, which had always struck Raj as a child's language, full of soft, cooing sounds, and Shay seemed to be following along fine enough. That was the other reason for Rupa. Raj's mother had wanted her grandson to learn her language. Raj hardly spoke to Shay in Bengali, so it was Rupa's task to bring the language to his son.

After the park and lunch, he put Shay down for his nap.

"There's some business I have to attend to," he told Rupa when Shay was asleep.

"Of course," she said. "I'm here now."

It was a thrill to leave his boy with Rupa. He wasn't sure if he could, but now he had. That she wouldn't tell Bethany was the sweetest part.

He walked to the other side of the park, where rents were a little more affordable and the greenery less plentiful. It had been here that, during one of his early-morning runs as a new father, he'd met Molly Choi. She was running as he was, and they matched each other's pace on the straightaway and struck up a conversation. Even though they were measuring a good clip, he could smell a cloud of lavender every time he leaned close to hear something she'd said. She was neither as pretty nor as worldly as Bethany, he came to discover, but she was better in bed. Though he wore a wedding ring, she never asked about his story. Back when he was enjoying press junkets and finding himself in the occasional one-night stand, there was no expectation of further intimacy, and the same was true of his encounters with Molly. Their get-togethers confirmed his feeling that he was simply acting out his nature. He had only recently begun to think this way, believing that there was little choice for him to do anything else but to respond to Molly's text that read *U Free?*—for it was in his constitution.

This afternoon, even though he'd explained to Molly in advance that he'd be free all week during the day hours, even though he knew that she herself had arranged to "work from home," he desisted. Ten feet from the musty hallway of her prewar building, he texted her back, *Kid won't go dwn. Sorry!* The kid he'd told her about, just not the wife. He jogged back across the length of Prospect Park, nearly trampled at one point by a spandex-clad cyclist. He realized he'd left his child—his precious, voluble creature—in the hands of a person he barely knew. His jog turned into a sprint.

When he got home, Shay was up from his nap and roaming in the kitchen. He was trying to explain that he only wanted to eat animal crackers. Rupa was cutting the fig-size grapes Bethany had bought into little pieces.

"He just got up," she said, continuing to slice even as she held his gaze, a display of culinary competence he found endearing. "He only wants to eat sweet things."

"We have to be careful about that," he said breathlessly. There was no fire to put out. He was relieved, though no fire to put out was also a little disappointing.

"Once he finishes his snack, would it be possible for me to make a call?" she asked.

"To India?"

"What's India?" Shay interrupted. He seemed to enjoy the challenge of having to learn their new language.

"It's the far, faraway place where Rupa and I came from," he said in English.

"Where did Mommy come from?"

"The far, faraway place called Missouri. They speak strangely there and barely know how to spell."

"It's just that it's getting late," Rupa said. "Over there, I mean. You could just call your mother on video. She'll have everyone come over."

"Hold on, skipper," he told his little boy. "We're establishing cross-Atlantic communications."

His mother answered the video chat, her face so overly close to the camera that he was level with the blackheads on her nose. "Beta, it's almost midnight. What is the matter?"

"I didn't realize it was so late," he said. Most of the times they connected it was she who called at times that suited her.

"Ma," Rupa said, squeezing beside him so he could feel the press of her hip on his. "Can I speak with her?"

"Who?" Raj asked.

"Hold on," his mother said, grumbling as she pointed the camera away and began to dress.

"Is that Grandma?" Shay asked, trying to burrow between their bodies.

"Oh," Raj's mother said, returning moments later. "It seems they've been waiting by my door."

"Who?" Raj asked again.

His mother panned the camera to show all the faces that had entered her room. He hadn't been home in over a decade and didn't recognize a soul. There was a gang of them, squinting into the screen.

"I don't see Lakshmi," Rupa said.

A little girl's face emerged into the camera. She was wearing a lacy dress that could've been used for a christening, entirely too hot for the weather. "Hi, Ma," she said.

"Who's that?" Shay and Raj said almost as one.

"That's my daughter," Rupa said. "She's turning five next week. Can I have a minute to talk with her? I want to introduce her to little Shay."

"Your what?"

"My child. Did Ma not explain?"

"Of course! Ma, I'm going to call you on your cell." He locked himself in his bedroom and considered what he'd say to his mother. This was her idea, though he'd been the one to sell it to Bethany.

Apparently, she'd left out a little detail. He had assumed that Rupa was unattached, not a mother herself. They'd contracted someone to watch their child while her own remained a world away.

"Completely unacceptable," he said when he'd gotten hold of his mother on his cell phone. "Why didn't you tell me she had a little girl? I thought she was, like, twenty-two or something."

"She is twenty-two," his mother said. "It just so happens that she started early. Pretty common for village people, actually."

"But you didn't tell me!" he said.

"You didn't ask," his mother replied. "Anyway, what does it matter? She has a history. All people do. That is why she is doing the job. With the money she gets, she'll start sending Lakshmi to private school. Six months is not a long time, you know. There's hardly a change in that time."

Perhaps that was true of him. Once he'd landed his job at the *Times,* he'd steadily put in enough hours to be neither fired nor promoted. *Do enough* was his mantra. It had been like that for most of his life until Shay was born, and he'd decided to go part-time to become the primary caregiver, a duty he'd come to regret. In his life, little seemed to change in six months, but for Shay, the same period of time had meant the difference between incoherent babbling and semicoherent speech. Lakshmi was a little older, but still. "There's something not right about it. I'm dreading telling Bethany," Raj said.

"Why would you tell Bethany?" his mother asked as if he were the dunce in the room.

"We don't keep things from each other," he said, thinking of Molly Choi's violet bedsheets.

"Then you are stupider than you look," his mother said. "Anyway, what will you do? Send her back? If you want, I can arrange her ticket to return home next week."

"Oh," he said, feeling a shiver run through his heart. Besides Molly Choi, he'd planned a host of activities that were to be timed with Rupa's visit. The potential loss of those afternoons at the bar, or at the beach, or winding his way through the couples' intimacy workshops he'd signed himself and Bethany up for, was too much to bear. "It's just that I need to wrap my head around this. Anyway, it's late over there. Goodbye, Ma."

When Bethany came home that night, she flashed a smile that signaled just how bone-tired she was. They'd entered the news world at the same time, but she'd desperately wanted to climb the ranks. So she had. From running features to becoming managing editor of a travel journal and then editor-at-large of a magazine that did travel entrepreneurship, a term he still barely understood. Whatever it meant, she still paid the bulk of the rent.

They'd prepared dinner in her honor. When motivated, Raj knew how to make a meal delight all the senses, and tonight he was. Motivated, that is. They'd all three made a trip to the market, where Rupa had marveled at the ubiquity of every fruit and vegetable, wrapped her sari around her shoulders as they passed through the frozen aisle. She made a few suggestions along the way, picking up bitter gourd, which he'd tempura-battered as an appetizer.

"What's that saying? The fastest way to a girl's heart is through her stomach?" Bethany said, relishing the gazpacho he'd made with heirloom tomatoes and fresh lavender.

"We had such a nice day," he said. "Didn't we, little man?"

Shay vehemently shook his head *no*.

"We went to the park, we got groceries, we acquainted Rupa with the neighborhood."

"Yes," Rupa added. "Yes, very good."

"Oh, I'm so glad things are working out!" Bethany said.

That night, Rupa again put Shay to bed, and this time, his boy put up less of a fight. Raj thought of telling his wife that he'd learned something of Rupa's history, but the dinner had gone so well that he let the moment pass.

He lay with Bethany in the dark of their bedroom, cluttered from the detritus of their travels, the trinkets all around him—the stars from Mexico with little inner lights, which they'd hung from the ceiling. Occasionally, they lit those lights and had sex, though this had been abated by Shay's coming, or simply by the exhaustion of their bodies, the familiar smells and snores. This night, he tried again by stroking Bethany's thigh. She murmured something.

"What is it, darling?" he asked. But it passed like a signal from a faraway planet.

The summer burned on. Bethany took a trip to Iceland, where her ancestors came from, for the sake of covering a music festival, and reported that even the far north was suffering from a heat wave. When she returned, she seemed more relaxed, rejuvenated, even. In her absence, Rupa had continued to learn the neighborhood. A month into her tenure, she'd even improved her English. She'd made friends with the bodega owner down the block, who regally opened the door just for her and Shay.

Raj and Bethany had reached the age when most of their friends had either tied the knot or committed to the single life the city offered. There were, however, still a few in-betweens— divorced men and women who threw potlucks to celebrate the second coming, or partnerships that were made for the sake of the children promised. It was for one of these that they'd been invited to Maine.

When he suggested that they try to leave Rupa alone with Shay for the weekend, Bethany threw her shoe at him.

"She hardly speaks English!" Bethany yelled. "What if something happens? How will she communicate?"

"She'll call me on the cell, and I'll translate," he said. "Besides, she's been picking up a few words." *Give me two mangoes for price one,* he'd heard her say to the bodega owner, who had mysteriously complied. He'd enjoyed the role of translator, his language the primary link to the person who was keeping their child safe. This frustrated Bethany; he knew that. She spoke three languages but not the one she'd need to understand what her son was now beginning to learn.

So Rupa came along, as did Shay. Raj's mood soured from the moment he picked up the minivan, which was the only rental left that could fit all of them. Driving it through the Palisades and onto I-95, he felt ancient. He'd turned forty the year before, but the gray had started to accumulate in his beard seasons earlier. Every time Shay cried or had a tantrum in the car, he felt another little strand of himself wither into old age.

Helen, the bride-to-be, had attended Bethany's alma mater, and in bygone summers, Bethany had spent weeks at their house on the lake. Now they'd rented a cabin next to the wedding plot. It was also on the lake but allowed for more privacy. There'd been an option for them to stay with other families at the wedding, but Bethany had declined. He suspected it was because she was embarrassed about Rupa, who still rotated through the same three saris she'd brought from India, fastidiously washing each day's garments in the bathtub.

They arrived on a Friday afternoon. With the wedding not until Sunday, they had a whole day to laze around the lake. The water felt too cold to him and to Rupa also, who for once declined to follow Shay as he ran from the beach into the clear water, instead letting Bethany run alongside her son. His wife was at home here. Even in Iceland, she said, she'd bathed in the fjords, and their son had inherited his mother's gift for cold waters.

"Have you ever been to the sea in India?" he asked Rupa.

"I was in North Kolkata. I was in my village, and now I'm here. Nowhere in between."

"Oh," he said. He was going to tell her a story about the time his parents had taken him to a seaside resort as a child, which no longer felt apropos. "Well, do you like it here?"

"The lake is beautiful, yes."

"No, I mean America," he said. "Do you like being with our family?"

She looked at him for a long moment. Even in the hour they'd been outside, her skin had bronzed in the sun. "Your little boy has a good heart," she said. "But I miss my Lakshmi."

Since that first call with his mother, he'd almost forgotten about the existence of her own child. She hadn't asked to see her daughter again, and he hadn't offered. It had seemed for the best. Once the time to tell Bethany the truth had passed, a gentle forgetting was all anyone could hope for. Even when his mother had called to check up on Shay and Rupa, they'd never again discussed Lakshmi. He wondered now who was taking care of her—a grandmother, an aunt, the uncle who chauffeured his mother around?

"We can call her again when we get back to Brooklyn," he said. He would have offered they try this weekend in Maine, but his cell phone didn't work and neither did the Wi-Fi, Helen's family having chosen to forgo installing a satellite dish or doing anything that would interrupt their connection to the bucolic setting.

When Shay took his nap, Raj and Bethany visited Helen and Rob, her husband-to-be, in their house. Rob fixed margaritas for everyone, and Helen shared their honeymoon plans for Tahiti.

"A bungalow on the beach is exactly what I need after all this. It's on stilts, so it sways whenever there's a wave, which means you sleep more deeply."

Rob licked the salt off his margarita glass. He was into watches that told him things about his body. At the moment, he was testing and wearing three separate ones, one of which caught the light from the lake and glowed like an orb. "So, who's the refugee?" he asked.

"Hey, that's not nice," said Helen. "Unless, of course, she is a refugee, which is perfectly fine, of course. There are countries where horrible things happen, and we shouldn't close our doors to everyone."

"She's not a refugee. She's here on a legal visa," Raj said.

"More to the point," Bethany said. "She's here to take care of Shay. Plus, she's being paid for by Raj's mother, so cheers to that."

They all clinked glasses, including Raj, who pretended he was enjoying the joke as much as anyone. Slowly, he zoned himself out of the conversation, smiling at the right times so no one would notice. There was an extraordinary amount of pink Himalayan salt on the lip of his glass, and he took his time to surreptitiously lick it off.

It was nearly evening when they thought to return to their cabin. Bethany was the one who'd realized, even though she'd had one more margarita than he, that the afternoon had flown by. "He's up from his nap, I'm sure—our little man," Bethany said. The tequila failed to mask the anxiety in her voice.

"Don't worry. The Import's there, and she's more responsible than both you and me," he said, which he'd meant to elicit a chuckle, but no one joined in.

They walked back to their cabin as the sun began to set on the lake. Even the old house next to theirs, where no one lived, which was being subsumed by the land, seemed as if it were made of impressions and follies, the nails on the clawed wood of the docks shining like white teeth.

The door to their cabin was open—no one bothered to lock doors here—but the house was quiet.

"Shay, baby?" Bethany called. She couldn't help but sound chirpy whenever she was worried, but Raj knew the difference.

"Maybe they're playing hide-and-seek?" he offered.

They searched through all the rooms. Shay's stuffed octopus was in his crib. His diaper bag with its travel toys was missing, as was Rupa's peacoat, which was too warm for the weather but which she'd brought anyway.

"Obviously, they went for a walk," Raj said. Even he had begun to feel it in his belly, the beginning of trouble. He'd always had a knack, as a reporter on the beat, for knowing, for instance, when to leave a protest before it became unruly. He thought of himself as a survivor, someone who made it through life's turbulences through the grace of this sixth sense.

Once again, Bethany restarted her cell phone, but there was

still no service. "One of these houses must have a landline. We could call the police, get them to help us," she said.

"That's a little premature, isn't it?" Raj said. He led them into the twilight, unsure of how to begin their search.

"We'll split up," Bethany said, taking charge. "I'll go get Helen. You look in the other direction."

The other direction meant the road that led off the island. "Road" was an exaggeration, though. It was a graveled stretch of land; there weren't even barriers to keep cars from falling into the water. As it darkened, he used his cell phone as a flashlight. The lock screen photo was one of Shay at seven months, an epoch before, when they'd barely been sleeping through the night, and when he'd questioned his life choices, as he was doing now, walking alone on that path where few of the cabins were lit.

He kept telling himself that Rupa was a village girl, which meant she knew something more about the darkness than he did. Probably, she was not even afraid, wherever she was.

Nearing the end of the island, he saw a canoe in the middle of the lake. He couldn't tell if it was Rupa and his little boy until he shined his light toward them and heard a response.

"*Oar in the water,*" Rupa called.

"Okay, you stay where you are!" he yelled back, as if they had a choice. He ran back toward the cabin and found Helen, Bethany, and Rob carrying life vests and a giant flashlight.

"I found them," he said triumphantly. "They went out on a boat and lost their oars, so they're just floating there. They're perfectly safe."

"You saw Shay? He's all right?"

"I heard Rupa. She said everything was fine," he said. In fact, he hadn't seen his boy or heard from him, the boat too far in the water to make out faces. Years later, sitting with his therapist, he would also begin to question whether, in fact, he'd heard Rupa. *Oar in the water.* He couldn't think of the Bengali phrase for that, and Rupa wouldn't have said it in English.

"I'll get our boat," Rob said.

They all squeezed into a motorized dinghy that had been beached on Helen's dock. The oarless canoe was still there, floating perhaps a little farther away from the island.

"I've got some rope, so we can just tie them to us," Helen said.

They seemed so capable in a crisis, these two. He hoped it would make for a memorable nuptial story they'd embellish with humor and retell for years to come.

For what seemed like minutes, Bethany hadn't said a word. He held her hand, felt her quickened pulse. She would as likely choke him now as give him the time of day. A reckoning was what she was planning, though he didn't know the details. He wanted to calm her and seem strong. She flexed her wrist and took his hand away as if it were a soiled napkin.

Nearing the boat, Rob dimmed the lights. It was still hard to see, but there was Rupa waving at them.

"You will go into that boat," Bethany said quietly. "You will bring my boy back. I don't care if you leave her there."

Rob steered the boats close together. When he lurched into the canoe, Raj saw Shay asleep in cat pose. Rupa had a hand on his forehead. She didn't seem at all surprised to see him. That's when he noticed the oar lying in the middle of the canoe. He kneeled to examine it for any defects, but it seemed right as mud.

"What are you doing out here?" he asked.

"I didn't want to remain inside," she said. "He was having a fit. We needed air."

"But it's dark, and I called you from the shore. Didn't you hear me?"

She gazed into the dark water. The slant of her face reminded him of a hunting knife held in shadows, a thin, sharp instrument. His knees began to shake. The stars edged closer to the lake, or so it felt, as if on this night, the cosmos was aiming to suffocate him.

Finally, she returned to him and spoke in a voice so low that only he could hear: "You worry at the wrong times and about the wrong things."

"What is she saying?" Bethany shouted. "What did she do to my son?"

"What you should worry about is a woman who fails to love you," said Rupa. She put the hood of her sari over her head, rocked in her seat as if muttering a prayer.

"Bring him here right now," Bethany called.

Rupa stood to her full height. Perhaps there'd been a river in the village, for she balanced in the canoe like a natural. She bent to pass him Shay. For a moment, her callused hands met his before he brought his boy back into the dinghy. Helen attached a rope to the canoe and they set off for the shore.

Back in his mother's arms, Shay awoke. He seemed startled by the moonlight. The night was alive with the chorus of bullfrogs and crickets and the hum of a myriad of other insects. For a long moment, he remained quiet. "Why are there so many frogs?" he finally said.

The love for his little boy roared out of Raj. "There are a million frogs here," he said in his first language, which had become for them like a secret tongue, but Bethany was holding Shay to her breast, cooing into his ear as if he were a baby newly emerged from the womb. Behind them, he could see Rupa clearly: a cheap nose ring, a dark face in the pale light. They were pulling her toward the shore as if she were their prisoner, but it was not like that at all. She had come of her own intent. It was that you could know a person only so well. Then their own ideas would muddy the water. Then you'd have to return them to where they belonged.

Amber Caron
Didi

WHEN MY BROTHER CALLS it's about his daughter, Didi. She is seventeen, out of control. Total nightmare to be around. Lacks respect for the rules. Out all night with friends he doesn't know, with boys she's just met.

"She came home at three thirty this morning in a pair of high heels," he says. "Last week she returned without any shoes at all."

It's not just her footwear. Don't even get him started about her shorts. Her shirts, too. Too short, too tight, big bold words printed across the front: *Juicy* and *Unwrap Me* and the one that stunned him into silence, drove him to pick up the phone and call me: *Save Water, Shower with Someone's Boyfriend.*

I laugh. It's not funny, he tells me. Nothing about this is funny.

He's tried everything. He's bought her new clothes. T-shirts—thick T-shirts, cotton T-shirts—and by the next day she's taken liberties with the scissors. Gashes across the back. A deep V into the neck. The arms are gone, the front tied in a knot above her belly button. Which is pierced. Did he mention that? That his daughter lay flat on her back to let some guy drive a hole through her stomach with a needle he sterilized on his stove?

"Her mother," he says. Her poor mother. She doesn't even

know what to do anymore. At wit's end. Haunted by images of Didi facedown in a ditch, shirt up over her head, her body bloody and cold.

What my brother doesn't say and what we both know: he doesn't deserve a child like this, but I probably do. Maybe I feel bad for her. Maybe I sense in this phone call that he wants to send her away to a place far off in the wilderness, far away from everything, to dig ditches in the desert or climb mountains with other troubled teens. All in the name of tough love.

"Okay," I say, "fine. Send her here. Just for a month. Just to reset."

Immediately, I regret it, realizing my brother is probably taking advantage of me.

My husband tells me I'm being paranoid, a little selfish.

"It's just a month," he says. "We can do anything for a month."

When Didi arrives, I take a week off from work, leave my lab in the hands of my graduate students, give them a single instruction: don't let anything die. The first thing I notice is that Didi is small, makes herself even smaller by curling up on a single couch cushion. She crosses her arms even when standing in large rooms. Tucks her legs under her body when she sits at the kitchen table, pushes her silverware under the lip of her dinner plate to take up even less space. Everything about her is scrunched, compact. And there is no sign of those clothes. What Didi wears is boring at best, nothing worth commenting on or worrying about. Ill-fitting blue jeans. Baggy tank tops. Sometimes she wears a baseball hat that comes down over her ears and makes her look even younger than she is.

Still, no matter what she wears, Didi's days are no longer her own. I take her with me to run errands. I tour her around Westport. We see movies in the middle of the day. I drive her out to the beach so she can see the Pacific coast. Just once, because I can't help it, I take her to the lab with me so I can check on the shipment of mantis shrimp that has just arrived. I show her one of the buckets, a single shrimp inside it. People are normally surprised by how big they are, but Didi doesn't move away, doesn't wince, so I pick one up.

"This thing has the fastest animal movement on the planet," I tell her. "They use this appendage like a crossbow. Wind it up real tight and then let it go, killing prey in a single whack."

"You do tests on them?" she asks. "Like experiments and things?"

I nod. "We've clocked that movement at eighty-three miles an hour."

"Does it hurt them? When you test?"

I return the shrimp to the bucket. I don't tell her about our next study, the one our lab is already behind on, where we will remove their eyes from their bodies to better understand how they see color.

"Well," I say. "We're getting better at controlling for that."

At home, Didi reads. Occasionally she'll get up to get a glass of water, to fetch something to eat, to find a sunnier spot in the house. She tears through the books she's brought. Biographies of musicians. Short histories of Western philosophy. When she finally puts the books down to come to the table and eat, she asks lofty questions. How can we all be more like Simone Weil? Like Mother Teresa? I bite my lip. When she finishes philosophizing, Didi offers impulsive confessions. She's never swum in a lake before. She's never been on a roller coaster that goes backward. She taught herself to ride a bike.

At the end of the first week, I tell Evan I think it is going to be okay. "She's a little weird," I say, "but it might actually be fun to have her around." I climb into bed beside him. I run my hand across his chest and hold on to his shoulder. Even though he's showered, he still smells like the nursery—the trees he repots, the garden herbs he sells to customers.

"I don't know," Evan says. "Something about her makes me nervous."

"What do you mean?"

"Have you noticed—" he says. He stops. We listen as a door down the hall opens and closes. Didi is in the bathroom. He lowers his voice to a whisper. "It's like she's set up mirrors all around her. Like she's constantly watching herself every time she moves."

The next morning I call my brother. I ask him if he is sure he sent the right child.

"Don't let your guard down," he says. "This is what she does."

In Didi's second week, I return to the lab because two of our specimens have already died and my graduate students can't figure out why. Before I leave, I write my office number on a piece of paper. Under it, my cell phone number and the number to the department just in case she can't reach me and needs to leave a message with the lab assistant. I magnet it to the refrigerator and tell her it is there. She says she'll call if she needs anything.

"Or just let Evan know," I tell her. "He took the day off, so he'll be around."

When I return that afternoon, I find her in the living room, curled up on a single cushion of the couch. She barely looks up from the book in her lap when I walk in. Finally, when I interrupt her, she turns to face me, blinks her eyes.

"Fine," she says, as though this word speaks to an entire day.

When I pry, she sighs, puts her finger between the pages to save her place, and shows me the cover. Another biography. A ballet dancer I've never heard of.

"Do you still dance?" I ask her, remembering all the recitals I missed.

"No," she says. "I quit when I was ten."

"You used to love it," I say.

She shrugs. "I was bored. And everyone else got better."

She puts the book on the couch and gets up to go to the fridge.

"Should we go to the pool?" I ask. I'm doubting even her belly button ring now. I think maybe my brother has made that up as well. "Free swim starts at seven."

Didi returns from the kitchen. She has an apple in her hand.

"I didn't bring a bathing suit," she says.

"I have lots. You can borrow one."

Didi scans me from head to toe, takes a bite of her apple.

"Or we could run down to the mall," I say, "and get you a new one if you want."

"I'm good," she says. She picks up the book and keeps reading.

"Where'd that come from?" I ask. "I don't remember buying apples."

"Grocery store," she says. "I walked down there today."

"Alone?" I ask.

"Yeah."

"The whole way?"

"It's not that far."

"I must have been on the phone with my parents," Evan says that night as he clears the table. "I didn't even know she was gone."

"You can't do that," I whisper. "When you're here, you have to watch her." My hands are deep in soapy water, and I am scrubbing the forks with a sponge.

"Val, she's seventeen," he says, slipping our dirty plates into the sink.

"You said you were okay with this. You said you were fine using your sick days, keeping an eye on her."

"And I did. We had lunch together. I checked on her twice. I made some calls. She read."

He dips a washcloth in the water, wipes the counter, and moves to the table.

"But we agreed you'd call me if she needed something. And you even said that you were a little worried. That whole mirror thing. You were concerned."

"We didn't need anything. I talked to my parents. Called my sister. Anyway, it was the middle of the day. How much trouble can she actually get in?"

I turn to him, hands soapy.

"That's not the point," I say.

"Then what is the point?"

"That something *could* have happened to her. That she *could* have gotten into trouble."

"Like what?" he says. "It's Westport. It's not like we live in the most thrilling place."

He hangs the wet washcloth on the hook above the sink. I grab his hand, but he doesn't look at me.

"What does that have to do with it?" I say.

"It's nothing. I'm just saying there isn't much trouble for her to get into here. It's quiet."

"You mean boring. You mean it's not Chicago."

Finally, he turns to me. "Listen, can we just drop this? Please? She's fine. We're fine. Maybe tomorrow we can set up a camera and you can observe us both from work, turn us into one of your little experiments, make sure we're doing everything exactly the way you want us to."

"Don't mock me," I say.

The mirror thing. I want Evan to explain it further. I want him to point it out to me so I can see what he sees, because all I see is a girl pulling her knees to her chin, her arms around her shins. Like she's trying to tuck in her heart. She takes up less and less space at the table each morning. Sits on her hands as we watch movies in the living room. When she takes popcorn from the bowl she chooses one kernel at a time. She lets it dissolve in her mouth before she chews. When I go into her bedroom each morning, it looks like she hasn't shifted in bed, like she didn't move from the first place her body touched. This morning, when I look in on her, I see she is sleeping on top of the quilt with no covers at all.

When she comes out, I am at the table eating breakfast and I ask her if the bed is okay, if she is comfortable in the guest room. She says yes, it's great. She hasn't slept so well in a long time.

"Do you not sleep well at home?" I ask.

"Not really," she says. "Mom refuses to run the AC."

"Are you too warm here?" I ask. "We can put the AC on at night."

"That's okay. I'm mostly comfortable," she says. "Although I might open my window a little tonight, if you don't mind."

When I get home from the lab they are both on the couch watching the TV on mute. I am late; at the end of the day, I successfully removed a specimen's hard, beadlike eye, but when I tried to transfer it to a test tube, rushing, it popped out and I lost it. On the TV, I see footage of an attack somewhere in Iran, and Didi is telling Evan about the Iranian poet she has been reading. He looks genuinely interested. I don't interrupt. Instead, I put my bag down quietly, taking a seat on the chair beside Evan, and listen as she talks about the way the poet broke a traditional form to make a political statement about the injustice of the current regime. When Didi finishes, she goes to her bedroom to get her coat, and Evan raises his eyebrows and mouths *wow*. He leans over to kiss me on my forehead, my nose, my lips, and when Didi returns we all walk into town for pizza.

The waiter is excited to see us. He scolds Evan and me for not coming more often, and he welcomes Didi to town, to the restaurant. He tells her everything on the menu is good, that she can't go wrong, which is exactly the same thing he tells us every time we come here. Whatever we order, it is always, in his words, a very fine choice.

Didi defers to us. She will eat anything, she says, and so we order two pizzas and a salad to share. As we wait, I try not to watch the TV behind Didi and Evan where they are showing the aftermath of the bombing. It's bad. More than four hundred dead. They keep showing the same image of a young boy with a bloody face. I'm certain it's not his blood. His face isn't at all scratched, but the boy is clearly stunned. I try to refocus on Evan and Didi's conversation. He is wondering about future plans. Has she thought about college?

"Not a lot," she says. "I'm thinking about taking a gap year."

"Be careful," Evan says. "Those don't always work out."

He is speaking from experience. She asks him what he means.

"I had plans," he says. "I was going to backpack around Europe with my girlfriend. Take the train from Spain to Italy to Germany. Up through Scandinavia. Had it all planned out. Had the plane ticket in my pocket. Two weeks out and she dumps me. Turns out she had applied to college and was going to Boston without me. She was waiting to tell me until all her financial aid came through. That trip abroad? That was her backup plan. *I* was her backup plan."

"So you didn't go?" Didi asks. "Why didn't you just go alone?"

"Wasn't like that. Wasn't about the trip. It was about her. Us."

"And the girlfriend?"

Evan looks at me with a grin.

"She came running back, eventually."

"No!" Didi says. "It was you! You did that to him, Aunt Val?! That's so cruel!"

Evan smiles even wider and turns back to Didi. "I was okay," he says. "She did the smart thing."

The waiter delivers both pizzas and the salad to the table. He serves us each our first piece. We toast with our water glasses.

"To gap years," I say, and they both laugh.

"Well," Evan says, "you've heard my warning. But what do you have planned? Hopefully nothing with a cruel-hearted high school sweetheart."

Didi shakes her head.

"No," she says. "Nothing like that. I don't even know really. I just thought it might be nice to have a break from school for a little bit."

She picks the mushrooms off her pizza. Puts them in a tidy pile on the side of her plate.

"It's kind of nice here," she says, not looking up at us. She moves on to the sausage, puts it in a separate pile. "It's quiet, at least. Not as hot as Texas."

She cuts her crust into bird-sized bites and chews one slowly.

Calculated, I think. Maybe that's what Evan means with the whole mirror thing. Every move. Every word. Every gesture. It is all very calculated.

"Yeah, Westport is nice," Evan says.

The waiter returns. He asks Didi if everything is okay. If there was something wrong with the pizza. If he can get her anything else.

"It was so good," she says, handing him the plate, her pizza picked over but not eaten. "So delicious."

At the end of the meal, I suggest we walk home and have dessert on the porch. It is a beautiful night. A coastal breeze has come inland. We pay up. As we leave, the waiter runs after us with the box of pizza we left on the table. He apologizes to Didi again, is concerned she hasn't had enough to eat.

"I'm worried you will float away," he says.

She promises him she had plenty to eat. She pats her stomach to convince him.

As we walk home, Didi and Evan are back on the Iranian poet. More lofty questions: What do you think is the role of the poet during such violence? What is the role of *any* artist, for that matter?

At home, Evan brings a bottle of wine onto the porch. Didi says she needs to call her parents.

"It's only eight," I say. "Come eat pie with us."

"I promised I'd check in."

"One piece. Look," I say, holding up the plate. "From the bakery. Look how beautiful it is."

She agrees, reluctantly. On the porch, she sits on the edge of her seat, picking at the cherries while Evan and I each take a second piece, a second glass of wine. She finishes it though, the entire slice of pie. And then she clears our dishes for us. I hear her at the sink washing them. She comes back out to say she's turning in. She's going to go to her room, call her dad. She will probably read after that.

I smile at her. "Tell him we say hi."

Evan and I talk about our days—the shipment of hostas that arrived at the garden center, how he had to unload them alone; how I lost the shrimp eye and am behind on our data collection—and I hear Didi's voice coming through the night. It's soft, but I can tell it's the voice of someone who is happy. It's also a young voice. So young. Almost babyish, as though she is talking to a dog, coaxing it to her with a treat. Her window is open. I stop talking. I am straining to hear her words.

"Hello?" Evan says, waving in my direction. "Where are you, Val?"

"Have you ever heard a girl talk to her parents like that? In a voice like that?"

"You would be a terrible mother," he says.

"Wouldn't I? Overbearing. Overprotective."

"A total spy," he says.

This has been a joke between us. I don't believe it is untrue.

"Still," I say. "Admit it. It's a little weird. The whole thing at dinner. Picking at her food like that."

He admits it. Yes, it was strange. We stay up late, long after Didi's voice goes quiet and her light shuts off.

"You had to tell her that story," I say. I am smiling.

"We could still do it," he says. "Take a gap year. Travel around by train. Find ourselves and all that."

This isn't the first time he has proposed the idea. He brought it with him when he eventually followed me to Boston. And to Minneapolis for grad school. And to Chicago for my postdoc. And now here to Westport for my job. For him to bring it up now, I know it means he is bored, restless, generally unsatisfied with the fact that we have landed in a town he doesn't like but is, once again, making work.

"Maybe for my sabbatical," I say.

"In five years?" he asks, exasperated.

I know it is the wrong thing to say. His has been the harder path, I know this. The constant moving. The random jobs he's accepted not because they will lead anywhere but because they pay rent. The year working construction in Boston. The year as a substitute teacher. Three years waiting tables. And now the garden center, where he works alongside high school students, unloading trees and plants, hauling them into place at the nursery and then hauling them into the cars and trucks of customers.

"What if I *had* gone?" Evan asks. It is his attempt at a lofty question. "What if I had boarded that plane and spent the year traveling alone? What if I hadn't been there when you came home that first Christmas?"

I have no answer. I sip my wine.

I look in on Didi after midnight, just before I go to bed, and she is there, her back to the wall, curled up in a ball, the window open, the breeze cool, covers pushed to the bottom of the bed.

I remember a neighbor in Chicago. A woman with triplets, all boys, eighteen months old. We had just moved in, and I was unpacking boxes one day when she came running to our door. She was locked out. She had slipped out to have a cigarette—*Not even a full one,* she said. *Just two drags*—and the door clicked behind her. Her boys were inside. She had already called the landlord. He was on the way with a key. We stood at her living room window and watched her triplets slink around on their stomachs, rise to their hands and knees, and begin to crawl. There was no gate to the kitchen. The bathroom door was wide open. A set of wooden stairs led to the second floor. She was crying, cursing herself for being so stupid, for being so careless, tapping on the window, trying to get the boys to look at her. I grabbed a rock from the yard. *If they get too close to the kitchen or the stairs,* I told her, *I'll put it through the window*. She nodded. She sang to the boys through the glass. They crawled toward us. They smiled at their mother. They extended their arms, wanting to be picked up. They cried. Finally, the landlord arrived with the key, and I walked back to my house with a racing heart, the heavy rock still in my hand, thinking this must be what parenthood is like all the time.

In the morning, before I leave for work, I knock gently. It's supposed to reach ninety degrees today, and my plan is to go to the lab for a few hours, come home at lunch, and bring Didi to the store so she can get a bathing suit and we can spend the afternoon at the lake. That's what my calendar says will happen.

I knock again, but Didi doesn't respond, and so I knock a little louder, and then I let myself in. She isn't there. I'm thinking that she must have slipped into the bathroom after me. She woke early because she went to sleep early. I move down the hall to the bathroom, but she isn't there either. I check the back porch, which is as we left it last night. Two wineglasses. An empty bottle of red.

Even when I say it to Evan it doesn't really seem possible.

Her clothes. Her makeup. Gone. Her shampoo is gone from the shower. Her retainer from the bathroom sink. Hair ties. Everything, gone.

There's nothing in the closet, no shoes by the door, and all I can say—all I can *think* to say—is, "She was just here, she was just here. She can't just disappear."

Evan already has the phone in his hand. He is calling Didi, and I can hear the phone ring. It goes to voicemail, a mechanical female voice rattling off the digits of Didi's number. Evan hangs up.

"Try again," I tell him.

"Val," he says.

"Do it," I tell him.

He is scrolling through names in his contact list. He presses my brother's name.

"No," I say, taking the phone from him. "Not yet."

"Maybe he's heard from her. Maybe she said something last night when she talked to him."

"She didn't call him last night," I say. "No girl talks to her father with a voice like that. You heard her. You heard that voice."

He nods. He knows I'm right.

We sit on the couch and think of all the possibilities, and then Evan leaves the house to check the bus stop, every business in town.

Before he closes the door, almost as an afterthought, he instructs me to do what I already know I must: "Call your brother."

Of course he hasn't heard from her.

While he yells at me, I walk out onto the driveway and stand there as though she'll show up while I'm on the phone, so I can tell him it's all been a big mistake, a huge misunderstanding. I consider all the things my brother has told me about her, all the things he's telling me again.

Teenagers do this stuff every day, I hear myself telling him. Teenagers disappear and come back when they're hungry.

She's not a dog, he is saying. She's not a *goddamn dog*.

"I just mean—"

"I thought things were going well. I thought everyone was having a *great* time."

"They were," I say. "We are."

It goes on like this until Evan returns, without Didi, and he gets out of the car and tells me there's no sign of her anywhere, that it might be time to call the police.

Two officers arrive within minutes. I have seen one of them—the woman—in uniform, walking up and down streets, putting tickets on people's windshields. How I hated her in those moments when she just stood watching the meter, counting down, waiting for the time to run out, so she could print a ticket and slide it under the wiper. Now it's not hate I feel but an intense need to speak directly to her rather than the other officer—a man I've never seen before.

"My niece is gone," I say as she leads me back inside, taking out her notepad and her pen, asking me to tell them when we last saw her, who in the area she knows, how long she has been here, what she was last wearing.

"What does that matter?" I reply. "What she was wearing?"

The woman looks at me. She doesn't skip a beat.

"For identification purposes," she says. Before I can apologize, Evan is trying to describe her clothes. Baggy jeans. Loose T-shirts. Sometimes a ball cap. As he speaks, all I can think is, *Please let her be okay. Please, please. Let this nice woman, Officer Peterson, find her.*

The police ask to look around. They are in and out of our bedroom. In and out of Didi's room. The bathroom. The porch. They ask about the bottle of wine. The glasses. They check windows and doors. I follow them around the house. I follow this woman, especially. She inquires about locks and alarm systems.

"Do you always keep it open?" she says of Didi's window.

It takes me a second to make sense of her question. "You think someone came in and took her?" I ask.

"We have to consider everything," she says. "But between you and me, I doubt it."

I want this woman to tell me again and again in her matter-of-fact voice, just as she's telling me now: "Listen, this happens a lot. Teenagers leave. Disappear for a day or two. They usually show up."

And that's what I was trying to say to my brother. Not that they return when they're hungry but that they usually show up.

"Her father thinks she's a bad kid, but he's wrong," I say. "She tries to make herself small. She moves from one sunny spot to another all day, reading biographies of ballerinas and books about Iranian poets. And when she moves, it's like she's set up mirrors all around her. Like she's always watching herself."

Officer Peterson looks up from her pad. "What do you mean?" she says.

I don't tell her that I think Didi's actions seem calculated, borderline manipulative. I don't want her to think badly of my niece. *I* don't want to think badly of her.

"I only mean that she's careful," I say. "Incredibly alert."

I catch her looking behind me, beyond me, and I turn and see Evan showing the other officer where we store the bikes. The shed is full, both bikes parked in their separate corners.

I pick up the phone because it is ringing, and I am certain it will be Didi. But it's my brother, and he is listing off times, and I am confused until I realize he is on a computer, looking at flights, booking something to Portland.

My brother has never been on a plane. He rarely leaves East Texas. He works on the oil rig where our father worked, where our grandfather worked. He has taken care of our sick parents. Has given everything he has to his daughter. Has worked long hours to give her private dance lessons.

"Listen, you might be overreacting," I tell him, trying to project calm, trying to remain confident. "She'll probably show up."

He hangs up on me.

The police leave. I go into Didi's room. I pull back the covers on the bed. I look for anything she might have left behind, any kind of clue. Suddenly I am furious at my brother. He knew. He knew she would do this, and he sent her here anyway. Surely he is also a little responsible for this. I pick up the pillow. I pull the sheets taut. I make the bed. She was here just last night. Sleeping in this bed. Evan is beside me now.

"We'll find her," he says.

It's a trope, I tell him. It's a cliché. Girls always disappear. They make themselves small, and then they disappear.

"And if they don't disappear, they go insane. That's it. Those are the only two options we get."

"I thought the cliché was that girls were always in pursuit of boys," Evan says.

"So we have three options!" I yell.

That I am mad at him is inexplicable, incomprehensible. This isn't his fault. No more than it is my fault. And yet, I think, if only he had been less cavalier about the whole thing, had been more concerned about the walk to the grocery store, her coy voice on the phone.

His hands are on my shoulders. His fingers are pushing at the muscles, only he's missing the muscle and hitting the bone, and I shrug off his hands and walk away, down the hall, into the kitchen, where the dishes have been washed and are sitting neatly in the drying rack. He is behind me.

"She knew," I say. "Last night when we went for pizza, and she ate pie with us, and she cleared our plates, and she washed them. She had already planned to leave. I know it."

"She knew the second she arrived, Val."

I don't want this to be true. I don't want to believe it.

Evan is going to retrace our steps.

"From the last three weeks?" I ask. "All of them?"

"You stay," he says, kissing me on the forehead. "In case she comes back."

My brother calls again. He asks for our address. He wants to know how he is supposed to get from the airport to our house, which is an hour and a half away.

"Rent a car," I say.

And because I know what he is thinking, I tell him we'll pay for it.

Evan and I sit on the porch. We wait. This is what you do on the first day while you wait for a teenager to return, which they usually do, almost always do.

You check the local newspaper headlines. You drive around the neighborhood.

You turn on the TV in the middle of the day, expecting to see her face, her body.

You try to distract yourself with small tasks.

You create false deadlines. She will be back by noon. And when she doesn't arrive, it's by three. Then dinner becomes your arbitrary marker, and you push dinner later and later until your husband puts a burger and fries in front of you.

You feel you shouldn't eat it. You feel you don't deserve it.

But you eat it because you haven't eaten all day and you are hungry.

I watch my brother, a short, balding man with a beard, get out of the car. He looks different. Older and tired and more like our father than I have ever noticed.

I expect the trunk to pop open, for him to pull out his suitcase, but instead I see my brother swing a backpack over one shoulder as he walks to where I am standing at the front door. And now

I am crying. Because all he's brought is a backpack. Because it's been three years since I've seen him. Because his daughter is missing. Because it's his first time on an airplane, for this. Because he warned me, and I didn't believe him.

He wraps his arms around me, and I feel like I don't deserve this either. His comfort. But I take it. It has always been this way with us. Fierce on the phone. Quick with blame. All of that gone when we see each other.

That night, we all pretend to sleep, and in the morning, while I'm still in bed, covers pulled up around my face, eyes closed because I am tired, I hear Evan in the bathroom. He is showering. Shaving. I hear the toothbrush against the sink. And then he is standing at the closet. He is dressing. I sit up in bed.

"You can't," I say, but I know as soon as I say it that he will. He has to. If he calls in sick again he will lose his job.

The police station is empty. Just a small waiting room with three seats. An officer sits behind a desk. I hope my brother is comforted by how quiet it is in here. I hope he feels, as I do, that this nice man behind the counter is going to help us. I tell him that my brother has just arrived, that my niece hasn't been seen in over thirty-six hours, and that we need to talk with Officer Peterson.

"She's not on duty," he says. "You'll have to talk with me." My brother stands with his hands in his pockets. As he talks with this new officer, I listen.

Yes, she has done this before, many times, about a year ago it started. Every few months. Out all night. Gone for days at a time. Once much longer—more than a week. That was during winter break.

I look at him. What he is saying—none of it makes sense. It's not the same girl, I want to say.

After we leave the police station, we stop for coffee, and when we get back in the car, I make the absurd offer to give him a tour of town. Maybe a drive out to the beach. He has never seen the Pacific Ocean.

"I told you. You couldn't take your eyes off her. I told you. You can't leave her alone."

"We were sleeping," I say.

"Before that? All those other days?"

I lie: "We never left her side."

We go home and sit on the stoop outside the house, waiting. I ask him about his job, and he says what he always says: it's a paycheck. He asks me about mine, and I go on for too long and in too much detail about how we think mantis shrimp have a different kind of color vision, how we're trying to get a reading from photoreceptor cells but can't even fit a recording device onto them because they're so small. When I look at him, I can see I've lost him.

"She wants to come live here next year," I say. "After she graduates, if she decides to take a gap year."

"Is that what she told you?" he says.

I nod. I'm trying to gauge whether he is hurt or angry or relieved, but he just shakes his head. He laughs a little.

"She doesn't have enough credits to graduate next year," he says. "She's still considered a sophomore."

We sit for a long time, watching cars drive by the house. Across the street two dogs bark at the fence. The owner comes out. Tells them to get inside, to cut it out. A kid rides by on a bike. Another one follows on a skateboard. They are singing a song that is popular this summer, one that is played over and over on the radio.

Evan comes home at five fifteen. He doesn't say it, but I can tell he has had a bad day. He kisses me and pats my brother on the shoulder.

"Anything?" Evan asks.

"Nothing," he says.

. . .

That evening, the police call. They ask us to come down to the station. They have a few more questions. They have something we should see.

We are in the car and down the road before anyone speaks.

"Did he say what it is?" Evan asks. "What they want to show us?"

"A picture of some kind," my brother says. "They wouldn't tell me more than that."

A picture, I think. Of Didi alone? At the airport, boarding a plane? Getting into a strange car? Her body, my god. Would they ask us to come down to identify a picture of her body? Would they be so casual about it on the phone?

I hope, when we walk through the police station doors, that Officer Peterson will be there to greet us. She's not. It's a different officer. Someone we've never talked to before, and it's my brother he needs to speak to. They disappear down the hall, and Evan and I sit on chairs in the waiting room. I reach for his hand.

"Was your day okay?" I ask.

He turns to me. I think he will tell me about the apple trees he pruned incorrectly or how he overfertilized an entire shipment of succulents. I'm expecting news of broken terra-cotta pots or bamboo sticks that never arrived.

"When you left," he says, "this is what it felt like. Exactly like this."

The officer behind the bulletproof window stretches, arms overhead, and yawns. It takes me longer than it should to realize we aren't talking about Evan's day, or the plants he tended to, or the nursery at all.

I shake my head. "You knew where I was going," I say. "You could have called me. You could have come to visit whenever you wanted."

"I'm not talking about college, Val. I'm talking about all those other times you disappeared, before you left for college—those nights you didn't call, the weekends you just vanished. And later, all those research trips, how you extended them again and again, sometimes without even telling me, sometimes for weeks at a time."

We have had this conversation before. More than once. Dozens of times. But I see something new in his face now, not a bitterness but a sadness, and I am convinced this is the first step to his leaving me—maybe for a year, maybe longer. Before I can say anything to talk him out of it, my brother is coming back down the hall, the officer behind him.

My brother shakes his head. "Wasn't her," he says, and I can see he is near tears, shocked by what he has been forced to look at.

We drive home in silence.

It all ends just as Officer Peterson promised.

We drive back to the house from the police station, and she is there. My brother is out of the car before I even come to a full stop. I sit in the driver's seat while he goes to her. Evan doesn't move. He sits beside me. We watch.

I wonder how many times this scene has played out. How many times has a girl returned to find no one is waiting for her?

And what is it you want to know? Whether my brother hits her? (He doesn't.) Whether she is crying? (She isn't.) Or do you want to know where she was, what she was doing? (She will refuse to say.) Is she harmed? (Not in any way that I can tell. No scrapes or bruises. No broken bones. No blood.)

Because you are wondering. Because people always wonder, because under these circumstances, it matters what she is wearing, by which I mean it matters to me:

My clothes. A pair of jeans—black and tight and cropped. A white T-shirt, baggy and see-through, a baby-blue tank top underneath. Black summer sandals. Beige stitching at the seams. Thin leather straps that loop around her heels, hug her toes, and, I am certain, have left her blistered. I leave Evan in the car, and I go to her. I pull her to me. I feel her body against mine, rigid and small and hard. Her heart pounds against my palm. I fold her in. I tuck her in as close as I can and hold her for as long as she lets me. When she begins to pull away, I let go, certain there is nothing I can say, nothing I can do, to make her stay. So I do the only thing I can. I pull her hands out of her pockets. I push her shoulders back. I am not gentle.

Francisco González

Serranos

THE TRAILER PARK was our domain. We were nine sets of
parents, with a dozen children. On the other side, we had
all lived in the same village. Now we lived in Ranch View Mobile
Estates, on the outskirts of Buellton. The owner had posted a sign
at the entrance that said FIXER-UPPERS AVAILABLE! and another
that said THIS COULD BE HOME! We knew because our children,
who were literate, had told us.

At Ranch View Mobile Estates, there was no code enforcement
and no regulation enforcement. A scattering of oaks and syca-
mores fought for their lives among heaps of used, broken, empty
things: huge propane tanks, PVC pipes, busted stoves, crippled
tractors. When we walked around our neighborhood, we did so
with the occasional sound of shattered glass crunching underfoot.

But the trailer park was a good place to raise children. Each
family had its own Shasta, Forester, Kenskill, or Spartan. Rent was
only a few hundred dollars per month. And the entrance could
not be seen from the county road, which made it difficult to find,
even if you'd been told where to go.

A wall of corrugated tin surrounded our five-acre community.
We had fashioned secret exits along its perimeter, where we'd

loosened the bolts that joined the sheets of metal. In the event of a raid, we could jiggle the bolts, slide a panel, and take flight into the woods.

Although we had been ten years in the valley, and no longer thought of ourselves as foreigners, our precautions had long ago become a part of us. We avoided banks, police stations, doctors' offices. We had stopped attending Mass, since we'd heard the stories of worshippers seized at the steps of churches. And we visited Albertsons or Safeway only in groups of three at most. We couldn't risk losing too many adults; someone had to remain to watch over our daughters and sons.

We were civilized people. We were not like the migrants who stumbled through the valley, alone or in small bands. They'd wander the roadsides, begging for work in alleys or parking lots. They'd toil a week or two on ranches. Now and then, we caught sight of them sleeping rough in the shade of trees, in creek beds, or beneath bridges. Very few of them managed to harden to the labor, put down roots, and endure as we had.

When the strangers walked into Ranch View Mobile Estates, we thought they'd arrived by mistake. There were eight of them. They lugged fifty-pound packs, bedrolls, and polyester blankets; they wore huaraches on their feet. We nearly approached them to ask if they needed directions, but they knew where they were going. They had keys to the vacant Holiday Rambler and began to move in.

The Holiday Rambler was one of those enormous 1960s trailers. It had a makeshift plywood porch. Its broken windows were boarded up, and its flanks blackened by a fire that must have burned before our time. We were shocked that human beings would make that rig their home.

At first glance, the strangers all appeared to be young men in their early twenties. But then we noticed a woman among them who had long gray hair. Her presence eased our fears. If the youths had traveled with an elder and taken care of her, surely they couldn't be so bad.

Nevertheless, we agreed that the worst thing you can have in your proximity is other people. We observed the strangers' every move as they made improvements to the derelict trailer. They pulled the weeds that obscured it. They chased away the family of possums that lived in its undercarriage. They unboarded its windows and used old rags to shine its corroded aluminum exterior until the trailer looked bigger, and parts of it reflected light.

The strangers knocked on our doors and made their introductions. Rather, it was the gray-haired woman who introduced them, while the seven young men stood behind her in silence. The woman wore a woven cotton dress with the sleeves torn, and a crimson rebozo around her shoulders. She moved and carried herself like a prizefighter in the ring. She seemed to be in charge.

She said, "I am Mother Paz. And these are my sons."

Immediately we were skeptical. The young men did not resemble their supposed parent, nor did they resemble one another. That, and Mother Paz appeared far too old to be their mother. Despite this, when she referred to them as "sons," she sounded so confident that none of us could bring ourselves to challenge her.

One by one, we presented ourselves to our new neighbors and shook their hands, which were every bit as rugged as ours. It was hard to communicate with the young men. Their words were plated with an accent we didn't recognize. But Mother Paz spoke for them, and she spoke our language well. She told us they had come from the Sierra Madre de Chiapas.

"So you're Serranos," we said. "Tell us, how bad are things in Chiapas?"

This was a rhetorical question. We knew about the peasants

who had risen up against the government and been crushed. We knew about Subcomandante Marcos, and Red Mask, and the massacre of Acteal. It was the stuff of legend.

The old woman, who styled herself a mother, grinned at us, and yet we detected a gloom passing behind her eyes. We could tell she was pretending not to be upset, so we pivoted.

We asked the Serranos if they needed jobs. We explained that we earned our keep three miles up the road, at a boutique winery of some renown, where grapevines crowned the terraced hills. The winery also had horses, hens, and goats. We cared for the animals, and we cared for the grapes; we poured samples for tourists: reds, rosés, whites.

We mentioned that our boss might need a few extra hands, since it was now April, and fruit would soon appear on the vines. "We can set you up," we offered, "as long as you deliver." We didn't know what sorts of people grew up in the southern mountains, or what manner of work they'd be skilled at, but we hoped we might win them over by doing them a favor.

Mother Paz shook her head.

"Thank you, but we have all of us farmed for the last time."

Arrangements had been made: they would work at the new Greek restaurant.

The Greek restaurant was on the far side of Los Olivos, which meant that the Serranos had to commute more than six miles each way on foot. They left in the small hours before dawn and got back after dark. We predicted, correctly, that their routine was not sustainable.

A few weeks into it, we were all dining at the picnic tables at the center of the trailer park, when the Serranos approached us. Mother Paz asked if we knew of an easier way to reach Los Olivos—a bus, perhaps. No, we assured her; there was no public transportation in this corner of the valley. We were used to walking to the winery, and our children were used to walking a half mile to their high school.

Mother Paz snapped her fingers. "I should have known—there's always one stitch in the rug that I miss. I've got another idea, though."

She'd heard about the Department of Motor Vehicles. She and her sons would probably go there and obtain driver's licenses. If they saved for a few months, she figured they could buy a used car. Nothing fancy—something small would do.

We couldn't stop ourselves from laughing. We informed the Serranos that they wouldn't be driving on California roads, not in this lifetime. Only citizens were allowed to have licenses. And even citizens had to take tests, fill out forms, and speak English if they wanted to get behind the wheel of a car. The process was so convoluted, so overfilled with restrictions, that it would be simpler to hijack a crop duster and fly to work instead.

Mother Paz was incredulous. "Those rules are absurdities!" she cried.

Again, we laughed.

"You're not wrong," we said. "Even so, you're in the North now, and every dance is a different dance."

The following Saturday, the Serranos left the park in the chill of dawn. When they returned several hours later, they were walking single-speed bicycles with knobby tires. The bicycles were teal or hot pink or lime green, and low to the ground. Some of them had tasseled handlebars; clearly they were built for kids.

We didn't know how to ride bicycles, and neither did our children. It was immediately obvious that the Serranos didn't either, though they wasted no time in trying.

They practiced in the evenings. Three or four of them would roll through the trailer park, pushing themselves along with their feet, while the rest used flashlights to illuminate the path ahead.

We were glad they had sense enough to wear helmets. Some of the riders managed to lift their legs for a few seconds, but they seemed to spend most of their time crashing to the ground and shouting words that we assumed to be profanities.

Mother Paz, who was clumsier than the rest, crashed so many times that her helmet finally broke in two. The young men helped her up, and she shook dirt from her dress.

"Remember the proverb," she said. " 'The Devil fell and lost his grace, but not his pride.' "

Minutes later, she was at it again.

In the days that followed, the Serranos began to add accessories to their useless bikes: reflectors, baskets, luggage racks, bells. A few of them tied artificial roses to their top tubes. Then came the American flags, the miniature ones you could buy at Walmart; the Serranos attached these to the backs of their seats.

There was something particularly annoying about the flags, which seemed to imply that we needed to be reminded of where we lived. Or perhaps the Serranos were foolish enough to believe that stars and stripes would save them if they got in trouble in the world beyond Ranch View Mobile Estates.

Spring gave way to an early summer. Squashes and tomatoes ripened in the fields on either side of the county road, and grapes swelled in the vineyards. It wasn't hard then to ignore the Serranos. Our shifts were longer and busier; visitors flocked to the winery in buses and expensive cars. Our boss would lecture them on acidity, tannins, and flavor compounds. Meanwhile, we'd hustle back and forth with fresh glasses and bottles, getting them drunk. Some of the tourists seemed to shit money. The older they were, the more they drank, the more they tipped us.

On Friday afternoons, we'd line up at the front office, and our boss would pay us in cash. He'd remark that Spanish people were good workers, and we were confused as to why he would say that, because we had never met anyone from Spain. When we asked our children to explain, they rolled their eyes and said, "He's too stupid to live."

Our children transacted mysteries that were beyond our knowledge and past our learning. They were good at English, so good that they could memorize rap lyrics. They could even identify peculiar accents just by overhearing a few words; they'd gesture at chattering tourists and tell us, "That man is probably from France," or "That one sounds British."

On Sundays, our children read the local papers to us, translating on the spot. They'd decode the content from cover to cover. Gossip. Sports. Crime. Politics. It made us giddy to see these displays of intelligence.

Sometimes our children would ask us, "Do you ever wish you could read? Or speak perfect English?"

And we would joke, "We wish you couldn't. So you'd understand what it's like for us."

One day, we returned from the winery to find the Serranos riding their tiny bicycles through the trailer park—without crashing. The seven young men rode single file, with Mother Paz leading them, and they were all whooping and laughing. Somehow they'd solved the puzzle of balance.

We stood there watching the Serranos. They formed an odd parade, with their American flags fluttering behind them. One of the young men had duct-taped a portable radio to his seat post and was blasting country music. Mother Paz glided past us, cackling. She looked almost like a witch on a broomstick.

The spectacle of the bicycles so excited our children that some of them began to clap and cheer for the Serranos, but we found this irritating and demanded their silence.

. . .

Every weekday morning, we trudged to work on the shoulder of the county road, while our neighbors followed the same road to Los Olivos on their bicycles. They usually passed by without saying much, which was fine with us. We had no real desire to converse with them. We would have preferred to keep them on nodding terms, at most.

Occasionally, though, one or more of them would slow down to match our pace and spoil our mood with talk. They boasted that it now took them only thirty minutes to reach the Greek restaurant, "or twenty, if you really step on it." They could visit any of the surrounding towns: Santa Ynez, Ballard, Los Alamos. They'd been to the Santa Maria Target, where the aisles were so long that you couldn't see the end of them. And they'd been to a theater in Solvang, where they'd watched a movie about a million penguins mating. The movie had inspired them. Someday, they said, they might try their luck at crossing the mountain pass into coastal Santa Barbara. They had never seen the ocean, but wanted to.

Privately, we agreed that the Serranos were idiots to put themselves at risk in their petty adventuring. We were content to keep a low profile and focus on our work. While we moved drip tape, mucked corrals, and sprayed chemicals between the vines, we'd fall back on our fantasies. Our children would grow up to be suited professionals, stacking money. With a little luck, we would end up living in their two- or three-story houses. Then there would be nothing left to do but play with our grandkids, push their strollers, and rest our bones.

In June, the Serranos invited gabachas into the trailer park. The gabachas were roughly the same age as the young men, and drove not bikes but ramshackle cars. They'd pull into our community and stroll past us as if they had every right, as if we were furnishings in their living room. Sometimes they brought plastic bags of mota and six-packs of beer, and they'd sit on the porch of the Holiday Rambler, drinking and smoking with the Serranos. There were at least four or five gabachas, though they were hard to count, because we couldn't tell them apart. They all had brown hair with blond highlights. They all wore lipstick and short skirts, and had tattoos. They'd all get drunk and talk too loud, and when they laughed, they'd tip their heads back and open their mouths wide, like donkeys.

The Holiday Rambler had next to nothing in the way of insulation, so we could tell right away when the sex began. On weekends, pairs of Serranos and gabachas would enter the trailer in shifts, and we could hear their coaxing, moaning, and grunting. The Holiday Rambler's walls jounced and swayed until we wished it would collapse. But it was built to last.

We decided to make our displeasure known to the Serranos. Since we were conscious of our numerical superiority, we agreed it would be best if only three of us approached them. A group of that size could impart seriousness, without the implicit hostility of a larger crowd.

On a Saturday morning, the chosen three of us found Mother Paz sunbathing on a lawn chair beside the Holiday Rambler. She wore a pair of sunglasses, a high-waisted bikini bottom, and a T-shirt with Superman leaping out of it.

It was a small matter, we said. But did she think her boys could be a touch more discreet? With their exchanges?

We had decided beforehand that *exchanges* was the most suitable word in our arsenal. Its vagueness would spare the conversers from directly acknowledging the dope, the boozing, and the carnality.

But Mother Paz only said, "You know how young people are."

We had hoped for a simple conversation. Briefly, we considered whether this woman's grasp of our language was really as strong as we'd thought. Then we noticed the telltale rocking of the Holiday Rambler starting up, and, along with it, the braying of a gabacha.

This prompted us to say that yes, youths can forget themselves, and they can forget their neighbors, and sometimes it takes an elder to set them right again.

Mother Paz removed her glasses and folded them.

"Scripture tells us that love does no wrong to a neighbor, and therefore love is the fulfilling of the law."

We were struggling to keep our cool; we were in no mood for a religious debate.

"Our children look up to you," we admitted. "You're showing them things they shouldn't see and shouldn't hear."

"I'll take that message back to my sons. But I can't make any promises."

When we instructed our children to keep their distance from the Serranos, they asked us to explain why.

"They seem to be hardworking people," we said, "but we don't want you to be entangled in the things they do when they're not working."

"They're really nice to us, though," our children said. "We play lotería or soccer with them when you're not around. And Mother Paz brings us baklava from the restaurant."

"She's nobody's mother."

"Who cares? She's our friend."

"Why not make some real friends, kids your own age? When school starts again, invite some classmates over—we'd be happy to meet them."

"Our classmates avoid us. They say we smell like trash because we sleep in a landfill."

"This is a trailer park, a neighborhood. They should know the difference."

"Difference? What 'difference'?"

Our children became furious. They were sick of spending empty summer days surrounded by rubbish, explaining obvious facts to us. They suggested that we were jealous of the Serranos since "you're boring, and they're fearless. And you can't control them the way you control us."

We were hurt, and sad that our influence was no longer what it had once been, but we were not entirely surprised. Our children had entered their teens, and we had expected defiance on their part. Some of our coworkers at the winery, the ones who lived in other communities, had shared stories of their sons and daughters dropping out of school, experimenting with narcotics, dating hoodlums. We couldn't imagine that our children would sink so low, but they were bound to find new ways of testing us. Naturally, we were tempted to punish them. Our own parents wouldn't have tolerated such flagrant disrespect. They would have taken belts to us, or whips, or electrical cords—whatever happened to be within reach. In the end, though, we kept our hands down and let our children be. This was a phase that would pass in its own time.

Grape tending kept us occupied well into the evenings. We trimmed clusters, discarding immature fruit. We planted bell beans, oats, and daikon beside the vines to lure away insects. The air was heavy with the scent of fresh manure and turned earth, which smelled to us like prosperity and renewed our optimism.

One night a commotion woke us from our shallow sleep. There was the sound of something like whistling and popping, and we noticed intermittent bursts of light coming through our curtains.

"Stay inside," we told our children. "We'll handle this."

When we opened our doors and stepped out, we were horrified: the eight Serranos—along with a few gabachas—were shooting bombettes and flash powder and multicolored jumping jacks. They were spinning flame wheels and fiery balls that screamed into the air. An immense plume of smoke had risen from our neighborhood.

"Stop!" we begged. "Stop all of this!"

Mother Paz came forward.

"Friends, it's *Independence Day*," she said.

We tried reasoning with her. Hadn't she heard of *zero tolerance*? The fireworks were illegal. And they were especially dangerous at this time of year, when a single spark could set the entire valley ablaze. The display was visible for miles around. If a malicious outsider should see it and call the police, we'd all be taken away.

We implored Mother Paz to trust us and benefit from our advice. In order to persist in the North, you had to hush your impulses. You had to withdraw from the world until nobody gave a damn about you.

Mother Paz delved into our faces; there was no shame in hers.

"I've been told that tonight is a night to celebrate. Maybe you should relax for once."

Enraged, we told her, "Maybe you should live in a place where you don't have neighbors, so you don't have to act like neighbors!"

"All right, fuckers! I don't know anything about anything—is that what you want to hear?"

The seven younger Serranos had been observing our exchange. From their wide-eyed expressions, we could tell they understood our anger, if not our vocabulary. Mother Paz turned to them, barked something in their language. They extinguished their firecrackers, and the gabachas followed suit, until all was dark again.

That weekend, the Serranos avoided us. They stayed behind the door of the Holiday Rambler.

On Sunday evening, we held a meeting in the Becerra family's trailer. All eighteen of us crammed ourselves into the kitchen/bedroom/living room.

We said, "These Serranos have come to spread chaos! They're pissing on us, and we're kneeling here with open mouths!"

Only one set of parents dissented, counseling forgiveness.

"They're our brethren," they said, "not our adversaries. Haven't we all crossed the same border? Aren't we all just workers following the work?" They suggested that this was a teachable moment for our children. This was an opportunity to put a good lesson into their hearts, and into the hearts of our neighbors.

The rest of us wouldn't have it. Our animosity was only hardened by that sort of talk. Forgiveness be damned—those beasts hadn't even apologized. And it wasn't our job to teach them how to apologize, or think, or be passable humans. Now was the time to stand up, raise our voices, and yield no ground.

We said, "If it comes to battle, so be it: we have the numbers!"

We would tell the Serranos to pack their bags. We would order them to leave Ranch View Mobile Estates immediately.

All eighteen of us marched across the trailer park. Since we wanted to appear as formidable as possible, we had changed into our best pants, guayaberas, and dresses—the things we'd worn to one another's weddings, our children's baptisms, and weekly Masses, back when we were still brave enough to attend church. A few of us also strapped machetes to our hips. They were tucked into leather sheaths, and we didn't plan on using them, but we thought they'd add considerable authority to our demands.

We intended to give our neighbors the type of shock they wouldn't forget. Candlelight flickered in the windows of their trailer, the focal point of our wrath. When we reached its porch, we assumed the most vicious expressions in our power, and pounded on the door. It swung open.

A gust of warmth and humidity escaped the Holiday Rambler. We were greeted by Mother Paz and her sons. They wore aprons and chef's coats. Behind them, on a small table, sat a host of saucers and bowls caked in flour. Pepper stems and seeds were piled neatly on a rectangular cutting board. We saw wooden spoons, spatulas, and dough scrapers soaking in a washbasin.

Three of the young men held a massive earthenware pot. They lifted its lid, and gesticulated in a way that said, *Have a look*.

The pot contained several dozen rectangular dark green pouches, which were fat and smooth and beaded with moisture. They looked like vegetables from another world.

Mother Paz noticed our bewilderment.

"Some tamales for you, prepared in the southern style," she said. "They're wrapped in the fronds of a banana tree. Don't wait too long—eat them while they're hot."

A few of us tried to speak, but we couldn't bring our denunciations into being. We were stupefied.

Food is sacred to our people, and has been for numberless generations. Its presence governs our behavior. You can't attack someone when they've cooked fresh provisions for you and opened their hands; tradition tells us that it would be as bad as striking down the healer who binds your wounds. Maybe the Serranos were aware of this, or maybe they weren't. In any case, we were constrained by our principles and unwilling to commit sacrilege.

So when at last we found our voices again, we had no choice but to thank our neighbors. We accepted the earthenware pot. Of course we hadn't forgiven Mother Paz and her sons, and our differences were far from settled, but they had pulled our fangs and bought themselves time. We divided the strange tamales between us—half a dozen per family—and returned to our homes, dressed in our finery.

The tamales, which had been made by this so-called mother and her so-called sons, were the best we had ever eaten. Their flavor bloomed in stages. Beneath the leaves, the cornmeal was soft and buttery. This was followed by a tangy second layer that surprised us with a hint of tamarind. The most intense delight lay at the core of each tamal, where a spicy flourish whispered across our taste buds.

Our children ate with us. They asked, "How come you've never made tamales like these?" and laughed when we had no answer. We considered that perhaps our ancestors had passed down the wrong recipes, and these were the first true tamales we had tasted; maybe all the rest had been mockeries. We licked and scraped the banana leaves, extracting every trace of their essence. It was happiness pumping through our bodies.

Our neighbors were uncivilized. They were unpolished. But you don't need so much polish when you're sincere.

The Migra came for the Serranos on the ninth of July.

They had raided Santa Ynez, southeast of us. And they had been seen in Buellton. Still, we hadn't expected their agents to bother with a town as small as Los Olivos, which had only a thousand inhabitants. For some reason the Migra—or else the town itself—wanted to make an example out of the Greek restaurant.

The details oozed into our knowledge from various sources. We learned them from coworkers at the winery, and from cashiers at Albertsons, the ones who spoke our language. And our children told us what they could, when the *Santa Barbara Independent* printed a brief article about the raid.

We listened as our children translated: The raid had happened around six P.M., during the dinner rush. The Migra had taken ten restaurant employees into custody. They had fired two shots in the process, since a few suspects had resisted capture. One suspect had been hospitalized with "minor injuries."

Our children turned a page, then another, and frowned. "There's nothing more—that's all it says."

An amateur photographer had been dining at the restaurant at the time of the raid, and we examined the black-and-white photos she'd snapped. You could see trucks and vans and pistol-wielding agents with bulletproof vests, who were escorting three hand-cuffed men out of the restaurant. The young men must have been taken completely by surprise; they hadn't even removed their hair-nets or their latex kitchen gloves. They'd averted their faces from the eye of the camera, and we couldn't make out their expressions, but we recognized them as our neighbors.

Our children announced their plan to walk into Los Olivos. "We're going to check things out," they said.

They pointed out the fact that only three Serranos had appeared in the paper. Maybe the other five had eluded the Migra and gone into hiding. Maybe they needed help.

It took us a few moments to realize that our children were serious.

"This is a game to you?"

"We should go," they said. "We're American-born, and we can't be taken away."

"Don't be so sure!"

We recited the names of friends and relatives who had thought they were safe but had vanished all the same. We stressed that men, women, and children were known to die in Migra prisons. And captives died just as often when sadistic agents turned them loose in hellholes like Agua Prieta, Reynosa, and Ciudad Juárez, where people like ourselves were food for wolves.

"At this rate, the newspaper will run an article about a gang of thumb-suckers who should have listened to their parents!" we said.

Our children held their ground. They crossed their arms.

"This is the right thing to do, and it's the least we can do for our neighbors," they said.

We couldn't back them down, so we began to beg. We wept and wailed. We embraced them and refused to release them.

Then, too, we were proud of our daughters and sons, even

though we wouldn't reveal it. The years had sculpted their character. They were so strong that siding against them was like siding against nature. Someday perhaps we ourselves would be dragged away, and they would need that strength to survive in this country without us.

Our children's voices softened.

"If the Migra got their hands on you, we'd scour the earth," they said. "We'd find you, no matter what."

And with that, we let them go.

Raided businesses often make a show of reinventing themselves. After several expeditions to Los Olivos, our children reported this to be the case with the Greek restaurant. For a week, it stayed dark inside. Then a crew of workers undertook a series of renovations. There was a lot of drilling and hammering, lifting and moving. The workers repainted the façade, and it became powder blue instead of brown. They replaced the plastic OPEN sign with a neon OPEN sign, which was bright enough to be seen from down the block. They filled holes in the parking lot, paved it with fresh tar, and etched new lines between the parking spaces.

In the second or third week after the raid, the gabachas reappeared at Ranch View Mobile Estates. Sometimes they sat alone on the porch of the Holiday Rambler, hugging themselves. Sometimes they came in pairs and loitered together. When they spoke, they spoke in murmurs. Every now and then, they'd try the door, even though they already knew it was locked. Perhaps they just wanted to touch something that their lovers' hands had touched.

A month after the raid, our children informed us that the Greek restaurant had started doing business again. Its double doors were propped open. A large banner appeared across its awning. It said

GRAND REOPENING in big letters, and UNDER NEW MANAGEMENT in smaller ones.

The Holiday Rambler's curtains remained closed behind its windows. There were days when clouds rumbled, and their sprinkling brought up nettles and smutgrass around the trailer, until it appeared to be sinking into the weeds. We could still see the path leading to the home of our erstwhile neighbors, which had been imprinted by the weight of their comings and goings. Abandoned laundry fluttered on their clothesline, and when night calmed the breath of the trailer park, we could hear T-shirts slapping against pant legs.

Our children stopped looking for the Serranos. But they couldn't stop dreaming about them.

In one dream the Serranos lived in a zoo, where each of them was housed in a small cage with steel bars; when you got too close, they'd roar in the way that mountain lions roar.

In another dream Mother Paz couldn't see you, even when you stood right in front of her. She'd wander around the trailer park muttering, "Almost."

Our children tossed and turned in their sleep. They woke up gasping, and we kneeled beside their beds, held their hands, and soothed them just as we had when they were babies. We told them they needed not worry. The Serranos were nothing if not resourceful; they were quick on their feet. "And wherever they've ended up, they're surely together," we lied.

When our children were out of earshot, we confided our true feelings to one another. The dreams had provoked in us a new sense of disquiet. They were exactly the sorts of dreams you might have about the dead, when they reach out from the hereafter.

Now when we went to work, we slogged through the woods and up the Santa Ynez riverbed, which is parched all but two months of the year. August was the height of rattlesnake season, and we had to watch our steps, but none of us wanted to follow the county road anymore. We felt endangered by the eyes of passing motorists.

A harvest day arrived, and we rose before dawn to prepare ourselves for long hours among the vines. While our children were fast asleep, we covered up with hats, bandanas, neckerchiefs, and long-sleeved shirts. We packed coolers with food and water and gathered at the picnic tables. We were about to leave.

Just then, we spotted Mother Paz.

We were terrified at first. If someone had told us that we were seeing a wayward spirit, we would have believed them. But Mother Paz was really there, riding through the entrance to Ranch View Mobile Estates on her pink bicycle with its American flag. She rode alone. She wore no helmet, and her long gray hair swirled freely in the wind. We were astonished—somehow she'd escaped.

The Migra worked in mysterious ways. Once, in Lompoc, they'd barged in on a wedding banquet and taken more than forty people, but spared the singer and his band. Another time, they'd raided a plum orchard outside Los Alamos and arrested only the male workers, leaving the women behind. It was hard to discern any logic in their doings. Agents took parents and left children; they took children and left parents. Perhaps they had decided that Mother Paz was old and would die soon anyway, and did not think she was worth their trouble.

The violet sky advised us that we were supposed to be at the vineyard, yet none of us made a move. Mother Paz dismounted her bicycle a stone's throw from the Holiday Rambler and let it fall to the ground. Her face was dirty. She looked barely awake and far away; she was panting like the wounded.

Stupidly, we asked, "Where are your sons?"

Mother Paz brushed past us without a word. She must have hoped that the events of the last several weeks hadn't been real and that the young Serranos would be waiting for her, and she didn't have any space in her thoughts for us. She pulled a key from her pocket. A moment later, she hobbled into her home.

We acted strong, enclosed in the trailer park, but we knew we were prey. Neighbors brought our fears to life. It was easy to hate them; we couldn't bear to love them, since they never lasted long. The heat of day was upon us, defining our shadows as we approached the Holiday Rambler. We decided it would be enough, for us, not to be forgotten. Gently, we knocked on the door.

Caroline Kim

Hiding Spot

IT WAS A GOOD HIDING SPOT. Too good. Mrs. Lee stood in her closet with her hands on her hips, squeezing her eyes shut, telling herself to "think, think." She could almost see it, see herself folding tissue paper around her wedding rings, pushing them down into a blue velvet pouch that also held her wedding pearls and a white jade ring passed down from her mother. Yes, she could almost even feel herself pulling the yellow drawstring tightly closed and putting it all . . . where?

In a box? Under something? *In* something? Scornfully, she remembered congratulating herself for picking such a good hiding spot because no one would think to look there. She felt like a character in a folktale, an old fool, tripped up by her own cleverness.

It was only three months ago that she had hidden her jewelry, in the days before she and Mr. Lee went on a cruise to Alaska. They weren't the vacationing type, but one day while Mr. Lee was reading the *Chosun Ilbo* online, he saw an ad for a cruise line offering incredible deals. "It'll feel like we're losing money if we don't go," he said. The only catch was that the cruise left in just a few days from Seattle. No problem. Isn't this why they'd retired from their dry-cleaning business the year before? They certainly didn't have to worry about anyone missing them. Not a single person would be affected if they left at a moment's notice. So they flew from Atlanta to San Francisco to Seattle and spent a week in a tiny, closet-sized room with no windows, disembarking in the mornings to take other, smaller boats out to where they took pictures of melting glaciers and smelly, wild-looking sled dogs. Mr. Lee couldn't sleep because of the nonstop humming of the ship, which Mrs. Lee hardly noticed. While he spent hours lying in their tiny room watching Korean dramas and reading newspapers on his laptop, Mrs. Lee sat out on the top deck watching people brave the chilly air to swim in the pools or sit in the foamy waters of the hot tub, which Mr. Lee called "people soup." The only good parts were the entertainment and the profligate amount of food on the ship, which Mrs. Lee found unnerving, though it did not stop her or Mr. Lee from stuffing themselves at all hours of the day and night.

When they returned home, Mrs. Lee didn't look for her rings right away. But on the evening they were invited to a dol by the Chois, whose plump grandson was turning one, Mrs. Lee discovered she couldn't remember where she'd hidden her rings. At first she didn't worry. Her memory had just turned shy, refusing to reveal what she needed to know when she was too focused on it. This had happened to her her whole life. Thinking too much about one thing made it flee instead of getting it nailed down. She figured the pouch would turn up eventually when she was looking for something else.

But now there was an urgency. She needed to find her rings because Ken had shown up the night before, with a girl, no less. Ken, the son she hadn't seen for two years.

Mrs. Lee moved quietly through the house because Ken and the girl were still sleeping. Mr. Lee was at the YMCA getting in his laps before the pool became crowded. Their new house was a lot smaller than their last; they had downsized a year back after taking a good long look at their finances. But the two of them were fine in a small bungalow with just the two bedrooms, the larger one for sleeping, the smaller one as Mrs. Lee's craft room, where Ken and his girl were now sleeping. She kept a bookcase of yarn and a sewing machine on a desk in there, a comfortable chair where she knit hats and blankets, sewed baby-sized quilts for her church to donate. But there was also Ken's old futon, which Mrs. Lee normally kept folded up like a couch and sometimes took a nap on, though not too often because naps felt like dying in a way that sleeping at night did not. As she passed she held her breath as she listened at the door and heard nothing, conscious of the cheap plywood doors in her new house. She continued into the kitchen and turned on the electric kettle. Ken looked like he had gained weight, which was a good thing because he had looked so thin and weak the last time when they drove him down to Florida to the treatment center. Mr. Lee was so disappointed in Ken he avoided looking him in the face, but Mrs. Lee couldn't stop staring at him, looking for the young man who used to smile so readily it worried her. She thought it made him vulnerable to being taken advantage of, and in the end, hadn't she been right about that?

Looking out the window above the sink, she saw her neighbor Alice walking slowly back and forth, pushing her mower. The woman was at least seventy-five but it was only a slight exaggeration to say that she was stronger than men half her age. Mrs. Lee thought she would probably die the way a man would, a sudden heart attack, an old tree falling down. That made her think of wood and then bookcases and now she had a vague memory of being on her knees, putting her head down to look into some dark space . . . under the bookshelf in the living room? Quickly, she walked from the kitchen to the small living room where their old furniture took up too much space. The bookshelf she was thinking of was wedged next to the fireplace and filled with her husband's books on the Korean War.

Ignoring the stiffness she felt in her limbs, she bent down and put her ear to the hardwood floor but saw nothing in the darkness. Why didn't she bring a flashlight? She extended an arm, sweeping her hand underneath, feeling sticky dust and nothing else. When she pulled her arm out, she saw the body of a large daddy longlegs sticking to the back of her hand and she carried it to the sink, sent it rushing down the pipes. *At least you died of old age,* she thought. That was a gift on its own. She washed her hands thoroughly.

She returned to making her instant coffee, revising her memory of a few minutes earlier. The image of it being under a bookshelf was still strong, the sensation of bending down still sharp (and not just because she'd just done it), the feeling of *aha! nobody will ever look here!* clear as a bell.

If not that bookshelf, another one? The one in her bedroom with the Korean novels her sister sent from Korea, which she never read? The one in her craft room with her yarn and knitting books? Mrs. Lee's heart started thumping and she put a hand over it as if to contain it, closing her eyes and taking big deep breaths just like the woman teaching yoga at the YMCA had shown her. "Picture your lungs as a balloon," the woman had said. "Now fill the balloon slowly and deeply." Then, holding her thumb and forefinger together, she had pinched the end of her pretend balloon and said, "Now let the air out slowly, slowly, slowly, until the balloon is empty. Do it again. Keep doing it."

Mrs. Lee tried to concentrate on imagining that her lungs were two pink balloons but she could not get the image of the blue velvet pouch out of her mind. It was a royal blue, not easily seen against the dark brown wood of the floor if anyone happened to look underneath. Most people wouldn't. But drug addicts were not most people. Drug addicts were intuitive at ferreting out things of value. The last time they saw Ken was after they'd brought him home from the rehab center. Three days later he left with three thousand dollars they'd hidden in a Florsheim shoebox under stacks of old letters from her family in Korea, when they still wrote letters to each other instead of posting pictures on Facebook.

Before that happened it would never have occurred to the Lees to hide their money from Ken. He had always been such a responsible child. They could hardly believe it even when it did happen. Mr. Lee said he didn't want to talk about Ken anymore. Mrs. Lee finally understood that their son was caught in a sickness, the worst kind, that pushed you to feed off the people you loved like leeches. Mr. Lee repeated to Mrs. Lee that they had no more son, and adjusted himself accordingly, erasing Ken from his mind. Having a son who stole from them was worse than being childless.

It was a tragedy. That's what all the articles Mrs. Lee read on the internet and in the women's magazines told her. It was heartening to know that she wasn't the only mother suffering from this drug epidemic, but the stories scared her terribly. Such sad lives that ruined so many others. To be caught in a hunger like that. It almost seemed death was preferable.

Mrs. Lee decided to wake Ken and his girlfriend by making a loud breakfast. She pulled out her beaten-up pans and set them heavily on the stove. She padded back and forth from the pantry, which was in the cramped laundry room next to the kitchen, and began making pancakes and bacon. She believed this was what all Americans wanted to eat for breakfast. Korean people made no distinctions between their meals like Americans did. It was perfectly normal to eat whatever you ate for dinner the night before as breakfast the next morning. But she didn't see Ken as Korean anymore. He was American now. An American addict.

"Morning," Ken said, coming alone out of the room, closing

the door softly behind him. Now Mrs. Lee had to admit he looked older, softer, like butter left out on the counter. Still, she was glad that he'd gained some weight back. But he was a man now, a stranger to them.

"Good morning," Mrs. Lee said, more cheerfully than she felt. She was uncertain around him, moving around too much, waving him to a chair, setting a plate of pancakes and bacon before him, spilling orange juice as she poured it.

"Careful, careful," he said. He looked at the plate before him, appreciating it, and smiled at his mother. "It looks good," he said. "Thank you."

"I make more. I have lots of batter."

Ken knew she was feeling uncertain about him by the fact that she was speaking in English. He nodded. "Wait until Celeste wakes up. She'll be hungry too."

"Nice girl?" she asked. She set a cup of instant coffee in front of Ken. Sat down with her half-drunk cup.

Mrs. Lee thought back to when they'd picked Ken up at the expensive rehabilitation facility they'd paid for. To her eyes, he hadn't looked like an addict. As he sat in the front seat next to his father, both of them silent, she thought he looked more like a grad student in the freshly ironed button-down shirt she had brought him. Much like her husband had looked when he was at Yonsei University all those long years ago.

Ken smiled looking down at the tan coffee, heavily sugared and creamered. "Very nice," he said. "And smart. She used to go to Emory."

"Used to?"

"She's back in school, but not at Emory. She's studying to be a nurse now."

"That's good," Mrs. Lee said. But the truth was she wished Ken had shown up alone.

"What about you? We never hear from you." She had switched to Korean.

Ken grimaced. "I'm sorry about that," he answered in English. He cut up his pancakes without eating.

"We don't even know where you live."

"I live in Austin," he said. "With Celeste. I'm okay now. I'm a manager at a movie theater."

Mrs. Lee nodded without saying anything. She pictured Ken scooping popcorn into buckets, smiling and saying thank you to customers. He had never wanted to work in the dry cleaners after school. He'd been too shy to wait on customers. She used to want him to be a doctor or businessman, but her expectations for him were low now. If he could support himself working at a movie theater, why not?

"It's a small theater," Ken said, shrugging, "but I like it. It's tough finding a job with a record, I'm lucky to have found this. I like it."

"You watch movies," Mrs. Lee said.

"Yeah, I do."

"That's good," Mrs. Lee said.

They sat in an awkward silence, not knowing anymore how to talk to each other. Twenty times Mrs. Lee was about to ask if Ken needed money but didn't.

"Where's Dad?" Ken asked.

"At the YMCA. He goes swimming there."

"Really?" Ken said with wonder. "I didn't even know he could swim."

"Yah, lots of things you don't know about us." It came out sounding more accusatory than Mrs. Lee intended. She'd meant to say that they didn't know enough about each other. The truth was she felt bad about the way her husband had ignored Ken when he arrived the night before. She would have preferred for him to get angry and lash out at Ken, but he wasn't that kind of man. Not anymore. Long days and nights working at the dry cleaners, dealing with customers who were angry or dismissive, had eaten away at him, whittled him down to someone who only wanted life to be agreeable. The only things he cared about now were reading historical books, watching war documentaries and films, going swimming every day at the Y, and hanging out with a few old war buddies Sunday mornings at the Dunkin' Donuts. He had stopped going to church over the past year, saying he didn't want to waste his life with stuff like that anymore. "What kind of stuff?" Mrs. Lee had asked. "With wanting. Trying. Feeling bad about things I can't change." Mrs. Lee had to think hard to remember the man she married. Was this the man whose face used to turn dark red when he drank, who once beat Ken when he came home high and was laughing at them, kicking him as he lay curled up on the living room rug until Ken threw up?

At the same time, Mrs. Lee and Ken heard a door open and close, then soft padding on the carpeted hallway. The girl appeared in the doorway to the kitchen wearing an oversized men's T-shirt as a nightgown, pulling her long, reddish hair into a ponytail. "Good morning, Mrs. Lee," she said.

Mrs. Lee's heart sank looking at this girl. She had no experience with young white girls, couldn't guess at what they thought or cared about. At least this one was going to be a nurse, someone who wanted to heal and not hurt. But wouldn't she be around a lot of drugs?

Ken's face lit up when he saw the girl. It filled Mrs. Lee with dread.

"Morning, beautiful," Ken said.

All Mrs. Lee could think about was checking under the bookcase in her craft room. She hurriedly set a plate piled high with pancakes and bacon in front of the girl ("Whoa," said the girl), and then excused herself to go to the bathroom. She walked into the hallway, waited until she could hear their voices in conversation, and then opened the door to the craft room as quietly as possible. The bed was still unmade, a suitcase opened in one corner of the room, spilling clothes and what looked like a pile of women's lacy underwear. How long did they plan on staying? Mrs. Lee smelled the scent of unfamiliar shampoo and something else. Were they smoking in the room?

She didn't have time to consider that. Instead she knelt down before the bookcase and ran a hand underneath it, feeling empty space. She leaned her head down for a closer look. She saw a dark shape far in the corner.

"Ma?" Ken asked at the door. "What are you doing?"

"Me?" Mrs. Lee sat up, trying to pretend everything was normal. "I . . . I dropped a needle here yesterday . . . before you come here. I didn't want you or the girl to step on it."

"We'll be careful," Ken said. "I'll keep an eye out for it." He leaned against the door frame, and said, "I was thinking about taking Celeste out for a drive. Show her the old house, where I went to school and all that."

"Great idea!" Mrs. Lee said, overly enthusiastic. "Then you come back here?"

"Sure," Ken said. "I'll bring back some dinner. What do you feel like?"

"Anything," Mrs. Lee said.

"Chinese?"

"Your father loves Chinese."

"Chinese it is then," Ken said, nodding.

Mrs. Lee got up from the floor, dusted off her knees, feeling foolish.

"We'll keep an eye out for that needle," Ken said.

"Oh, don't worry about it," Mrs. Lee said. "Not important. Watch where you're stepping."

Ken moved aside to let his mother pass. In the hallway, he touched her shoulder gently. "Ma," Ken said, "just a minute." He shook his head, and his face turned red. "I just want to say how sorry I am. I . . . haven't been a good son. But I want you to know that things are different now." He opened and closed his mouth as if he wanted to say more but didn't.

Trembling, Mrs. Lee patted Ken's arm. "It's okay, Ken. You were sick. Me and Daddy know that. We love you. We glad you okay. All we want is for you to be happy. Okay? You're our son."

They both heard a stifled cough. Celeste was standing at the end of the hall, grinning at them. "That's beautiful," she said. "I want you to know, Mrs. Lee, what a good man Ken is. I'm so lucky to have met him. And I want you to know that I'll take good care of him, just like you did." Much taller than Mrs. Lee, she came over and folded herself over Mrs. Lee in a hug that wedged Mrs. Lee's face into her armpit.

Mrs. Lee submitted to the hug and patted the girl's back. The girl really didn't seem so bad and Mrs. Lee was glad that Ken wasn't alone. At least he spent every day with someone he loved. It was a lot more than most people had. But as she turned to go into her bedroom, she heard the girl whisper, "Did you tell her yet?" and all her misgivings about Ken and the girl came rushing back.

When the surprise of Ken and the girl showing up at their door had been absorbed, and after Mrs. Lee had turned the futon into a bed for them and gotten them settled, she found Mr. Lee already in bed with the lights out.

"Are you sleeping?" she asked.

"Not anymore."

Mrs. Lee undressed in the dark.

"I know what you're thinking," she said. "But Ken won't steal from us. He's our son."

"He was our son the last time he stole from us."

"But he seems different now."

"People don't change."

Didn't they? Mrs. Lee remembered how her husband used to spin her around to Frank Sinatra and how he used to laugh at *The Three Stooges*.

"Maybe we should never have moved to America."

Mr. Lee gave a big sigh. "I'm sorry, I can't do it. I can't give Ken another chance."

"Must be nice," she said.

As soon as Ken and his girl left the house, Mrs. Lee went into the craft room and retrieved the blue pouch from the darkness under the bookcase. She smudged the dust off the velvet and shook out the contents. The pearls slid out in a lump, but she had to pull on the tissue paper to get it out of the pouch. She unwrapped her rings and weighed them in her palm but didn't put them on. She shook the blue pouch; nothing else came out. The white jade ring wasn't there. Mrs. Lee wondered if she had even put it in there but knew with certainty that she had. Did Ken take it or did the girl? Mrs. Lee's heart felt like it was being smothered from the inside. Her knees hurt from the wood floor so she got up slowly. She felt ancient, as exhausted as if she had worked a fourteen-hour day like she used to. What had been the purpose of such work? Such a life? She and her husband meant it all for their son. Maybe Mr. Lee was right. He was a rotten apple and proximity to him would infect them with his rottenness too. Maybe he wasn't the one who needed to change, she was. On the other hand, who cared about a ring compared to a child? So what if he stole from her? If only he knew that she would give him everything if he asked.

With some difficulty, Mrs. Lee wedged her wedding ring on. The skin around it bulged unpleasantly and reminded her why she had stopped wearing it in the first place. It was only a replacement ring anyway, even if it was far more valuable than the original. The first one had been sold, along with most of their other valuables, to fund their move to America. It had taken fifteen years of working long days, of buying the laundromat first and then the dry cleaners, to save up for another ring. Mrs. Lee had scoffed every time her husband mentioned it over the years, saying she didn't need a fancy ring, what long-married person wanted to advertise that they were married anyway? But every so often when they were at the mall, Mr. Lee pulled his wife into a Zales asking to see this one and that one, did she prefer emerald cut or princess?, and she understood that the ring was more about the man than the woman. That it was just another way of asserting his manhood.

She stood in front of the window and let the sunlight fall on the almost-full-carat diamond, turning her hand this way and that to throw rainbow glimmers on the walls. She wondered if Ken was thinking of marrying Celeste, what it would feel like to have a white American daughter, what their half-Korean kids would look like, and then the next generation if they also married non-Koreans, until soon nobody looked Korean at all. It made her sad and then angry at herself. What did it really matter? Human beings were human beings. That's all that was important.

Mr. Lee came home for his usual lunch of soup, rice, and whatever banchan Mrs. Lee found in the refrigerator. Ever since Mr. Lee retired, he'd kept to a strict schedule. Every weekday, he swam at the Y, then crossed the street to Starbucks, where he sat by the window with a newspaper and a small black coffee.

He grunted when Mrs. Lee told him that Ken and his girlfriend had gone sightseeing around town. "What's there to see here?" he said, gesturing with his soup spoon to take in the whole of the Atlanta suburb they lived in.

"He wants to show her where he grew up," Mrs. Lee said. "Young people are like that when they're in love. They want to know everything about each other."

Mr. Lee grunted again, spilling soup as he ate quickly, a reflex left over from growing up during wartime.

"Slow down," Mrs. Lee said, pouring him a glass of barley water. She was on a diet, eating only a small breakfast midmorning, toast or an egg, and then nothing until dinner. She hated the thickening of her waist, the way it made her coming mortality more real.

"He's getting old to be falling in love. He's almost forty!"

"He's thirty-five. How would you like it if I added five years to your age?"

"You're always defending him. That's why he's still not an adult."

"You're the one who wanted to have him!"

His spoon froze midair. "So, you think it's my fault."

The thing she'd been trying so hard not to say had slipped out. That's the way it was. When you tried to push things away you gave them the strength to push back. "It's not your fault! It's not anybody's fault! Ken's a good person!"

"Ha! Would a good person steal from his parents?"

"Who cares? It's only money! You care more about money than people! What kind of human being are you?" Mrs. Lee felt an urgent need to move. "I'm going for a walk!" she said, and headed for the door. She had just enough sense to exchange her house slippers for her sneakers and grab her hat before she hurried out. The October day was bright and still very warm, though some of the trees had started to change color. She walked without a sense of wanting to go anywhere, turning in random directions whenever she got to a corner.

She remembered the panic she'd felt when she'd found out she was pregnant with Ken. They were new immigrants then who had just used all the money they had to cover the down payment on a barely functioning laundromat. But it wasn't just that. Only when she was pregnant did she realize with certainty that she did not want to have children. She had always assumed the desire would kick in at some point, like the process of puberty or adult teeth coming in, like menopause. It was just part of the natural cycle of life. But none of it felt natural to her. Motherhood almost always felt like a chore, a job to her, one she tried to be a success at, partly because of the guilt she felt. What of this had Ken felt? Had he turned to drugs to fill a lack he felt in his life, a lack he couldn't even name because he'd never known what he was missing?

He was a good boy all through school, never giving them any reason to be concerned. He had even received an almost full package to Stanford. She looked back at the way she and her husband used to congratulate themselves on a job well done, how they had insincerely waved away their church friends' envy, and she saw two fools standing on quicksand thinking it was concrete. Was it the pressure of being in a school full of geniuses, surrounded by the ultra-privileged, or being in California after growing up in the South, or a genetic predisposition to addiction that got turned on like a light switch, or, or . . . ? They didn't even know Ken's addictions started in college until much later, when he could no longer hide it from them, when the calls had started to come late at night for small loans though they'd assumed he made a decent living as a programmer. But he said living in California was expensive, that he was unlucky with the expenses that kept popping up—rent increases, car repairs, expensive nights out with coworkers and superiors. Don't they pay for that? Mr. Lee had asked, thinking of the way things were done in Korea. The company dinners, sure, Ken had said, but not for the drinks they had afterward, when the important relationships were cemented, when future promotions were decided. And Mr. Lee had thought to himself, Ah, well, things aren't so different after all.

Mrs. Lee found herself at a busy intersection. She had been so lost in thought, she hadn't realized that she'd walked out of her neighborhood. That meant she'd walked a couple of miles already and now she felt tired and thirsty. She saw a small café across the street next to a nail parlor. She pressed the WALK button and waited, watching the faces of the drivers passing, most of them blank and unreadable, but one car passed with a young girl clearly singing loudly, her mouth wide open, though Mrs.

Lee couldn't hear her voice. She smiled, briefly wondering what it would have been like to have had a daughter. Would she have felt closer to her?

Ken was a good son but he had never shared much of himself with her or her husband. And then she remembered a moment when he was perhaps five that filled her with shame. Ken cried easily when he was young, or at least that's the way it had seemed to her, but maybe he only did the normal amount of crying. After all, she really didn't have anyone to compare him to. She couldn't even remember why he was crying that time, maybe he had tripped and hurt his knee, no, it was his hand, she suddenly saw in her mind five-year-old Ken holding one hand protectively with the other. He was looking at her, his eyes big with tears, his mouth open with ragged cries, and she'd watched him impassively without going to him, without putting a look of sympathy, never mind empathy, on her face. Just watched him from a distance like he was a kid on TV, a kid she had no relation to, no responsibility for, while knowing that he was waiting for her to come to him, to hug and comfort him, and she had held back purposefully, until finally he'd had to close the space between them himself and threw himself into her arms. Even then she'd hesitated for the briefest of moments before folding him to her, smoothing back his hair, opening up his hand to look at the cut, to kiss and blow on it, before taking him inside to clean and bandage it. She'd thought he wouldn't remember anything from that moment, but was that the beginning of his pulling away, into himself, asking less of her? That wasn't the only moment like that, of course. There were many other times when she hesitated a moment too long, when she remained herself rather than Ken's mother. It was wrong, she could see that now, but it was also something she couldn't help.

When the WALK signal finally came on and she started moving, she felt a sudden urge to keep walking, past the coffee shop, past the strip mall where she got her nails done, past the gas station she and her husband had once considered buying, walking walking walking out of this life and into another. But she was tired and thirsty and pushed away such thinking, ridiculous and exciting as it was, and entered the coffee shop, bells jangling cheerily with the opening of the door.

Mrs. Lee was not an ambitious woman; that is, she had never felt herself called to do anything in particular, something that would count as leaving her stamp on the world. In fact, if pressed, she would say she wanted the opposite; once she left this world she wanted to leave nothing of herself behind. She had often chafed under the roles assigned to her—wife, mother—and life seemed to be no more than a series of tasks that took up time until one's body failed. She remembered seeing her grandmother bed-bound after a lifetime of work that had twisted her body in ugly ways—humpbacked, gnarled like a tree that had always had to fight for sunlight.

But even more difficult than that had been how living with others made her feel pressed in, like being on an elevator with too many people. She was conscious of holding herself in, the presence of others a corset that kept her from breathing freely. Early afternoon at the dry cleaners had always been her favorite time of day. Mr. Lee, who had opened up at six in the morning, would go home to take a nap, Ken was safely at school, and customers were busy doing other things. She would sit slowly eating her lunch at the counter, watching the street through the window, people walking their dogs, getting in and out of their cars, always eating, drinking, talking on the phone, and she loved the separation she felt from the world then, letting herself get lost in her own thoughts, not even of anything important, just idle thoughts that made her feel alive and present, that made her feel just like the bird she saw making an arc at the top of the windowpane. It was peace she felt then, not being anything for anybody, not even herself. That was freedom. That was what she supposed Ken was chasing through drugs and alcohol.

Ken and Celeste arrived home just after dark. Ken's face was still flushed from the whiskey sours they'd had at the Elephant Room, the dive bar a couple of blocks away from his parents' dry cleaners that he'd never been to before today. In the morning they'd gone to see Ken's childhood home, a brick colonial with black shutters that looked exactly the way Ken remembered. The only difference was that there was a Ford pickup in the driveway with an American flag sticker on the back window. It was the same and yet he couldn't fathom having grown up there, treading the wall-to-wall carpet from his bedroom to the kitchen. Even though it didn't make sense, he blamed the ring in his front pocket, the jade ring he'd taken out of the pouch underneath the bookcase. That morning as he bent down for the jeans he'd thrown on the floor the night before, something yellow caught his eye. It was a bit of yellow string holding a pouch closed. He wasn't surprised to open the pouch and see his mother's rings. She had hidden things all his life; besides cash and jewelry, he'd found a collection of keys, a small box with his baby teeth, a notebook with Korean writing, little hotel-sized shampoos and soaps wrapped up in a silk handkerchief, and old black-and-white photos of a Korean man he'd never seen before. If he really thought about it, she did that with herself too, keeping parts of herself hidden from him and his father.

He had no intention of keeping the ring, or selling it. He didn't know why he'd even put the ring in his pocket. A flash of resentment. It weighed on him all day and now he couldn't wait to return it, to be rid of it. The anxiety it caused him made him want to escape himself. That was a dangerous feeling. He forced himself to sit still until the feeling passed. They sat outside his old house until Ken thought he saw someone look out the window.

Afterward, he'd driven Celeste around his high school, the Friendly's where he went after school with his friends, the cemetery and the golf course where kids drank on the weekends when he was in high school and probably still did, aware the whole time of the ring in his pocket giving off heat. After driving past his parents' dry cleaners, he was grateful when Celeste suggested stopping for a drink.

Now he felt his mother taking in his reddened eyes with her clear ones.

"Where's Chinese food?" Mrs. Lee asked, speaking in English as a polite gesture toward Celeste.

Ken smacked his forehead. "I forgot, Ma. I'll go right now. What's your favorite place?"

Mr. Lee came in from the living room where he'd been watching the evening news, his glasses perched low on his nose.

"Hi, Dad," Ken said.

"No food?" Mr. Lee said.

"I told Ma I'd go get it now. What's your favorite place?"

"It's late, Ken," Mr. Lee said. He turned to his wife and spoke in Korean, telling her to heat up some leftovers.

"No, no, Dad. I said I'd get it. Here." He whipped out his phone and started going through Yelp. "There's a place about a mile away that gets four stars. That's good for a Chinese restaurant."

When he said the name, Mrs. Lee shook her head and said, "That place is no good. No taste in their dishes. We like Wall of China."

"Wall of China, Wall of China," Ken said under his breath as he scrolled through the listings on his phone. "It only gets three stars."

"What is this star business?" Ken's father asked.

"It's a rating system," Celeste said. She'd taken off her shoes and was holding them in her hands. "Five is the best."

"Only three stars?" Mrs. Lee said. "Food there is so good."

"That settles it," Ken said. He turned to Celeste. "Why don't you stay here and take a shower and I'll go out to get it."

"Are you sure?" she asked. She leaned over and kissed Ken on the mouth. His parents looked away.

Mrs. Lee said, "I write down for you what we want. Your father love the ma po tofu."

Mr. Lee shrugged and wandered back to his chair in the living room.

Ken stood in the small entrance to the house with his shoes still on, waiting for his mother to return with a list. He felt like a teenager again, caught in a lie, and he felt an overwhelming urge to try to make everything right, try to make everyone feel good, especially his parents. And then he wanted to swallow, smoke, or shoot something inside him that would make all feelings go away. Anxiety was making his extremities tingle. He remembered his therapist telling him to picture something calming, whatever was soothing to him. The first thing that came to mind was an orange, a large, round, juicy-looking orange promising refreshment. He thought of it now, perfectly dimpled all over, glinting with a slight wet sheen.

When Mrs. Lee returned with her list, Ken said, "I'm sorry I forgot, Ma. You must be hungry."

"No, no." Mrs. Lee waved his apology away. "Don't worry." She wondered if drugs had ruined his brain, made him forgetful. Without thinking she said, "You're a good son, a good boy." She used to say this to him often when he brought home Mother's Day and Valentine's Day cards from school, made with yarn and stickers and thick white glue. She threw them away when he wasn't looking. Later he gave her cheap drugstore perfume for Christmas, and later, translations of popular American books in Korean. He was always thoughtful.

Ken looked guiltily at his mother's veined hands, her ringless fingers. "I'd better go," he said. "Dad must be starving."

"I go with you," his mother said suddenly, grabbing her jacket from the coatrack near the door, pushing her feet into her battered black shoes, the backs permanently broken down.

When Ken stood there and didn't say anything, she said, "C'mon. What you waiting for? Let's go." She called loudly to her husband in the living room and he grunted in reply.

"Ma, it's not necessary," Ken said.

"I know," she said. "I don't care what necessary."

"Tell me about Celeste," Mrs. Lee said in the car. "You gonna marry her?"

"Yes," Ken said without thinking.

"She pregnant?" his mother asked.

Ken stared at her. "How did you know?"

"Watch the road!" Mrs. Lee said. "Oh, boy, poor girl."

Ken didn't ask what she meant by that.

"You better grow up, Ken."

"I know. I am."

"You really quit drugs?"

"Yes."

"I'm glad you quit." She directed him to the highway and told him which exit to get off at. "It was hard?"

"Nah, it was easy." Ken looked over at her and smiled. She smiled back. What would be the point of telling her what he had gone through, getting fired from one job after another, selling off his things one at a time, living on friends' couches until he was too embarrassed to face them again, leaving thank-you notes on top of neatly folded sheets on the couch.

Mrs. Lee knew he was joking, knew he didn't want to talk about it. "You think this time it work?"

"I think so," Ken said. "But I have to make the decision again every day."

Mrs. Lee nodded. "Make sense." She thought of how she used to buy scratch tickets every day until she realized how much she was spending and how she was hiding it from her husband. It was hard to quit buying them, hard to quit the hope that her life could be changed all at once with a huge influx of money. Finally, she'd had to figure out a new route to the dry cleaners so that she wouldn't drive by the Circle K anymore. Of course there were other Circle Ks but that one had been hers.

Mrs. Lee reminded Ken of the exit and told him which strip mall to turn into. They pulled into a space facing the restaurant and stared at the bright red neon of the lights spelling out the restaurant's name. The first letter was unlit so the sign said ALL OF CHINA.

Ken turned off the car but neither got out.

"Ken, you take Halmani's ring?" Mrs. Lee asked without looking at him.

He hesitated only for the briefest of moments. "Yes," he said. "I wasn't stealing it. I just put it in my pocket by accident. I wasn't going to keep it," he said, knowing how lame he sounded. He took it out of his pocket and put it on her open palm.

Mrs. Lee fingered the smooth roundness. She thought about how this was one more thing she could never tell her husband.

"This ring important to me." She tried to push down the anger she felt; instead she began to shake.

"I know, Ma. I'm so sorry." Ken looked down at his hands on the steering wheel. When she didn't answer, he turned to look at her. "Ma, are you okay? Are you sick?"

She looked hard at Ken in the reddened light from the restaurant's sign, but she could only see half of his face. He looked so open, so guilty. She felt a moment of despair, recognizing how alike they felt. She should be the one apologizing to him. She thought of how he'd hidden himself away from them, not wanting to burden them with his addictions, until he needed money for rehab. Despite how American he seemed, he was still Korean in that way. She felt for the first time how difficult it must have been to grow up in two cultures that often seemed so opposed to each other. She wanted to tell Ken that she wished she could do it all over again. Instead she said, "Yah, I'm okay. I'm okay, Ken. You take the ring. You keep. You going to be fine. You fine already. You going to be a wonderful father. We be here. You need anything, you let me and Daddy know."

She took his right hand off the steering wheel, opened it, and placed the jade ring on his palm. "You take it, Ken. It belong to you now. Give to Celeste or somebody else. Don't worry, someday I like her a lot." She smiled at him until, just like when he was a child, he smiled back.

Katherine D. Stutzman

Junior

Tʜᴇ ɴᴇᴡs ᴏꜰ ᴛʜᴇ ᴅᴀᴍ ᴄᴏᴍᴇs, and Junior Ogilvy does not alter his routine. He rises in the dark as he has always done, lights a lamp, and carries it up the stairs to the room where his father sleeps. The iron bed has been painted white, but now the paint has chipped and the black iron shows through in many places. The bed fills the room, leaving space only for a washstand in the corner. Junior goes to the washstand, pours a little water into the enameled basin, allows the light of the lamp and the sound of the water to wake his father. He waits to see if his father will be able to put his feet on the floor and stand without help. His father, Henry Ogilvy, does not like to be helped more than is necessary.

When he finishes waking his father, Junior goes to the kitchen. He fries bacon, makes coffee, fries eggs and bread in the drippings from the bacon. He puts the food on two plates and sits down at the table, waiting and listening as his father makes his way down. Soon, he thinks, his father will no longer be able to manage the stairs.

The rest of the day, as always, is spent in work: feeding and milking the cows, keeping his eye on the calf that has been born late in the season and that, he fears, will not survive the winter. He and his father once did this work side by side; now he works alone. Junior sells their milk to Bob Weld in town, just as they have done for years.

From the porch of his farmhouse, Junior can look out over the Herne River and the town of Willards Mill, across the valley to the long rows of apple trees in the Cranfield orchard on the other side. The window in his father's room faces the other way, toward the upper pasture and the line of trees beyond. Now, in late August 1919, when the news comes that the Herne will be dammed and Willards Mill flooded, the view from his father's room is of browning grass and trees that are beginning to change their color. From the porch, the Herne is difficult to see at all as it flows with late-summer shallowness through the town. Junior sits on his porch in the evening, after milking and before going in to cook supper for his father and himself. He looks between the rooftops to catch a glimpse of the river. When he was eight years old, a boy in the year ahead of him drowned in the river. Not when the water was low and brown like it is now, but in spring, when the river turns black and rushing. Junior has not thought of that boy in many years, but now the incident comes back to his mind.

Two days after he learns the news, Junior tells his father that the courts have ruled and the dam will be built after all. "It's official," he says. "They'll flood us." Henry grunts, returns his attention to the egg on his plate. Later, as he walks to the barn, Junior shakes his head and laughs. He doesn't know what else he expected.

It is not hard for Junior to imagine the dam itself or what it will take to build it: the construction, the men working. But it is hard for him to imagine the water that will fill Willards Mill. When he tries to picture a lake, its surface shining and unbroken, stretching over the town, he cannot do it. He knows he will have to leave, of course; he realizes that he will need to find a new farm and start elsewhere, or find some other type of work that he can do. But he cannot seem to push his thoughts any farther into that rudimentary plan.

As the weather cools and Junior begins the process of drying off the cows, something changes in his father. In the mornings he is the same, and he spends his daylight hours by the window, looking out at the reddening trees, but at night he slips into a low fever and often cries out. It unnerves Junior to hear these cries, for his father sounds like not an old man but a boy. The cries are sometimes wordless, but at other times he calls to his mother or to someone named Alfie. Junior has never heard him mention the name Alfie in his waking life.

When the nightmares have been going on for two weeks, Junior asks Dr. Culler to come to the farm and examine his father. The doctor tells him only what he has already suspected: that there is little to be done for a patient of Henry's advanced age, that Henry will die, the only question is when. The doctor also tells him that nightmares are normal in a feverish patient, and gives Junior a blue glass bottle of drops to help his father sleep more easily. Junior pays Dr. Culler with three pounds of butter.

Then comes a morning when Henry falls on the stairs. Junior hears the sound and finds his father sprawled, unable to stand. Junior lifts him to his feet and is surprised by how easy it is for him, how little his father weighs now. Henry is bruised but does not seem to be seriously injured. Junior helps him back to his bed, brings him his breakfast and a glass of milk. "Go on. They need you," Henry says, and Junior knows he means the cows.

The time of the nightmares ends. Henry sleeps lightly but quietly now, sleep covering him like the first thin dusting of snow for the year. He no longer comes downstairs and is only rarely asleep when Junior comes into his room in the mornings. He lies in his iron bed, looks at Junior out of eyes that are blue and swimming, and does not speak.

In November of that year, Junior receives a letter from his sister Rebecca, married to a military man at Fort Drum. Junior does not open the letter right away, but sets it on the table in the kitchen, where its envelope looks clean and bright against the greasy wood. He looks at the letter while he eats breakfast and supper, admiring the neatness of her handwriting but unwilling to learn her message. When he finally opens it, he does so in the morning, feeling that it will be better to carry the letter's contents out into the cold, into the barn, among the cows with their breath steaming from their nostrils, rather than carrying it into his little room under the stairs and into his sleep.

In the letter Rebecca says that she has heard of the dam that is, by then, already in progress, and she knows that Willards Mill is to be evacuated and flooded. She tells Junior to bring their father to her house near the fort, where he can be made comfortable in his old age. Then Junior will be free to find a new farm, or a new job, a new place to live, whatever it is he plans to do when he can no longer live in Willards Mill.

He does not know how to respond to this letter. He feels a heavy reluctance to move his father from the farmhouse, but he can't find a way to explain this to Rebecca. She is two years younger than him and almost entirely unknown. After their mother died, she was raised in town by their Pomeroy grandparents; Junior was left on the farm to be brought up among grief and silence and cows. He holds her letter in his hand and remembers a time when she was seven or eight years old, and their grandparents brought her to the farm for a visit. It was summer; she had worn a green dress. He and she had stood in the kitchen and watched the adults drink coffee until he told her he would take her to the barn and show her the calves. Rebecca had been surprised by the size of them—perhaps, Junior thinks now, she had expected them to be no bigger than kittens or puppies—and afraid of their mouths and damp noses, but she had petted their hips and sides. She had turned to him with bright eyes in the hot, dim barn and exclaimed that the calves were so much softer than she had thought. But when they got back to the kitchen, their grandmother had asked Rebecca what she thought of the calves and she had only shrugged.

Junior allows so much time to pass without responding to his sister's letter that it becomes clear he is not going to respond. He knows that his father will die—he does not expect him to live through the winter— and he thinks it better that he die in the iron bed in the room upstairs, with the window that now looks over gray fields and leafless trees, a brittle landscape waiting for the deep snow that is coming. Junior doesn't know what his sister's house looks like, or what the room she would put their father in is like, or what the window looks out on. Nor does he know what he himself would do once his father was installed in Rebecca's house waiting to die.

Eventually another letter comes, in which Rebecca suggests politely that perhaps he had not received her earlier correspondence. Two weeks after that there is another. More letters come, and they grow more insistent. Finally she writes and tells Junior that he is irresponsible, that she will do nothing to help him. Junior puts this letter into the stove in the kitchen and goes out to sit in the barn in the cold. He does not think of himself as irresponsible and knows that he is not. Yet he has no plan to leave.

The late calf—the one he thought would not survive the winter—does not; he finds it dead one morning in December, after the coldest night they have yet had. On Christmas Day he buys a chicken from Gerry Smeals's poultry farm and roasts it in the oven. He eats slices of it with gravy at the kitchen table, then shreds some of the meat into a small dish and takes it upstairs to feed his father. Henry stares at his son and eats three bites of the shredded chicken with gravy. Then he abruptly closes his eyes and falls asleep. Nearly every day, Junior expects to find that his father has died, but the old man lives on, lying in his iron bed, his body a bundle of sticks.

The thaw begins, and the fields outside his father's window become dark and wet, with patches of old snow lingering in the shadows of the trees. Junior sells his little herd to a larger dairy farm near Lowville. He keeps the mule and the flat cart he used to transport milk for sale; those will be useful to him when the time comes to leave. But wherever he goes, he will go without the cows. Looking across the river now, Junior sees only the empty ruin of what had been the orchard, the trees chopped down, the rootstock dug up to be replanted somewhere else. One day he sees a group of men at work in the cemetery, digging up the graves so that they can be reburied somewhere else. He goes every day for a week and watches the work, leaning on the cemetery fence. He had not considered that even the dead would need to evacuate their homes.

Junior brings Dr. Culler to the farmhouse again. The doctor tells him it will not be long now.

He goes into town, to Sevald's Hardware, and finds the store in disorder. There is little left on the shelves, and open crates litter the floor, partially filled with the last remaining merchandise. He finds old Mr. Sevald, the father of a boy he was friends with many years ago, and asks him if there is lumber left. Mr. Sevald looks at him, tells him there are only scraps, but he can take what he needs. Junior carries the lumber back to the farm and in the empty barn he uses Henry's tools to build Henry's coffin.

Most people leave Willards Mill with the arrival of spring. The only people still in town are those without connections: the hired apple-pickers who have no more apples to pick, the former bartender at the Willard Hotel whose bar has closed with the hotel, those men who have never held steady jobs in Willards Mill and will likely never hold steady jobs anywhere else. These men do not need plans; they can go at any time, and so they wait for the feeling to strike.

Junior goes into town sometimes and walks the empty streets, looking at the way different houses have been left—some neatly, their rooms empty, their doors and shutters fastened, and others carelessly, doors thrown defiantly open, as if in leaving the owners had wanted to underscore the fact that nothing done in Willards

Mill could matter anymore. Sometimes, Junior sees other men in town. He never speaks to the people he sees. It always seems that they don't want to speak to him any more than he wants to speak to them.

When he is not walking, he stays in the farmhouse, sometimes sitting by his father's bed, sometimes looking out the kitchen window, moving from room to room and worrying. He does not know what he will do if his father does not die by the time the water begins rising. He imagines himself trying to carry the dying man out of the house, his father crying out in pain as Junior takes him—where? Or else he imagines searching through the streets for one of those furtive figures he sometimes sees, and having to ask that man for help in moving his father. He feels that the body in the iron bed will never die, that his father's life will smolder forever in the room upstairs, until the water rises right around the bed. Junior paces the house, his mind full of these thoughts, and then he climbs the stairs with broth for his father to drink.

Six days since Junior has last seen someone else in Willards Mill, he comes into the wooden room carrying a glass of water. When he puts out his hand to raise his father's head, he finds that he is cold. He brings the coffin that he made in the barn and lifts his father into it. The old man has lost so much flesh that it is no trouble to lift him. Junior nails the lid over his father and goes out of the room, closing the door carefully behind him. He has done it wrong, he realizes; now he will need to carry the box with his father in it down the stairs. He sits in the kitchen, waits, though he doesn't know what for.

Eventually he climbs the stairs back up to the wooden room with the iron bed and the wooden box in it, with the window that looks out over the green fields of June. He picks up the box and wrestles it down the stairs, jarring it twice against the wall as he goes. He takes it out and sets it on the cart, then goes back into the house for the suitcase of his own belongings that has been packed and waiting by the door for days. He hitches the mule to the cart and walks away from the farmhouse where he has lived his entire life.

When at last Junior Ogilvy leaves Willards Mill, he does not go down through town and away along the River Road. He walks beside his mule out behind the farmhouse and across the pasture. He will find his way up and over the hill, to another valley, to a place where he can put his father into the ground and begin again.

Juliana Leite

Translated from the Portuguese by
Zoë Perry

My Good Friend

Sunday evening

ABOUT THE ROOF REPAIR, I have nothing new to report. The tiles were supposed to arrive yesterday; they did not. I rang that young man at the store to give him a piece of my mind, but he's always so nice that I forget I called to quarrel. He told me the news about his mother (new boyfriend). We chatted for fifteen minutes, and it wasn't until I hung up the phone that I realized I'd once again neglected to give him an earful. Meanwhile, the roof is still in shambles. It continues to leak, and of course now the walls are following suit—they're covered in great big stains. Once the roof is done, I'll need to fix the walls. One thing at a time. I can't complain, though. All this leads to phone calls, conversations. If it weren't for the roof tiles, I'd never have found out the boy's mother has a boyfriend—it's Celso, the one who drove a Ford Corcel when we were young. The boy at the store told me his mother is happy because she always had such a crush on Celso's Corcel, and it's just a shame the car's long since been sold, she said. "All things in good time" was what the boy told me on the phone. He was talking about his mother's relationship, but a bit about my roof tiles, too.

Today I had lunch with my good friend. It's been two months since he had that fall, in his hallway. My friend thinks it's been more than two months, a lot longer, but that's because he's always in pain, etc. To this day, he can't say how it happened—it wasn't loose shoelaces this time, apparently. When he fell, my friend slammed his shoulder against the door and just lay there on the floor stunned, not knowing who he was or who that newly broken shoulder belonged to. The doctors gave him one of those slings that straps your arm against your body, and then they wrapped everything up so he couldn't spread or even raise his wing.

After that my friend's memory started to go. No one knows exactly why this happened—he didn't hit his head on anything. My friend was terribly frightened because in the moment he tripped, he had time to realize he was going to hit the door on his way down, and that it was going to do some damage. He must have managed to duck his head and shield it from the impact, but he doesn't remember. He says it must have been nothing more than a reflex. He protected his head, but the fright made him lose his memory.

My good friend is the one with uneven eyes. I've mentioned him here before by other names: my hunched-over friend, my friend whose parents were from Pernambuco, my toolmaker friend, my friend Suzy's husband—they're all one and the same. Right after his fall, when we spoke on the phone, he still remembered me perfectly, but a few minutes later he asked me, "Suzy, is that you, dear?" So I had to remind my friend who I was, and that Suzy was long gone.

After he fell and broke his shoulder, we had to go a few weekends without our get-togethers, without our precious lunches. My friend's children came to take care of him and so it wasn't right for me to come around as often as I usually do. My friend didn't ask me to do that—I mean, he didn't ask me not to stop by. I just preferred it that way. His four children came to town—two by plane, as I understand it. They saw their father with a broken shoulder and couldn't think of anything besides medications and physical therapy. They don't even know how to cook, and so my friend, who's so fond of food, spent weeks eating cheese sandwiches. They didn't even get him fresh rolls from the bakery, just sliced bread, and they only sometimes added a slice of tomato. My friend told me this only after his children had left. He said I'd done the right thing by not visiting, or else I would have been forced to eat one of *those* sandwiches, too.

My friend's children always seem a lot nicer on the phone. They talk to me for a few minutes, call me Auntie, give me the latest on my friend's health. But then they say they need to hang up, and poof, they're gone. In the last few seconds of the call, I say I love each of them, I say I love them as always. They don't say, "I love you" back, but they mean no harm. "As always" covers a very long period of time—maybe what they'd need is a cutoff date, so they could reply without feeling embarrassed.

They were very distressed by my friend's fall, of course they were, scared, afraid. So if, on top of everything else, they found out that my friend and I had been having lunch together every weekend, and that we even had dessert, they wouldn't just be distressed, they'd be furious. They'd remind their father he's diabetic. The kids found the Pyrex dish I'd used to transport the flan for our last lunch in the kitchen cupboard, and asked my friend if that Pyrex dish belonged to me. My friend denied it, and to sound more convincing he said he and I barely see each other now, because I'm an old lady who has trouble getting around, who spends most of her time in bed—that's what he said. I don't blame my friend for lying to his children—after all, he knows very well what those children of his are like. But he didn't have to throw me to the wolves like that, as if I don't even put on perfume anymore.

Well, my friend called me a few days ago and said his children had left. Two by plane and two by car. He was silent on the phone for a while, searching for something to say, but then he remembered the reason for his call and said he had the food and the beer ready, waiting for me, so I didn't have to worry about a thing. He said, "Don't worry about a thing," referring to the food and drink but also to the absence of his children. He would make his vegetable loaf, from that Turkish or Balinese recipe, I can't remember which, a dish I really like because it has olives. We'd have time to talk about his shoulder, about my roof, and also about something he'd been thinking about, he told me. I didn't ask what it was, I was afraid it had to do with his children, probably some complaint, etc. My friend said that what he had to tell me was important, and this puzzled me because, after all, he doesn't usually refer to his children's grievances that way, as important or unimportant. But perhaps it had nothing to do with that. I hurriedly agreed to my good friend's invitation and tied a perfumed scarf around my neck.

It's very different talking to my good friend at his house and not over the phone, as we've had to do for the past few weeks. When we have to talk on the phone, with the kids around, we're a little more perfunctory. We talk about the simple things, about the present. If he hadn't been so closely watched, my friend would have used the calls to complain about Raul, his son the newsagent, who announces all the news before my friend can read his morning paper. My friend takes his coffee and sits down at the kitchen table to read his nice newspaper, but before he's even had a chance to skim the headlines Raul comes in and reports everything in that day's edition, in detail. My friend gets so frustrated he doesn't even finish his coffee.

But my friend couldn't tell me about any of this before now, because his kids were always around when I called. He'd just tell me about his shoulder, the pain, the drugs, and he'd ask me something about roof tiles, leaks. He always sounded very clear-headed and serious in those moments when he asked me about the leaks—he sounded like an expert. In the presence of his children that sort of thing happens—our friendship tenses up and we both sound very aboveboard and like experts on things that matter very little.

Everything is so different when my friend and I meet for lunch at his place. There we have hours and hours, and there's no one watching over us. How I'd missed my good friend lately! I ended up watching a lot of movies, but it's not the same thing. My friend always gives me a hug as soon as I get to his house. It's so nice to hug someone who arrives at your home smelling good, with a beautiful blue scarf around their neck—who could ever say they don't like that? My friend feels like smiling for no apparent reason. I really enjoy being at my friend's house because he makes me feel at home. He cooks something from a country we've never been to and turns on the fan, and the breeze and the exotic smell of the food make us feel like we're on a train trip. He calmly tells me about his vegetable garden and soon I'm so excited I can't sleep when I get home. I've written about this before, a few pages back, about his huge cabbages, the beets.

After talking about his vegetables, we inevitably talk about the past. We don't mean to, but before we know it, it's happening. It's like a piece of fruit on a tree ripening in reverse: we look at each other, my good friend and I, and then the fruit turns green again, back to its unripe state. Today was the first day he didn't mistake me for Suzy since he took that fall. We spent time together, we ate, we talked normally without my friend ever thinking I was his wife. Anyway, in his house there's always that picture of Suzy in the living room, right there on the little table next to the sofa. If my friend felt confused at any moment, he could look closely at that photograph to tell us apart. Suzy was as beautiful as the singers on the radio—she had magnificent curly hair, while I have no curls and I don't look like I sing either.

When I go to eat with my friend, I usually take a flan or a coconut custard for dessert, always with plums in syrup because my friend adores plums in syrup. It's just that since his fall he's forgotten about that adoration of his; he told me on the phone that he doesn't remember liking plums that much. That put me in a real predicament. I used to use those plums to express my love for my friend, through the finest imported plums, which I'd take him on the weekends. Suddenly I had to find a replacement to show him my love.

Just yesterday I went into town and had three flavors of strudel wrapped up at that bakery where they make Hungarian pastries. I'm not talking about the new bakery, the one with the annoying neon sign, but the old one on the street behind the market. I try not to stay inside that place for long, because the sweets attract mosquitoes and those mosquitoes are enough to drive you to violence. They still sell those same packets of shortbread there, but they seem to keep moving them higher and higher up, out of the customers' reach. The lady at the counter told me that they've always been on the same shelf, at the same height, which only goes to show I've shrunk. I go to that bakery because their pastries are well-known around town for being freshly made every morning. Just one look at a bag from that shop and presto, you know you're getting something fresh. In the town where we live, some things might be old, like me and my good friend, but pastries can never be. Pastries have certain obligations and one of them is that they must be fresh, especially on weekends. I suspected some strudel might be a very effective way of saying "I love you" to my friend after his fall, maybe even better than the plums. Ultimately, I wasn't wrong.

Today I left home early because I wanted to get to my friend's house as soon as possible. I'd hardly slept. I was up at five in the morning, eating my toast and spritzing perfume on my handkerchief. Then I read a few pages of that book about the gardener—finally the winter chapter is ending, some pine trees have appeared now, pine trees and seriema birds, but I couldn't read much, because I was anxious and that gardener is too calm, the pages move along and he just talks more and more slowly. I looked out the window, it was already pouring down rain, as expected. I put

on my coat, grabbed my umbrella—the one I got for Christmas—
and walked down the street, leaning into the wind. In this town,
if you don't do that, you'll fall backward and you won't be able to
get back up, like a beetle. The only reason I didn't go faster was
because that might have endangered the strudel, snug inside my
tote bag.

As soon as I got to his house, my good friend had to push hard
on the kitchen door, which opens outward, so that I could finally
enter, thrust inside by the howling wind. He hugged me tight,
squishing the pastry a little in the bag, surely forgetting there
might have been a custard or flan in there. I was soaking wet and
my friend told me to hurry and take off my coat, so I wouldn't
catch a cold or worse. He helped me, pulling my coat up, freeing
my head like a stuck cork. My friend's house was warm and tidy,
with the fresh scent of Pine-Sol and butter, which is his way of
telling me that, for his part, our love still stands, even if he doesn't
remember it sometimes.

Roger the cat came to greet me, and when I peered into the
living room, there was Suzy in her picture frame, next to a vase of
yellow begonias. My friend told me he'd had to fight over those
flowers at the market this morning, because they had been the
only yellow ones. I walked over to say hello to Suzy and kissed her
on the cheek through the glass.

My good friend was preparing the food. He looked at his watch
and opened two cans of beer. We usually start drinking at eleven.
If it's before that, we have coffee or juice or whatever's in the
fridge, to kill time. Whenever we start drinking our beers, well,
what happens is we start talking about loneliness. About widow-
hood and loneliness, although these specific words are never said.
These aren't sad or melancholy conversations, no, no, you would
be wrong to imagine that. On the contrary, we drink and rejoice,
because at last there's somebody who understands just how similar loneliness and contentment can become over time. My good
friend and I have both been widowed for so long, we've figured

out how to settle into our circumstances, we've learned how to do that. We reminisce about times with Suzy and times with my husband as if we were looking at a puzzle with some pieces that have gotten lost, God knows where. We ask each other, "Do you remember that, dear?" or "And that time at the lake, do you remember, sweetie?," testing which of us is getting more senile with each encounter.

My good friend and I take such good care of each other that of course it's love. But we don't use that word, because of the kids. Our friendship goes back to before our marriages, it's always poured out of everything and embraced all the people we chose along the way. The more my friend and I loved our spouses, the more we loved each other, too, as though both loves heightened and nurtured each other, even if one of them had come first. Suzy and my husband, they looked at us from the outside and in their own way understood what was going on. They didn't grumble, at least not all the time. They realized that the closeness my friend and I shared was sultry and velvety at times, but that it was also dull and tightly drawn, like a chicken wire fence.

We got married the same year, 1957. Suzy and I were the same age and had more or less the same body—she had slightly fuller breasts. We decided to save money by wearing the same dress, which was tied around the waist with a ribbon, and to change the look a little we bought different-colored ribbons—mine was sky blue and Suzy's pale yellow. I'd been trying to grow out my hair for a few months, at Suzy's suggestion—she told me that with long hair I could pin a flower or a pretty barrette in it for the ceremony. I preferred short hair, a bob, but I went along with my friend, because Suzy knew how to primp and preen like a lady, how to make those magnificent curls, wear perfumed handkerchiefs, etc. I'd tell people, "Oh yeah, I'm growing my hair long for my wedding," and Suzy would grin as she explained her plan to pin in a pretty barrette, a flower, or a paper swan.

Back then, my fiancé and my good friend were young men

and looked a bit alike. Both of them had thick, shaggy beards, like most boys in those days. They were thin and about the same height. Sometimes people mixed them up, especially if their backs were turned. But my good friend carried a denim backpack wherever he went, and so the backpack made it clear who was who. That backpack smelled awful and so his back also smelled awful, but it was a smell you soon got used to and grew fond of.

When Suzy agreed to marry him, my good friend was ecstatic and said he'd wear a red suit to the church, an outfit he'd bought for cheap from a circus dealer. He'd often make up these stories and I'd confirm every detail, as if I myself had seen the suit, which wasn't exactly red but burgundy, with a lighter colored stripe down the side of the trousers. Suzy was nervous about the burgundy, and about the stripe thing, because she didn't want a flamboyant groom, she wanted a groom like her cousin's, that boy who'd fainted at the altar. In those days, fainting at the altar was seen as a good thing, a kind of sign that the groom was lovestruck in the proper way. In the end, my good friend entered the church wearing a light gray suit with a white satin flower on the lapel that I'd made as a gift. There's a photo where he, Suzy, and I are at the altar; she's adjusting the flower on his lapel and I'm holding the bouquet for her.

It's almost hard to believe my good friend and I were ever that young—I mean, it's hard to believe that that moment in time existed in this very same life, where we're now old. When my friend feels confused, he asks me if there's ever been a time when he didn't have this pain in his shoulder, when his shoulder was just an ordinary, painless shoulder, and I show him the old photos where he has a denim backpack slung over his shoulder. He still remembers the backpack, the stink on his back.

I got married just a few months after my good friend. Back then we all married young because we wanted to have sex—it was more respectable to have sex once you were married, in our day. Afterward, we rented neighboring houses for our families, and that's why we lived as one tight-knit group of people, all mixed together. My good friend and Suzy started having kids in 1958 and didn't stop until 1963. We watched their four kids grow up little by little, and we also watched each one move on to adulthood. To this day I call them "the kids" because it's simpler that way. My friend's children live far away nowadays, and they're very nice, although in the past they've said very unpleasant and nasty things to me and my friend. The children said these things to both of us when Suzy was dying—they were sad and angry and all of it came bubbling to the bitter surface.

Suzy's health spiraled quickly, and that's when the kids first started to talk about my friendship with my friend. They'd say the word *friendship* and make little air quotes. They snarked about the closeness we shared when we took care of Suzy together, in the bed and in the bath, and when she was hospitalized. Suzy preferred when my friend and I bathed her, because, after all, we'd known her naked body for a long time, we'd seen that beloved body in all its phases. The children talked about us in secret, and we knew everything, because, after all, we'd been talking about them for even longer, since they were little, as all parents do. We were the parents, and we'd had a lot more practice whispering about things behind their backs.

Those kids saw Suzy dying and they wanted my friend and me to do something, to find a way to turn it all around, or else to die in her place. And if we couldn't do that, well, they wanted us to grow pale, so pale we'd become transparent around their mother's bed. They wanted to look at that bed and see only their convalescing mother, not their mother and our intimacy on top of her. My good friend and I would spoon Suzy, with her in the middle. We held hands, the three of us, and then we went to sleep. The children would tiptoe into the bedroom to take a closer look at those intertwined fingers, at our three hands joined at Suzy's hip. They suspected that there, hidden between our fingers, were all sorts of old things, things they'd only now realized and that would become too visible if they didn't do something to stop it. Suzy was about to leave us, but the two of us weren't going anywhere. We'd both be alive a little longer and would still hold those *things* between our fingers. Didn't we think we were betraying Suzy by staying alive?

Once, during the night, Raul snuck into the bedroom and read a few pages of my diary, which was on the dresser. He read almost the whole thing. In the morning, over coffee, he said I described too many mundane details and what those pages needed was a little action. It'd be better if I put in some more action, Raul told me, because then whoever read it might also have some fun, unwind, you know, and not just have to wade through all my innermost thoughts, one after another. I should think about it—that's what Raul said.

When we meet at his house for lunch, my good friend and I rarely talk about the things his children have accused us of, because it's always better to forget their words so we can forgive them. We are infinitely willing to forgive those kids, especially when everything they say is veiled, or whispered. We don't speak about it—that way we can keep our forgiveness from chafing.

I was thinking about all these things while setting the table for lunch at my friend's house today. The kids had been with him there just a few days ago, had taken care of my good friend and talked to me on the phone like that, like I was their aunt. I felt a bit of disgust for those kids grow inside me as I spread out the tablecloth, but luckily my friend looked at me and all he saw was someone setting the table. The tablecloth is still the one we bought on the family trip to Campos do Jordão. Suzy bought one and I copied her and bought another just like it but a little smaller. Suzy knew how to take care of a home, and when she was with me she would often slow down, so I could imitate her without rushing. The sunflowers on the tablecloth are faded, but we have such vivid memories from when they were still new and bright yellow that it's as if they haven't faded at all. The fabric has that candle burn from Raul's twelfth birthday—that was such a nice birthday. My husband and I gave him a hooded sweatshirt and some stickers to put on his window.

My good friend was taking the vegetable loaf out of the oven when he looked at me and said my eyes were a lot paler today than they had been the last time we saw each other. He told me that as we get old our eyes do lose their color, just like our hair, but that it's supposed to be something gradual and almost imperceptible. "Your eyes are getting lighter in no time flat," my friend told me, and held my face to get a closer look. He looked at me and I looked at him too. Then we sat down to eat the loaf, each with another can of beer.

My good friend had made the loaf with plenty of cabbage because his garden won't stop producing cabbages, he told me. He had also made a lettuce salad with a few small fuchsia-colored flowers. He's been growing edible flowers since Suzy died, and now they're at their peak, he said. The yellow ones bloom in May and the fuchsia ones in June, which is why my good friend spends at least two months of the year eating flowers every day. We're from a time when people didn't eat flowers, and now we're in a time when people do eat flowers, and what a magnificent difference between those times.

Roger came to sit under the table to get the crumbs. He's getting fatter, Roger the cat, because he's been eating rice—I bet he's been eating rice. The food was so steaming hot that we had to stop talking and eat in silence, both of us blowing on it. My friend and I get out of breath when we do this, and we have to focus on the task, like people at the bottom of a flight of stairs.

It's wonderful to be with my good friend because the silence is never uncomfortable or awkward, like it is when we're around his children. The last time I was with the children, we had to constantly come up with new topics to talk about, tacking on anecdotes to keep silence from taking hold, because then they might look a little too hard at me and my friend. During those encounters, I'm the one who has to be a chatterbox, especially about my husband, because bringing up my husband always calms those kids down a little. They're reassured by that kind of subject, because they knew my husband very well, of course—they even called him Uncle. Those children, they know how much I loved my husband and how pleasant and sweet smelling the two of us were on weekends. Sometimes we even got them shaved ice from the newsstand, or yogurt. The children remember these stories and are reassured by them, and that's always when I offer them some more grape juice. When the children are around, there's always grape juice, and we all sit there licking our purple mustaches after each sip.

But today at my friend's house the children were not with us, and so we felt relaxed enough to sit in silence, blowing on our food, chewing it slowly. My friend stuffed the lettuce leaves into his mouth whole, unceremoniously sticking out his tongue to capture an entire leaf. I could watch him without having to hide or look away. That was very nice.

Soon after, I served the dessert on two small gold-edged plates. We both went into the living room and sat on the couch to eat beside Suzy. My friend's eyes rolled back with every bite of strudel. He scarfed it down, barely taking a breath. He only paused briefly to praise how fresh and crisp the pastry was, and then suddenly he choked on a crumb. My friend started to cough and cough, harder and harder, startling me and forcing me to slap his back. The crumb came out only after several long seconds, and when that happened my friend was so upset he started to cry. I made him drink a glass of water and he told me he couldn't imagine choking to death or dying from a fall, and yet all those things had been happening to him lately. He calmed down after a few minutes and then laid his head in my lap. He wiped the tears with his fingers and dried them on my slacks.

My friend was silent as he gulped his own saliva down, the way we often do after we choke. But after a while he was still swallowing, and then I realized he must actually be getting ready to tell me something—he was getting his tongue ready. My friend had his head in my lap, right in front of Suzy's portrait, when he said, "Sweetie, I want you to come live here with me." He said that and then he said, "It's time," and looked at me after he stopped looking at Suzy. It didn't seem like he was still choking.

I started to tremble. I wasn't wearing my coat. I clutched at my friend's sofa so I'd stop trembling. Maybe my friend was losing his mind from all the painkillers. Maybe, with the fall, he'd forgotten what our love was, this thing we share but only at a distance. Surely he'd forgotten about his children. Or maybe he thought that now, more than anything, the two of us should be together, so I would be nearby for the next tumble or the next time he choked—maybe he was being proactive. Suddenly I thought my friend, lying there on the sofa, might be right. I was trembling. There was a bite of strudel left on my plate. I looked at Suzy, at her magnificent head of curls. Suddenly between the three of us there was a feeling of shared love, and not that same far-off love, our usual one. Roger the cat came over.

I thought I was ready to say something. I was ready. I was about to say something when I put the last piece of strudel in my mouth. My friend had fallen asleep on my lap by this point, the way little boys fall asleep after crying a lot. His mouth was open and his breath smelled of beer and strudel. I sat there quietly, waiting for him to wake up from his nap, thinking I really was ready to say something.

But a few minutes later, or maybe it was half an hour, the phone rang and my friend woke up with a start. One of his children was on the other end of the line. He wanted to know how his father's day was going, whether he'd had one of those cheese sandwiches for lunch, the ones he and his siblings had left in the fridge. My good friend assured him that, yes, he'd eaten two of the sandwiches for lunch and was now taking a nap on the couch before he took his afternoon medicine. I got up to put the gold-edged plates in the sink and my good friend motioned for me not to worry about that. Then he turned to the window and continued talking to his son. Based on the conversation, I don't think it was Raul; it was one of the boys who'd left by plane.

I looked outside and saw the afternoon had already turned to dusk. I waved at Suzy from afar, grabbed my umbrella, and pushed open the kitchen door into the wind. I left my friend talking at the window. I thought about walking home but ended up taking the bus because I don't see very well at dusk, and I might have tripped. Luckily it didn't take long. When I got back home, there was a message from my friend on the answering machine saying I'd left something in his kitchen, my coat. It still wasn't completely dry. He'd keep the coat at his house, my friend said in the message, and I could pick it up later, whenever I liked, or at our next lunch. It's my best coat.

It is now nine thirty at night. I still need to wash my feet and take those drops that help me sleep properly. Thirty weeks exactly—that's how long it's been since the roof started leaking. I'm jotting that down here, so I won't forget how long I've been waiting for those tiles. I tend to forget how long I've been waiting for things after a good night's sleep. Tomorrow morning I'm going to call that young man at the store and this time he'll have to give me an answer. He'll see. His mother was going to the movies with her new boyfriend this weekend, he told me; I'll finally find out what the film was.

Kate DiCamillo

The Castle of Rose Tellin

PEN REMEMBERS IT ALL. It was 1968. They took a family
vacation to Sanibel. Pen's father drove the station wagon. He
held the wheel tightly and gritted his teeth and smoked cigarettes
when he wasn't gritting his teeth.

Pen's mother sat in the front seat. She wore a blue scarf and
black sunglasses and kept saying, "Slow down, Cal. What's the
point in speeding? This is a vacation, right? You're supposed to be
relaxing. That's what the doctor said. Relax."

Pen and her brother, Thomas, sat in the back seat.

It was a big back seat; but Pen felt crowded, as if there were
more people in the car than there actually were.

Before they left for Sanibel, Pen and her mother had gone to
the circus together, just the two of them, and Pen had watched in
disbelief and horror as clown after clown climbed out of a very
small car.

"Infinity," Thomas had explained to her once, "is where nothing ever ends. It's where everything just goes on and on."

It was an infinity of clowns, and Pen was terrified.

She had started to cry.

Her mother said, "Jesus Christ, I've never seen a kid cry about
the clown car. And I've seen everything."

This was something her mother said a lot: "I've seen everything! I've seen it all!"

But at the same time, she kept having to say, "I've never seen anything like it."

It was confusing. Who knew what she had actually seen?

In any case, Pen couldn't stop thinking about all the clowns packed into that tiny car. It made her queasy stomached to consider them—their white faces and sad mouths and big, round noses.

"Pen looks funny," said Thomas.

"Be more specific," said Pen's father.

"Her face is green," said Thomas.

Pen vomited. And then she vomited again.

The seating in the car was rearranged. Thomas moved up front.

Pen sat alone in the middle of the back seat with the windows rolled down. She forgot about the clowns for a while.

When they arrived in Sanibel, invisible flies were waiting for them.

The flies bit them as soon as they stepped out of the station wagon.

Pen and Thomas and her mother and father all slapped at their faces, their arms and legs.

"What the hell?" said Pen's father as he twirled around, waving his hands.

It was funny, watching him, but Pen knew not to laugh.

The lady who was renting them the house came toward them smiling and slapping at her face. "You must be the famous judge," she said, holding out her hand to Pen's father. "What an honor to have you and your family here. I'm Mrs. Colwood."

Mrs. Colwood shook Pen's father's hand. She shook Pen's mother's hand.

She patted Pen on the head.

"You get used to the flies," said Mrs. Colwood. "And it's worth it! Oh my goodness, is it ever worth it! The views here are unparalleled. You're right on the water, as you can see."

"Actually," said Thomas later, when he and Pen were sitting together on the couch in the living room, "if you ask me, we're too close to the water for comfort. There are enormous fish lurking out there. They're man-eating fish and they're just waiting for us to make a mistake."

Thomas was nine years old—three years older than Pen.

He knew more than she did.

Or he pretended like he knew more. Also, he made things up.

They ate dinner together at a glass-top table in the dining room. Pen found it disconcerting to look down and see her feet. They looked so small, too small for the job of carrying her through the world.

Pen and her father were on one side of the table and Thomas and her mother were on the other.

From Pen's side of the table, you could see the water.

The sun was setting. It hung over the water in a thoughtful, reluctant way—as if there were something it had meant to do and hadn't gotten done.

"Everyone to bed," said her father when dinner was over. "It's been a long day."

"It's been a long day is right," said her mother as she laced a pair of boxing gloves onto Pen's hands. "The days are always long around here."

It was a rule—her father's rule—that Pen had to sleep in boxing gloves to keep her from sucking her fingers at night.

The boxing gloves were orange. They had kangaroos printed on them. Which was supposed to make them fun somehow, but the gloves weren't fun at all.

In the middle of the night, Pen would wake up holding her boxing-gloved hands in front of her face and think: Who took my hands? How can I get them back?

It was a relief each morning when Pen's mother unlaced the gloves and Pen found that her hands still existed.

"You'll be grateful to me someday," her father said at the

breakfast table as Pen sat beside him facing the sea. "You don't want to ruin the shape of your mouth, do you? You need to have a pretty mouth."

Thomas said, "But how can you ruin the shape of your mouth?"

"By running it all the time," said her father. "So why don't you shut up for once? Learn to keep your own counsel."

Pen looked past Thomas. She stared at the Gulf of Mexico. The water was so blue it had become green. It looked like a painting. She saw a dolphin leap out of the water.

"Can people ride dolphins?" said Pen.

"No," said Thomas.

"But I saw a picture once of someone riding a dolphin," said Pen.

"It was made-up then," said Thomas. "Dolphins aren't as nice as they look. They have teeth. Everything out there is dangerous."

Pen's father pushed his chair back from the table and lit a cigarette.

"Stop smoking," said Pen's mother. "That was another thing the doctor suggested. Give up cigarettes."

Pen's father blew a smoke ring above his head; when Pen looked up at it, he winked at her and smiled.

"Yep," he said. "Stop smoking. That will help with the stress for sure."

After breakfast, Pen went up to her room and crawled under the bed and sucked her fingers until she felt calmer.

"Fee fi fo fum!" her father shouted from downstairs. "Let's get out on that beach and have some fun!"

Pen rolled out from under the bed. She got out of her pajamas and put on her bathing suit, but by the time she made it down the stairs and outside, Thomas had locked himself in the station wagon.

Her father was standing very close to the windshield shouting, "Unlock the door, you little shit! Unlock the door now!"

Her mother stood next to her father. She had on her blue scarf and her dark sunglasses. "Stop yelling," she said. "It's not doing any good."

Pen's father had a cigarette in one hand. The other hand was curled into a fist that he was using to beat on the windshield. Sweat was pouring down his face.

The invisible flies were biting. Pen's father stopped pounding on the windshield so that he could spend some time slapping at his face and arms.

Meanwhile, Thomas sat in the car, in the driver's seat, with his arms folded, staring off into the distance.

"I've never seen anything like it," said Pen's mother.

After what seemed like a very long time, Thomas opened the door and climbed out of the station wagon.

"What is your problem?" shouted Pen's father as Thomas walked past him. "Tell me. What is it? Huh? What's your problem?"

"Let it go, Cal," said Pen's mother. "This is supposed to be a vacation. Remember?"

"Yes," said her father. "I remember."

"Why don't you just do what he wants?" Pen said to Thomas later, when they were sitting on the seawall.

"Look," said her brother. "I'm working on a way to get us out of here, okay?"

"How?" said Pen.

Thomas turned and looked at her. "I think I can make the car fly," he said. "You know. Like Chitty Chitty Bang Bang."

"Oh," said Pen.

They had watched *Chitty Chitty Bang Bang* at the Goldbergs' house on the Goldbergs' TV.

Pen's father didn't believe in TV, and so they didn't have one.

Her mother didn't believe in TV, either. Or that was what she said.

But once, Pen and her mother were downtown together and they had walked by a store with a whole wall of TVs, and all of them were showing the same thing: a bunch of ladies standing in a row, dressed in spangly costumes, kicking their legs up in the air and smiling.

Her mother had dropped Pen's hand and stopped and stared at the TVs. She said, "That was me."

Pen looked up at the wall of dancing women.

"I used to do that," said her mother. "I was a chorus girl. A Darzy girl. This was a long time ago. Before your father showed up. He put a stop to all that, of course."

"Oh," said Pen.

"But my legs were made for it," said her mother. "That was what Fred Darzy said. And he was the best there was."

Pen and her mother stood in front of the TVs for a long time.

The smiling, kicking ladies kept smiling and kicking, kicking and smiling. They didn't look like they ever intended to stop.

"I had a real spark," said her mother.

"I'm going to start with the ignition," said Thomas as he and Pen sat together on the seawall. "He hides the keys, so I need to figure out a way to start the car without them. I need a screwdriver, I guess. And some wires."

"And wings," said Pen. "You need wings. Chitty Chitty Bang Bang had wings."

"One step at a time," said her brother.

That night, before she went to sleep, Pen held the boxing gloves up in front of her face and studied them.

The gloves weren't really to stop people from sucking their fingers. That wasn't what they were made for. They were made for people to hit other people. The gloves were for hurting people.

You wore them so that you could hit someone and hurt them without hurting them too much.

One time, Pen's father had gotten so mad at Thomas that he had picked him up by the hair.

"I did it so that I wouldn't really hurt him," her father had explained to her mother afterward. "It was a reasoned, calculated move, a way to get my point across."

What had his point been?

Pen couldn't remember.

But when she asked Thomas if it hurt to get picked up by the hair, he said, "Yes. It hurt a lot."

Pen studied the smiling kangaroos on the boxing gloves. The kangaroos had on boxing gloves, too. And the kangaroos' boxing gloves had kangaroos printed on them. And even though she couldn't see it, Pen thought that the kangaroos on the kangaroos' gloves probably had kangaroos printed on them, too.

It was an infinity of kangaroos and boxing gloves.

Which was alarming.

But not as alarming as an infinity of clowns.

The next morning, they all went to the beach together.

They sat on lawn chairs. It was cold.

Little crabs went in and out of holes in the sand. The crabs were translucent, almost invisible. They looked like ghosts.

"Why don't you two make a sandcastle?" said Pen's mother.

"I'm reading," said Thomas.

He was dressed in a sweatshirt and jeans.

"Where's your swimsuit?" said Pen's father.

"Leave him alone, Cal," said her mother.

"I'm not bothering him," said her father. "I'm asking him a question. A reasonable question. We're at a beach. People wear swimsuits at the beach."

"Make a sandcastle, Pen," said her mother.

Pen got out of her chair and knelt in the sand.

"Am I bothering you?" Pen's father said to Thomas.

Her brother looked up from his magazine.

A ghost crab ducked into a hole.

"Yes," said Thomas. "You're bothering me."

Pen's father stood and lunged forward. He picked Thomas up by the ears and lifted him up out of his lawn chair.

"Jesus Christ," said her mother. "Put him down, Cal."

Her father gritted his teeth. He held on to Thomas's ears.

Thomas smiled a big, terrible smile. Tears rolled down the sides of his face.

"Stop it," whispered Pen.

Her father slowly lowered Thomas to the sand beside Pen.

"Pick up your chairs," said Pen's mother when Thomas was back on the ground. "We're leaving."

"Don't worry," Thomas said to Pen as they walked up to the house, "he can't stop me. He won't stop me."

Thomas's ears were red. It looked as if someone had tried to set him on fire.

Pen slipped her hand in his.

Later that day, they all got in the station wagon to drive to town for ice-cream cones.

"What the hell?" said Pen's father. "Look at this."

Pen's mother leaned over and looked where her father was pointing. She lowered her sunglasses.

"See that? There's scratches all over the steering column! And something is stuck in the ignition. Somebody tried to steal this car!"

Pen put her fingers in her mouth. Thomas started to hum.

"I'm calling the cops," said her father. "I can't believe this."

Thomas leaned over and whispered in Pen's ear, "I'm going to make a break for it. You should run, too. We should all run."

And then he opened the door and he was gone.

Pen's father turned his head slowly in the direction of Thomas. He turned his head back again and stared straight ahead.

There were only three of them in the car now.

For some reason, three seemed like a scarier number than infinity.

After the circus, Pen had asked Thomas about the clowns—about how so many of them could fit in one small car.

"They don't," said Thomas. "There's a trapdoor under the car. And they climb up out of that."

"What's a trapdoor?" Pen had asked.

"It's a hidden door," said Thomas. "Hidden doors are every-where. Hidden doors are all over the place but no one ever talks about them."

Pen knew that her brother made up a lot of things, but for some reason she felt as though he was telling the truth about trapdoors.

"I'm going to kick the shit out of him," said Pen's father from the front seat.

"Oh, calm down," said Pen's mother. "Isn't that the whole point of this trip? For you to calm down?"

Invisible flies came in through the open back door. They started biting Pen's face and neck.

Pen's father beat his hands on the steering wheel and then he got out of the car and slammed the door.

Pen and her mother sat and waited—one of them in the front seat and the other in the back.

"I suppose I'll have to go find your brother," said her mother. She got out of the car and then Pen was alone.

She sat there until the tow truck arrived, its yellow lights flash-ing.

The man who drove the tow truck had a patch on his shirt that said GENE in cursive letters. When he saw Pen sitting in the car, he said, "Hey there, cutie. You're going to have to get out of the car now."

Gene gave her a yellow lollipop. "You don't need that," said her father. He took the lollipop from Pen. "It'll just rot your teeth."

"Okay," said Pen, and she stood beside her father and watched while the car got hooked up to the tow truck.

"Your brother has some real problems," said her father. He took hold of her hand. "He's not like you and me, you know. He would never be able to appreciate a Picasso."

The Goldbergs, in addition to owning a TV, had a painting by Picasso. The Picasso hung on the wall in the dining room. The painting was called *Weeping Woman,* but the crying lady's face was not put together right. It looked like a face, and also not like a face.

Pen's father had walked into the dining room once and seen Pen standing in front of the painting, staring up at it.

He said, "That's a famous painting you're looking at, Pen. It's called *Weeping Woman*. It's by a man named Picasso."

"Oh," said Pen.

"What do you think the painting is about, huh? Any thoughts?"

And Pen had said, "The lady is broken and she's trying to put herself back together but she can't figure out how to do it."

"You've got a good eye, Penelope," her father said. "You're like me. You see things." He had taken hold of her hand. "You know that I'm the one who named you, right? Penelope. Because Penelope was the one who waited. Penelope was the one who was faithful. I looked at your face when you were born and I knew you would never betray me." He squeezed her hand.

Now, as the tow truck pulled away, dragging the station wagon behind it, Pen's father kept hold of her hand. He squeezed it harder and harder.

The mechanic was able to replace the ignition on the station wagon. He made shiny new keys for the car, and Thomas had to stand on one foot in a corner of the house, staring into nothing with his hands over his head, for a solid hour. That was his punishment.

"Next time," said Thomas to Pen as he stood in the corner, "I will succeed."

"No talking," said Pen's father. "Penelope, leave him alone. He deserves to be punished."

"But there's no stopping me," whispered Thomas over and over again, "there is no stopping, no stopping me, no stopping me at all."

The next morning, before anyone else was awake, Thomas took the new car keys from the table by the door. He went out to the station wagon. He opened all the doors so that they would act as wings. He got behind the wheel and cranked the ignition and stepped on the gas and drove the station wagon out of the driveway and through a hedge and over the seawall and down to the water.

By the time Pen and her mother and father made it outside, Thomas was already out of the car and running down the beach. He was running very fast.

"I will kill him," said Pen's father in a calm and decisive voice, the voice he used when he talked to his secretary, the voice of reason and judgment. He leapt over the seawall and chased after Thomas. When he caught him, he punched him in the stomach again and again.

Pen looked up at her mother. She waited for her to say, "I've never seen anything like it."

Instead, her mother screamed a loud, terrible, long scream; and then she was running down the beach, too, her nightgown billowing around her.

Pen stayed where she was. She was still wearing the boxing gloves. Her hands felt too heavy to lift.

The next day, Pen and Thomas flew back home to Philadelphia with their mother.

Before they left, they went down to the beach—this was after the car was towed, after Pen's father had disappeared.

They went down to the water, the three of them, so that Pen could get rid of her boxing gloves.

It was her mother's idea.

"Do you hate these as much as I do?" she had said to Pen when she was packing their suitcases.

Pen nodded.

"Good," said her mother. "We'll get rid of them then."

Pen threw the gloves into the water. They floated, bobbing on the surface.

"It will take a while," said her mother. "But they'll disappear."

It wasn't as cold as the day before. They sat together on the beach, the three of them. Thomas read his magazine. Her mother held her face up to the sun.

Pen worked on a sandcastle. She collected tiny pink shells that looked like butterfly wings. The shells were strewn everywhere on the beach. They were infinite, and Pen used them to decorate her castle.

"That's pretty," her mother said to her. "That's a very pretty castle, Pen." It turned out that Pen's father had checked himself into a mental institution. Later, they went to visit him. A nurse named Linda led the three of them through a series of locked doors and down a long hallway into a room with a TV and armchairs and folding chairs and tables with puzzles on them.

Her father cried when he saw them. He pulled Thomas to him and hugged him.

"Penelope," said her father. "Come here. Let me hold you."

She went toward him. She let herself be held. Afterward, Linda the nurse gave Pen a striped piece of gum that tasted like fruit.

Pen chewed the gum as she walked down the long hallway through the doors and out into the world.

Her brother remembers none of this.

Or he says he remembers none of it.

"But you destroyed the car," said Pen. "You tried to turn it into Chitty Chitty Bang Bang."

"Well, I remember Chitty Chitty Bang Bang," said Thomas. "And the Child Catcher."

"The Child Catcher," said Pen.

"Yeah," said her brother. "Because kids were against the law, remember? They all had to hide in the grotto of rose castle."

And suddenly, Pen was back on the beach in Sanibel, building a castle with a great hidden room beneath it, a place where the children could hide. She added pink shells to the exterior, making the castle as beautiful as she could—so beautiful that no one would ever think to look beneath it.

"Does this shell have a name?" she had asked her mother.

"It's a rose tellin," said her mother.

Pen liked the way the words sounded. She had used them to make a song.

"Rose tellin, rose tellin," she sang to herself as she worked. "I am Rose Tellin, building a castle in the sand."

Each time she looked up from the castle, she saw that the boxing gloves had gone farther away.

Soon, just as her mother had promised, she couldn't see them at all.

They had disappeared entirely.

Colin Barrett

Rain

A s scully and Charlie Vaughan passed under the trees in the town square, the afternoon seemed to switch on and off around them. It had rained while they were in the shops and the leaves above their heads had that dark, weighted gleam they got after rain, the sun a fitful flicker in the gloomy upper tangles of the branches. The stretch of footpath that ran beneath the trees was only lightly spattered where the rain had succeeded in dripping through the foliage; the rest of the footpath, exposed to the elements, was a blasted wash of concrete, scoured to a dark shine.

Scully, sixteen, was hefting a bag of ice on her shoulder. Charlie, Scully's thirteen-year-old sister, was carrying two shopping bags containing a two-liter bottle of Coke and a big carton of milk; several packets of chocolate digestive biscuits; a bunch of unripe, hard green bananas; a slab of butter; cheese; a squirty thing of mayonnaise; and a box of tea bags.

There was a small fountain in one corner of the square. As they often did, separately and together, the Vaughan sisters paused to inspect the stone bowl of water. With a familiar, and by now almost gratifying, charge of disappointment, Scully immediately saw that the small dull discs littering the trembling floor of the fountain were almost all coppers. Worthless ones and twos, nothing you'd chance a wet elbow for.

Next to the fountain was an old, mutilated public pay phone.

"See that?" Scully said.

"What?" Charlie said.

"That," Scully said. There was a rectangular white card, a little smaller than a postcard, taped to the pay phone's battered housing.

"What's that, now?" Charlie said, leaning in and screwing up her eyes. A sentence was printed in black type on the card.

IF ASHA CALLS TELL HER TO GO HOME, Charlie read. "Who's Asha?"

Scully let the bag down onto the footpath. Her neck and jaw on her left side stung, and the collar of her T-shirt was damp and nubbled, like a teething baby had been chewing at it.

"That note's been there for the last week," she said. "I've been trying to work it out."

"What's there to work out?" Charlie asked. "If Asha calls, you tell her go home."

"It's just that whoever made this note put it here because they reckon there's a decent chance Asha will call this particular phone," Scully said.

"Okay," Charlie said.

"But why would Asha be ringing this pay phone?" Scully asked. "She must be ringing to talk to someone. Someone *specific,* someone she has to go through the hassle of contacting on a public pay phone."

"So the note is for that person," Charlie reasoned.

"Or for me. You. Whoever happens to answer when Asha calls."

"And then we tell her: go home!" Charlie said.

"It's been at me," Scully said, "how the person who wrote this knows enough about Asha to know there's a decent chance she's making calls to this pay phone. But for some reason they can't locate or contact Asha directly themselves, or else why go through the effort of putting up this note in the first place?"

Charlie blinked and thought about this. She pressed the heel of her palm against her temple and ran it up into her hairline. Her hair was short and dark and went up in skunky puffs. As her fingers swept over her hairs they sprang back up. Charlie's eyes looked small and preoccupied. It was only then that Scully realized Charlie wasn't wearing her glasses, that she must have left them back at the apartment.

"Maybe she's like a runaway, and it's a note from a parent?" Charlie suggested. "Who knows she's around, but they don't know where."

"But the way they put it," Scully said. "*Go home*. Not *come home*. Like it's an order. And an angry one."

"Parents give orders."

"But if you wanted someone who ran away to come back . . ."

"That'll be a bag of water you're carrying if we don't get going soon," Charlie said after a while.

Scully hauled the bag of ice back up onto her shoulder and adjusted her grip to make sure it was secure. They resumed their course and left the square. As they made their way along the streets of the town, Scully had to regularly transfer the bag of ice from one shoulder to the other. Soon both of her shoulders were cold and wet and buzzing with numbness, like a punched lip.

They arrived at the woods on the edge of town and crossed a small ditch onto a path of pale brown dirt. The path climbed a hill into the woods. The trees in this part of the woods were almost all conifers, their needles glimmering with rain and their tops pointing straight up.

"You ever even used a pay phone?" Charlie asked as they walked through the trees.

Charlie's question made Scully remember a scene from a movie; a car in an American city at night, screeching to a stop in a dark side street. A man hurriedly exited the car and dashed into a telephone box. The telephone box was illuminated with a scathing brightness, like a medical booth in which large, living things were sterilized. The man had thick, anguished eyebrows. Scully remembered a close-up of his hairy-knuckled hand as he nervously slid a coin into the slot, each hair on his knuckles dark and distinct, like a coil of black thread sewn into his skin. She remembered the noise the coin made as it descended through the belly of the phone; a hollow *ratatat* like a pebble rolling along a corrugated roof before dropping off the edge into nothing.

The sisters entered a clearing, and soon were coming down the other side of the hill, toward the parking lot at the rear of the block of apartments where they lived.

Scully did not remember anything else about the movie, just that scene, and the lonely rolling noise of the coin in the pay phone.

There was no fence around the car park, allowing them to walk straight onto the tarmac. The car park was, as usual, near empty. The apartment building was run-down, its cream façade faded and stained gray. The sisters took the exterior stairs to the second floor, blunt tufts of grass sprouting from the cracks in the concrete steps. At the door to the apartment, Charlie slipped off her left runner, shook out a key, and opened the door. From the short hallway, they could hear Rain holding court in the kitchen, speaking at a volume and intensity someone unfamiliar with him might have mistaken for anger. But that was just how Rain sounded when he was happy.

"I'm as well pull out the lot of them and be done!" he scoffed as they entered the kitchen. He was talking to his friend Victor Reilly and Scully and Charlie's mother, Mel.

Rain was sitting at one end of the little kitchen table set against the wall. Victor was sitting opposite. Victor worked with Rain as a security guard in the psychiatric hospital just outside the town, though both had the day off today, and were dressed in their civvies. It was four in the afternoon and they were drinking whiskey and Cokes. Mel was at the counter, noisily sawing the top off a plastic shampoo bottle with a bread knife.

"Pull out what?" Charlie asked Rain, dumping her bags on the kitchen table.

Rain looked squarely at Charlie and Scully, then grimaced, baring his teeth in a sudden yellow clench, like he was in pain. He had a coin in his hand and clinked it against a tooth.

"This babby is refusing to go to the dentist," Mel said.

"Teeth are a burden," Rain said, rummaging through the shopping bags and tearing open one of the packets of chocolate digestives. "I reckon I should pull the lot of them and put a set of wooden ones in instead. Be done with it all for once and for good. What do you think, girls?" He took a bite of a biscuit and pushed the packet to Victor, who raised a brief hand in refusal.

"That sounds dumb," said Charlie.

Scully popped the freezer door and arranged a space among the various parcels of frozen food already crammed in there. At the back of the freezer she could hear the cooling fan, its vanes shagged with ice, ticking strenuously. A bank of stubbled ice had almost completely encased the freezer's rear wall.

"This yoke needs defrosting," she said as she worked the bag of ice into the space she had cleared.

"I know that," Rain said defensively. "I've a video on the phone I'm going to watch."

"How was town?" Mel asked.

"It rained," Charlie said. "But we missed it."

With a final stroke of the bread knife the top of the plastic shampoo bottle came off in Mel's hands. There were two halved bottles already on the counter. Scully watched as Mel used a teaspoon to scrape the gel stuck in the bottle into one of the bottle halves. This was one of Mel's tricks for getting that last bit of mileage out of the shampoo. There was always a final amount of gel you couldn't squeeze out of the bottle, so what Mel would do was save up several bottles and once she'd enough take all their heads off and combine their remaining gel. The bottles tended to be a mix of different brands, whatever was on sale at a given time, so they all smelled different, but that didn't matter. The compounded, floral smell of the gels mixed in the confines of the kitchen with the foul chemical tang of the varnish Rain had lately begun applying to his nails in a bid to deter himself from biting them.

"Rain, rain, go away," Rain singsonged, to no one in particular.

Rain was around fifty, but Scully did not know for sure. His face was meaty and pitted. There was a swollen, reddened quality to his features, as if he had recently recovered from an allergic attack, except he always looked like that. He had a bitty, gray-flecked beard and bullish brow, a crushed prominent nose, and shining dark eyes set deep in his head. His real name was Johnny Tell. Rain was the name Mel had given him back when they first met, because he looked like a German film director she had liked named Rainer. The name stuck.

"No upkeep is what you want," he said, baring his teeth again and again tapping the coin against one. "It's the upkeep of things does you in the end."

Then he closed his eyes and rested his head against the wall behind him, as if suddenly exhausted. Tacked on the wall over Rain's head were several drawings done by Mel. Mel and Rain had both been—and technically still were—artists, though Rain seemed to have stopped painting ever since he had gone full-time in the hospital. Scully was glad she didn't have to see his work so much anymore. Rain had painted abstracts, near identical pictures featuring dense, somber swabs of muted color that looked depressing and dreary, like pictures of migraines or terrible weather. Mel's pictures were charcoal and pencil sketches of body parts; sections of torsos, faces with precisely smudged mouths and wary, animate eyes, disembodied hands and feet flexing and gesturing in white space. Scully understood that art wasn't necessarily about being able to draw things skillfully and accurately—the sense she had always gotten was that among those circles responsible for such judgments, Rain's work was held in much higher esteem than her mother's—but Mel could draw, and draw well. Maybe it was not a requirement to be able to draw well in order to be an artist, but Scully reckoned there were few artists around who could draw so well as her mother. Rain couldn't, for example. For a while, back when he still regularly painted, he had introduced into his compositions something approximating human figures, but they had never looked right. They had weird proportions and crude, sloppy detailing, which he insisted was all on purpose.

"Did you see anyone?" Rain said.

"Who would we see?" Scully said.

"Somebody interesting."

"We met no one I would call interesting."

"Everybody's interesting," Rain rejoined, as if it was the girls' fault for failing to generate an anecdote-worthy exchange with some local.

There was a noise in the hall, a creaturely patter, and Rain's two-year-old daughter, Tessa, bare-legged in a nappy, came through the doorway in a racing waddle. She was coming straight at Scully, who dropped into a nearby seat and steered her knees just in time to catch the child between her legs. Tessa was in a Cookie Monster T-shirt. She had a rashy, raw-lipped mouth, pale brown hair as thin and fine as an elderly person's. She was wearing a pair of glasses too big for her face, balanced precariously on the nub of her tiny nose.

"Here," Scully said, snatching the glasses from Tessa's face and handing them off to Charlie.

Natalie, Tessa's mother, followed the child in.

"Tessa, stop," Natalie said tiredly, though the child wasn't doing anything just now other than idling between Scully's legs.

"She's all right," Scully said.

"She needs shooting with a tranquilizer is what she needs," Natalie said.

"You get tea bags?" she asked Charlie.

"Uh-huh," Charlie said as she fixed her glasses back on her face.

Natalie lifted the kettle out of its cradle, held it under the tap in the sink, and ran the water until the spout began to drool. She did not ask anyone else if they wanted tea as she took a mug from the press and fixed herself a cup. She turned around, leaned against the counter, and glared unhappily at Rain and Victor. Natalie was Mel's younger sister, Scully and Charlie's aunt. She was a tall woman in her midthirties, long limbed and sinewy, the tendons in her neck rising taut as corset boning when she spoke. Her left knee was strapped into an athletic brace. She was the goalkeeper and captain of the local women's football team. She'd done something to her knee in a match the previous weekend.

"I had a dream once that a bunch of my teeth fell out," Scully said.

"Many people have that dream," Rain said. "I've had it, many times. They reckon it's a dream about money. When you're worried about money you dream about your teeth falling out. Do you have money worries, Scully?"

Scully thought about that.

"I don't think so," she said. "I mean, I'd like to have lots of it."

"I'd like that too," Rain said.

All of a sudden, Victor sprung silently from his chair and swooped in to grab Tessa from between Scully's legs.

"Hup ba," Victor said to Tessa as she twisted around in his arms to see who had grabbed her, then he tossed her clean into the air.

Scully watched Tessa's body go up, spin, and come back down headfirst. Her heart froze as she foresaw the awful wallop of skull against lino, but at the last second Victor caught Tessa by the ankles and held her hanging upside down in the air, her head swinging a foot from the ground as she cackled in a hysteria of happy fear. Victor worked her body clockwise, limb by limb, until she was upright in his arms again.

"There you are! I didn't know where you went," he said. He eased her back down onto the floor, shooed her away, and took his seat with a wild smile on his face. Victor was a good deal younger than Rain, only in his midtwenties. He had a long forehead and was fair-haired, with a generally quiet and deferential demeanor. But now and then, out of nervousness, or some agitated inner surplus of energy, he was prone to saying or doing something sudden and inexplicable, such as the stunt he had just pulled with Tessa.

"The child is not a bag of fucking spuds, you prick," Natalie said.

"Stop now," Rain said calmly. "Victor was only playing. Did you like that, Tessa? Did you?"

Tessa shied at his question and stepped in behind Natalie.

"Enough of this," Rain said. "Hand me my sword, Victor."

He indicated the key chain dangling from a hook on the sill behind Victor's head. Victor took down the key chain and passed it to Rain.

Rain climbed up out of his seat, opened the freezer door, removed the bag of ice, and brought it to the table. With the glimmering silver wedge of the little palette knife he kept on his key chain, he slit the bag open.

"It was considered a great dishonor," he said as he hacked free several cubes, "when a Roman centurion misplaced his sword, or let it be taken from him."

He dropped the ice into their glasses, topped up the drinks, and returned the ice to the freezer.

"Actually, we did see something interesting today," Charlie said. "A message left on that pay phone by the fountain in the square."

"There is a pay phone still there, isn't there," Rain mused as he attached the key chain to a belt loop of his trousers.

Scully looked at Charlie. She could see that Charlie, in her innocence, was going to tell them all about the note on the pay phone. Scully wished she wouldn't. She wanted to keep the message about Asha between herself and Charlie. Her sense, though she couldn't explain it, was that the message contained another message, hidden in plain sight within it, and that if they thought hard and long enough about it, they could work it out.

"Someone is missing," Charlie continued. "You ever meet anyone around town called Asha?"

"Could be I've met one or two Ashas in my time," Rain said. "This is the person who is missing?"

"The message on the phone said *Asha come home*."

"It said *go home*," Scully corrected.

"Was the Asha you know young?" Charlie said to Rain. "We reckon she must be a kid who ran away on her parents."

"Really, I never met an Asha," Rain said, "and though you're right it's probably a kid, that doesn't have to be the case. An adult can run away too, only nobody ever calls it that."

"What do they call it, then?" Charlie asked in earnest.

Rain held his tongue and smiled. Scully knew he wouldn't answer. He took great pleasure in taking a thought, tying it into a knot in front of everybody, and then just leaving it down.

"I was thinking," he announced, "that Charlie and Scully could come to the pub, if they wanted."

"Charlie's too young for the pub," Mel said.

"Charlie's too young to drink in the pub. But Charlie may come to the pub if she pleases."

"I'd like to go," Charlie said, "if I'm allowed."

"Well, I don't think so," Mel said.

"We're going to watch a film," Natalie said, her jaw gone tight. "After Tessa is down, we can have Coke and digestives."

"They've Coke in the pub," Rain said. "They might even have digestives."

Rain placed the coin he had been ticking against his teeth down on the table, balancing it on its side like a wheel, and set it rolling toward the table edge. Scully came up out of her seat and caught the coin just as it dropped. The coin was of a yellow-brown, almost mustard hue, with an embossed harp on one side and a horse in profile on the other, the valuation 20p inscribed above the horse. It was old money, money from before the last millennium, and had been out of circulation for a long time.

"What do you reckon, Scully?" Rain said.

Scully glanced at her mother's and Natalie's wary faces. Usually, it was only Rain that went out. At night, Scully and Charlie stayed in with Mel and Natalie and watched films. That was how it had been for ages, but now Rain appeared to be changing the rules.

He had set the situation up in an interesting way. There was no way Charlie would want to go with the men on her own, which meant the decision was still finally Scully's. But Scully could now make that decision under the pretense of looking out for her little sister—though she actually did want to look out for her little sister! Scully did not love Rain. Maybe she did not even really like him, but after all these years she was used to him, very, very used to him, and if you paid attention, he did teach you things like this, disguised little ways of getting what you wanted.

Scully slipped the coin into her pocket, because there was nothing else to do with it now that she had it. She looked into the face of her little sister, and saw, as she always did, the sweet heedless openness of it, the hunger for more of the world than they were allowed. Scully could read Charlie's thoughts, just like Charlie could read hers. Scully did not believe this, she knew it. It was just a fact, as solid and hard as the coin in her pocket.

"I'll go if Charlie goes," she said.

"And I'll go if Scully goes," Charlie said, just like Scully knew she would.

Robin Romm

Marital Problems

VICTOR AND I CROUCH in the yard, trying to find where our five-year-old daughter, Lucy, has buried the bird. She made it a coffin—sweet, except that she made it out of my husband's father's binocular case. My husband didn't know his father, a birder—a deadbeat birder to be more precise. So the binocular case came to him in a roundabout way a few months ago.

Junk from the kitchen remodel litters our yard—an old sink, pieces of hacked-apart tile—a hazard, a disgrace, a child's wonderland. As we search, Victor piles the debris in the corner.

"That fucking guy," he says, trying to move a cast-iron sink basin.

We've been remodeling our kitchen for the better part of a year. That makes us sound fancier than we are. In truth, a guy's installing IKEA cabinets and tile we got at a seconds sale. New lights, new wiring. For this budget refresher, I interviewed seven men in Carhartts, many of them hazy pupiled, a few of them so expensive I couldn't bear to relay the bids to Victor. I settled on Marco.

Victor would like to sue Marco for leaving us without a working kitchen for months on end. Victor would like to take a cosmic flyswatter and squish him against the wall. Cork him in a bottle and sink him to the bottom of the sea.

"I think Marco's having marital problems," I tell him, moving a rock and peering under it, testing to see if the earth's been disturbed.

"Whatever," my husband says. "He can still find some guys to move this shit." He has dirt on the top part of his shaggy sideburn. If he swipes at his brow again, he'll wipe it into his eye. I don't mention this to him. "His wife has nothing to do with this job." Victor takes a piece of wood and hurls it at the corner. "Anyway, what makes you say that?"

"I can just tell," I say.

Whenever I predict the dramas of other men, Victor frowns and squints. He doesn't care, really, if I know such things about my female friends. He'll often jump into the fray with that sort of gossip. He loves a good postpartum depression story, a colicky baby, an eating disorder. But when I surmise a man's emasculating salary, his attraction to domineering women, his obvious lust for a clichéd paramour—a nanny, a personal trainer—Victor recoils. *You don't know that,* he'll say, and it becomes clear to me, the boy he was at sixteen.

"He wants to talk about it, but I never ask," I say.

Marco's hair curls around his forehead and his lips form surprisingly soft little pillows above a very perfect knob of a chin. He looks like Hansel all grown up, a fairy-tale boy with his tool kit and leather belt and paint-spattered ladder. Except that he isn't happy, our Marco. He hasn't figured out how to throw the witch in the oven. Instead, he finds himself married to her.

This is, at any rate, my theory, assembled through tattered bits of small talk. His wife, a Brazilian woman named Rosie, wants kids. Marco mentioned this once while doctoring his coffee. But he doesn't want the complication. He had a daughter from another marriage, and that child was the reason for the divorce. Marco always talks to me—no matter the subject (hardware, contracts, his wife)—with a sultry little smirk.

I get the sense that Marco figures if he lingers in the kitchen long enough, I'll finally lose my inhibition. My obvious attraction to his compact body, those muscles that look carved from soap, will overwhelm me. I'll descend the stairs in a negligee, a look of raunchy hunger thickening my gaze. But I don't feel like telling this to my husband. It'll make him even more furious at the asshole hijacking our home. He'll ratchet up the rhetoric against Marco until we have no choice but to fire him. And who will complete this half-finished budget remodel in this expensive city if not Marco?

Lucy didn't actually bury the bird. Had she buried it, we could ask her where. Instead, while Victor and I attended an actual funeral for a colleague of mine who died of ovarian cancer at thirty-two, Lucy put the dead bird in its coffin and then lost interest in it. The babysitter, a woman we hired through a service, didn't want to leave a dead bird lying around, so she went ahead and buried it. The babysitter hasn't responded to my emails or calls, and so somewhere in the yard lies the bird. Or so Lucy told us. She's frequently entranced by the notion that truth is a malleable thing, so who knows what to believe.

Most of our yard is compact soil, nearly claylike. Any disruption to it causes lumps and crumbs, which makes this bird burial particularly perplexing. We've tried places that appear to be stirred up, mostly near the fence or under vines, but so far they've yielded nothing.

"He might just be depressed," my husband says. "Or hate being a contractor."

"Maybe," I say.

"Or maybe he doesn't like you."

"No, Marco likes me."

"I don't know why you think you know everything," my husband says. "Did he tell you that he has marital problems?"

"He definitely has marital problems. Think about it. When we ask him to do something, he sulks, he looks at the ground and acts like he hasn't heard. The kitchen job was an eight-week job. He's been here nine months, and it's not even done. When you follow up to see if a small task has been completed, he just stares. Can you imagine being his wife?"

"Yeah, that's true," my husband says. "What a dick that guy is."

"He's not a dick. He's just really passive. And slightly incompetent."

"Why do you defend him?" Victor asks.

"I'm not," I say.

"I should kick that guy's ass," my husband says. I try to imagine my husband taking down Marco. Victor used to have muscles like Popeye, bulbs sprouting seemingly off bone. But over the years he's become just plain skinny, with a small and polite little potbelly, a purse of flesh that Lucy likes to lie against while they read.

"Victor." I say his name sharply, like I'm snipping a thread.

The person Victor would really like to beat up, of course, is the deadbeat birder, but any man who comes around and tries to pull a fast one gets a tiny dose of Victor's ancient, private rage.

Several months ago, we got a call from a biological half brother of Victor's who'd located Victor through a DNA testing service. Victor had sent off for results a few years prior, inspired by a longing for a clan after his mother died.

But he never did much with the information, so it surprised us when the half brother, Quinn, emailed and asked if Victor wanted to meet. He detoured to Portland after a friend's wedding in Port Townsend, showed up for dinner bearing flowers, a bottle of expensive wine, their father's binoculars, and a dog-eared copy of *Birds of America*.

He worked as a paralegal for a big firm in San Jose. I thought he might be gay, though he never said as much. He exuded a tidiness, the kind that usually means that no woman washes your boxer shorts or puts away your laundry, enabling you to enjoy a lifetime of hetero-slovenliness; a tidiness that comes from doing all that bodily and sartorial maintenance yourself. He charmed us both. Lucy kept walking around his chair, gripping the back rung and shyly smiling, though Quinn didn't know what to do with a child and kept inching his chair closer to the table.

I can only tell you what's going on in the marriages of other people; I'm not sure what's going on in my own. It's Saturday, and our "morning alone time" has come to a close. We spent it all out here, looking for the binocular case. Maybe my marriage is like a beautiful weathervane on a regal barn, its edges soft, its tin turning turquoise and black. It used to spin beautifully, but the center's grown rusty. Maybe that's a dumb metaphor. That metaphor requires me to extend it, to say that these alone hours are the WD-40 we need. Maybe we're less weathervane and more tomato plant and this whole thing is fertilizer, or maybe we're just aging and sometimes I notice that my eyes are more revealed, the skin around them thin like that of a tomatillo. A hardness comes through places that used to be supple, and when Victor reaches for me in bed, it only feels like habit, the way we reach for our toothbrushes, and because I'm not a toothbrush, I turn away. I want to circumvent this fate, though I don't have the body for bustiers or the energy for finding politically acceptable, palatable, not completely obnoxious porn.

Last night, Lucy's friend Madeline slept over so that her mother, Danielle, could go on a date. Madeline had no idea that she'd been evacuated in order for her mother's house to become a den of seduction, but yesterday, when Danielle dropped off Madeline, she managed to show me her newly waxed legs.

Danielle was vague about the man, but I imagine he's some kind of artsy professional, an architect with a quick wit and intense libido. He stands in the kitchen—that gorgeous, airy kitchen—after a dinner of artichokes and oysters. Danielle's wavy red-blond hair is a little mussed, the strap of her slinky dress halfway down her arm. The bodice peels away slightly from her sternum, exposing a black lace bra. She steps out of her shoes, and he pulls down on the strap assuredly, until the breast reveals itself, a ripe peach in its netting, propped and framed. And he bites at it and she presses his head down toward her widening legs and he yanks the zipper of her dress, pulling it off like tissue paper to get to her underwear, also lace and easily removed. Then he hoists her up to that beautiful marble kitchen island, spreads her legs, and goes at her like a ravenous teenager. Then when she's just about to come, he enters her, both of them groaning, wailing, convulsing as if being electrocuted—maybe the lights above them even go out, and semen spatters her fancy Scandinavian knife block.

In exchange for last night with Madeline, Danielle took Lucy this morning. Victor and I didn't crawl into bed together the second she left, though I still find him lovely, his black hair flecked with white and silver, his sharp jawline that could be used to trace right angles. Frequently, women at the grocery store chat him up. Once, a realtor closed the door to a bedroom of a house we were looking at buying—this was before Lucy, when I still worked my ruthless job at the domestic violence shelter and had to send Victor out to peruse new listings—and propositioned him. "What exactly did she say?" I wanted to know. Victor shrugged. "She said, *This bedroom has good energy*, or something. *If you would like to try it out*. What does it matter?" My husband backed away from her and politely suggested that our family might not need her services after all.

Or maybe they slept together in that ranch house. Maybe usually moral and righteous Victor couldn't resist such low-hanging fruit and let this forward, frothy agent suck him off in the slatted light of cheap blinds. Maybe they fucked in the bedroom closet, so hard they both left with rug burns. It's a little bit fun to feel the pain when I picture it.

But anyway, I have to retrieve Lucy from Danielle's. I brush the dirt off my jeans. I'm about to declare the binocular case a goner—we may or may not find it, but we definitely won't find it by despairing with shovels in our yard—when Marco comes through the back gate.

"We were just talking about you," Victor says, smiling his big, fake, flashy smile. Marco nods.

"I think I left my drill," he says.

"You didn't," Victor says. "There's no drill in there."

"I think I left it under the sink," Marco says. "I'm just going to go check."

"Did you fix the hole under there?" Victor asks. He stands, finally flicks the dirt off his face. I watch the fleck fly off and vanish before it ever hits the ground.

"Basically," says Marco.

Victor follows him up the stairs and into the house, legs a little stiff, head down like a domineering dog.

I put the tools back in the shed. Two crows scream above the walnut tree.

I'd be lying if I said I didn't, occasionally, follow Marco's fantasy to its logical conclusion. I descend the staircase in a negligee or whatever, leggings and a T-shirt. I walk close to him, and he reaches out and puts a warm, callused palm on my lower back. Then his hands are everywhere at once, up my stomach and over my breasts—which are my old breasts, my pre-baby breasts that spring from my bony ribs. I watch his face as he looks at them, these breasts that could be in glossy magazines. And I tear his plaid shirt without worrying about how much it costs or how to sew the buttons back on. His pecs look like rolling hills of sand dunes and the smell of him is not a smell so much as a cloud of sex. His finger slides into my underwear, where my vagina is still so very intact, not the scarred-up and slightly intimidating place it became after Lucy's protracted entrance to the world.

"The hole under the sink must be redone," my husband says,

"and the caulk's already come up. Why? What kind of caulk did you use?"

Marco looks studiously under the sink with a blankness as vast as the sea.

Danielle lives in the big lavender house at the end of the block, the kind of grand old house that used to stand alone overlooking farmland or some kind of estate, before all the smaller bungalows were built around it in the 1940s. Danielle is—and I'm not spinning yarns—a gasping expert. She used to do voice work in Hollywood until she became famous for expressing surprise. Now, apparently, she can freelance from Portland, flying out to Los Angeles to gasp every once in a while—an oral stunt man. Or it's something like that. Maybe I wasn't fully listening when she explained it to me. Though she's not yet thirty-four, she appears to be financially set, whether from the gasping or the divorce or an inheritance or a trust fund, I have no idea.

"Hi, Paige!" she says as she opens the door. She's wearing an oversized, mustard-colored sweater that looks like a thrift store find and probably cost three hundred dollars.

Her house, free of dust motes, cat hair, and the general detritus of modern life, always smells of lemons gently fading into some kind of sage or woodsmoke. Whenever we have Madeline over to our house, I become very aware of the rip in our secondhand tweed sofa and the vague smell of decaying food that emanates from our kitchen compost bin.

Lucy appears, a big brown splotch on her strawberry T-shirt. She's eating a piece of baguette.

"Brie," she says, opening the baguette and showing me a whitish lump. Then she touches her shoulder to my legs and darts off.

I follow Danielle into the kitchen. The girls have been playing with Madeline's all-wood, Waldorf-inspired dollhouse, complete with tiny, nontoxic beds and dressers. Lucy returns to it, kneeling in the corner of the living room where it sits upon a custom children's table with tiny elephants carved into the legs.

Here is an indisputable fact: Lucy, my daughter, is so much prettier than Madeline. No matter our squat and dim house, our debris-strewn yard. Madeline has tight red curls and a soft, smeary nose with nostrils that you can see straight into. Probably, she looks like her father. Lucy, my brilliant, quick-witted child, has Victor's dark hair. The gloss in her nearly black eyes is like wet obsidian, deep and soulful and bright. And she moves with a gazelle's ease, this baby of mine, this sleek little girl. Sometimes I wish we had not been so old when we had her, but it had been an ordeal—two years of fertility doctors, a miscarriage, the whole nine yards. We were lucky, with my aging eggs and Victor's sleepy sperm, to have a child at all. Had I known the babies I was capable of producing, I might have started at twenty, had a whole army.

Danielle takes out a big wheel of brie, a bowl of cherries, and a plate of cured meats, half-eaten and covered in plastic wrap.

"Wow," I say. "You really know how to snack."

Danielle smiles with only half her mouth so that her dimple deepens into a black abyss.

Danielle is beautiful, too. People everywhere wave at her, smile, think they know her when in fact, that's not why she caught their eye. Her huge forehead announces her thick, honey-colored hair that in some lights gives way to a strawberry blond. It's wavy, and she wears it in a nest-y bun, with tendrils climbing down her neck as if she's a living, breathing sweet-pea vine. She's not terribly thin—a refreshing trait in this city of bone-broth-sipping anorexics. Her curves just make her look sensual. She once told me she breastfed Madeline for thirty-one months. Men, babies, whole towns could probably live off that body for a while, so glossy with nutrients.

"So, how was the date?" I ask, glancing at the kitchen island, which does actually seem to be a little out of order, the basket of fruit moved near the toaster, a wadded towel by the knife block.

"The guy's great. So . . . attentive." She lowers her voice. "It's been a while. I thought I'd aged out of that kind of thing."

The girls come crashing into the kitchen with a bug net and a tiny doll that has gotten ensnared in the string. I take it and start to untangle her, but her tiny plastic fingers have something disgusting and sticky on them that's making the string come apart.

Danielle leans back slightly, hand on her lower back, as if to express that she's a little sore, what with all the contortions.

Danielle sees a feminist counselor via Skype, a woman who believes in Danielle's inborn human potential, her capacity to make a six-figure salary gasping, her inner magnetism that will attract a well-rounded and compassionate man. Six times a year, Danielle travels to a women's gathering in Ojai where they do things like talk to their ancestors in a hall of mirrors, thanking them and handing them unwanted baggage. They eat clean food and hike and sing and visualize themselves in fantastic futures. More than once, she's asked if I want to come with her. More than once, I have felt myself startle, as if she has offered to cover me in scalding glue. But Danielle *believes*—believes that you can manifest the good things in life through positive thinking, that her bad marriage resulted from her erroneous inner narrative. My mother, a botanist with a zest for life, a passion for Latin dance and freshwater pearls, died of a staph infection when I was ten. Enough said.

"Can I stay a little longer, Mom?" Lucy asks, holding the baguette. She hands me the brie. Danielle holds out her hand. She puts the white wad in the pristine compost container—handmade pottery—by her sink.

"I don't have that much going on," Danielle says. "She can stay. Madeline and I had planned to go the pool, but—"

"I want to go to the pool!" Madeline says.

"We have to find the binocular case, or your father may blow a gasket," I say to Lucy, because I can't think of another extraction technique.

"I know where that is," Madeline says.

"You do?" I say.

"Yeah," Madeline says. "We were playing with it the other day. We were making a mouse house."

"Oh yeah," says my daughter.

"Did you bury it?" I ask.

"No," says Madeline.

"Where is it?"

"Ummmm," Madeline says, making a cute face and tilting her head. "Ummmmm," then she giggles.

"Would you be able to show me?" I ask.

"Ummmm," Madeline says again, trying to prompt me to smile at her as though she's the most astonishing delight. I give her the requisite smile. "I don't know," she says.

"We could walk over," Danielle says, "and you can see if you can remember. Then go to the pool after, okay, Mads?"

"Is it in the backyard?" I ask as we near the house.

"Yeah," Madeline says. "I think so." So I let the girls in through the back gate. Madeline rushes over to the birdbath in a corner of the yard covered in ivy. She starts rooting around. We already looked there.

Danielle keeps glancing toward the street, where Marco parked his gray truck, one wheel on the curb.

"Want a glass of water?" I ask. She follows me up the back stairs into the kitchen, where Victor stands, holding a screwdriver. He gives me a look.

I met Victor one thousand years ago in San Francisco when we both worked at a bike co-op. He repaired bikes. I rang people up. Can that really be true? Did we used to sleep together on an old futon under a huge window overlooking Valencia Street, which was just butcher shops and thrift stores once upon a time? A friend recently sent me a picture of the old butcher shop, still a butcher shop, but now all wood and gleaming chrome with eleven-dollar-a-pound artisanal hot dogs.

I know the look, of course. It means, what a jackass; it means, I hate contractors; it means, I should kick this guy's ass. A small puddle of water has accumulated on our floor.

I've always loved my husband. Well, actually, at first I thought he was a tiresome pedant, inserting Marxist theory into every conversation. And then after a month or two of furtive make-out sessions in the repair room of the co-op, I loved him. He knew how to be still. He knew how to listen, even if he didn't always do it. Lying next to him after sex, I just felt at ease, not filled with the sharp melancholy I'd previously known. And for a moment, watching him stand there with that screwdriver and that look, a tenderness fills me. It flares up whenever it wants, this alliance, this feisty monogamous urge.

And then the toilet flushes.

Marco rounds the bend to the kitchen, his face harboring shadows, deep in some argument with Victor. But then he notices Danielle, standing there like she's the rarest of buds, thrusting fresh and new out of that baggy outfit, holding the water glass in such a way that it reveals the loveliness of her wrists, and he halts, then does something surreptitious with his hands. He beams a smile at Danielle as he does it, but it doesn't distract me; he has removed his wedding band, slipped it into his pocket. Did Victor see it? Yes, absolutely.

"Oh!" Danielle says, and with this one utterance her breasts seem to enlarge, grow rounder, and she leans back on our counter, which is improperly grouted to the wall. Her neck, when she leans like this, exposes itself, so long and vulnerable and white.

"I didn't realize you were working over here at Paige and Victor's!" she says, and I scour my brain to remember what I've said about this terrible remodel. Surely I've bitched about it.

"Just finishing up the job," he says, which is interesting to hear. I can see Victor putting it all together, even though I didn't tell him why Madeline spent the night. "You two know each other?" he asks.

Danielle pushes off the counter and yanks the clip out of her bun. Then she coils her hair again and fastens it tighter, no tendrils hanging down.

"We do," Danielle says.

Marco nods. "I was just finishing up here for the day," he says. "Want to walk me to my truck?"

Victor and I exchange a look that communicates pretty much everything that anyone would need to know about the current situation.

Danielle glances toward the back door. Outside, her daughter looks for the bird with my daughter.

Danielle has told me a little bit about her ex, a Hollywood manager named Elijah, a charmer, a talker, though when at home alone with Danielle, he barely spoke. After she got pregnant, he wouldn't touch her.

Danielle told me this last summer. The girls played and we drank wine on her driveway, looking at the flowers she'd planted in the new garden boxes.

"That must have been terrible," I said, and she looked down the street and began openly weeping.

I didn't know what to do. How do you deal with people like this, so quick to feel their feelings, as if they curate and file them carefully so that whenever they think a thought, they can find the corresponding emotion? I can't even begin to imagine how exhausting that must be. I put my hand on her arm, though really, I wanted her to give me more details: a fecund and nubile Danielle, her round belly harboring kicking, squirming life, her whole body pounding with the need to fuck—on the ground, in the bed, doggy style, pretzeled up, her pregnancy hormones giving her clitoris a new and defiant will of its own—and this husband tensing up, curling his lip as if her vagina had an odor. Masturbating into rags that he let her find and toss into the hamper.

"God," Danielle said, gazing at her black-eyed Susans, her bluebells, and her daisies. I waited for her to continue, to tell me that it had hurt to be rejected but she'd learned to love herself, or learned that motherhood was worth it, or learned whatever it is— whatever made the whole thing feel epiphanic—but she never finished the thought. Instead, she excused herself, turned and started to walk inside the house, stepped in something, kicked off her sandal, sniffed and sighed and, with the stick of a child's pinwheel that had been spinning in the flowerbed, dislodged a piece of cat shit from the sole.

That night, I slid Victor's boxers down and imagined Danielle, pregnant and randy, tits heavy with the anticipation of milk, belly a vein-streaked orb, as Victor pressed himself into me. When I came, I imagined her coming, the way her face might look, sweaty and pink, that pretty hair stuck to her neck.

"I'd love to have another baby," she'd told me on another morning, as Madeline and Lucy put on their shoes in my hallway.

"Still plenty of time," I said to her, and she smiled and nodded, and that night I cut my hand chopping tomatoes, a deep gash that stained my white shorts and made me so angry I could barely bandage it up.

"I can walk you out, sure," Danielle says, a little too fast. She sets the glass on the counter. Marco nods at Victor.

"Hey," Victor says. He points at the water on the floor. "You can't leave a leaking pipe until tomorrow."

"Oh, I can't work tomorrow," says Marco. "I'll have to turn the water off at the source and come back Tuesday."

"It's the *kitchen sink*," says Victor. "You need to fix the pipe." Victor's face is starting to get red above his dark beard.

Marco shrugs.

"What kind of contractor leaves a puddle of water on the kitchen floor for days on end? In a house that is lived in? In a house with a child? I'm sick of this shit, Marco. You'll stay here until the sink works. And then you'll finish the rest of this work and clean the fucking yard."

I glance at Danielle, chin angled down now, her neck no longer the focal point. Will she gasp?

"Look, man," Marco says, "this kitchen is totally functional. And the demo was a lot more work than I thought. And you got a good price. If you want more done, we can renegotiate. But you can't be cheap. I need to eat, too."

"Functional? What does 'functional' mean to you? Generally, to most of the world, it means that things function."

Once, when we were living in Hayes Valley, a meth-addled lunatic leapt out from behind a building and grabbed my breasts. Victor punched him in the face, just like that. The world turned a sparkling aquamarine when he did it. I felt so loved, which was not the reaction I meant to have.

"I did everything I was contracted to do. That light wasn't in the bid. And the sink would work except you have bad pipes, and that wasn't in the bid either. I'd need to add several hundred for parts and labor. Closer to a thousand, actually. And I can't do it right now, man."

"We hired you to remodel the kitchen. The lights and sink and counters were definitely in the bid. Don't get screwy with me, *man*. I'm just not in the mood."

Marco moves his shoulders back. All the little synapses in his brain flick and dance. But he can't think of what to say.

"I'm finished with this job," says Marco. "I quit."

"You *quit*?" says Victor. "You can't quit. You have a contract and our money. I'll alert the contractor's board. Go ahead and try to quit."

"I'm—" Danielle starts. She's doing something funny with the heels of her palms, pressing them together. "I'm . . . sure you can find a way to resolve this. What exactly is the problem?"

"We found the bird!" says Lucy, bursting through the back door. Then I see the dead bird in her hands.

"Oh, Jesus, Lucy!" I pull the cabinet open to pull out the trash bin and the hinge breaks.

"You couldn't even make this shit up," says Victor.

"Those were the hinges in the bid," says Marco, his lips so soft above that blond goatee he's nurturing, that little patch of fur he probably dragged into Danielle's private swamps last night, his chin as obdurate as any child's. "You could have chosen classier things," he says.

Victor puts the screwdriver down.

"You want to talk about classy?" says Victor. He stands too straight, a little too close to Marco, who also stands too straight. "Why don't you show your girlfriend here your wedding ring."

Marco's head angles back from his neck, his chin juts. And for a minute, the pair of them stand like that.

The night that Victor's half brother came for dinner with the expensive wine, I made spaghetti and cleaned the house as Victor played airplane with Lucy with a little too much gaiety. The spring night air flirted, the crocus buds in the yard poked their heads from glistening soil, a light rain hit the roof, and the brilliant green moss sang its color to the world.

I could see some similarities between Quinn and Victor, as we sat there in the flickering candlelight. Their hands, for example, had the same tulip-shaped fingernails and oddly angled thumbs. And there was a resemblance across the brow and in the curve of the nostrils. But Quinn was much smaller in stature, with reedy bones and sandy-colored hair. We all pretended that the dinner had no bizarre undertones as we discussed Quinn's law firm and Victor's job at the environmental nonprofit, the dire political landscape and the climate.

"You didn't miss much," Quinn finally said. Lucy had gone to bed. The wineglasses looked frosted with fingerprints, the dishes mostly cleared. "He was the worst—my mother got a little inheritance from her father's printing business after he died, and he convinced her to let him put it into his self-produced country album." He reached for his phone and showed Victor a photo of it, a man's bearded face garlanded by roses, the lighting soft, his name in hot-pink gothic font at the bottom: EDDIE JOEL DUSSEL. "Of course it made no money, though he bankrupted us making, like, ninety-five thousand cassette copies and mailing them all over the world. One station played his song 'Roses and Poses' as a joke and he flew into a rage, breaking the door off our fridge. My mother had no spine—took him back, took him back. Finally, he ran off with some guitar student of his, barely eighteen. They had a daughter, Ocean Wave Dussel—she's twenty-two now. I tracked her down, too, in a prison in Indiana."

I'd never seen the look that came across Victor's face before and I've never seen it since. It made me stand up and put my hands on his shoulders, then on his chest. He didn't reach for me.

"Sounds rough, Quinn," I said.

"Oh, you know," Quinn said. "You have to play with the hand you're dealt. I just wanted you to know. I just thought, probably, you wondered what you missed. I would have. And I'm here to tell you, it wasn't anything. Just a frustrated, damaged asshole with efficient sperm."

And then he gave Victor the binoculars and the book. For about a month, the binoculars lay in the corner of the dining room. Then one day, I noticed them in the bedroom. Then in the closet. Then we both noticed them in Lucy's room.

The men face each other and I'm tempted to laugh, to break the tension somehow. Marco's puffed himself up so he's almost as tall as Victor. His blond hair stands off his head. Did he really meet Danielle through mutual friends? The idea of Marco with friends amuses me. What does he do for fun? Play kickball? Race go-karts? I'd only ever imagined him skulking home to his wife, the caustic things the wife would say, the silence he'd use like a barricade. But surely he owns other outfits, not just Carhartts.

Marco takes a step back and punches Victor in the face.

I don't know who gasps with more authority, me or Danielle. But Lucy yelps and covers her face with her hands and Madeline, strangely, claps her hands, just once, but loudly.

I jump toward Victor, but he's calmly taking out his cell phone. So I go to Lucy and pick her up. She presses her face into my neck, but quickly pulls back to stare at the men.

"I'm sorry, man, I'm sorry," says Marco. He's red and his hands are shaking. "I lost my temper, man."

While Marco watches, Victor narrates the situation to the police. Assault, he calmly says. Punched by the contractor, Marco Schumaker. He gives our home address.

Danielle holds Madeline close, her beautiful mouth twisting downward, seeing that she will, again, go to sleep on her fancy sheets alone. Marco pleads with Victor not to talk to the cops. He promises to finish the sink, to upgrade the hinges. Says something about a kickback and 15 percent. The dead bird rests on top of an egg carton and some plastic wrap. I wonder, for the first time, if the binoculars even had a case. Now that I think about it, I can see Quinn handing them to Victor with nothing around them.

Lucy continues to watch her father. Her stoic daddy with the same eyes as her looks as tall as Paul Bunyan, his back straight and long. As he stands there, not talking, Marco yammers. Soon, in the cartoon of Lucy's retelling, Marco will be the size of a doll, then the size of a mouse, then he will not be there at all.

When Lucy was small, Victor spent every morning with her, reading to her, singing to her, dancing to the Cure or Prince. He never traveled. He never missed a morning. He still looks her straight in the eyes when he talks to her. *Dada* was her first word. Even though it annoyed me, I could understand the depth of his pride.

Tonight, Victor will explain to her that some people are ass-holes. He will make her white teddy bear do the cha-cha. And then he will eventually come to bed, and we'll go over this day, and I'll talk him out of pressing charges.

I look at the bird. It's pretty, with its grayish tufts and its tiny yellow beak. I have no idea what kind of bird it is. Some backyard dweller, ubiquitous, food for the hawks and cats. So close at hand, you wouldn't need binoculars to find it.

Allegra Goodman
The Last Grownup

S HE HEARD THEIR FOOTSTEPS on the stairs. Water running in their bathroom. She sensed her daughters everywhere, but it was just her imagination. They were gone. Of course, they would come back. They were safe, and it was just till Sunday. It wasn't death—it only felt like that. Her friends said, Now you can rest! You can think! You can work out! Theoretically, she could have done these things. She could have been thinking and going to the gym and resting, but when the girls left with their father Debra sat on the couch and cried. Which was fine. Crying was good. Divorce was hard! All she had to do was call, and her sister Becca would come right over, but Debra didn't want sympathy, so no one saw her tears except the dog.

Max was a Samoyed, and pure of heart. If anyone was injured, he came running. When Lily fell headfirst from her bike, Max had rushed to lick her better. But where was Debra hurt? She couldn't explain, so she buried her face in his white fur.

Eventually, Debra got up and preheated the oven to four twenty-five. She poured a bag of frozen shoestring fries onto a cookie sheet. A sprinkle of salt, a dollop of ketchup, and that was dinner, which she ate right on the couch. It wasn't good for her, but she was listening to her body, and her body said, Who cares?

She called her parents down in Florida, and her mom said, "Hi, honey. How are you doing?"

"I'm okay," Debra said, balancing her plate on the arm of the couch.

"Ed?" her mom said. "Debra's on the phone."

Debra's dad picked up and said, "What's new?"

"Our paperwork is finished."

"It's finalized?" Her mom was disbelieving. It had been so long. "Done."

She could hear her parents mulling what to say. The paperwork was done, and it was weird and painful, like picking off a scab, because the marriage itself had ended two years before.

"Well, that's a relief," her mom said.

But Debra's dad spoke in the voice he reserved for his deepest disappointments. "All right. That's that."

"I'm wondering," Debra's mom ventured. "Should I take down your wedding picture?"

"Cindy," her dad chided.

"You've still got that picture up?" Debra said.

Her mom sounded embarrassed. "I was just—"

Debra said, "It's fine. Either way."

"You don't mind?"

"Why should I mind a picture?" Debra asked, although in retrospect she thought her beaded gown unfortunate. "I have the whole album."

"You look at your album?" her mother said, gasping.

"No, but I'm not going to get rid of it. The girls might want it! I'm not erasing history."

Silence, and she knew that her mom was gazing at the photo in its gilt frame. "You look so happy."

"I *was* happy," Debra said.

"And Richard was so young!"

"Yes, Mom. He was young." Debra almost laughed—and then she felt guilty for mocking, even inwardly, because how could her parents know what to say? How could anybody? What clueless things would Debra tell her own daughters? They were in tenth and seventh grade, and, obviously, a million years from marrying, let alone divorcing—but if they did. Would you admit the truth? Debra asked herself. Would you say this was not what I imagined? This was never what I hoped for you?

Debra took out the trash and picked up a package by the door. New earbuds for Sophie, who had lost hers. Then she took Max out to romp and sniff and chase his rubber ball in the backyard. The girls never set foot here anymore. At sixteen and thirteen, their days of racing and foraging were done, but Max never outgrew anything.

"*You* need a yard, Maxy. Yes, you do!" She threw the ball, and he streaked off, untiring. Did he wonder where the girls had gone? Debra was sure he missed them, and she was glad he didn't know it would get worse. In just two and a half years, Sophie would leave for college, Lily would follow, and then what? Debra didn't want to sell the house, but could she and Max afford to stay? Would he even live that long? Oh, no!

Admittedly, Debra tended toward the worst-case scenario. It made Richard crazy, because she was always, as he said, fast-forwarding. But she had foresight. She prepared. She planned meals and vacations, scheduled lessons, preregistered for summer camp. Slow down, Richard would beg her. Cut back, get help! Of course, he never considered helping. When they fought he said, But you insist on doing everything.

This was true. No one had ever told Debra to stay home and do everything; that came from her. Nothing compelled her but her conscience and her common sense. When the girls were babies, she gave up free time and exercise. When they were older, she gave up her job, because two people could not work the kind of hours they did and see their children while they were awake. And because she wanted to eat real food. And because she did not want to outsource every single aspect of her life. And because those were years you could not get back, and because she hoped someday to return, if not to law, to something new. Education? Social justice? Counseling?

Together, Debra and Max examined icy puddles under the girls' old climbing structure and green slide. It was exhilarating to think of all the possibilities—how she might teach or advocate for immigrants—but when she thought of Richard she saw his future as domestic. He would remarry. It was obvious to her—to everyone. He was already living with his girlfriend, Heather, who was smart and beautiful and sane. The girls adored her; Debra approved. As for Richard, he was better than he had ever been. Eating healthy, losing weight. The girls said he'd stopped sneaking cigarettes.

"Good for you," Debra had told him a few days earlier.

"Yeah, I'm doing it," Richard said.

She looked at him with sudden insight. He was taking the plunge. The paperwork was done. "You're going to propose!"

He looked startled. "I meant quitting."

"Oh! I'm sorry."

"I wouldn't propose without talking to the girls." He was reddening around the ears.

She nodded. "That's smart."

"We want them to be—"

"Yeah," she said.

"Comfortable. We want it to be natural."

"They'll be ecstatic," she encouraged him.

"Thanks," he said.

A sweet moment, a really good exchange. "I was proud of us," Debra told her therapist, Suzanne, the next day. Truly, she was happy for Richard, and relieved that he was done dating women half his age. Heather was someone Debra could work with. Someone she could respect.

It was a good thing. It was the right thing—and at the same time she knew that Richard's remarriage would sting. The greater good would be another loss. "Does that even make sense?" she'd asked Suzanne.

"Totally."

"But what can I do about it?"

"Do you always have to do something?" Suzanne answered.

And Debra sighed, because she knew that sometimes there was nothing to be done with feelings but to feel them. There was nothing to be done about her ex-husband and his new relationship except to watch events unfold. Debra understood all that. (She was good at therapy.) If only Richard and Heather would hurry up and get it over with.

That evening, Lily called from Richard's place. "Guess what?" she said, and Debra's heart leapt. This was it.

"What?" Debra said.

"We're making pizza from scratch."

"Oh."

"We should do this sometime," Lily told her.

"Okay. Sure!" Debra heard laughter in the background.

"Mom, we have to get a pizza stone."

"We have one."

"But it broke," Lily reminded her. "We should get another one."

"Okay."

"Then after dinner we're getting gelato."

That was when Richard and Heather would tell the girls, except they wouldn't tell them; they would ask. They would sit together, the four of them, and Richard would say, Girls, we have a question for you. Or Heather would speak humbly: I will never replace your mom, but I want to ask you if I can be on your team and support you forever. Or they would say together, Girls, we have a present for you. You don't have to wear them all the time—or ever—but we want to give you these necklaces.

Debra could imagine it every which way, the squeals of delight, the delicate gold chains, everything sensitive and meaningful. Richard would be kneeling, or Heather—or both of them! And there would be hugs and happy tears. "Have a wonderful time," Debra told Lily now. "Let me know how it goes."

"Bye, Mom. Love you."

Lily always said goodbye like that, and Sophie, too. Love you, they chirped on every occasion—even when they called to say that the carpool was late. Love you, love you, until the words meant nothing. They might as well have said, Talk soon. Where did that come from? Summer camp? It irked her, although it didn't bother anybody else. Plenty of parents spoke to their kids that way as well. Becca declared, "I always say 'Love you' to my kids, because who knows what could happen? What if you were hit by a bus? Wouldn't you want your last words to be 'Love you'?"

Debra said, "Not if it's just habit." Love you. Killed by a bus. The whole thing made her sad. She walked through the empty house. Then she vacuumed the first floor and cleaned the girls' rooms.

The kids won't learn to clean up after themselves if you do it for them, Richard used to remind her. He had been scrupulous about telling the girls to do whatever task Debra required. *Do as I say, not as I do.*

She shook her head and picked up laundry from the floor. School clothes, leotards, balled-up tights. Lily's rug was sea green, Sophie's fluffy white. She'd said she wanted white like Maxy's fur, and that was what she got. Her rug was furry, and it shed. Legos used to disappear in it. What was that, caught in the white shag? An earbud right at the foot of Sophie's bed. And there was the other one. Debra almost called to say, I found them! Right after the new ones were delivered! But she resisted.

They'd be at the gelato place by now. Finishing up. Driving back to Richard's condo. Debra expected the news any second, but nobody called.

How was the gelato? she texted at last.

Good, Lily texted back.

When the girls returned, nothing had changed. Richard and Heather were not engaged. Debra had been fast-forwarding again.

"Have you ever had cherry amaretto?" Sophie asked.

"Is that what you got?"

"We tried Heather's."

Debra tried to picture Heather with a fruit flavor. Heather seemed more cookies and cream.

"It was weird," Lily said.

But nothing else seemed strange to them. In fact, they were lighter, happier than when they had left. Trust Heather—a trail runner and a hiker—to leave kids better than she'd found them. The girls hugged Max, went up to their rooms, and did their homework. Even Lily, who worried at night, did not seem sad at all, and curled up in bed with her book about girls learning to be witches, or possibly princesses, at boarding school.

And life was good, and it was ordinary. It was school and ballet and groceries and dinner and pre-algebra and world history, and the next weekend Debra had the girls, and she made waffles. All was calm until the following Thursday.

Then Richard came in and played with Max while the girls were dragging their bags downstairs, and he said in a low voice, "Debra, I have to tell you something."

That was a bad sign. "Go out to the car," Debra called to the girls as Richard started pacing. He forgot Max completely. "What is it?" Debra asked.

"Well . . . ," he began.

"Is it Heather?"

"Yes."

She froze. Were he and Heather breaking up? Now? Now that the girls were used to her? Had he really screwed up this relationship already? "You didn't."

"Didn't what?" He shot back, instantly defensive.

"Richard. What's going on?"

He hesitated for just a second, and then he said, "We're expecting."

"Wait, what?" The words didn't even register at first.

"We're expecting a baby in January."

"But I thought you were— You aren't even— Aren't you getting engaged?"

"We're planning to."

"And when are you going to tell the girls? And when will you get married?"

"I wanted to ask you about telling them. I mean, it's good news."

She took a breath. "It's a lot of good news at once."

"Exactly."

"Congratulations!"

"Thank you."

"I'm just—I was just surprised."

"We didn't want to wait too long."

Wait? she thought. You didn't wait at all.

"Lissa—"

"Who?"

"Heather's sister is having a terrible time getting pregnant."

Debra stood there bewildered, because why were they talking about Heather's sister's infertility?

"When are you getting married?"

"After the baby."

"Okay," she said slowly. She had foreseen engagement, and then marriage, not an instant family.

He said, "Are you worried it will be weird for the girls?"

"Well, yeah."

"Because you think it's wrong to have a baby first?"

"No." She wasn't going to be the bad guy, the moralistic one, the evil fairy at the christening! She realized something now. The king's first wife—that's who the evil fairy would have been. But that wasn't Debra. Not at all. She just needed a minute. She had never imagined Heather in a rush, or Richard so nervous and so glad, and she felt a pang, hearing his good fortune. Once upon a time, Debra had wanted a third child, but Richard had objected, and she had listened.

"It's just so much at once."

"That's why we want to talk to them."

The front door opened. "Dad," Sophie said.

Lily called from the open car, "You're taking forever."

He called back, "One second."

"Let's figure out a plan," Debra told Richard.

"Great!" He was speaking in that cheerful tone he adopted when the kids were near.

Debra said, "Team meeting."

The three of them met at the Abandoned Luncheonette. Richard sipped kombucha and Debra had black coffee and Heather had nothing.

"Why don't you try the water?" Debra suggested.

And Heather smiled. She appreciated Debra's sense of humor. Of course she did, because she was perfect—even if she looked a little pale.

"How are you feeling?" Debra asked.

"Eh," Heather said, and Richard took her hand.

"She's a trouper." Richard could have been talking about Lily, but Heather didn't seem offended.

Debra asked, "Are you going to find out whether it's a boy or a girl?"

They spoke at the same time. "I think so," Richard said.

"I'm not sure," Heather said.

"Well, either way," Richard said.

Debra interjected, "But you're going to tell the girls that you're expecting."

"Of course!" Heather said.

Richard said, "We have to."

"Here's the thing," Debra told them, and now she saw Richard getting tense. He hated hearing a thing. "I think you should get engaged first and then let a little time pass before telling them about the . . . I think it's important for them to know—"

"That we're all in this together," Heather said.

"Exactly."

"That this is forever," Heather said.

Debra said, "Right."

As for Richard, he said nothing. He would do what Heather wanted. He, who had insisted he could not handle a third child. This was different. Debra understood that. This wasn't a third child born into their old family with their old wars. He and Heather were a new beginning. This was the way of things, that women had their babies and they stopped, while men lived like starfish, constantly regenerating.

"I love the girls so much," Heather was saying. "I want to include them when we get engaged."

I got that part right, Debra thought.

Heather said, "I want to dedicate myself to them."

You're great, Debra thought. You really are. And, at the same time, you have no idea. Parenting times three. The sleepless nights ahead, the tantrums and book reports and standardized tests and the million ways that kids in middle school are mean.

Heather said, "We'll write a family proposal."

"Thank you," Debra said, and meant it. "I think that will be wonderful," she told Heather, because why scare her? And the new baby would be beautiful. She envied Heather that, although she was grateful for the daughters that she had.

"I'm glad we did this!" Heather said, when they were walking to the cars. Richard hugged his future fiancée's shoulders. He kissed her ear.

And Debra didn't feel alone at all. She didn't mind watching.

She just felt like the last grownup on earth as she called after them, "I'm glad we're all on the same page."

The next weekend, she was forewarned and forearmed. She had in her possession a folder with the proposal. Heather had sent it, so Debra was like the press corps with the full text of the speech the president was about to give. And, better than the press, she had printed two copies on archival paper. Even as her daughters were off listening to Richard and Heather pledge their troth, Debra was sitting at the kitchen table framing the documents, so that each girl would have a copy in her room:

FAMILY PROPOSAL

We propose to be there for each other every day.

To respect differences and appreciate each person for who they are.

To make sure everyone in our family is seen and heard.

To honor each other's feelings.

To be on one team.

Debra's phone was ringing. It was Lily, and she was on speaker. Debra could hear Sophie and Heather and Richard in the background talking as Lily shouted, "We're engaged!"

"Mazel tov!"

"And we're expecting!" Sophie added.

"Oh, wow," Debra said automatically. So much for letting a little time pass. "That's so great."

"Mom!" Sophie said. "You already knew, didn't you?"

"I can neither confirm nor deny," Debra said, and she heard

Heather saying Ha! "This is so great!" Debra repeated. "This is really, really wonderful." She said it, but her body ached. Her arms, her legs, her heart.

"It's going to be a girl," Lily said.

Debra said, "They told you?"

"Lily just wants it to be a girl."

That was Sophie's older-sister voice.

The phone was ringing over there at Richard's place. Debra could hear it in the background. "Sorry, it's my parents," Heather said. "Mom? Hi!"

"We should talk to them," Richard said.

"And we need to make dinner," Heather reminded him.

Crashing sounds and laughter. Heather's voice: "Yes! We're here with the girls. We all proposed to each other!"

"Okay. I have to go," Lily told Debra after a minute. "Love you!"

Everyone was happy. Everyone was young. As for Debra, she was relieved. She was actually glad that Richard and Heather had shared all their news at once. She almost wished they'd revealed the gender, too, and named the baby, and that their perfect child was in school, and Richard was showing just how involved he could be the second time around. I have so much more patience now, he would say, as older parents always did. I am so much calmer. Debra wished it had all happened already, so she didn't have to watch.

In the twilight, she got the leash and took Max for a walk. The earth was damp, the grass tender. The neighbor kids were biking up and down the street, looping in parabolas. She stood watching, as she called her sister.

"Hey," she said.

Immediately, Becca said, "The deed is done?"

"Yup."

"And how was it?"

"It was great. It was beautiful."

"Were you there? You sound like you were there."

"No! I wasn't there. I heard from the girls. And they also know about the baby."

"I thought Richard was waiting to tell them."

"Apparently not."

"I thought you had that big meeting."

"We did, and Richard sat there agreeing to everything."

There was a pause, and then Becca said, "He's just bad."

"He isn't bad," Debra said numbly.

"Yes, he is!"

"He's inconsiderate," Debra said. "That doesn't make him bad."

"Whatever," Becca said. "You can call it what you want. He blindsided you!"

"No, Max!" Debra called. He was straining at the leash, barking at a beagle. "He's getting violent," Debra told Becca. "I have to go."

"Max isn't violent."

"He has a thing about little dogs." Debra was maligning her own sweet Max just to get off the phone.

"Hey, Debra. It's okay to be angry," said Becca, who taught creative movement. "You can scream! You can dance it out."

Debra pulled Max across the street. "Yeah, I don't think I'm in that kind of shape right now."

"No, anyone can do this! Listen, it takes two seconds. Plant your feet."

Debra planted her feet on the sidewalk as Max looked quizzically at her.

"Breathe in and tighten your whole body. Make fists."

"Uh-huh."

"Then open your hands. Release your breath. Let go."

Debra opened her left hand, because she was still holding the leash in her right. She exhaled. Then she said, "Let what go?"

"The whole thing."

"Oh."

"I can show you some other ones," Becca said. "That's just a mini-ritual. Anyone can practice that at whatever level. Just try it whenever you feel the need."

"Thanks," Debra said. "Will do."

She took Max home and let him run around while she sat on the girls' old swing. He was looking for his ball. Several times he ran up as if to ask, Where did it go?

Max sniffed her knees. He wanted her to hunt, but she said, "I can't, Max. Sometimes you have to rest. You know?" His ears pricked up; he could detect even a hint of sadness. "It's okay. It will be okay. I promise. You keep looking, and if you still can't find your ball I'll buy a new one. And then as soon as I buy a new one the old one will turn up." Max buried his head in her lap as she said, "I don't know why it happens. It's funny, right? But that's just how it goes."

Dave Eggers

The Honor of Your Presence

HELEN HEARD A SWISH and a crackle from beyond her window, and knew her uncle Peter had arrived. Always he showed up like this, like a restless child, racing to her house on a bicycle, dropping it carelessly into the juniper bush. He was sixty-two years old.

"Hellie?" he called.

"Back here," she answered, and saw his bald head glide past her lemon tree.

He opened the screen door and flew in. He was wearing madras shorts, an oversized polo shirt, and canvas boat shoes. The loose skin around his knees jiggled as he swept his eyes around Helen's office and finally collapsed on the futon. "Too hot out there to be biking," he said.

Helen regarded him. Uncle Peter was pale, pink, built like a tennis player, and covered in brown freckles. His chest was just short of concave, his back the slightest bit bent. He walked with a loping gait that brought to mind a shaggy hippie with no particular place to be.

"I don't know how you stand it out here in the middle of nowhere," he said. "Especially with you being so young and vibrant."

Helen did not usually consider herself so young and vibrant—she was thirty-one and had not exercised meaningfully in eighteen months—but she took the compliment, stored it away, knew she would visit it often.

She saw few people, and those she knew, professional acquaintances and distant cousins, were reserved and disinclined to make such pronouncements. She'd grown up in this town, Tres Pinos, between Killey Alley and Quien Sabe Road. It was scarcely a town, more of a stopover, but as soon as she could walk she'd found, among its few children, three friends, and they'd stayed together for the next few decades, a tight pentagon of unquestioning loyalty. But in the last few years, they'd both moved away, Maria married and dragged to Connecticut, and Leonor gone to nursing school days before the pandemic. Helen was alone, in a suddenly silent world. Then came Peter.

Uncle Peter was known as a wild card, a character, a piece of work. He'd lived in London most of Helen's life, working in the theater as a stagehand and set painter, never accumulating family or wealth. For thirty-two years he'd rented a one-bedroom in Shoreditch, until Covid, when work dried up, his savings dwindled, and he'd spent his last thousand to come back to California. Like all things in the family, the reappearance of Peter Mahoney after three decades was treated with a shrug. Now he was living in Helen's garage in Tres Pinos, just inland and over the hills from Monterey in the oak-choked armpit between two parched yellow hills. He seemed perfectly content there. He had no material needs, it seemed. His only grievance was the heat.

"Yup, too hot for the bike," he said. Peter filled any silence with a reiteration, slightly altered, of whatever he'd just said.

"What're you working on?" he asked, and was instantly off the futon and at Helen's shoulder.

Helen was a designer specializing in event invitations of the high-end category. The brunt of her business was weddings, but she'd worked on fundraisers, galas, reunions, quinceañeras.

The pandemic had flattened the business for the better part of two years, though the many false starts, almost-openings, had worked, oddly, in her favor. Clients ordered invitations, canceled, and ordered them again when the event was rescheduled. She discounted the second go-round, of course, but she had to charge something; her rates were already far lower than those of her competitors. She had steady work because she was on time, she was good—always good, not always great—and her overhead was low.

Overall, the purgatory of Covid had soured her on the industry—the gross expense of these gatherings, the largely fruitless pursuit of merriment and meaning. What if everything, permanently, were scaled back, or outright canceled? She mused this way daily. The towering stresses and exorbitant cost of these Babylonian weddings and fundraisers had gotten out of control. Maybe the pandemic was humbling us toward a more rational scale for our gatherings. Meet up with a few friends under a tree. Get married at city hall and take a few pictures. Wasn't that enough? Parties were stressful, chaotic, invariably a lesser version of a dream. Things got broken, the food arrived cold, the music was too loud, the lead singer's outfit overshadowed the bride's. The invitations, on the other hand, could be perfect. They were inert, contained. They were the carefully worded promise of a glorious event never realized.

"You ever go to any of these parties?" Peter picked up a finished invitation, embossed and with gilt edges.

"No," Helen said.

"But couldn't you just make an extra invitation?" Peter asked, and swept his hand toward her printer.

"First, this isn't where they're printed," Helen said, and explained the difference between a desktop inkjet printer and letterpress. That printing was done by a woman named Gwen, who worked out of a converted barn in San Ramon, a hundred miles northeast. Helen sent the digital files to Gwen, Gwen did the letterpress by hand and then sent the finished invitations to the client. If the invitations or envelopes required calligraphy, that was done by a man named Guillermo, who lived even farther north, in a trio of trailers on the mohair shores of Lake Berryessa. And everything started with Sona, the event coordinator who sent them all business. She was legendary—detail obsessed, uncompromising, and the most miserable person any of them knew.

"So how do *you* get copies?" Peter asked, and nodded at Helen's wall, where invitations to past events were pinned.

"Gwen always prints a few extras for me."

Peter gave her an imploring look.

"I'm not going to a wedding I'm not invited to," Helen said. "Sona would fire me in a second."

"Not a *wedding*," Peter said. "But what about that one?" He pointed to an invitation to the Monterey Bay Aquarium's summer fundraiser, the Big Splash. "There must be a thousand people going. No one would notice us."

"No," Helen said. "And not with you."

"I could die any day. You should take me," he said.

"You're not sick. Are you sick?"

Staring at her sweating, wild-eyed uncle, Helen realized she knew very little about him. She had five uncles on her mother's side alone, and these uncles had begat at least thirty cousins. Peter, this London uncle, *could* be dying. The way information flowed in their family—sporadic, incomplete, unreliable—he or anyone could have had days to live and she wouldn't have known it.

"Did I tell you about my friend who died of an aneurysm?" he asked.

"The guy at the tire shop in town?" Helen asked.

For some reason, Peter had befriended a man named Gus, the second-in-command at the local tire store. Pudgy, boyish, and mostly bald, he was anywhere between thirty-five and fifty. Wherever Helen saw him, he looked happy, eager, wholly content, like a boy lined up at the ice cream truck, money in hand. Gus came around Peter's garage every Sunday morning and stayed till ten P.M., the two of them sitting in the dappled shade of the live oaks, drinking spiked lemonade. What they talked about for twelve hours at a stretch was an unsolvable enigma.

"No. That's Gus," Peter said, and dropped himself back onto the futon. "Gus had a stroke, but he's fine. The guy who died of the aneurysm really died. He was exactly my age."

"Sixty-two."

"Well, this was four years ago. So fifty-eight. Quite sobering."

"So now you've vowed to go to parties to which you're not invited."

"Not specifically, no. But it's the kind of opportunity we'd both be mad to pass up."

Mad was one of Peter's few Britishisms. In thirty years in London, he'd picked up *mad* to supplant the American *crazy*, and he sometimes *fancied* things. Otherwise, there was almost no evidence he'd been gone so long.

"So I assume it's a go?" he said. Peter clasped his freckled hands behind his head. Gangly and constantly moving, wherever he was, Peter seemed at once ill at ease and absolutely comfortable in his skin.

"No," Helen said, and went back to her screen, hoping he'd take the cue and leave. And maybe take a shower. She'd been picking up on a ripe smell in the room and now realized it was him. Peter stood again and hovered over her shoulder. The odor was fruity, acidic. She held her breath, and he moved back to the wall of proofs.

"Too many of my friends have died," he said. He unpinned the Big Splash invitation and held it like a reliquary. "And it's a costume party! This can be something we look forward to," he said, running his aristocratic fingers over the thick board, its deep embossing. "Something extraordinary to do in a short life."

Peter found a folding chair and arranged it next to Helen.

"Helen," he said, looking at every part of her face and hair. In the noonday light, his blue eyes were incandescent. "Your problem is that you spread word of celebrations, without getting to join in."

"That's not my problem," she answered. Her problem, the one that had preoccupied her for months, was that her house was on septic, and the septic tank was under the house, and the tank was full.

"You spend too much time alone," he said. "I don't want you to have regrets. I have so many. So many things I'd do differently."

She'd never seen him look so serious.

"You're not serious," she said.

"No, I'm not serious," he laughed, and his face burst open. "I'm not serious, no. But the reason I don't have regrets is because I took advantage of stuff like this. Fun stuff where no one's harmed."

"I think you're bored out here in the hills," she said. "Maybe you should go to the city." She was thinking of San Francisco, but he thought of London.

"I'm not ready to go back," he said. "But out here, yes, in Tres Pinos I am absolutely bored. And it's so hot. Let's go over the mountains and to the sea."

Peter ordered the costumes from an Etsy person, using Helen's credit card, and thanked Helen profusely for covering the cost. He'd ordered a leopard seal for himself, a whale shark for Helen.

Now, on a gusty gray Monterey afternoon, they were parked a quarter mile from the aquarium, standing on the road's gravel shoulder, changing. She was miserable. Peter was giddy. Beyond her was the Pacific, pale and frothing.

Somehow she didn't think any of this would actually happen— that the costumes would arrive, that they'd actually get in the car and drive an hour to sneak into a gala. Now she regretted not thinking harder about the marine mammal she'd chosen. The costume was enormous.

"I'll be knocking over trays and glasses all night," she said, seeing her vast reflection in the window of her Nissan.

"I bet it's warm in there," he said, meaning inside her costume, which was made of synthetic material Helen was certain wouldn't breathe, and was likely flammable.

Peter was bent over, twisting his feet through his costume, which was lean and convincing.

"Why is yours so much better than mine?" she asked.

"Yours is great! Can you walk?" he asked.

She waddled along the road.

"Perfect," he said. "You said you wanted your face hidden. It's definitely hidden."

That had been the first of the demands she'd made. They would not eat or drink at the event, either, she insisted; that would be stealing. The third demand was that they would endeavor to be quiet and invisible, and would leave the moment anything felt strange for them or their hosts.

"Yup, your face is impossible to see," he said.

Now dressed, Peter made for the museum without looking back. He had a way of drifting away, chin aloft, from whomever he was with. Years ago, at the funeral of his own mother, Helen's grandmother, he'd walked away from the burial—during the burial—hands behind his back, reading other gravestones. At the reception afterward, he praised the ceremony as glorious, dignified, perfect—as if no one had seen him leave.

They approached the museum's entrance. She was already soaked in sweat. Outside, dozens of adults and children were gathered, all dressed as fish and dolphins and sea captains. There was a family of penguins, the last of which was no bigger than a bowling pin.

"Will you wait a second?" Helen asked.

He stopped. She waddled to him.

"What will you say if someone asks why you're there?"

"I'm rich and I love fish," he said.

"Don't say that, please," she said. "Don't say anything memorable or funny."

"Nothing memorable or funny, got it," he said.

"If I'm found out," she said, "I'll never work again. Sona might even be there." Helen didn't think this was true, that her boss would attend such a thing, but now it seemed a grave possibility. She wanted badly to go home. Helen never went where she was not invited. Not in high school, not in college, not ever.

"We're fine," Peter said. "No one can possibly see you."

"Don't talk to anyone," Helen said. "I know how chatty you are."

Peter made a mouth-zipping gesture with a spotted fin, and got in line behind the bowling-pin penguin. By shifting her head left and right, Helen could make out the greeters just outside the aquarium entrance. They were two young women in crisp white dress shirts, black pants, and sky-blue Covid masks. Each held a tablet and seemed to be checking the guests against the list.

"We're not on the list," Helen said.

"The paper invite will work," Peter said. "Only a real guest would have one."

Helen's thighs were sweating.

"You have ours?" Peter asked.

Helen could feel the oversized, cardstock invitation in her waistband. With no pockets big enough to hold it, she'd stuck it between her pants and stomach. Her right hand retreated from the fin and, in the costume's vast hollow, she grabbed the invitation and pushed it up through the costume's mouth, where she retrieved it with her left fin.

Peter took it, and they moved toward the door, finding themselves behind a tall man dressed as a hammerhead. He entered without incident, and when it was their turn, one of the greeters took the invitation from Peter's fin and said, "Welcome," without even glancing at it.

"Told you," Peter said.

Outside it had been cold and gray, but inside there was amber light from Chinese lanterns, Lizzo's "Water Me" blasting through the grand atrium, and a bearded waiter was offering them champagne.

"Yup, I told you," Peter said, and then was gone. Not gone, but going. She caught his silky, spotted shape, chin up, meandering into the crowd as if summoned.

Helen waddled toward the bearded waiter and asked for a glass. He offered her his tray, she took a flute and looked for somewhere to sit. She could make it through any social predicament as long as she was sitting. She found a padded bench and slowly lowered herself until her costume billowed out in front of her. Now her face was deeper in shadow, and she felt like she was both within the party and watching from some misshapen closet.

She sipped on her champagne and took it all in. There were children everywhere—hundreds of them. She had not expected children. They were dressed as dolphins and orcas and squids, and there was a small dance floor, where three adolescent girls in jellyfish costumes were twisting before the DJ, a teenager dressed as a manatee. Next to him was another man, disguised as a midcentury sailor, with a scarf and bell-bottoms.

"Vegan pasta puffs."

A different waiter was standing over her. Helen extended her hand through the whale shark mouth and took two pasta puffs and a napkin.

"Thank you," she said.

"What's that?" the waiter said.

She pictured herself at the bottom of a well, screaming to be heard. "Thank you!" she yelled, and the waiter smiled and spun off.

Another waiter followed with more champagne; she took a fresh glass. For years Helen believed events like this would be insufferable, bizarrely counterproductive. Why not use all the money spent on the event to fund the actual cause? Sona had explained the spend-money-to-make-money concept to her, but Helen remained unconvinced. Still, this was fun. It was unpretentious, like an oversized multigenerational birthday party. There was a coloring station, and a shallow pool where guests could touch mollusks and skates, and there was a kind of laboratory for the making of exotic marine-themed cocktails. But where was Peter? She turned and heard a crash.

Her tail had knocked a plate off her bench. She maneuvered her head-hole until she saw that she'd sent it hurtling ten yards into the lobby. But the plate was plastic, and hadn't had food on it, and it was quickly gathered up by a passing waitress. Every bit of contentment she'd felt moments before turned to sour self-loathing. Helen had always been tall and awkward in her body; her mother had promised grace would come, but grace had not come. She needed to leave. Or half-leave. To go outside.

She rose, steadied herself, planning to find her way to the deck. Shit, she hissed from her hollow. She was already tipsy. She should have eaten dinner. Costume tipsy was different than everyday tipsy. Shit, shit. She walked slowly through the main room, trying to make her languorous pace true to a whale shark. Weren't they slow? They were! They were! She stepped steadily, as in a procession of one. All the while she stayed close to the perimeter, running her fins along the surface of walls and columns until she came upon the dance floor. Its minefield of flailing bodies was just before the door to the deck; she only had to get across without knocking over an adolescent jellyfish-girl.

"You okay?" a voice said.

She turned suddenly, thrusting her snout into the head of the midcentury sailor. "Sorry!" she said, and from the darkness of her cavern tried to ascertain the damage to him. While finding him unharmed, she saw a Polish flag on his shoulder. But did Poland *have* a navy?

"Not a problem," he said, and shook his face theatrically, like a boxer recovering from a sucker punch. He was a beautiful thing, with huge brown eyes and a delicate jaw. She expected him to quickly move away, but he lingered.

"Are these girls digging your dance moves, sailor?" Helen said. She customarily, reflexively, said aggressive things to handsome men.

His face registered real surprise, then outrage, as if the full weight of the false accusation had finally landed. "I'm the party starter," he said. "This is my *job*."

Helen's face burned, and she cursed her terrible mind and horrible mouth. She yelled another "Sorry" from the depths of her disguise, and then waddled to the back door and burst through to the deck. In the ocean air she found her way to the redwood railing and collapsed against it. Once every year or two, she encountered someone she found alluring, and her mouth spewed bile. How could she remember not to do something like that, given it only happened once every few years? And wasn't it natural enough— the spouting of hateful banter at a perfect and friendly face? She was out of practice, had been out of practice for the better part of a decade.

Helen had only truly adored one person, and that had been a mistake, a small-town mistake obvious to all but her. How stupid to fall for Maria's brother. He was four years older, and she and Leonor had grown up seeing him as the unassuming, unattainable model of masculinity. But then he'd returned from college, and when she was eighteen, he made himself suddenly attainable—to Helen. For a summer they acted on ten years of latent desire, in a private frenzy, most of it outdoors. Then she went to college downstate, he took a job in Dubai, and he never looked back. She thought he might look back, and for years she was ready for him to look back, but he never turned around.

From the safety of her cave-mouth, she peeked through the glass and at the dance floor, to see how the Polish sailor was faring. He was back to party-starting, bouncing up and down with a toddler on his shoulders.

"Fuck, this is wonderful," Peter said. He had sidled up next to her. His flippers were on the wooden railing. "Don't you think?"

"I'm on the fence," she said. It took him a second to get the joke. He lifted his seal-snout.

"Hellie, don't you *long*?"

"Don't I long?" she asked, looking at a seagull eating someone's forgotten sushi, jabbing at it on the wet, blue deck.

"Don't you *long*?" he asked again, stretching the word out this time and giving it a guttural edge. His eyes met hers in a kind of challenge.

"Yes," she said. "Sure. All the time. Did it this morning."

"You have to long for *some*thing," he said, looking straight down to the inky sea. "Longing is such pleasure. It's like chocolate and cannabis in a hot tub—only you don't have any of those things. It's *wanting* all those things, and also wanting meaning, and love, and the sense that you're on a reckless adventure, seeing things that have never been seen."

"Okay," she said. She really didn't know this man. Was he about to confess something to her? He was gay, she assumed, but this had never been said. Maybe he was bi?

"Hellie, I want to know what you long for," he said. He took her fat gray fin in his flipper and looked at it.

A rush of thoughts came to Helen. She actually had an answer. Just a few days ago, while sleeping through the first bright hours of morning, she'd had a vivid dream (all her most vivid dreams were in the morning). In it, she was lying on a bed, high in the air. The bed was on a kind of pedestal, forty feet up, in the middle of a meadow, and outside it was night, a gauzy lavender night, and the stars and planets were out, and there was someone next to her who was soft and gentle and radiating love and giddiness, and the face was smiling, eyes delighted. It seemed a woman's face, but that's all she knew.

Helen wanted to tell him this, but before she could, he spotted the champagne glass in her other fin. It was near-empty.

"You broke your rule!" he said. "You said we couldn't eat or drink. I'll be right back." And he was off, headed to the outdoor bar at the end of the deck.

Helen was alone again, and anonymous, and aglow with champagne and a handful of crackers and carrots she'd taken into her mouth-cavern. She walked back inside, and moved slowly, dreamily, through the galleries of bright blue glass, where barracudas, belugas, sailfish, and turtles moved like dazed tourists in their crowded tanks. After an hour she found herself among a small group of guests watching a magician do impossible tricks at close range. He was not in costume, but in all black—black pants, black shirt, black vest, black beard.

He was engaged with a silver-haired man in an admiral's outfit. After some banter, the magician pulled a gold coin from his own mouth, and this gold coin had on it the name of the silver-haired man standing before him.

"That's the most astounding thing I've ever seen," the silver-haired man said. "And I own a professional hockey team." As he and the magician talked about hockey and close magic, a regal woman of about sixty, dressed as a scaly sea goddess, took notice of Helen.

"Are you here alone, hon?" she asked. Helen assumed she was the hockey man's wife. As their eyes met, her stare hardened from sympathetic to suspicious.

"No, my uncle's here somewhere," Helen mumbled, and her thighs began to sweat again. She looked intensely into the aquarium, as if he might swim by.

"Your uncle, do we know him?" the sea goddess asked, fingering a glittering necklace. Her eyes were ice blue, her fingers like pink talons. Helen was certain the sea goddess knew she was uninvited. This was why she didn't come to these things—this feeling of not being fully welcome. Everywhere, there were levels of welcome, and the owner of the hockey team, whose name was on the coin in the magician's mouth, was at the top, his sea goddess at his side. And they looked down to the muddy ocean floor to see Helen, hiding in her mouth-cavern.

"You probably know him," Helen said. "He owns a hockey team, too. Isn't that weird? Field hockey, but still. Let me go get him."

She took the stairs recklessly and found refuge near a tall aquarium full of jellyfish, falling like snow. Something brushed the back of her leg, and she turned to find an enormous octopus, seven feet high and with all eight tentacles, gliding by. The person inside was wholly hidden, even their legs, and the effect was so magical that Helen felt a tingling rush of gratitude; people went to such lengths to make something like that, some beautiful and useless deception.

Just as the octopus turned a rounded corner, the Polish sailor emerged from a nearby bathroom, checking his zipper. Finding it satisfactory, he looked up and saw Helen. In three quick strides he was standing close, his face made more extraordinary in the soft peach light of the jellyfish tank.

"I wasn't dancing with the kids for *fun*," he said. "It's my *job*," he said again.

"I know, I know!" Helen said, and pelted him with clumsy apologies for the next few minutes. Finally he softened.

"I'm Bartek. Are you here alone?" he asked. He was half-Polish, and his grandfather was actual-Polish, he said, and the uniform he wore was his grandfather's. He touched the medals on his chest, declaring them real. She found this unaccountably sexy, and brought her face closer to the whale-mouth, hoping Bartek might see her eyes smiling at him.

She told Bartek about Uncle Peter, mentioning his habit of abandoning her, in hopes that Bartek might feel, out of chivalry, an obligation to stay with her. She didn't know if his party-starting was finished—did someone else finish what he had started? Was there a party-ender? Because she knew the event ended at nine, and that soon she'd have to take a drunken Peter home, she only wanted to glean some knowledge about Bartek that would ensure she could find him again.

"I live up in Redding, actually," he said, "but I'm working at a thing in Gilroy next weekend. I think it's open to the public. Maybe you should come."

Again her mouth tried to say something terrible to him, something nasty about Gilroy, but this time she fought the impulse and said she would try.

He provided the details, and the lights dimmed and then went horrifically bright, indicating the night was over. Peter arrived, drunker than Helen thought possible, holding an ice-cream sandwich in his leopard-seal fin. Seeing the Polish sailor up close, Peter saluted, slurred a few words of greeting in a newfound British accent, and Bartek, sober and tired, excused himself and spun away.

On the way home, Peter kept his head out the window, grinning into the wind like a dog. "Everything about that was worth it," he yelled.

In the past, after Helen had attended any social event where she'd had alcohol and spoken words to people, she'd spend weeks lamenting every catty or ignorant thing she'd said, every clumsy walk to and from the bathroom, every person she'd kissed in the lobby while the overnight janitor polished the floors with a spinning green machine. And it had all gotten far worse when her friends left town. There was no one to reassure her she had not behaved like an idiot.

But after the party in Monterey, no such regrets had haunted her. Her name had not been known, her face was hidden, she could not possibly get caught or face consequences. She could move freely and see all and go home, and only she knew it had happened. It was invisibility and flight. She was entertaining the possibility of a long public life dressed as a whale shark when she heard the shush of Peter's bicycle landing in her juniper.

"Hellie?" he called out.

His bald head sped past her lemon tree and appeared, with the rest of him, in her office.

"So," he said, as he studied her wall, where six new proofs were taped. "Anything good coming up?"

"No," she said. She had not ruled out going to another event, but had ruled out going with Peter. He was too careless, and he vastly increased the risk of discovery. But she had decided not to tell him this, or about the Gilroy event, which she'd been considering attending.

"What about this one?" he asked. He pointed to an invitation to a corporate event in San Jose. His eyes darted over the page. "It's an afternoon thing for the whole family," he said. "And Billy Idol's playing! Don't you want to see Billy Idol?"

She did want to see Billy Idol.

"No," she said.

"Did I ever tell you I know his nephew? He was a lighting tech in London. He had a goiter, which I thought unusual."

Peter had pulled the invitation off the wall.

"Don't," Helen said. "They have a guest list for that one. And each invite has the person's name done by a calligrapher. There's no way to sneak in."

"Is this the list?" Peter asked. He'd found the printout on her worktable. Sona had sent it to her, and Helen was supposed to send it to the calligrapher.

"Why not just add me to this?" he asked.

"You know I can't do that."

"Did you get this digitally?" Peter asked.

"Yes," she said.

"So just add me and print it out again. My last name's different than yours. No one could possibly connect this to you. You add my name to this list on your computer, you print it out again, you send it to the calligrapher. Easy."

"No."

"You can be my plus-one."

"The event is too small," Helen said.

"It doesn't look small," Peter said. "It says it's at a fairgrounds. You can't have a small event at a fairgrounds. Can you ask Gwen how many invites she's printing?"

"How do you know about Gwen?"

"You told me about her. Your letterpress friend."

"Well, she's not my friend. I've never met her," Helen said.

"You've never met her? How often do you get out socially, Hellie?"

Helen said nothing. He knew she never went out. They saw each other, heard each other, every day in their armpit-valley.

"Sorry. That was out of bounds," he said. "I just thought we had fun last time. Didn't we?"

"It was fine," she said.

"Fine. Okay. And this one's outside, and it's Billy Idol. Far more casual. It's like sneaking into a county fair. No one cares."

They did not go to Billy Idol. But the only way to get Peter off her back about Billy Idol was to take him to Gilroy, where Bartek's next gig would be. The Gilroy Garlic Festival had an opening-night party, and this seemed an easy compromise.

But she couldn't be complicit. She needed some measure of plausible deniability, so she had looked away from her keyboard and let Peter type his name onto the calligrapher's list. Somehow it mitigated her guilt, and he'd gotten his invite in the mail like anyone else. She was just his plus-one. It was all absurd, but she was as invisible as before, and now they were pulling off the highway to enter Gilroy.

"You have the invite?" she asked.

Peter held it up. It had been beautifully handwritten by Guillermo, but seeing Peter's name on that envelope turned her stomach. Printing an extra invite was one thing; this was a more florid kind of fraud.

The late afternoon heat was still coming off the pavement.

Growing up in Tres Pinos, Helen thought of Gilroy as the big city—the place everyone wanted to leave Tres Pinos for. She hadn't been there in years, and now half the town's businesses were dead by Covid, boarded up.

"I don't remember this place," Peter said. "And I don't smell the garlic. Did it ever smell of garlic?"

It did, often, smell of garlic. And to compensate, someone, a hundred years ago, decided to embrace it—to make Gilroy the Garlic Capital of the World. It was on every sign, every T-shirt, and they'd made the harvest a time of citywide celebration. The opening gala was being held at the Ramada, and when they pulled into the lot, older adults in bright cowboy costumes wound their way through trucks and SUVs, heading toward the Ramada's cul-de-sac. A new surge of Covid was blasting through the region, so guests had been asked to wear masks, and were encouraged to wear bandanas over the masks. *Let's Make This Outlaw!* the email update pleaded.

"Can you do mine?" Peter asked. He handed her his bandana, black with gold lacing. She tied it on, and she turned to let him fix hers. Knowing only her eyes would be visible to Bartek, she'd spent an hour on them, using far more eyeliner and mascara than she'd ever dared before.

"Liz Taylor!" Peter said.

"It's not too much?" she asked.

"No. And I like the pants. Sorta seventies-country. Very East End, 1983."

Helen did not know what that meant, but took it to mean something British. She'd found, online, a pair of silky royal-blue pants with white Western stitching. They were tight in the thighs, loose at the ankles, and made in Serbia.

"Now can I do something?" he asked.

Flush from his compliments, she agreed.

"Your posture is shit," he said, and her confidence shattered.

He stood at her side and pulled her shoulders back, squinting.

Wanting to curse him and run, she only managed a breathless grunt.

"Better!" He stepped back. "Chin straight," he said, and inched her chin up with his knuckle.

All this in the parking lot. Helen looked around. No one was watching.

"*So* much better," he said.

"I don't stoop," she said. People thought she stooped, had been saying this since she was thirteen. Her mother had long ago given up the fight.

"Not anymore you don't," he said. "I know you were tall as a girl, but you're not so tall now. Five nine?"

"About." She was five ten and a half.

"There was an actress in London," Peter said, "you know her now, but I knew her when she was just out of Royal Shakespeare. She was six foot barefoot and hunched a bit, like you. The director insisted she stand straight up. She was playing Medea—definitely a tall woman's part. She straightened up and my god, she was like a Corinthian column."

"I don't want to be a Corinthian column," she said.

"I know. But Medea? Let's see you walk like Medea," he said.

"No," Helen said. She didn't know how Medea walked, and she was finished with all this. "Can we just go inside?"

"We can," he said, and he was at the door of the Ramada in seconds, leaving her far behind. Peter was wearing black jeans and a brown suede shirt with black stitching. He'd borrowed it from Gus, and looked fully the part of a working farmhand cleaned up for a night in town. She caught up with him at the doorway, where a pair of women in their seventies were sitting on high wooden stools.

"Hello, handsome!" one said.

"Hello, gorgeous!" Peter said. The British accent was back in force. He handed the invitation to the woman, who didn't look at it. She waved them through.

"All that work, all that intrigue," Helen said.

"We are but dust," Peter said.

The room was beige and sterile, lightly decorated by what appeared to be four different people trying to evoke four different eras. The large garlic cutouts on the walls looked vaginal, the flowers on the tables were dried but not yet dead, there were six ice sculptures of dubious stability, and the waitstaff looked like casino dealers—in black formalwear with red ties.

The hundred or so guests were huddled by the walls or milling around the tables where raffle items were offered. On the opposite corner of the ballroom was a sorry dance floor, and in the middle of it, Bartek. Helen had to assume it was Bartek. In a white Stetson and sky-blue jeans, the figure he cut was wholly different than at the aquarium. In that costume, he'd been masculine and convincing—a meat-eating exemplar of a remorseless superpower. Tonight he looked like a Branson backup dancer.

"Hello, young lady," he said, loudly. There was something performative and general in his voice that strongly implied that he didn't recognize her.

"Bartek," she said. His look was blank. "It's Helen. We met at the aquarium."

"The aquarium?" He looked around, as if he'd find one there, in the ballroom.

"In Monterey. By the jellyfish. I was a whale—"

"Oh!" he yelled. "Yes, I know!" Now he knew. Did he really know? "You came!" he said, slightly less loud now. He was wearing a red bandana over an N95. "Do you live here in Gilroy?" he asked, while looking over her shoulder. Two women had just entered the ballroom, one of them holding a clipboard.

"Stay here," he said. "I'll be right back."

There had been no recognition, no spark. Screw it. Bartek was a bust. Helen was ready to leave. During Covid you could leave moments after arriving and no one could question it. Everyone was ghosting, canceling, not bothering. It was a pandemic well suited to her natural inclinations.

She looked around the room for her uncle. He was standing at the raffle table with a soft-bellied man about his age. They were inspecting one of the offerings, a week at a ski-in house in Tahoe.

"Do you ski?" she asked, and Peter practically jumped, his eyes white. The man next to him turned, too, and Helen realized it was Gus, his friend from the tire shop. He had a suede cowboy hat by his side. He put it on and tipped it to her.

"Hi, Gus," she said.

"Hi, Helen," he said.

"You paid to go to this?" she asked.

Gus looked at Peter, who looked at the ceiling.

Finally she put it together.

"You put him on the list, too," she said.

Peter was not apologetic. If anything, he seemed to be blaming Helen. Of course he would abuse the moment she'd given him at her keyboard.

"Don't worry," he said. "Gus won't tell."

Gus crossed his heart with his pudgy finger.

"I'm leaving," she said.

"I'm staying," Peter said. "We drove an hour."

She walked away, now truly wanting to exit, but then found two things she wanted in one place: the bar, and Bartek. He was talking to the bartender, a woman of about forty wearing a tight Western shirt the color of butter.

A couple was at the bar, complaining loudly about the cost of their babysitter, dinner for the babysitter, then their Uber and dinner before the event. "All for this!" the woman, a slinky blonde, said, and swept her hand around the joyless room.

"There's just no point," the man said under his fake handlebar mustache.

They left, and Bartek stared daggers at their retreat.

"Sauv blanc, please," Helen said to the bartender, who seemed wholly unaffected by the couple's bleating.

"Sure, sweetie," the woman said.

Helen had a weakness for terms of casual endearment like this. The women who used them had to be warm, confident, loving. What a gift, to be able to pull off a *sweetie* with a stranger.

She lifted her chin to Bartek. "Ready to party-start?"

Again he looked at Helen as if he'd never seen her before, so she took a long pull on her wine and turned toward the bartender. The woman's hair was reddish, probably dyed, pulled back into a ponytail. Her face was round, cheeks rosy, and that chest—it was enormous.

"I think so," Bartek said. "How about you?"

He still had no idea who Helen was.

"Am *I* ready to party-start?" she asked.

He nodded, looked beyond her, then back at her. He smiled politely, clearly accustomed to talking to drunken strangers who wanted their songs played, who wanted to stomp around to "Come On Eileen" at their high school reunion.

"This is a tough crowd," he said, and eyed the empty dance floor as a general would a battlefield. "Kids make it easier. I think you're the youngest person here."

He glanced her way, studying her briefly. Still nothing.

"Well, I better go," Bartek said, and made a quick diagonal across the ballroom to his post.

The busty bartender had refilled Helen's glass already, a generous second pour, and had added a pink napkin around the stem. Bartek had left without a drink, and by this Helen assumed that he'd been visiting the bar for the bartender, not a beverage. Helen wilted. She could not compete with a pretty, shapely person like this, a woman with the curves of a fertility idol and the sunny manner of a kindergarten teacher.

"Thanks," she said to her, and looked for somewhere to sit. In the corner of the ballroom, she saw a zigzag row of folding chairs, and next to it, an abandoned wheelchair.

"You bet, hon," the bartender said, and held her gaze for a moment just longer than casual.

Helen shuffled away and sat on the chair farthest from the wheelchair. She sipped her sauv blanc and stole a few glances toward the bartender, who was by then surrounded by a group of elderly drinkers. The room filled until a hundred or so were wandering unhappily between the bar and the raffle table. It was a truly terrible party. There was too much space, too much floor.

"Hey hey, party people!" Bartek said from his microphone, and encouraged the attendees to gather near the stage. "No stamping, please," he added, and laughed to himself for an inordinately long time. A woman introduced herself as the deputy mayor and made solemn remarks about garlic, and then introduced a succession of board members past and present. The last speaker cued Bartek, who began with "Billie Jean," which had no takers. "September Song" had no effect. Helen returned to her conclusion that most gatherings were horrific wastes of time and money and goodwill.

She couldn't find Peter and Gus. Maybe they'd left. Bartek was likely going home with the big-pour bartender, and Helen was happy for them. They were in the same industry, making do with an insufferable species that tried in vain to have fun. Even if she had to wait in the car for an hour or two, she had to leave this room. Heading toward the exit, Helen glanced back at Bartek and his tragic dance floor, and saw a man on all fours.

At first she assumed one of the septuagenarians had fallen, but then another man—oh god, it was Peter—came out of nowhere and leapfrogged over the man on all fours, who of course was Gus.

Helen couldn't watch, couldn't look away. She stood in the middle of the ballroom, mouth agape. Gus got up from the floor, and he and Peter took a second to compose themselves, then reassembled, now standing side by side. They launched into what seemed to be a coordinated dance, featuring much swooping of arms and more leapfrogging. The rest of the attendees began wandering over to the dance floor, as they would a car crash.

"Is someone having a seizure?" a woman near Helen asked.

For the next half hour, the funereal gathering became a party, with Peter and Gus at the center of it, performing a sequence of maneuvers loosely resembling square dancing, then breakdancing, and frequently falling back on leapfrogging. Somehow their sweating, grinning, grimacing, and frantic work convinced a few dozen couples to venture onto the dance floor.

Afterward, Peter and Gus found the folding chairs Helen had claimed earlier, and they asked for two gin and tonics each, and water, too, which Helen was happy to get from the bartender. When Helen visited her this second time, she saw her name, Terri, on a name tag stuck on her chest. The name tag hadn't been there before, Helen was sure, and now the highest button on Terri's shirt had been released, revealing an opulent curve of flesh, and a bit of underwire bra. Helen looked away, suddenly flushed.

"You with those two?" Terri asked.

Helen turned back to her, to that open and rosy face, and felt like she'd jumped in an ocean at sunrise. It was too much.

"My uncle and his friend," Helen said. "There's something wrong with them."

Terri watched the two men. Peter had his arm over the back of Gus's chair. Gus was leaning forward, massaging his knee.

"I guess at that age you can be less inhibited," Terri said.

As Terri looked at them, Helen allowed herself to look at Terri. Her eyes were dark and merry, her cheeks round and full.

"Weird thing is, I don't think they've had a drink yet," Helen said.

Terri laughed. She tilted her head, assessing Helen. "I like how you carry yourself," she said. "I have a friend your height who's always hunched over like a flamingo. But you own it."

If only you knew, Helen thought. An hour ago, I was hunched over, then my London uncle fixed me, citing Corinthian columns and Medea.

"I have a break in half an hour," Terri said, filling Helen's glass again. "Want to hang outside?"

When her break arrived, Helen was tipsy, and followed Terri to the bumper of her Subaru, where they vaped and laughed about Terri's ex, a career Marine with crippling anxiety and an edibles addiction. Helen told Terri far too much about her years of growing isolation, and all the while she knew she was saying too much, was painting a picture of herself as a pathetic shut-in who went to garlic events with her uncle. She stood up, feeling embarrassed.

"What time is it?" Helen asked. "Don't you have to be back soon?"

"Kiss me," Terri said, and in one fluid motion she grabbed Helen's shirt, pulled her down, and kissed her with an open and ravenous mouth.

"That okay?" she asked.

Helen was stunned and wanted more. She leaned down and, with her hands behind her back—it seemed more polite, less presumptive—she kissed Terri longer, softer, grabbing at her lips with her teeth, briefly tasting red wine on her tongue. When they finished, Helen was gasping, half-blind. Her hands had found their way into Terri's shirt, under her bra, caught like rabbits under a fence.

Terri leaned away. "Gotta work," she said. "To be continued. Follow me home. I have a big shower." Then she hustled back into the Ramada, straightening her buttons.

Helen staggered inside and found Peter and Gus. They were placing fake bids on auction items—vacations in Kauai and Tahoe. "I'm taking the car," she said. "You guys can Uber. Don't ask questions. You owe me."

Helen drank water and coffee and felt sharp by the time Terri packed up the bar, started her Subaru, and waved for her to follow. She drove behind, watching Terri's taillights leave Gilroy proper and turn up into the San Gabriel foothills. All along Helen pictured herself pressed against Terri, her chest to her back, in Terri's big shower—all that water, everything so smooth.

But when Terri pulled into her ranch house driveway, her headlights swept over a crowd of teenagers, their silhouettes spidery, their shadows striping the yellow stucco.

Terri jumped out of her car and plowed through the crowd and into the house. Helen waited in her own car, on the street, watching teenagers lope off to their cars and bikes. After ten minutes, Terri hadn't emerged.

Helen thought it through. The night was over. Terri had a kid, or more than one kid, and the kids—teenagers!—had thrown a party, thinking she'd be coming home later. Now they were arguing, and Terri was punishing them, and assessing damage, and clearing the house. There would be no big shower.

She texted Terri, saying she was leaving. Terri didn't answer. An hour later, after Helen was back in Tres Pinos, in bed, having masturbated twice, she got a response. *Sorry. Long story. Idiot daughter of mine.* A minute passed, then another ding. *They broke my parents' wedding plate.* Helen consoled her, they went to bed, and the next morning, just after dawn, Terri texted again. *Have to be up in SF for a gig this week, an old-timey costume thing, but see you when I get back?*

Peter was on Helen's futon again.

"It shouldn't be so hot here, not so close to the coast," he said. He was wearing yellow tennis shoes and salmon-colored shorts. He put his shoes on the futon, then took them off. He cracked his knuckles and rubbed his eyes.

"Nope, shouldn't be so hot," he said.

"So did you guys work all those moves out before, or . . . ?" she asked.

"Nah, just spontaneous," Peter said. "Like jazz." Then he was up like a leprechaun, suddenly peering over her shoulder at her wall of proofs.

"No more parties," she said.

"I'm thinking no more Ramadas from now on," he said. "We need something a bit classier."

"I'm done," Helen said.

"I like the costume ones," he said. He was pawing through the boxes at Helen's feet. "Ooh, look at this one!" he said, and picked up a stray invitation for a fundraiser for the Palace of Fine Arts in San Francisco. The Palace, a pseudo-Roman dome and collection of columns around a man-made pond, had been erected in haste in 1915, for the Panama-Pacific International Exposition— a kind of World Expo to celebrate the opening of the Panama Canal. It was the only part of the expo that still remained, and it needed constant work to keep it standing.

"Those went out months ago," she said.

He continued reading from the invitation. "Orchestra. Dancing. Period-specific attire. And this is in three days! I'm going."

"You can't go," Helen said.

"It says you need to present the invite at the door. Is that a period-specific thing, too? That's perfect for us. You have more of these?"

"No," she said.

He laughed to himself. "You know, I actually have a top hat! From *My Fair Lady*."

"Where's Gus? Isn't Gus missing you? You should go work out more dance routines."

"Gus has Covid," Peter said. "Probably from Gilroy. He's actually pretty sick. He went to the hospital."

"Oh god, I'm sorry," Helen said. She really should never open her mouth; a very small percentage of the things she said were the right things to have said. The silence in the room stretched out.

Peter inhaled. "Yup, Gus got the Covid," he said.

"All the more reason to skip this one," Helen said. "Wait a month and then we can go to another event. For now, though, we need to cool it before someone notices. And you should be close to Gus. Does the hospital let you visit?"

Peter gave her a confused look. "He's not still *in* the hospital. I said he went *to* the hospital. But the line for testing there was too long, so he went home and did a rapid one."

"And he's positive."

"Oh you know Gus, he's always upbeat."

Helen took a breath. Peter was near the door, and she thought of shoving him through.

"You'll wait this one out?" she asked.

"If you say so," he said.

After he was gone, Helen returned to the task she was in the middle of when he arrived: finding a costume for the 1915 party. She needed everything—corset, dress, shoes, parasol, fan. The event, partly outdoors, wasn't requiring masks, so she'd decided she needed casual face-coverings, diversions, anything to ensure some level of anonymity. She knew almost no one in San Francisco, so she was not too concerned with being discovered, but then again, all crime sprees ended when the criminals got sloppy.

Terri had not invited her to join her in the city, but Helen had done some cursory research and guessed that the old-timey party Terri mentioned was this Palace of Fine Arts thing. And she was feeling restless, reckless, not herself. The drive was only a few hours, and she wanted to see Terri again, wanted it to be weird and bold. She wanted to see what Terri looked like in one of those tight white shirts with the flowing sleeves and the high collars. Thinking about it, on the highway, was getting Helen hot; she rolled down the window and thought about all the things she hadn't worked out, like where she was staying that night, when she'd go home, and what to do, how to live, if Terri, like Bartek, forgot her completely.

The event's website had promised a changing room where attendants would be available to contend with corsets and hoops, so Helen parked as close as she could to the Palace of Fine Arts—across the highway, near the beach, squeezed in a row of campers and windsurfers—and rushed to the building holding two garbage bags full of corsets and bustles. There were two women at the door, and Helen presented her invitation, the one Peter had inspected. It was the proof, and the only extra invitation printed. One of the young women accepted it, said, "Good luck," and directed Helen to the changing room.

The Palace of Fine Arts was a wide-open space, round and the size of a small armory. The women's changing area was indeed between two basketball hoops, and there, at least forty women were assembled, back to front, pulling and grunting and laughing. The age range was vast, from eighteen to seventy-five. About a dozen women were in their twenties, their hair coiled high, their necks exposed. The discomfort was great, but the effect was transfixing. The clothing flattered every body type, every face. A woman of Helen's size and shape, but twenty years older, approached her with kind eyes. She was already dressed.

"You need help?"

Helen unpacked her corset and the woman took it expertly in hand, fitting it carefully around Helen's ribs. From there, the woman's hands were quick and skilled. She pulled and threaded while humming softly to herself.

"Nothing left to tie," the woman finally said. "Is that your parasol?" she asked. "Indoors, at night, it's a stretch, but it's a lovely thing. I'm Barbara. Are you here alone?"

"I am," Helen said, thinking of Terri. Was she with Terri? She dropped the parasol and began nudging it under a nearby divan. "You?"

"I'm with my son," Barbara said. "You should meet him. He's stuck with me." The woman smiled while picking a strand of hair from Helen's sleeve. "Don't hold that against him. He's a normal person. If I see you out there, I'll introduce you."

Barbara squeezed her hand and strode off, her dress flowing, breathing beneath her like a living thing.

Helen found a free seat at one of the vanities and finished her makeup. She took cues from the other women around her, none

of whom seemed quite sure if the colors should be demure or pro-
nounced. Helen sat, looking at herself, bewildered. She was pow-
dering her face, dressed like a turn-of-the-century heiress. What
the fuck was she doing?

Finished, she went outside, joining a trickle of partygoers making their way down a bending walkway. The strains of a small
orchestra wafted from a doorway ahead, and at the entrance of a
great hall, she paused. Sona really could be at this party. In fact,
if she came to any party at all, it would be this one. Helen had
brought a cloth mask, tucked into her sleeve. She put it on.

The hall was vast, alive with a hundred thousand lights. Chan-
deliers hung from the ceiling, which was covered in elaborate
bunting of violet and cream and gold to simulate sky and clouds
and god-light. The music was orchestral, jaunty, of the era, Helen
assumed, played by a vast band in tuxedoes. A woman bassoonist
with cascading white hair was soloing. Helen roamed through the
room, looking for Terri. She skirted the tables covered in white
cloth, exuberant arrangements of lilies and roses bursting from
each center. A woman in a blood-red costume walked by, smelling strongly of lilac, to join two friends in sunflower-yellow flap-
per dresses, and an announcement came over that the orchestra
would be playing a composition written for the 1915 fair. When
the three women began dancing, Helen was suddenly overcome.
This is glorious, Helen thought. So many parties were just half-
gestures toward merriment, but this was something different.
There was glee in the eyes of everyone in the room, a sense that
they were in the midst of something very odd, very ambitious,
but which had been pulled off far beyond anyone's expectations.
The effort and expense for all this, for one fleeting night, was
obscene, and yet Helen felt that she would fight anyone who said
it wasn't worth it.

The music stopped and a woman in a dress of the palest purple
emerged, tapping her glass with a fork. "Now for some—gasp—
organized fun," she said. "At an event like this, there would have

been a number of group dances the attendees would have known. Which of course we do not know. But we happen to have a wonderful teacher who will familiarize us with a few of these dances. I promise you it will be painless." She first introduced the "Pan-Pacific One-Step," which required the two dancers to hold hands very high, over the shoulder, and then do a sort of Charleston with their legs. Two professional dancers demonstrated, then continued demonstrating while the rest of the attendees were urged to join them. A man next to Helen, about sixty and without hair anywhere—not on his head, not on his eyebrows—asked Helen if he might accompany her, and she was too startled to refuse. He was wearing white gloves.

They struggled through the number, his movements graceful but hers labored with the undercarriage and her hair, which was coming undone. She couldn't breathe, so took off her mask. No one, it seemed, was wearing masks anymore. He spun her, stepped on her toes and heels, apologizing each time, and finally, for the last half-minute, they were something like graceful. Afterward he thanked her and excused himself, joining a large throng of people his age at the bar.

Helen wandered the room, which began to feel smaller. From a distance she caught sight of a bartender who looked a bit like Terri, but older, with a high mound of white-gray hair. Could that be Terri in a wig? She investigated closer; it wasn't Terri. By then she'd visited every bar in the room, checked the face of every waitress, every place Terri might have been working, and she was nowhere.

And Helen had forgotten to eat. She was hungry, coming down from her champagne high, and very tired. She sat on a period-appropriate divan, under a fragrant fern, and glowered. She'd lost her mask, and felt exposed again. She'd driven a hundred miles for this, gotten dressed in this ludicrous way, chasing a woman based on the faintest clue.

"Everyone together!" a voice said. Helen knew this voice. She followed the sound to the foyer, where a group of women in black dresses were gathered, posing for a photo. Their dresses were identical, slinky black gowns with spaghetti straps, and when they all turned to their left, Helen finally understood. *Madame X.* The painting had been exhibited at the original exposition, and now all the party's Mesdames X were taking a group photo. And just as the photographer counted down from three, an older man appeared in the frame, leaping from the wings, and that older man was Peter.

"Someone had to be John Singer Sargent!" he said, and after the Mesdames X laughed dutifully and shooed him away, his eyes met Helen's. He was wearing a tuxedo with tails, a high white collar, and a fake mustache. He looked utterly natural in it. His face was a radiant pink.

"Hi, Hellie!" Peter said, utterly free of shame. "I didn't think you'd be here." He hugged her, smelling of cologne and cigars. He pulled back, surprised to see the fury in her eyes.

There were a few dozen people near, so she parsed her words. "I thought we agreed you weren't coming. To this. Or anything."

"Sure, but then I wanted to," he said brightly, and signaled to a waiter passing by with champagne. He took two flutes and gave one to Helen. "And I figured you weren't coming, so it wouldn't do any harm. Your main concern was my getting you in trouble, right? But if you weren't coming, then I couldn't get you in trouble."

The logic was unassailable, and she was angrier than before. "But how did you get in?"

"Gwen helped me," he said.

"Gwen?"

"Oh, I just remembered you two haven't met." He peered at the mass of Mesdames. "Gwen?"

One of the heads turned and a woman's huge brown eyes lit up.

Peter pointed to Helen and mouthed her name, and Gwen came rushing over.

"I can't believe it!" she said, and pumped Helen's hand. "I didn't think you were coming. We finally meet! You're younger than I thought."

Helen was struck dumb. She stared at Gwen, with her long neck and delicate features. Gwen worked out of a converted barn; irrationally, Helen had always pictured her in overalls. But here she was with silky raven-black hair, dark eyes, and, next to her nostril, an astonishing mole.

"This is so messed up. Was this Peter's idea?" Helen asked.

"He got in touch, yes," Gwen said. "You know Gus has been sick, so—"

"How the hell do you know *Gus*?"

"Don't *you* know Gus?" Gwen asked.

"Yes, *I* know Gus!" Helen said, and a pair of elderly suffragettes looked their way. Helen lowered her voice. "What does Gus have to do with this?"

"Well," Gwen explained, "Gus really wanted to come to this event, given he's an amateur historian, and after he had that big Covid scare."

"He finally got into the hospital to do a real test," Peter explained.

"He didn't actually have Covid, thank god."

"But it was so sweet," Gwen continued, "how Peter said Gus really loved this era, and wanted to come up to the city and enjoy it all. I know it's unorthodox, Helen, but no one's being harmed, right? Here he is now."

It was Gus.

"Jesus Christ," Helen said.

He strode up in a burgundy suit and black top hat. Seeing Helen, he tipped it toward her and smiled broadly. It was the top hat from London.

"That's Peter's, I assume?" Helen said.

"How'd you know?" Gus said.

"If Sona's here," Helen said, "we're all fired."

"Sona's not here," Gwen said. "And she wouldn't fire us all. She definitely wouldn't fire Guillermo. She loves Guillermo."

"Not Guillermo," Helen said.

"You've never met him in person, right?" Gwen said, and hailed a tall man in an elaborately waxed beard.

"Guillermo, meet Helen," Gwen said.

Guillermo stretched his arms out for a hug, eyes closed. He was drunk. "Helen! Shit! Finally, all of us together! I can't believe—"

Helen wheeled toward Peter. "Was this you?"

"It was him!" Guillermo said. "It took your *uncle* to finally get us all together!"

Peter leaned toward Helen. "You look mad," he muttered.

"Don't you realize how stupid this is?" Helen roared. She pointed at her colleagues, one by one, like a scolding nun. "Sona *comes* to these events. She's probably somewhere with a headset and a clipboard. With every additional moron—and you're all just towering morons—you're exponentially increasing the chances we'll all get caught."

"Helen," Gwen said. "You really think she'd recognize any of us in period costumes, and half of us in masks?"

No one was wearing masks, but Helen was too angry to point this out. "Excuse me a second," she said, and pulled Peter down the hall, until they were out of earshot, under a kerosene lamp.

"Check out my monocle." He pulled a monocle from his front pocket and tried to secure it in his eye socket. "I only have eye for you," he said.

"You're an idiot," she said. "I could lose my job. We have to get everyone to leave." Helen thought desperate thoughts. She could pull a fire alarm. Did they have fire alarms in 1915? She wanted to smash Peter's head with the kerosene lamp.

"Helen. Helen," Peter said, taking both her hands in his. "Nothing matters right now. You know this. Sona knows this, too. We have another year, at least, before anything matters again."

"It does matter," Helen said. "It matters to me, now."

"No. It's an experiment right now," he said. "We're experimenting. We're emerging, and no one cares, and everyone understands." He squeezed her hands and smiled. His eyes were so old, so bright.

"I'm leaving," Helen said.

She walked the length of the glittering Palace and burst through the front doors. The sun had recently set and the sky was streaked with a garish pink. She wanted only to get into her car and drive home. She was halfway to the parking lot, in her corset and hoop dress, before she realized she'd forgotten her street clothes inside the Palace. She doubled back and stomped through the basketball court, where she found her clothes neatly bundled up and tucked under a divan, next to the parasol.

It had to have been Barbara. Oh, Barbara. Her kindness took Helen's legs. She had to sit down on the divan. Okay, she thought. People aren't all terrible. Now she just had to make it home.

She gathered her belongings and went back into the night, the sky nearly black now, and crossed under the highway and rushed toward the beach, still in her hoop skirt and dress. She saw her car in the distance and was so grateful she laughed.

"This way, madame," a voice said.

A man in a gray tuxedo was suddenly in front of her, and with white-gloved hands was directing her to a colonnade of torches positioned on the beach. He seemed to be some kind of helper working the event.

"I'm heading home," she said. "Just getting my car."

"You know, you really should see this," the man said, abandoning all formality. "Fireworks start in a few minutes, and then they're doing a sort of sea battle on the bay. Lots of cannons and fake destruction. I saw the rehearsal earlier and it was bonkers."

Helen stood, breathing heavily. She really wanted to see all those things. She didn't want to start driving. The beach looked so calm. And there was probably a bar.

"See the cabana just over there?" the man asked. "That's for guests of the Pan-Pacific party. Get a drink and sit and watch the show."

It was so dark now that no one would see her, much less recognize her, not even Sona. So she tramped over to the cabana, where she found about thirty people dressed like her, and a latticework of overhead lights, and behind the bar, Terri. She was dressed in a snug white blouse, just as Helen had pictured and hoped for. Helen stopped breathing, watching Terri move, taking in her bright, cherubic face. Beyond, in the silver bay, two ships destined to fake-destroy each other were sailing slowly into place. Go, Helen told herself. But she couldn't move. She could only think about going home.

Then the first cannon fired. The sound was a crack—almost an accidental crack—then an assertive boom. People gasped, laughed. Then the second ship fake-fired back—but god it seemed real, Helen thought—and soon the cannons were exchanging fire with abandon, white flashes illuminating the burgeoning gun smoke. People clapped, screamed with delight. It was madness, totally unnecessary and reckless in every way. And because the aural plane had been busted open, and people were shrieking approvingly at a feigned sea battle full of fire and the delightful memory of bodies blown apart, Helen thought, Well, shit. She felt suddenly feral and free, so walked quickly, directly up to Terri's bar, snuck up behind her, put her hands on her hips, and said, "Hey, bartender."

Terri spun and swept her eyes all over Helen—her hair, dress, shoes, eyes again, lips. She threw her arms around Helen and squeezed her with bewildering strength, and Helen was so grateful to have left her house. There were so many things outside the house. Fuck my house, she thought. Over Terri's shoulder, the ship battle continued, the cannons sounding, the smoke rising, fire overtaking one ship's ghostly sails.

"How did you know I was here?" Terri asked.

"I didn't," Helen said. "I just had an invitation."

"Oh god, I'm hyperventilating," Terri said. "You look gorgeous."

She grabbed Helen's lower back and pulled her close, and their mouths took each other, lunged tongues and tasted each other, swallowed worlds and ended time. Finally Terri pulled away and composed herself. "So will you stay here with me? Pretend to bartend. Stay for the fireworks! Can you stay with me out here? It's not too weird?"

"No, no, no, no," Helen said. "I can definitely stay. I want to stay out here. I'm staying."

E. K. Ota

The Paper Artist

I F THAT WAS THE CASE, she wasn't to come back to them again. Muneo made this clear to his daughter in the front room of his parents' house, just north of Shimogamo Shrine. It was the house he'd been born in fifty-four years earlier; the house he'd lived in with his wife, Masako, for the past twenty-four years. His father and mother, no longer alive, were framed in pictures above the altar—large photographs, the black ink turned to a faded purple from years of exposure. Their expressions were unsmiling, severe.

She had shamed them, he continued. She had not only gotten herself pregnant, she had done it with a foreigner, a foolish one, by the looks of it, low-class and without prospects.

He did not look at the man his daughter had brought to them, who kept saying, in English, "What's going on, Mana?" and imploring her to interpret. He did not look at his daughter. When Masako had brought them in, he'd been gazing out at the garden, and he hadn't turned around to face them when they knelt down on the tatami in the formal *seiza* position. It was June, the rainy season. Since morning, water had drizzled from the low, stifling skies onto the rocks and pine and moss, turning everything darker and more vibrant. The hydrangeas were in bloom. Heavy raindrops slipped off bright blue clusters of flowers the size of human heads. Beneath the rain and heat, they bowed.

"If you don't take care of the baby and get rid of this man, don't think that you are welcome to show your face here again."

Mana looked at her father's erect back as he stared out into the garden. He was a small man but powerfully built, with a strong jaw and thick, black hair threaded with gray. His shoulders were still; she knew that if he had turned to meet them, she wouldn't have seen anger flashing in his eyes, his face contorted with rage. Her father was the master of control. He could sit *seiza* for hours. Once, when she was in elementary school and still in the habit of trying to please him, she had worked all day on a watercolor picture of an iron wind bell shaped like a frog. She had eagerly taken it to her father, who was in his studio at the back of the house. In their neighborhood and throughout Japan, even in countries she'd only read about in picture books, he was known as the paper artist. He was famous. By the time she was ten, she'd gleaned this, though it was mysterious how his many hours sequestered in solitude in the back room translated into recognition around the world.

"Father, look at what I made," she had said, bringing the watercolor picture to his desk, where he sat hunched over his work. She presented it to him gravely, but inside there was more than a little bit of excitement as he studied it beneath the lamplight. Instead of offering a comment, though, he had lifted the blade that was already in his hand and begun to rapidly slice slivers and strips of paper until the wind chime was almost completely cut away. He'd created a bird, she saw when he handed it back, its wings outstretched and flapping, tiny feathers scattered across the page. It looked alive. Its body seemed to move as it swiped at the bell with its wings and tugged with its thin, bony feet at the paper strip attached to the string dangling from the clapper. Her father had held the picture out without bothering to look at her.

The message was clear: her work had been unworthy; she was dismissed; she was not to disturb her father with such insignificant attempts again. Compared to the dramatic fury of the bird, her wind bell had seemed dull, heavy with unconvincing lines.

In the low, dim room, Mana raised her voice in protest, but hurling words at her father was as satisfying as throwing stones at water. He didn't turn around. He continued to stare out at the garden. When she started weeping and her words were choked up with tears, he asked her if she was done. Though he couldn't see her, she nodded. Was it true that she didn't want to get rid of the baby? Yes. Was it true that she purported love for this man? The man she'd brought to present to her father was looking in alarm at her tear-streaked face and tried to hold her hand, but Mana shrugged him off and wiped at her eyes with a piece of balled-up tissue. Already, the love and the passion she'd felt just the night before were fading beneath her father's derision. For as long as she could remember, he'd had that kind of power: whatever delight she found shriveled beneath his dismissive eyes. She hated him for it. This time, though, she wouldn't capitulate. This time, she wouldn't give him the satisfaction of turning her weaknesses into a pitiable parade. "Yes," she said, in answer to his question.

"Then we have nothing more to discuss."

"You were too hard on her," Masako said quietly after they had gone. She was clearing up the half-drunk cups of tea, the untouched sweets left behind on the lacquer tray she'd brought out for Mana and her boyfriend. Her husband was exacting. The precision that turned into a gift in his hands every time he created a sculpture out of paper and light and air was eviscerating in relationships. He was a proud man, pleased with nothing short of excellence in his own work and, by extension, his family. When he was young and not yet famous, he had made her an intricate paper necklace that she still had in one of her drawers, safeguarded in a glass box lined with velvet. Strands of delicate leafy vines and curled tendrils as fine as baby's hair were woven together, along with impossibly perfect passionflowers and hummingbirds that had made her smile in surprise when she first saw them. He had painted every single leaf and petal, and the hummingbirds had ruby throats, green wings flecked with real gold. Everything gleamed, preserved under a layer of clear varnish, so delicate that Masako, after placing it in the glass box, was afraid of ever lifting it out to touch it.

She was the daughter of a Tokyo government official. A slim woman with smooth skin and ink-black hair swept into a French twist, who managed to look cool and unperturbed despite the dreary heat of the rain. She had the subtle, self-effacing kind of elegance that was best perceived in retrospect, through the lens of accumulated events, like an aurora borealis flowing through the vast silences of photographs; toward her, Muneo rarely had a censorious word. He could be gentle, kind. But her daughter suffered: it pained Masako to think of what she'd endured all these years, and there were times when she wondered if it was her fault because she hadn't interfered.

"It had to be said. She's throwing away her life; she doesn't have time for a relationship or for a child; she's on her way to becoming a famous cellist."

"'The other cellist in the orchestra had more depth.' That's what you told her the last time you heard her play in the orchestra." Masako's hands tightened on the tray as she lifted it. She was upset, but the cups didn't rattle and give her away.

"She needed to practice more. She has talent, but because of a lack of diligence, it's not brought out."

"You could have told her that."

"What?"

"That she has talent. You could have at least looked at them, acknowledged the man who will be the father of your grandchild."

"She's being foolish. It's clear that she doesn't love him."

Masako shook her head. In the days leading up to the confrontation, Mana had talked about her boyfriend, pleading for her mother to intercede on their behalf. The man had been her English tutor at the conservatory. He was thoughtful and intelligent, a writer with some success already in the States, considering his young age.

"You don't know that."

"She'll realize it soon enough."

"Do you think you know the twists and turns of a woman's heart?"

"She'll be back."

In the mornings, Muneo paid homage to his parents. He got up early, at six A.M.—the same time every morning—and went downstairs to the altar, where he lit a stick of incense, rang the brass bell, clapped his hands. His father, too, had been famous: a well-known heart surgeon in Kyoto. In the Mizukami family, talent ran through the hands, which were nimble and decisive, capable of indefatigable precision long after others were exhausted. Mana, too, had been blessed with the gift. Even before she had learned how to talk, one day she'd gotten ahold of a pair of scissors and began cutting shapes out of the tablecloth. A square, a triangle. They were almost perfect. Masako had been angry, but while she scolded Mana, Muneo had slipped the cut-out shapes into his pocket. Later, in his studio, he had taken them out again and studied them beneath the lamplight with growing excitement. He did not know, then, that though his daughter had the capability, she lacked the character to match it.

In front of the altar, a curl of smoke rose from the lit incense stick toward the framed pictures of his parents. His father had expected him to become a surgeon, not an artist. Because of that, Muneo, too, had endured his share of confrontations. But he was grateful for that now. He pressed his palms together and bowed. His father's disapproval had sharpened him, whetting his appetite for excellence. In art school, he had stayed in while all the other students drank and partied. He went to bed later and was up before dawn, working on his various creations, and not even a year after graduating, he already had an exhibit in a major Tokyo gallery. "A paragon of precision" was what a critic had written: "Mizukami Muneo's art captures the great yearning of the human spirit to shed its earthly shell: the gorgeous sensation of mystery and liberation the moment flesh expires." He'd sent the pamphlet to his father, who did not reply and did not go. Years later, though, as his father lay dying in the upstairs bedroom, he had found that pamphlet, along with one for every single exhibit he'd ever showed, in the bottom drawer of his father's desk. They were filed away neatly in folders that corresponded to different years. There were newspaper clippings as well, he saw, glued to card stock so they wouldn't get crumpled or lost. To his astonishment, he even discovered a handful of ticket stubs.

Without his father, he wouldn't be the man that he was today. Muneo thought of this as he and Masako ate breakfast. As usual, they ate in silence while they listened to music, Frank Sinatra crooning about love and the moon. It was the same breakfast they'd eaten together every day for at least a decade: a slice of toasted milk bread, a cup of salad drizzled with Pietro dressing, plain yogurt flavored with a spoonful of blueberry jam, boiled sausage. The rude sounds of their chewing were obfuscated by the music, which also liberated them from talking so early in the day. Muneo had instituted this routine at the beginning of their marriage. In the first hours after waking, when his mind was most lucid and creative, he desired the freedom to leisurely tease out ideas that had flirted with him in dreams throughout the night. He loved the mornings. He loved the light that flowed between the eyelet curtains and refracted playfully upon crystal cups and bowls and plates in the display cases lining the wall. The rest of the house was perpetually in shadow; here alone, for an hour every morning, the light poured across the table, clear and translucent and warm, alighting upon the silver spoons in a flurry of effulgence, the curve of a plate, the copper tint of the jam jar lid, before finally settling in the depths of the blueberry jam. Numerous creations were born in these moments—if not, in some way or another, all of them—which was why his family had learned long ago not to disrupt him with mundane comments.

And yet, a few weeks after Mana's visit, one morning Masako broke into his reverie before they were even halfway done with breakfast. Mana and her boyfriend were moving to New York, she told him. She picked up a piece of lettuce and lifted it daintily to her lips with chopsticks. The light streamed through the window; it struck the crystal glasses on the table and cast a delicate, phosphorescent script across her face, which, Muneo knew without even looking up, would be expressionless, no matter how her emotions writhed below the surface. Unlike Mana, who had never learned to contain her feelings, Masako could control what she felt beautifully, shaping it the way monks raked sand into flawless ripples around rocks in temple gardens.

"They're leaving tomorrow."

The yogurt in his mouth went sour.

"She said they don't know when they're coming back. They want to get married. Her boyfriend is going to graduate school."

Muneo's hand kept moving his spoon from the bowl to his mouth until it scraped the last few streaks of yogurt off the bottom, then he set it aside without comment. So. This was what his daughter had chosen. He was disappointed. But he was a man of his word, and decisions had their consequences; it was a lesson she would learn now.

At the kitchen table, Masako didn't say anything else. Her husband was a stubborn man. She knew better than to suggest that they go to the wedding: they would not visit America, and they would not see their grandchild; her husband would never relax his pronouncement, even if he was tempted to revise it. For it was his pride on the line now, and it stung him that he had been disregarded. She could see the future unfolding clearly:

the silence that would pour out of the daughter-shaped hole in the middle of their household; the grimness with which her husband would set his face toward his work, how he'd assiduously cut out Mana from every conversation with relative, friend, and acquaintance. It reminded her of the first time they'd gone to his father in order to make amends. They'd been married two years, and Masako still hadn't met his family. She'd been terribly nervous; she could still remember how her stomach had clenched when they stepped onto the stone path leading to the doorway. In front of her, Muneo had carefully held a large box wrapped in dark blue *chirimen* cloth. It was a peace offering for his father: a lampshade he'd worked on for months that revolved slowly on a little pedestal around a lightbulb. The shape of a dragon had been cut out of the creamy mulberry paper. In a darkened room, the dragon slid across the walls, each carefully crafted scale a dazzle of light, its head and fiery eyes wreathed in glowing arabesques that had taken hours to painstakingly design. One slip of the hand and the whole thing would've had to be scrapped. When he'd shown it to her the week before, Masako had been delighted. The dragon undulated around their small studio apartment, and she'd pressed herself against the wall right where the dragon's jaw gaped wide, shrieking and laughing as Muneo staged exaggerated heroics to save her. She'd been six months pregnant then. When they had knelt in front of Muneo's father in the same front room in which they'd received Mana and her boyfriend, baby Mana, still in her womb, had kicked, and she'd felt nauseous enough with fear to vomit.

"It is not much, but I hope that in this gift you will see the first fruits of my meager talent," Muneo had said in formal Japanese, stiff with the requisite self-abnegation even though Masako knew that he was intensely proud of what he had created. Muneo had taken out the lamp and turned it on to demonstrate the moving lampshade, but the room was too big and the lamp too far away for the dragon to spring to life on the walls, its limbs liquid gold and elongated. As they watched it, Masako remembered the way they had played with such childish glee just the week before in their apartment. Now, though, Muneo's face was tense and somber. Unease moved deep down, stirring the baby in her womb, until it rose, and she could feel the molten heat of it just beneath her skin. In the large front room, so austere and spotless, the dragon had seemed subdued, much smaller and meeker than it had appeared in their apartment. After a few more revolutions, Muneo reached down and turned the lamp off, and the silence stretched and reverberated with unspoken emotion.

"Never in my life," began his father finally, in the low, controlled voice that Muneo would one day use with his own daughter, "did I think that a son of mine would become the maker of toys for children."

Masako kept in touch with Mana.

In October, she received a picture of Mana dressed in a lovely white dress with a satin skirt, a beaded and lacy sweetheart bodice. "It was a small wedding," Mana wrote. "Only Charlie's mom and stepdad came from Connecticut. A few of his college friends who live in the city attended as well." She described the lemon-raspberry wedding cake, drizzled with lemon syrup, each layer interspersed with buttercream, raspberries, or lemon curd (so sour, Masako thought, so rich), and she told Masako of her first visit to the home of Charlie's mom. "There were pictures of the family on all the bookcases and on the refrigerator and all over the walls!" she wrote, noting how different that was from Japan, where most households didn't put anything on the walls, except, perhaps, a calendar; family pictures were often formal portraits taken under the bright lights of a studio, touched up later so that everyone had perfectly glowing complexions. But in America, people tacked up photos of everything—a kid eating an ice-cream cone with chocolate smeared all over his face; toddlers rolling around on the grass in their diapers with the family dog; people with wide-open mouths and blurry bodies as they guffawed.

"Charlie's mom gave us a set of pots and pans," Mana continued, and Masako could almost hear her smile: "It was a shock for his mom to see him come back from Japan with a pregnant girlfriend who is now suddenly his wife, but she was kind to me. During dinner, Charlie's stepdad stood up and made a toast and teared up so much, he had to bring out a handkerchief to blow his nose."

The picture of the baby came in December. "Rina is her name," Mana wrote. "In America, babies are bundled up tightly in a cloth—'swaddled' they call it. They come out of the hospital like that with a little cotton cap. I think it looks terribly hot, and it seems Rina thinks so as well. Whenever I go to check on her, she has always managed to free one, if not both, of her arms."

Rina was an easy baby; she slept often. Mana, in contrast, had been fussy from the very beginning. Masako remembered how she would rock her daughter throughout the night. Every time it seemed as if it would be possible to lay Mana down, the moment Masako moved just a little bit, Mana would start crying. All she ever wanted was to be held and held.

"The baby's name is Rina," Masako reported to Muneo. The pucker around his mouth deepened, as if drawn tight as a drawstring bag around its contents. He made a sound in his throat as a substitute for acknowledgment, then pushed back his chair and cleared his plates from the breakfast table. He had work to do; he was preparing a new sculpture for a museum in London.

In his studio, it was hard for Muneo to concentrate. The work was delicate, demanding. He knelt on the floor, cutting out a tiger from a giant piece of washi paper. At the museum, the tiger would prowl above the museum guests, suspended from transparent nylon threads.

Its body was extremely fine, made out of swirling gold and black wisps and swells, graceful as ink seeping through water. It was his most ambitious work yet. Like his father, he used scalpel blades, which were thinner and sharper than razors, but they blunted so quickly that he had to change them every few minutes.

"*Otto,*" Muneo said, the second time he nearly accidentally sliced through a connecting segment. He sat back on his haunches. His hands were shaking with frustration. The bud of pressure in his chest that had materialized when Masako told him about the baby had been steadily inflating all morning. Muneo closed his eyes. For a few minutes, he focused on regulating his breathing. When his father was in the middle of a surgery, to be distracted was not an option. And so it was with him as well. Muneo lifted his scalpel and bent down.

In the beginning, Masako received messages and emails with pictures of the baby almost daily. Gradually, though, the communication from Mana started to taper off. By the time Rina was four, a month could pass without Masako hearing a word.

The messages that did come concerned Masako, even though the content was lighthearted, punctuated with exclamation points and playful emojis, funny anecdotes about Rina. Her daughter's address had changed three times since she had moved to New York, and after each move, the frequency in her communication dropped a little more. She had talked about Charlie and his mom and stepdad often in their first year of marriage, but after a while, Masako noticed that she didn't mention them. The insouciant tone of her daughter's emails felt forced: curated, Masako thought to herself when she'd finally asked after Charlie and had received a lengthy email back about a trip to the beach and how Rina had found a crab. Charlie, it seemed, had not gone on the trip, but Masako couldn't be sure because he simply was not mentioned.

After the sixth year, though, a melancholy note began to creep into Mana's stories and observations. Sometimes, she could see rats scuttling along the train tracks in the subways. In the winters, the snowbank next to their apartment got filthy if it didn't melt because it was next to a bar and accumulated the ash and cigarette butts from all the people smoking. The public bathrooms were sticky, and her upstairs neighbors sounded as if they were constantly dropping dishes and moving furniture across their floor. For the first time, Masako learned that when Rina was born, they'd lived down the street from the fire department. Though Rina was a good baby, the sirens woke her up almost every hour.

"Remember the wind bell you used to have in the garden?" Mana reminisced at the end of one particularly morose email. "The one made out of iron, shaped like a frog? Remember how you used to take it down at night so that it wouldn't wake up the neighbors? It seems outlandish to think of that now. In America, everyone and everything is so loud. The thing I remember most about home is the quiet."

"Please, come home and visit," Masako wrote back. "It's been over six years. I'd like to see you and my granddaughter."

"You know I can't" came Mana's reply, via LINE. "Father won't like it."

"Don't worry about him."

"He hasn't emailed or called me once."

"You don't have to see him."

"I've quit playing the cello. I've disappointed him."

"He'll be in London for two weeks at the end of March. I'll buy you and Rina a ticket. It'll be our secret." Masako's heart beat quickly against her chest, her fingers hesitating just a moment before she pressed send.

A day passed without a reply. Then another and another. Then finally, on Friday, she saw Mana had sent a message.

"Okay," it read. "We will come."

It felt like an affair, this meeting with Mana and Rina—a lover's assignation.

When Muneo was home, he and Masako had a set routine. They hardly went out to eat because he was always working. Also, he thought that eating outside was a frivolous waste of money when you could eat at home exactly what you wanted. He didn't cook. He didn't wash the dishes. He held the traditional convictions in their marriage that the woman was supposed to manage the household, freeing the man up to work and think. For her part, Masako was an excellent housekeeper, committed to cleanliness, a simple and elegant aesthetic, and an avoidance of excess. She herself had raised objections on occasion if they were visiting another city and Muneo wanted to take her to a fancy restaurant. Her family, though wealthy once, had fallen on hard times when she was a child. Since then, frugality had become her prevailing reflex, fueled by the understanding that all you have could be stripped away in an instant, so it was a good idea to be prepared. Still, she would have liked to eat out once in a while at the teahouses in Gion, to enjoy the grilled sweet eel at Kane-yo downtown.

In the weeks before Mana and Rina's visit, it occurred to her that finally, here was an occasion that made it permissible to do so. It was Rina's first time in Japan—how much there was to show her in Kyoto! As Masako vacuumed the first floor and took the comforters up to the balcony to beat out the dust, she felt flutters of excitement. When Mana was growing up, Masako had been careful not to spoil her. It was different with Rina, though. Who knew when she would be able to come back to Japan again? Who knew when Masako would get another chance to show her everything she loved?

That spring, when Muneo returned from London, he sensed that something had changed, but he couldn't put a finger on what it was. They took their meals and their midmorning tea at the same time as always. On Tuesdays and Thursdays, Masako held a flower-arranging class in the front room on the first floor. She went to the grocery store every other morning, and on Fridays, she volunteered at the neighborhood senior center, where the gathered elderly sang songs and heard presentations on safety from policemen. He could always tell when it was Masako coming home; there was the sound of her feet touching the ground as she dismounted from her bicycle; the strained exhalation, *yokkoisho,* as she lifted it onto the front step and placed it neatly next to his at the side of the entryway; the rattle of the door opening and closing; her feet shuffling into slippers; the creaking of the wooden floors as she moved through the hallway, and her voice carried to the back room where he worked, announcing that she was home.

Life continued on as before, and yet there was something ever so slightly off. Sometimes, if he came out of his studio unexpectedly, he found her in the living room, sitting on the floor, the glossy spread of a magazine open on the coffee table in front of her, although she wasn't looking at it. Instead, she gazed out the window, her features soft and dreamy in the muted glow of the light. If he made his presence known, she'd start and hurriedly gather up the magazine, saying brightly that here she was caught in a daydream when there was so much work to be done. Then she'd disappear upstairs, and he'd hear the balcony door open so that she could take in the washing.

Was he imagining it, or had her face been slightly pink when she'd stashed away the magazine? As if she were about to cry or had had a sip of alcohol. Muneo had never seen Masako drunk, and only once had he seen her cry. Years ago, her mother had gone to bed early one night, complaining of stomach problems, and died in her sleep from a heart attack. Masako and her mother had been close. When the news came, though, startling them in the early morning, she had not immediately given herself over to emotion. Instead, she had traveled over three hours by train to Chiba to make the necessary funeral arrangements; she had gone through the address book and called her relatives and her mother's friends. It was only after the funeral, when the new gravestone had been erected on a sunny slope that brought out its polish, that she allowed herself to grieve—silently, discreetly; she stood next to windows, staring outside, back turned to the people around her so as to disguise her tears until they dried. She did not convulse or give herself over to wailing like other women; not even her shoulders shook, Muneo remembered. There were just a few trickles, like stray raindrops. That was all.

"Whatever happened to that *hanten* I gave you?" Masako asked him out of the blue one night, and it took him a minute to figure out what she was talking about. It had been her gift to him before they'd even gotten married. They had met in Tokyo, at a gallery displaying his art. She had not known that he was the artist, and so when he approached her and asked her what she thought, she'd spoken candidly about how she could feel the yearning in the work, the great longing that the artist had encapsulated, but that it swept through the mind, brushed the soul, and couldn't quite penetrate the heart. Though that was to be expected, she supposed: she'd heard the artist was quite young. Then she'd asked him, jokingly, if paper artists got a lot of paper cuts. Muneo had held up his hands. For a long moment, she simply stared, then her eyes widened, and he saw the bright gleam of surprise before she bowed with a laugh.

They had met up almost weekly after that, for tea or dinner, or to walk in the park. Masako worked at a department store. For Muneo's birthday that first December together, she had bought him a *hanten,* and he wore the short cloth coat throughout the winter for years, until the fabric was soft and pilled and there were a few cigarette-sized holes in the sleeves from the days when they used to read and smoke in bed together. Some nights, Masako would fix them *monjayaki,* and while the cabbage and noodles and corn fried in a batter, they would turn on the radio and listen to jazz and drink beer—Masako only a few sips; Muneo downed one bottle after another until every centimeter of his body, from his toes to his eyelids and the tips of his ears, turned bright red, as if he'd been slapped or boiled alive.

Remembering this, it struck Muneo that those handful of years in his twenties had been an aberration; separated from his parents and intoxicated with his first professional success, the jittery excitement of his new relationship, he had given himself over to whimsy and excess in a way he hadn't before or since.

"The *hanten*?" Muneo said in response to her question. It was night and they were sitting in the living room, watching television. Muneo had already taken a bath, and his skin was clean and warm beneath his cotton pajamas. "Now that I think about it, I haven't seen it for years. Why do you ask?"

Masako absentmindedly patted at her flushed cheeks and forehead with the thin, damp towel that hung around her neck. Her eyes were on the television. They were watching a program about the food in foreign countries. Tonight, the feature was on poutine, a concoction of french fries and cheese curd and gravy enjoyed in Canada. "Just wondering," said Masako. "That's all."

Later that week, when Muneo was working in his studio, the memory of what had happened to the *hanten* suddenly came floating back to him. He'd gotten rid of it when they had moved into his parents' house. By then, his mother had already passed away, and his father, quite ill, was nearing the point where it was possible that he would join her.

"Are you sure you want to do this?" asked Masako when he told her he was thinking that they should go back to Kyoto. It was one of the few times in their marriage when she'd questioned his decision, but he explained that it was only a matter of course that he, the only son, should take up the responsibility of caring for his father. He believed in duty, in filial piety, in regarding his father with respect and honor, no matter what was said and done. Masako nodded quietly. She felt a twinge of trepidation but also admiration for Muneo and the strength of his conviction to do what was right no matter what the cost. Though it was thought of, Muneo's dragon lamp was not brought up between them. For years, Muneo didn't know what had happened to it. Then one day, he bumped into a woman from the neighborhood whom he knew by sight but had never talked with. She bowed politely and smiled, and they chatted about inconsequential topics. "I could never properly thank you," she said as they were about to part, "but the lamp you made was spectacular. Your father gave it to us as a gift when my son Taro was a boy. It helped him through many nights." Muneo looked at her in surprise. Her words blew through him, conjuring the sudden static of emotion. So this is what had happened. He'd wondered. For a little while, even, he'd had the fantasy that his father had secreted it away, only to take it out once in a while and view it privately at night. Up close, the workmanship was stunning. His father would have seen that.

The woman explained that as a child Taro had frequently suffered from nightmares, but having the dragon in his room was like having a personal guardian. His father was a great man, she added: they missed him. She shook her head sadly. He waited for her to say more. What had his father said when he'd given her the lamp? Did he say anything about his son? Muneo found these questions filling him with yearning, the way the wind fills a sail and carries it over unfathomable depths. Later, in his studio, he had remembered the way the woman's eyes changed as she looked at him. How the pleasantries had faded from her lips and she had taken him in, the barely suppressed emotion in his face, the way he had stuttered as he tried—and failed—to ask his questions, overcome by too much eagerness and longing and fear. He was not like his father: he had seen this understanding sink into her demeanor as the softness in her initial greeting dissipated and was replaced by the shiny, deflective kind of cheerfulness presented to strangers. He was not dignified like his father, the doctor—Muneo had read the thought that went through her mind: no, there was something wild about him, loose. But what did she expect after all? Of an artist?

In October, Masako was diagnosed with cancer. For a few months, she'd suffered from a persistent cough that worsened as time went on, and when she went to the doctor to get an X-ray, it revealed that the cancer was not only in her lungs but had spread to the rest of her body.

It was a strange autumn. In the garden, their Yoshino cherry tree was blooming, the first time it had ever done so out of season. Masako called it lovely, a gift in this time of suffering. Muneo thought otherwise. That it would bloom at this time of the year was unnatural and unnerving, and, according to the news, the phenomenon was being replicated elsewhere throughout Japan. Because the end-of-summer typhoons had stripped off all the leaves and the weeks that followed were unusually warm, the trees had been tricked into thinking it was spring; but the buds were few and sickly looking, as if there was something deep down that resisted the delusion.

Masako declined quickly. Her body wasted away, her smooth complexion growing rugged around her nostrils and mouth, her eyes sinking into shadowy sockets. Muneo learned to read the level of her discomfort in the corners of her lips, the furrows between her brows. From time to time, he patted her face with a cool towel or fed her ice chips with a spoon.

The prospect of losing her frightened him. Sometimes, in the shadowy hour of early evening, he felt terror run its icy fingers up his arms and tap on his heart like a pianist playing scales, toying with his emotions. It had been Masako who had urged him to keep going after his father's rejection. Masako had held him steady all these years; she alone knew how to read the minute vibrations that a subtle smile, a turn of the head, a pressed-thin lip generated in the warp and weft of a long marriage. There was no one as sensitive and incisive as Masako, no one as elegant or calm or tactful.

"Your mother is dying," he began the email to his daughter one morning after he found Masako coughing up blood. But then he stopped, perplexed and angry. He didn't know how to go on. The silence between them had built up like scar tissue over the years, and it was hard to cut through it now. It was important for his daughter to see her mother, though. He sensed this, no matter how much it grated against his pride, and time was running out. For Masako's sake, then, he set his face toward his objections, the way he'd done with exhaustion and disappointment and his father's censure before that, and grimly, he shouldered through them to the other side. "Come home," he wrote at last. "Your mother needs you. It's been long enough."

His daughter never replied.

In the aftermath of Masako's death, he threw himself into his work, pouring everything into his most ambitious sculpture yet: a muscular curve sweeping through the air like a smooth twist of metal, only it was made out of paper—millions of tiny granules that looked like sand. The middle of it was unbroken, solid, but at each end, the pale white grains of paper began to disperse, as if flung into the air, the way the ocean flings froth every time it flounces its heavy blue skirt. It was grueling, painstaking work. For hours nonstop, Muneo worked in his studio, wearing a surgical mask so that his breath wouldn't scatter each individually rolled particle of paper.

The sculpture debuted to great acclaim in New York in May. It was the height of Muneo's success. At the opening, he drank wine with the guests, maintaining the stoic silence he was famous for. "Stately," he had once been described as in a newspaper in London, and ever after, he had cultivated this persona, though in reality, he often felt ill at ease at these events, was afraid of speaking and betraying his awkward English.

The sculpture truly was sublime, though. As he stood in front of it before the opening of the show, he wished Masako were there to see it. Was this not finally a work of art that embodied the soul—the heart's swift-flowing and ecstatic but transient passions?

He thought of her often.

Though Muneo had always despised maudlin displays of emotion, he was beginning to understand how it was possible now. Thoughts of Masako always brought the tears close to the surface until his face felt puffy; although, after the initial wave of grief, he never cried. She had been a wonderful wife, a necessary companion to a stubborn and difficult husband. He knew that now. In the mornings before the altar, immense gratitude and respect welled up within him when he gazed at her calm and lovely countenance in the photograph that had been set up next to his parents', the ink still deep and fresh, and the feeling lingered with him as he went about his day.

His daughter he did not think of. His daughter he deemed unworthy of his attention.

And then—the letter came.

Dear Mr. Mizukami, it began in formal Japanese. *I apologize for my impertinence in sending you this letter even though you do not know me. I know it is the height of presumption to ask you such a personal question as this, but are you by any chance Mana Mizukami's father?*

The letter, written by a woman named Sayoko, went on to say that she had seen a brochure for his exhibit in New York (which she had attended and thoroughly enjoyed), and it occurred to her that he and Mana Mizukami might be related. If so, she felt it incumbent on her to notify him that Mana had been killed in a car accident the previous fall. Sayoko was the owner of a Japanese restaurant in Manhattan, and Mana had worked for her for the past three years, over the course of which they had become friends. When the accident happened, Sayoko did not know whom to contact, for Mana had spoken rarely of her family, and Sayoko did not have her family's contact information. Also, Mana had already divorced her husband when she had started working at the restaurant, and he was proving difficult to find. It had been a conundrum that Sayoko had agonized over for months, until she saw the brochure for Mr. Mizukami's exhibit and dared to believe that it was a miraculous answer to her prayer, for she remembered a conversation in which Mana had mentioned that her father was a paper artist. If he and Mana Mizukami were not related, she hoped that he would forgive her thoughtless intrusion into his life. She knew that he was a famous man, and very busy, and she did not want to burden him with the tragic incidents of other people's lives. If, however, they were related, she expressed her heartfelt condolences. She also desired to ask him what his wishes were pertaining to Mana's daughter, Rina. For the time being, Sayoko and her husband had guardianship of her. The girl was very sweet and quiet, and while they would very much like to continue to care for her in memory of her dear mother, both their time and their means were limited, as they had their business to attend to and two other children to raise, and it was also her belief that children flourished best when they were with family.

If it is true that you are Mana's father, please forgive me for the extended delay in relaying this unfortunate news, the letter concluded. *During Mana's time in New York, I have witnessed her persevere through many hardships with grace and courage; it is not easy to be a single mother in a foreign country. I was honored by her friendship and am grieved that a light like hers was snuffed out so early from this world. With utmost respect, Sayoko.*

In June, the child arrived. Her hair was light brown, slightly curled and frizzy around the temples; her cheeks were pink, but the rest of her face was very pale, and her eyes were slanted and dark and somber.

Their first night together, Muneo boiled instant noodles and flavored them from a packet that came in the package.

Across from him, the girl ate diligently. He was relieved that she knew how to use chopsticks, although she sucked up one noodle at a time, pausing in the middle to take a bite and chew before continuing on.

"In Japan, it's good to make noises when you eat noodles," Muneo told her, trying to make conversation, and he lifted a bundle of noodles from his bowl with his chopsticks and slurped them down whole in demonstration. He made a satisfied sound. "Like that," he said. "You don't even have to chew them. They just slide all the way down your throat into your stomach."

She stared at him. Then turned back to her bowl and continued progressing through her meal, noodle by noddle, in silence.

Was this how it was going to be from now on? The prospect of seeing Rina daily—of figuring out how to feed her and entertain her and take care of her when she was sick—made him tired and frightened. He had not been successful with Mana; did he dare think he could be so with her daughter?

More than ever, he wished that Masako were there beside him.

"What did you say?" In the aftermath of Rina's words, Muneo looked at his granddaughter, dumbfounded. They were sitting in front of the altar and Muneo had pointed out his parents' pictures and Masako's, who he had just told Rina was her grandma.

"I know," Rina repeated. "I met her before."

At the tone of her voice, the premonition of some feeling began to leak into Muneo's body, raising the little hairs on his arms before he understood why.

"You mean you saw her? Your mother had a picture of her that you used to look at? In New York?"

The little girl shook her head. "No, I *met* her."

"Where?"

"Here."

Muneo sat up straighter, felt an ice-cold finger clicking its nail all the way down his spine. Here? It was impossible. Had the girl seen a ghost?

"When? This past week? Last night?"

Sensing the agitation in his voice, the girl shook her head and went quiet, looking at the brass bell she held in her hands. She ran a finger around its lip.

A cloud of dimly perceived questions and observations began to gather in Muneo's thoughts, to coalesce and meld. He remembered that he had detected something different about Masako the spring before when he had come back from London, that she had seemed somehow, inexplicably, to be both grieving and happy. And then there was the girl herself. Ever since coming the week before, she had been at ease in the house, oddly so, not needing him to explain where the bathroom was and knowing where to find cups when she wanted water. At the grocery store, she had quickly found a package of azuki bean cakes that Masako had often bought, and on the way back home, she had seen a neighbor woman and waved. He had not thought much about it before, and yet now, little things accumulated and rearranged themselves into meaning in his mind. Their whole, long marriage—no, since that day he had met Masako at the museum, and she had told him exactly what she thought, and he held up his hands—they had hidden nothing from each other. Had they not?

"Is she coming back?" Rina asked, looking up again at the photograph, and he told her no, her grandmother was gone, and his granddaughter, accustomed to loss, nodded.

"Were the cherry trees blooming? When you saw Grandma?" he inquired, later, over lunch, after his emotions had stabilized. All morning, the thoughts had flickered and darted within him, but he kept them deep down beneath the surface; when he spoke, his voice was neutral, lightly inquisitive.

"Yeah," she said.

"And your mother was here, too, in this house?" he asked, after hesitating a moment.

Rina nodded.

Do you think you know the twists and turns of a woman's heart? His wife's words from long ago came floating back to him, and Muneo shivered in the warm, brightly lit kitchen. He had wanted to teach his daughter a lesson; he had wanted her to make something of herself, something she could be proud of. If he'd had a son, perhaps it would have been different. But a daughter—he gazed at Rina with apprehension.

"What did you do? When you were here?"

They had gone to a park, she said, with a big slide; they had eaten strawberry parfaits and gone to a temple and had shaved ice beneath a big umbrella: he imagined the three of them laughing together, the affection rushing strong and sweet and indestructible between them. Just as he had cut out Mana, so they had cut him out—and he hadn't even known.

You betrayed me, he accused Masako's portrait when he went to the altar next, and it sickened him to think that she had gone behind his back, that Masako and Mana had eaten together in the kitchen and given thanks that he was not there, swapping stories of his ridiculous pride, his awful intransigence. They would have told Rina that he was an artist; they would have allowed her to take a peek into his studio and would have picked up his tools and said it was too bad that people celebrated his talent even when they didn't know that it sprang from such a difficult, unworthy man.

Why didn't you say anything? he implored Masako silently, after the anger had given way to confusion, and he studied his wife's serene eyes, her gracious mouth, a face that was given to neither malice nor deception, and even as his chest grew leaden with the question, already he knew it was because he had not asked; he had not wanted to know; out of necessity as much as punishment, she had nurtured a secret life that had carried her and their daughter far away from him even before she died.

He could choose bitterness. But he would need every ounce of strength he had left to create a future that he and Rina could live in: this was the thought that went through him during the days that followed as he listened to Rina say, yes, she enjoyed going to the Golden Temple, yes, she would like to go to the bamboo forest again and to see the monkeys in Arashiyama, and that Grandma's omelet rice was the best thing she'd ever had, that Grandma had made it for her twice and decorated it with a happy face made out of ketchup.

As she spoke, she swung her legs and nodded her head. She had Mana's chin, Masako's eyes. Looking at her, Muneo felt his throat go swollen, his face tight.

It was so fun, seeing the monkeys at Arashiyama! Rina said, more talkative, it seemed, with every day that went by, and Muneo nodded, calm now, as a path through the summer began unfolding before them. In the right light, this, too, could be seen as a gift, was his thought as they sat together in the kitchen, eating noodles seasoned from a packet. Next week, they would see the monkeys. The week after that, they would go to the river and eat shaved ice. Maybe, he might even try making omelet rice sometime.

Yes, he said softly, tracing the edges of all those missing days.

He bet it was fun without him.

Tom Crewe

The Room-Service Waiter

THEY FOUND HIM where he had always been, living quietly on the rue Fournier. It was August. The man sitting across from Charles was a curator at the Louvre called Monsieur DuPont. He wore large rubbed spectacles and smoked seven cigarettes during the time he was in the house. His hair had sparks of gray in it—new ones leapt out when he turned his head in the sunlight bearing through the window. The cigarette smoke, ascending, was gold tinged; Charles was reminded of misty mornings when he was a child in Normandy, how the sun would glow behind the mist, and the cows sidle through like gods.

He told M. DuPont about these mornings. He was aware he did this often now, telling people things they hadn't asked to know. (He was getting old, past sixty.) In response, M. DuPont asked polite questions about his childhood—it suited his purpose, Charles realized, because it led him up to the hotel: When had Charles come to Paris? How had he got the job at Le Meurice? Did he remember his first meeting with the artist, Soutine?

M. DuPont was on his third cigarette. The room was a misty morning in Normandy. Charles was in a back corridor, a tray in his hands, cups shuddering, a streak of cold coffee running to the rim.

Did he remember the first meeting? He remembered the room. The smell of paint. His voice? Hard to say; he wasn't good with voices, he'd never been able to do impressions. He couldn't put his finger on the first time, no. Did he remember how he'd been asked? How many times, roughly, they had seen each other before then? It couldn't have been often, because Charles wasn't used to him yet, and you did get used to guests if they stayed long enough. Monsieur Soutine had asked very straightforwardly, man to man, like making any sort of deal; except Charles was young, he hadn't bartered the price up, but simply accepted what was offered. He would have done it for nothing, he suspected, knowing himself as he was then. It was exciting, having your portrait painted—it would be exciting now, still. He'd been flattered; he'd showed off about it to his pals, not too much or it might have started to seem funny, one man painting another in his hotel room. In fact, Charles remembered M. Soutine making a point of saying that he wanted him with his clothes on, in his uniform—that the uniform was the important part. He'd supposed that was true when he'd seen the picture, though he made no claims to be a judge.

M. Soutine was quiet when he was painting. Concentrating of course. Smoked a lot—like you, M. DuPont, Charles said to him, smiling. Sang a bit, can't remember what, not singing properly anyhow, sort of mumbling to a tune, out the corner of his mouth. There was the smell of the paint. The sound—he'd got used to the different sounds, the brush sliding this way or that, fast or slow, bigger or smaller amounts. He'd liked guessing, seeing him choose one color or another: what it was for, where it was going to end up. He got it wrong both ways. He'd guess the red would be for doing his waistcoat, and then it would go too high or too low; later he saw red on his ears, and on his hands.

The pose? He'd been asked to put his hands firmly on his hips—it was the way he used to stand, after bringing the food or the wine up: "Anything more, sir?" Looking round the room, trying to spot a problem he could solve without being asked, or discern some desire he could satisfy before it was spoken. With his hands on his hips. On the lookout.

He'd liked the job: being a waiter. Had liked the hotel, taken pride in it, fussed over it; swiftly removed any marks he found, picked bits off the floor, straightened the picture frames. It pleased him. Naturally the hotel wasn't as comfortable for staff as it was for guests—the back corridors and rooms were nothing like the rest of it. But the truth was that you spent the majority of your time in the nice parts, more time than most guests, so it wasn't crazy to think it belonged to you more. And if it belonged to you, it was worth looking after.

Still, it wasn't a job for a married man. And that's what he'd been from the nineteenth of May, 1928.

He'd met Josephine at the hotel. She was a chambermaid. He was angling for her already when he'd let himself be painted by M. Soutine. He'd stood there, listening to the brush on the canvas, sniffing the paint, hands on his hips, thinking of her, surveying the future. Asking himself: what's to be done? Wondering what problem he could solve, what desire he might be the answer to. They were both curious, later, about what had happened to his portrait. Josephine always said she'd like to see it, see him as he was then, thinking of her, scheming to catch her. This was when they were first married, when they had just opened their shop selling satchels on the rue Joubert; when all their memories were of falling in love and not of everything that came after, experience piling up like dirty laundry.

After his sixth cigarette, M. DuPont produced a photograph of the painting. He hadn't done so earlier, he said, because he wanted to be absolutely certain he had the right man. Even though he could tell as soon as Charles opened the door.

M. DuPont laid the photograph delicately on the coffee table. Charles laughed and his eyes unexpectedly filled with tears, so that the colors in the picture ran. When he blinked them away it became familiar again. He'd not seen it since it was painted, in

1927, more than forty years ago. He realized how much he had forgotten. How strong and bright the colors were: a greeny-blue behind, segments of red waistcoat on his big white shirt. And what a strange shape he'd made of him! His head and his ears stretched and rolled like dough, his arms out in great hoops. But it was undoubtedly him, as M. DuPont said. He recognized his old face.

"It's wonderful," he breathed.

"Truly," said M. DuPont. "Did you think so at the time?"

"Yes," Charles said. "I thought I was very wonderful."

When M. DuPont had gone, Charles opened the window and looked out onto the street. The shadows lying across it had a warm sleepy look. There were a few regulars sitting outside the bar. A car came past and he smelled the exhaust. He fancied a drink. Turning back into the room, he stared at the photograph left for him on the coffee table. There was to be an exhibition. There were lots of pictures like his, apparently—of waiters, pastry cooks, valets, bell-boys. He'd known he wasn't the only person at Le Meurice who'd been painted, but he hadn't realized how many hotels M. Soutine visited. He was very highly esteemed as an artist now.

Charles took his wallet from his bedroom, and then went into the hall and got his jacket off the peg. He hadn't needed to be told that M. Soutine had died; he'd learned it from a newspaper during the war or just after, when lots of people were dying and it hadn't seemed so important, only a shame. He must have thought about his portrait then, but merely as something from his own life. It had stopped existing in a real sense; he'd not imagined it being anywhere in particular. Now he knew that it was on its third owner already. They called it *The Room-Service Waiter*. Strange to think: That for all these years, even with the hotel long behind him, he'd been waiting on someone. And—as he walked out into the rue Fournier with a thirst in his throat—that M. Soutine had gone on being dead, all the way up to now.

. . .

It was spring before the invitation to the exhibition opening arrived. Charles was delighted to see it—he hadn't forgotten about it, not at all. Soon after, M. DuPont telephoned and asked if Charles would mind being interviewed by a newspaper. The interviewer was a woman journalist, only a little younger than Charles, very pleasant and interested and knowledgeable about M. Soutine's life. He told her everything he'd told M. DuPont— about the smell of paint, and the sounds of the brushes, and his pose, and how M. Soutine used to sing in that mumbling way, with a cigarette jogging at the corner of his mouth. And then he added the only other significant detail he'd remembered since the summer: that when the time for each session was up, M. Soutine would make one last stroke or touch on his canvas, look at Charles and at the picture, and quietly say, "Bravo." At first Charles imagined he was saying it to him—a thank-you, for having kept so still—but eventually he realized M. Soutine was saying it to himself.

The journalist liked this anecdote. So did Charles. It had returned to him unbidden one day when he was in his shop. (And yet it was somehow still the case that he could not remember M. Soutine's voice; could hear it, and not hear it. He had begun to wonder whether anyone's voice existed in his memory, or whether memory supplied only words.) Charles said "Bravo" now whenever he achieved anything—like buying milk before he ran out, or catching something before it hit the floor. The incongruity made him smile. He was like the valet to a famous man, repeating his master's little phrases in the dusty corners of his own life.

On the night of the opening, Charles dressed in his best suit. It was true, he thought again, looking in the mirror, that he was recognizably the same man as in the painting, even if in reality his head was a normal shape and size. He did not look so bad for his age. He still had his hair, and it had kept its color. He tweaked his red tie. His fingers were still nimble.

When he entered the gallery rooms, he could see M. DuPont standing at a distance. There was a huge number of people, far more than Charles was expecting. The noise was deafening, similar to a crowd walking down to a football game. The pictures hung back against the walls like policemen, discreetly keeping an eye on things. Charles could see at once that they were all by M. Soutine. Accepting wine from a waiter, he began to look for himself, moving through the crowd and from the first room into the second—unnoticed by M. DuPont, who was gesturing knowledgeably with a cigarette.

And then there he was, the Room-Service Waiter, hands on hips. Once more Charles's eyes filled with tears; this time, one escaped down his cheek and he had to catch it with his sleeve. It made a great difference, seeing the painting rather than the photograph. It was very real. Charles was very real, he and M. Soutine both. It was a part of their past, very private, that people were looking at. He wished, suddenly, that Josephine was here. It was a part of her past she had never seen. It occurred to him that he could have invited her. He had been allowed to bring a guest and had brought no one. He had become lonely in his mind, he knew: he no longer encountered other people even in his thoughts.

A young waiter came up and refilled his glass. While he poured, Charles caught his eye and pointed. "That's me."

The waiter finished pouring and looked at the picture, then back at Charles, smiling. "That is superb," he said. "You have scarcely changed, monsieur. How old were you then?"

"Twenty-four."

"That is only two years older than I am now."

The waiter asked whether the painter was here this evening and Charles replied that he'd been dead a long time. "What did he die of?" the young man asked.

"The war," Charles said. He made a half movement and took a drink, looking at his picture. "Well, it was hard not just for Jews. Many people died. It is a long time ago, thank God."

The waiter's face was sad, touched with confusion. "Yes, monsieur. What was he like?"

Charles told him about M. Soutine saying "Bravo" to himself. The waiter grinned and looked relieved. He pointed into the room with the neck of his bottle. "He was right to say it, wasn't he, monsieur?" Charles laughed and agreed that he was. The waiter filled his glass again before he went off.

Charles stayed standing in front of his picture until he had nearly finished his wine. He decided he would go over to M. DuPont. As he tried to locate him in the throng, waiting behind people, and for groups to notice him and let him through, he paid attention to the paintings. There were the others like his own, that he knew to expect, of hotel staff in their uniforms—garish and misshapen, but smart and pleased with themselves, as he looked pleased with himself. There were also some paintings of meat, strung up—slashes of red and white on blue backgrounds. One carcass looked a little like a waiter, hung upside down without a head. Charles shook his head now; it was wonderful to have spent time in the company of this great man, but also dreadful, to have thought so little of it, of him, for so long. He didn't remember asking M. Soutine a single question, unless it was how much he was going to pay him. And he could not remember his voice.

At last he found M. DuPont, still smoking and gesticulating, with a ring of people listening to him. Charles was sufficiently confident to tap him on the shoulder while he was speaking; he turned and his face scattered into a smile beneath his spectacles.

"Ah! Monsieur Bisset! You are here!" He kissed Charles on his cheeks and introduced him to the ring of people. "This man was painted by Soutine!" The ring responded enthusiastically, constricting and asking questions: addressing some to M. DuPont that Charles could have answered, and others to Charles that were fit only for M. DuPont. M. DuPont led them over to Charles's portrait, and they all exclaimed over it. The young waiter from before topped up everyone's glasses, smiling comprehendingly. Charles told them how it had been—about the smell and the sounds, about his pose and the cigarette and the singing. He almost forgot about "Bravo" but finished with it at the end. They all laughed. "It is a wonderful detail," M. DuPont said. "The sort of detail that really lives." Then, spying someone across the room, he grasped Charles's arm. "Here is a former colleague of yours, and another subject of Soutine. I did not want to spoil the surprise of this reunion."

Charles failed to recognize the man he was reunited with. He was ugly, short, and grossly fat—his underchin swelled out and dropped to his collar like a big fleshy napkin. They shook hands, but regarded each other blankly. M. DuPont looked disappointed. "Don't you remember each other?" He glanced between them. "Monsieur Renard was a bellboy at Le Meurice. And Monsieur Bisset was a room-service waiter."

"What is your first name?" Charles asked the man. He found his ugliness oppressive—the tight, swollen face with the eyes pushed in.

"Alexandre," the man replied. "And yours?"

Charles told him, but there was no answering flicker. By means of a few more groping questions it was established that they had crossed over at the hotel probably for only a month or two. Once this was understood they relaxed. They could not have been expected to remember each other. The past was full of blame and it was a relief when it could be avoided.

The three of them went to look at Alexandre's portrait. In it he was of course dressed in red from head to foot, being a bellboy (Charles wondered what came first, the uniforms or M. Soutine's interest in the color), but otherwise it was inconceivable that the person depicted was the same one standing here. The boy in the painting, with his little black moustache, was rasher-thin, with a spindly neck.

"There's not a trace of him in you!" Charles said. He'd had another glass of wine.

Alexandre laughed. "It's nice to be reminded," he said, "of when I had a neck."

Laughing too, Charles asked Alexandre what he could recollect of M. Soutine, telling him before he could answer about "Bravo." Alexandre pursed up his big face to think and said he didn't remember M. Soutine saying that. "What about him singing, with his cigarette in his mouth?" Charles asked. Yes, Alexandre remembered that. He remembered also that M. Soutine had a habit of tapping his foot on the floor, quite hard—it had stayed with him because he used to worry about the guests in the room below. Now it was Charles's turn to think and shake his head. He remembered the sound of brushstrokes, but not a tapping foot.

Their glasses charged, they began to discuss the hotel, some of its characters and what had happened to them. M. DuPont left. After a while, Charles thought to ask whether Alexandre remembered a chambermaid, Josephine. Pretty, with red hair.

"I remember her," Alexandre said. "She was the nicest of the lot."

"I married her," Charles said. He could not help blushing.

"I remember her going away to be married," Alexandre said. "So I must remember you after all."

"Come and see my picture!" Charles almost shouted in response.

He was growing excitedly proud of it, as if it were his son and it was his wedding day.

They walked across—it was easier now that so many people had left. Charles found he was lurching, but no matter. They stood in front of his picture. "I do remember you," Alexandre said. "It is bizarre: now I see both of you, I realize you have hardly changed, and yet, before, I'd have sworn we'd never met."

Charles was grinning, though sad that he still could not recall Alexandre from the old days. But then Alexandre had got so fat, and shaved off his moustache.

"You were very handsome, very dapper," Alexandre said, still looking at Charles's picture. "We younger lads envied you."

They carried on talking and drinking. Alexandre said that he worked for the post office, and Charles told Alexandre about his shop—how he first got into the trade when a friend was offloading some leather found in the river, still wrapped up and hardly damaged. Finally, Alexandre said he had to go. Charles was very drunk. They embraced and he felt the fat on Alexandre's back rise up in pouches under the pressure of his braces. "You look terrible, you know," he said to him without malice as they came apart.

Alexandre's eyes fled farther into his face. "I know, I know," he said, waving his hands in repudiation of himself.

"This," Charles said, taking Alexandre's underchin in his hand and wagging it from side to side, "this is far too much."

Alexandre stepped out of Charles's grip. "Yes," he said, wincing. "I have disappointed myself. It is hard to explain—" Abruptly he extended his hand, rather formally. "It was nice seeing you again."

The room was almost empty. Charles watched Alexandre amble slowly through it and into the next one, like a cow crossing a field. A man had begun to sweep the floor and the lights were brighter. M. Soutine's pictures seemed stunned, to be left alone.

Charles went back to examining his portrait. As he looked, he began to cry, and this time he let the tears wend over his lips and onto his tongue. After a few minutes he stopped and felt much better. Then he staggered out. By the cloakroom he found M. DuPont and embraced him fervently, planting great salty kisses on his cheeks. "You have changed my life," he told him, crying again, "—changed it utterly."

He hailed a cab and sang loudly all the way home with the window down, drinking up the cool night air and admiring the yellow lamplight. When he got in he made himself a sandwich and sat down at the kitchen table to eat it. He was immensely happy. It recurred to him, in his benevolence, that he should have asked Josephine. He had not seen her in thirty years, though she had informed him each time she changed her address. They were only married for ten, living here on the rue Fournier. There were no children, which Charles had blamed her for, but afterward she had two from her second husband, so he presumed it was his fault after all.

He finished his sandwich and found some paper. He wrote a letter to Josephine, telling her about M. DuPont and the picture. He would be honored if she were to go with him one day to see it, as they had always wanted to. People said he was hardly changed! He was sure she would think that he was. I hope you will say yes to this invitation, he concluded: I would so much like to see you again. Forgive me, Charles.

He sealed the letter in an envelope and left it on the table. Then he walked into his bedroom and stood swaying in front of the mirror. He smoothed his hair and tightened his tie and put his hands on his hips. "Bravo," he said quietly to the empty room. "Bravo."

Madeline ffitch

Seeing Through Maps

I WAS SPLITTING WOOD at sunset when the cat jumped up on the chopping block in front of me, arched her back, and took a long piss. My axe hung in the sky. The cat stared at me, tail up. I put my axe down and squatted before her. I hitched my gown to my waist. I sent my own stream into the brown leaves. The cat narrowed and widened her yellow eyes at me, which is what cats do because they can't blink. Our eyes locked as we added our nitrogen to the landmass. She broke first, streaking back into the woods. I've never seen a cat piss or shit, not once they are out of their resentful kittenhood. Cats are private about such things. I have kept cats all my life. I say kept because my neighbor in these woods reminds me that no one can own a cat, not really. He says I should be more careful about language. He says that words have power. My hope every day is that he will leave me in peace.

I swung my axe, trying to beat the dusk. I am particular about firewood. Sometimes firewood can feel like my whole life.

Tulip poplar wants to burn but it doesn't give off much heat. I use it for kindling. It splits like a wooden xylophone. Listen for that muffled bell toll.

White elm is scarce now and red elm leaves behind clinkers.

It will do. Across the grain, it's a rich color without being ornate, which some people appreciate.

Hickory rots at the center so you can split it in a circle, like unmaking a barrel.

If it's summertime and you're cutting live trees, you're screwed. You'll be burning green wood all winter. All those long dark days your wood will spit at you, refuse to catch, need constant tending, smoke you out of your place without keeping you warm, and that's not the worst of it. The worst of it is that green wood will build up creosote in your chimney, and your chimney will catch fire, and the fire will spread to your house, and your house will burn down and what will you do then.

My neighbor in these woods has already split, seasoned, and stacked all the wood he will burn this year. He did this last spring at the first thaw, as he has done every spring for the past twenty years. I don't cut live trees anymore. When I need to warm myself, I look for standing dead. All winter, I stay one fire ahead of the cold. I've never been good at planning. I don't know what's going to happen and I don't know why. I am, however, curious.

Oak will burn all night.

Persimmon is good hard wood but let it be. Wait for the first freeze and you'll get fruit like deflated jewels.

Ash was on the chopping block in front of me, soaked in the urine of the cat. The emerald ash borer, radiant and misplaced, has killed all the ash, so what to do but fell it and watch its bark fall off like meat from the bone. Green ash burns better than any other green wood, though it's useless to learn this. You should not burn green wood and you will not find an ash tree left alive.

Midswing, I saw it. Glistening in the piss. I bent to look. A drawing. A drawing in blue ink embedded in the tree rings. Nuanced borders, detailed topography, small as a badge. I had opened a tree and inside it found a map.

My neighbor used to have a book called *Seeing Through Maps*, written in a teacherly way that set my teeth on edge. "There are no rules for making maps," the book said, clearly a trick to get you to let down your guard. Of course there are rules. You'll be likely to break them. A map, by definition, is limiting. As with a journal, or any cavalier use of text, a map may help you remember things, but also invent a way of remembering them that makes you forget everything important. Instead of a journal, I made lists so banal that they unleashed my imagination in revolt against the tiresome record of my life. Instead of maps, I stayed home. I am certain my neighbor still has that book. He never gets rid of a damn thing that makes him feel good about himself.

There were two passages I could tolerate: "A map's quality is the function of its purpose." Also: "If you are making a map for your own purposes and do not care who else can read it—or do not *want* anyone else to be *able* to read it—the map need not even be intelligible to others."

I put my face close enough to smell the ammonia. The blue lines could have been a stamp, a tattoo, an island, a spit, an isthmus, a lake, a mountain of two lopsided circles. As a map it was unintelligible to me. Which, according to *Seeing Through Maps*, meant that I was not meant to understand it.

Is what I was thinking, leaning on my axe, when my neighbor appeared at the property line. I had marked those trees with orange blazes yet still I was not left alone. I could see him there, out of the corner of my eye, his patched coat that he'd made from three other coats, his tattered hood, his dirty scarf. "Permission to cross," he said.

"Do it, then," I said, and then I saw that he held his left hand awkwardly with his right as if it were an object separate from his body, and I saw that his left thumb was hanging from his left hand and that all the darkness he was flinging around, darker than dusk, was blood.

"I'm not sure I can drive myself to the emergency room," he said, approaching. He had the pallor of someone in shock but still I could hear the recrimination in his voice. I waited to hear how his severed thumb was my fault. I was curious. My neighbor used to be my husband and neither of us has forgotten it.

"I was splitting kindling and the hatchet slipped," my neighbor said. "You know, the hatchet that you gave me because you gave my first hatchet away." He slumped against a sycamore, a tree that can give you a cough.

It's true that I gave him a hatchet when we were first married, a beautiful curved instrument with a handle of striped walnut and a razor edge. It's true that some years ago I reclaimed the hatchet so I could give it to our other neighbor, the younger one. When you give a gift, it's important to give the best of what you have, not the least of what you have. My neighbor's hatchet was the best thing I had. Of course I replaced it, but he remained angry. It's easy to give the best of what you have when the best of what you have belongs to someone else, he said.

Maybe so. But if you had seen our young neighbor, a radiant person, you too would have given him a beautiful hatchet. You would have given him everything you had. Before he was our neighbor, he was our son. But it had been so long since I'd seen him, so long since I'd heard his voice, I was no longer sure whether I should call him our neighbor or call him something else, or no longer refer to him at all.

"That ash looks wet," my neighbor said, squinting past me at the round as if it was his damn eyeballs that had been severed.

"Don't talk," I said. "Conserve your strength." I tore a strip of cloth from my undergarment. My neighbor grunted as I tied his thumb back on the best I could. The blood soaked through the undergarment. I tore another strip. I tried not to breathe him in.

"Is it green?" he asked.

"I don't burn green wood," I said.

"Anymore," he said. "You don't burn green wood anymore. Let's at least be accurate."

"It's cat piss," I said. I let him lean on me as I guided him to the truck. I buckled his seat belt because he could not do it himself. I told him about the cat leaping onto the log, the eye contact, the stream of urine. I did not mention the map. I could see that through his pain he'd found something to focus on.

"The problem with you is that you have no respect for anything," he said as I coaxed the engine. "When animals act like that, you should stop what you are doing. You should call it a day. You should go inside and shut the door tightly and stoke your fire."

"But I didn't have any firewood," I said. The shocks were shot. The struts were rusted. At the bottom of the hill, the forest ended, and we waited at the railroad tracks as the coal train crept past, hopper car after hopper car, though I always looked for a boxcar, curious to see if someone might be inside.

"Chopping wood out of season," he said, shaking his head. "Then the cat pees on the chopping block at dusk. Then you thumb your nose at omens because you are desperate for warmth. Now you see what that leads to." He held up his thumb, trailing my undergarment.

Finally, the striped gate lifted. The light switched from red to green. I steered around the potholes, the ruts and deep ditches, to the highway. If my neighbor had bled out while waiting for the train to pass he would have found some way to reprimand me for that too.

He wasn't one to let a little thing like death stand in his way. It must be comforting to my neighbor to know with such certainty how one thing leads to another. Causality is one of the major world religions, one of the last great articles of faith. To me, it is one of the great mysteries. And what is causality but blame?

The emergency room was full of all the people we tried to avoid, I mean any people at all, in various states of visible and invisible distress.

"You should go now," my neighbor said. "You've got no wood and it's going to be a cold one."

"And how will you get home," I said, "in the freezing middle of the night with blood loss? You can't hitchhike with a thumb like that."

The on-duty nurse, in her rolling chair, asked all the questions that my neighbor answered no to. No regular doctor. No phone number. No emergency contact. No insurance. No income, not this month at least. The nurse rolled her chair, rolled her mouth around.

"The doctor will still see you of course," the nurse said. "But you will be expected to make a payment at the end of your visit."

I lowered my neighbor into a chair like a blue plastic bucket so he could leave a grease stain, which, like I said, no longer had anything to do with me.

"We should go," he said, closing his eyes and forgetting to hold his hand up.

"There's no shame in resting for a minute," I said. I took him by the elbow and guided his injured hand so that his uninjured hand could hold it. I certainly wasn't going to. My undergarment grew crispy at the edges. I knew he wanted me to take him home and nurse him. I knew he wanted my entire damn undergarment, strip by strip.

In the adjacent bucket seat, a woman bluely changed her baby's diaper, and the baby was not grateful at all, in fact the opposite.

"When my son was a baby," I told her, "I told him I was going to change him. I meant his diaper. But my husband at the time said, Don't tell him you're going to change him because then he'll believe we don't accept him as he is. He'll wonder if the universe fashioned him wrong." The mother was about to respond, I swear she was, but her baby then kicked orange poop at her so I will never know what she was going to say.

"We hope you change," I said to her baby, watching its mother wipe away the creamy shit while the baby screamed. "Because right now you are less than two feet long and you can't focus your eyes. You are entirely unreasonable and you are too loud for mixed company."

Words have power, my husband had said to me and to our similarly kicking soiled son. After that I stopped taking him seriously or I started taking him too seriously. Either one is the death of a marriage.

"There's no way I can pay for this," my neighbor said, grimacing.

"We could call him," I said.

"Who," he said, but I knew he knew. Before he left the woods, our young neighbor had told us both to get health insurance, an easy thing to tell people to do. He told us many things, most of which I can't remember because I thought he'd be there to remind me. He wanted us to stop replying to Do Not Reply text messages from collection agencies with sentences in all caps such as, *YOU WILL NEVER GET A RED CENT FROM ME*. It had been our health care strategy while raising him but apparently it was no longer good enough. He had called me exactly one time after I found his lean-to empty. Just to tell you I'm safe, he said. And to tell you I want you and Dad to take care of yourselves. He told me he had a job. A paying one. Something more real than being a consultant but less real than being a carpenter. Something in the middle. I can't remember. But I remember that he made more in a year than I had made in my whole life. I remember when he told me, how gentle it was. I could hear the whole forest around me, wondering what the hell money was, what the word *salary* meant, was it close to the word *salad* or maybe *salal*. I want to be happy, he said. I want you and Dad to be happy, too.

Stupid forest, I said. Doesn't understand what's really important. That's my idea of a joke. That's irony, which is like ironwood but easier for an axe to go through. My son has not called again. My text messages do not begin with Do Not Reply, but he does not reply.

A nurse called my neighbor's name. He tried to get to his feet but sat back down hard. I hauled him up and went with him into the back and the nurse put us behind a curtain, through which we could hear all the clamor and beeping, the frequencies and trouble and off-color jokes, the tapping and sighing and coughing that filled up that building, which is why we tried to avoid buildings, and each other. But here we were.

The nurse took my neighbor's vitals and asked him why he had filleted his hand. My neighbor looked at me as if I should be the one to answer.

"You're making me hungry with talk like that," I told her, because unlike my neighbor I understand humor. I understand that people who work in emergency rooms might want to use cooking or food metaphors to approach the horror that is human flesh. Unlike my neighbor I know that sometimes words have so much power that you can't talk about what you're talking about. You have to talk about something else.

The nurse left us alone, and my neighbor told me to reach into his pocket.

"Certainly not," I said.

"It's on my bad side," he said. "Help me out." In his foul pocket were six tiny persimmons. He used his good hand to take three of them.

"The persimmon tree is on my side of the line," I said.

"The fruit fell on my side of the line," he said.

We ate the persimmons. They revived my neighbor and they inspired in me a dastardly euphoria, unreplicable. They were exquisite.

When the young doctor came in, he tried to shake my neighbor's hand, then remembered, so he shook hands with me instead. "I'm Dr. Rahim," he said. "You must be the one making cannibal jokes. We love that kind of thing around here." Dr. Rahim and I shared a hearty laugh. He read my neighbor's name off a screen he held in his hand.

"Any relation to Duncan?" he asked, sitting down on his own rolling stool and unwrapping my blood-crusted undergarment. Neither my neighbor nor I said anything. "Had to ask," he said.

"Same last name. Small town." My neighbor closed his eyes, as if it wasn't his damn last name spilled over onto Duncan and me.

"We are Duncan's parents," I said.

"How about that? I love Duncan," Dr. Rahim said, inspecting my neighbor's wound. "Jesus, I've seen bratwurst more alive than this." He winked at me. "Let's see what we can do."

"I also love Duncan," I said.

"We were buddies in high school," Dr. Rahim said. "Duncan's much better at staying in touch than I am. Some people are so good at keeping up old relationships. Those high school days, though. When I think about how much trouble we used to get in." He laughed. My neighbor opened his eyes.

"What kind of trouble," he asked.

Dr. Rahim stopped laughing. "It was a long time ago," he said.

"Still," my neighbor said. "We are his parents. If he gets into trouble we need to know about it."

"Just teenager stuff," Dr. Rahim said. He looked at me, as if for assistance. But what did he think I should do? That man was only my neighbor. Only a distant pain. My relationship with my axe meant more to me than my relationship with him. Petting the cat was more interesting to me than my neighbor was. I had worked to edit our relationship back and back so that I barely knew him. Strictly speaking, he was none of my business.

Once, when my neighbor was still my husband, he caught me Velcroing Duncan's tiny shoes, which Duncan could do himself by then but which I preferred to do for him when I could get away with it. My husband explained to me that Velcroing Duncan's tiny shoes would lead to Duncan becoming prone to vices unimaginable and irreversible. Velcroing Duncan's tiny shoes was in fact one of the primary ills facing our dying culture. My husband asked several questions, including what was wrong with me.

Where to begin. Mean mom, distant father, doesn't know which colors flatter me, bad at dancing, bad baker, can only sing on key when no one is listening, only apologizes in order to get an apology in return, sad when it rains, can't shake the childish sentiment that rain is God's tears, doesn't believe in God, inattentive pet escort. But by that time he had taken his hatchet and slammed out of the house. He was intuitive, imaginative, generous in his ability to link causes to events in the most expansive and unlikely ways. Yes, sometimes that could be difficult. You can do hard things, he told Duncan, refusing to Velcro his tiny shoes. No one could ever accuse my husband of shrinking before difficulties.

Dr. Rahim touched each one of my neighbor's fingertips, in a way I had never done even when he was my husband. "You'll need stitches, of course," Dr. Rahim said. "Likely surgery too if you don't want the nerve damage to be permanent."

"I can't afford that," my neighbor said.

"Which," Dr. Rahim said.

"Either," my neighbor said.

"There's a charity thing the hospital does for indigent or uninsured patients. You can grab the paperwork on the way out."

"I don't need charity," my neighbor said.

Dr. Rahim frowned. "I understand the two of you may need to talk this over. Why don't I give you a few minutes." He once again gave me that significant look, which I had rejected my claim to years ago and did not in any way want back.

Dr. Rahim left, and my neighbor and I ate more persimmons. They were like if you never had to eat again. They were antipatriotic, anti-abundance. They were surrounded by blame but blameless. They were mostly pit, but all around the pit they were perfect.

"We should call him," I said.

"I did," he said.

"You did?" I asked. "When?"

"Before I came to find you," he said. "He was the first person I called."

"What did he say?"

"I left a message," he said.

"Do you think we were too hard on him?" I asked.

"No," he said. "At least, I wasn't."

"I actually meant you," I said. "I didn't mean me. What about when he climbed the persimmon tree and shook them all down before they were ready and as punishment you made him eat all the unripe fruit until he vomited? What about snapping him into his snowsuit and forcing him to play outside alone in a blizzard?"

"You call that a blizzard," my neighbor said.

"What about the nap tent? Knotting the zipper closed and letting him scream and cry sometimes for hours? Do you remember when he was too scared to hike with us in white fur coats along the ridge on a full moon and you made him do it anyway and he wet his pants? What about when you whipped him for insisting that everything was either a dog or a cat?"

Maple: cat. Elm: dog. Persimmon: dog. Dogwood: cat. Axe: dog. Hatchet: cat. Truck: dog. Creek: cat. Train: dog. Cat: cat. Squirrel: dog. Raccoon: dog. Spider: cat. It was a small thing, but it enraged my neighbor. Malingering, he called it. It was not honest, nor was it accurate. The one thing that stumped Duncan was a fox. To his father, he'd say that a fox was a dog. But to me he'd say a fox was a cat, because he knew I loved cats and he knew I loved foxes, although it's been so long since I've seen one that I think they might not live in our woods anymore, and Duncan doesn't live in our woods anymore either.

"The research shows it's not actually people's parents that make them who they are," my neighbor said. "It's other aspects of their environment."

"But what were the other aspects of Duncan's environment?" I asked. "You mean ash? Hickory? Oak?"

"His friends at school, for example," my neighbor said. "Dr. Rahim. You heard him, they used to get in trouble together, and we're only finding out about it now."

Dr. Rahim came back. He was looking at his phone. "I have some good news," he said.

"How much does it cost to amputate?" my neighbor asked.

"Duncan called," Dr. Rahim said.

"No, he didn't," I said.

"He texted me," Dr. Rahim said. "He said, *I hope you're taking good care of my folks. Let them know I'll pay for it. Don't let them try to stitch it themselves. Hahaha. But seriously.* I told him to contact billing, of course. I don't take care of all that. But I thought you'd want to know."

"He texted you?" I said.

"Yes," Dr. Rahim said.

"That's gratitude," my neighbor said. "Imagine that. The people who gave him life."

"He's paying your medical bill," I said.

"Money means nothing to me," my neighbor said.

"If you don't mind, I'm going to sew that up for you," Dr. Rahim said, taking his stool.

The nurse brought in a stainless steel tray. "From the cafeteria," she said, looking at me, but I was no longer in the mood.

Dr. Rahim readied the suture. The needle went in and out of my neighbor like he was a burlap sack filled with potatoes or sand. I could not believe such a bloodless man had blood beneath his cracked skin. He watched the suture, chewing on his filthy beard.

My neighbor and I never exchanged rings. Instead, I gave him the hatchet and he gave me the axe I swing to this day. It has some magic in it. I consider it the only other woman around because it's the only instrument that will do the work the way I want the work done. It's my only companion, now that Duncan is gone. When I gave Duncan the hatchet, he almost didn't take it.

It's Dad's prized possession, he said. How did you even get it from him?

I took it back, I said.

Does he know you have it? Duncan asked.

It belongs to you now, I said. But the hatchet did not make Duncan stay. He took it with him when he left.

My neighbor believes that blame, properly assigned, will bring our young neighbor home. What I wouldn't give to hold such a belief, or any belief at all. If I could rekindle my faith in causality, then what I would like is a map showing me how I got here. I would like a map directing me to Duncan. But no such map exists, or if it does, it's not a map I am meant to read. I stack wood for our young neighbor that is just the size for the woodstove in his lean-to. I keep his lean-to swept. I feed the cat, even though the cat is really Duncan's, even though no one can really own a cat. I wait. I'm punky on the inside, fungus filled. I'm eaten away, barely standing. I'm dead, and I'm burning, burning all the time.

"You're going to have to stay off this hand for a bit," the doctor said. "Hope you weren't depending on it for anything." He chuckled.

"Just kindling," my neighbor said. "My wood's all in."

"That's right," Dr. Rahim said. "I remember Duncan used to talk about how his family heated with wood. I was always a little envious. To me it seemed quite adventurous. But didn't he say your house burned down? Or someone's house? Before he was born?"

"He was born," I said.

"I built that house," my neighbor said.

"Duncan was three when it happened," I said.

"Passive voice," my neighbor said.

"No, it's not," I said.

"A hell of a thing to go through," Dr. Rahim said. To my neighbor he said, "Until the stitches come out, your wife's going to have to take care of your kindling."

"I'll split his kindling for him," I said. "But I'm not his wife."

My neighbor laughed.

"Forgive me," Dr. Rahim said.

"There's nothing to forgive," I said.

"Then I hope you won't mind me saying it's inspiring to see you two still have such a strong relationship, even after your divorce," Dr. Rahim said.

My neighbor and I stared at him. Divorce. What a powerful word.

Listen, we were like any other family. After the house burned, we took words apart and when we put them back together our relationship had changed. Our relationship to the word *house*. To the word *together*, to the word *live*, the word *son, neighbor, family*, to the word *because*, the word *before* and the word *after*. Eventually we lived on opposite sides of the forest. We drew Duncan a map so he could travel between us. As soon as he could, he constructed a lean-to. Please, he said, consider me as you would any other neighbor.

"Maybe this is too much information," Dr. Rahim said. "But my wife and I are considering that right now. Conscious uncoupling." It was too much information. We were simple people. The words we had already didn't work and there was no indication that new ones with more syllables would work any better. "Please give Duncan my best," Dr. Rahim said, depositing his latex gloves and his suturing materials into the biohazard container.

I drove my neighbor and his rotten hand home. He wolfed a pill prescribed by Dr. Rahim. For once he didn't speak. What was there to say? It's hard to do what other people want you to do. It's hard to give someone your best. It's hard to give someone the best of what you have. It's hard to live with someone and also love them. I can do hard things. I can say things like, How was your day, which is effusive enough for some people. I can even say, When do you think this cold snap will end, or, Hey are we doing Christmas this year, or, No just skip it, either way is fine with me. But words have power and mine were never powerful enough. Or they were too powerful. Either one is the death of a marriage.

Before the trees began, I steered the truck over the rise and dip of the railroad tracks, which made my neighbor curse. The striped gate was raised. The coal train was long gone. The animals hid in the dark of the forest, or they didn't.

When I gave him the hatchet, Duncan told me, You ignored what Dad did to me. You went along with it. Never once, he said. Never once did you stand up for me.

But just because you don't remember something doesn't mean that it never happened.

I do remember. Duncan was three. He was in the nap tent. He was meant to be napping. My husband had split and stacked two cords of wood. He'd told me which cord was seasoned and which cord was green. Burn the seasoned wood, he said. Let the green wood season, and I agreed. But in those days I had no relationship with the words *cord, ash, hickory, oak, cherry, maple,* let alone the word *green* or the word *seasoned.* To me those words were decoration, pleasant and folksy, with no real power. I must have been burning green wood all that winter, and into the spring.

That day, after my husband went out, I packed the stove. While the creosote built and bubbled in the chimney, I made a list:

Cat food
Lysol
Dish soap
Laundry
Propane
Diapers

I tried to remember what it took for me to get here and I wondered if I would ever leave.

I burned with curiosity.

After a while it became difficult to concentrate. I tried to stay curious, but my curiosity was interrupted by a noise.

It was a noise that had been there all along.

It was Duncan.

Duncan screaming in the nap tent.

Duncan growing claws.

Duncan clawing to get out.

Duncan speaking and speaking, speaking powerfully but without words. That time, I heard.

I looked once more at my list. I opened the stove. I tossed my banal list inside and watched it burst.

Then I undid the nap tent knot and I gathered my red and sweating boy, my panicked boy, my soiled boy. He doesn't remember. He doesn't remember that I stripped him of his diaper, and I cleaned him, and I changed him, and I wrapped him up and snugged him to my back. He doesn't remember that we left. That we walked down the hill, out of the woods, that we came to the tracks and a train was passing. Dog, Duncan said. Dog. I watched a hopper car, a hopper car, a hopper car, then a boxcar. The train slowed so that we could walk alongside it. I climbed with Duncan into the boxcar and the boxcar picked up speed.

We were leaving, we were leaving, and with that wonder inside me, I watched our forest stay behind.

Cat, Duncan said, waving his hand, and there was a fox. The fox was trotting from the forest as if she had somewhere to go, but she stopped at the tracks. She waited for the train to pass, but the train lurched. Stopped. Started. Stopped again. The fox, waiting, spread her hind legs, put her ass down, and prepared to shit. Poo, Duncan cried, and the fox looked up and saw us. The fox saw us see her shitting. I saw her see us see her. She flattened her ears. The way she looked at us, angry, embarrassed, shocked, we knew it was wrong that we watched her deposit her black logs packed with feathers and bones, insects and fruit and seeds. High above her a column of black smoke plumed over the trees.

I may have no respect for anything, even the universe, but for twenty years I have wondered and wondered how one thing leads to another. I have wondered where my story begins. The fox is where I return. Everyone knows that if by some misfortune you see a dog shitting, you should hook your index fingers together or else there will be a consequence. Some say a wart will sprout. Some say it will be worse. But a fox is not a dog. A fox is not a cat. Should we have hooked our fingers? Duncan's fingers were too small, and mine were wrapped around my baby boy.

The fox shit and then she dashed up the bank into the woods. The trees stood still. The boxcar stood still. Away down the tracks, I could still see the striped gate, beyond it our path home. We hadn't made it very far. The train didn't move. The temperature dropped. The sun went down. The wind picked up. Duncan said to me, Hungry. The boxcar said to me, Are you actually leaving? Do you know where you're going? Do you know what you'll do once you get there? Do you even have a map? I smelled the smoke. I burned with curiosity. But curiosity is something quite apart from the desire to know.

All I want is for you to be happy, I whispered to Duncan as I carried him back up the hill, toward the smoke and the man who would be my neighbor. My boy slept against me heavy as a river rock. I told him to be happy, but what did that mean? Only that amid the terror of such attachment, words don't work. Now Duncan is out there somewhere, another happiness-pursuer, another person who may believe he deserves something, anything besides blame. For that and for nothing else I will apologize.

I parked the truck at the edge of the forest. I put the emergency brake on. I chocked the wheel. I helped my helpless neighbor out onto the forest floor. He used his good hand to switch on his headlamp and we wound through the trees we had marked with orange blazes to define a home.

My woman axe waited faithfully against the ash I had felled and bucked into rounds and wheelbarrowed to the chopping block so that the cat could piss on it, so that the urine could turn to crystals, which after long-term exposure can be mysteriously bad for your health. This is the type of causality you can watch. You can see it crystallizing. You may forget about it, but years later

Dr. Rahim, or some other doctor who was a baby when your baby was a baby but who is now the one you trust your only body to, will look at you and break the bad news.

The cat slunk from the hut I built of particleboard and Tyvek near the burned-out foundation. Needily, she butted against my neighbor, who kicked her toward me. She put her rough tongue to my torn undergarment, curious.

My neighbor's beam caught the map in the ash.

"Spalting," he said.

"Spalting?"

"Those blue lines in the ash," he said. "Spalting. It's a process by which hardwood is eaten by fungi, requiring nitrogen, micronutrients, water, warmth, and air. It compromises the grain of the wood, but it's much sought-after by woodworkers, not for structure but for beauty."

"And for firewood," I said.

"You wouldn't catch me burning wood eaten up by fungus," he said.

"To me, it looks like a map," I said.

My neighbor bent closer, his thumb hovering upward. "You're right," he said. "It does look like a map."

What was I to do? And don't say be softened by the first words of affirmation he'd said to me in twenty years. Don't say invite him in.

What looked like a map was not a map. What looked like a map was spalting, which is a word like *sparrow*, like *salt*, like *salary*. Just a word that could be grown over and enveloped, repurposed and subsumed like all the others.

"Do you need help with your fire?" I asked.

"I'll manage," he said.

"Are you happy?" I asked. "I mean, living the way we do?"

"I'm not the happiness type," he said.

On that single affinity we had built a life.

Jess Walter
The Dark

IN THE DAYS BEFORE SHE DIED, Doug's wife had given him detailed instructions about how he should comport himself in his future romantic endeavors. ("Ellie," he said, "I do *not* want to talk about this.")

First, he was not to introduce their adult children to any women for at least a year. ("Ellie, please—") Second, he might have some Viagra on hand in case grief and guilt affected his performance. ("Jesus, Ellie!") Third—and somehow, this was the most important to her—Doug should beware of blond women in their sixties.

Now, almost two years after his wife's death, Doug Coates finds himself on his first date in forty years, sitting in a coffee shop across from a beautiful, sixty-year-old blonde.

She swirls her chai tea and smiles. "Children?"

"Oh, uh, yeah, two," says Doug. "Aaron works here in Spokane. As a city planner. Maya is a designer who lives with her wife in LA. Actually, in Santa Monica. Well, technically, Pacific Palisades. Or, you know, in between."

Actually-technically-in-between? Why is he dithering like this? What's the matter with him? His tongue feels like it's swollen, like he's just been to the dentist. When Doug was young, conversations with women came so naturally. He thinks he might even have been charming at one time. Smooth. Funny.

"Grandchildren?" the woman asks.

Doug concentrates, channeling his old smooth, funny self. "Not that I know of," he says, and then, for some reason, he winks.

Doug and the blond woman both cock their heads.

They look down awkwardly at their drinks, and for a long time, no one says anything.

"Not that you know of?" Aaron is delighted by his father's haplessness. Doug has driven straight to his son's house and is once again struck by how much Aaron looks like his mother when he laughs.

"Wait, wait." Aaron holds up a hand. "So, were you saying that you were so promiscuous in your youth that you fathered children you don't know about, who maybe fathered children *they* don't know about? Or that Maya and I are so promiscuous we're just out here dropping grandkids that you can't keep track of, like those women who leave babies in department store dressing rooms?"

Doug wonders if he missed a story about babies in department store dressing rooms. *What is wrong with this world?* "Honestly," Doug says, "I have no idea what I meant."

"So, tell me this, Mr. Suave," says Aaron, "are you planning to see this woman again?"

Doug sighs. "Not that I know of."

A week before the end, not long after Ellie gave Doug her awful dating advice, hospice sent over a nondenominational pastor. Doug was confused when he answered the door; he and Ellie had been clear about not wanting this. Doug was a geology professor who valued science over superstition. But Ellie had lapsed from her family's evangelical church as a teenager, and for her, the decision was more personal.

In the kitchen, Doug explained this to the pastor, a woman named Astrid. He spoke quietly, so as not to awaken Ellie from her morphine sleep. Doug said that while he appreciated Astrid coming by, they had been quite intentional in checking the *agnostic/atheist* box on the hospice forms. "We specified no last rites or—"

"Doug?" Ellie called from her bed in the living room. He was surprised at the power of her voice. They'd been speaking in whispers for days. "It's okay," his wife said. "I asked to see her."

Doug experienced something he later suspected was common to every married person: the fear that he didn't know his spouse nearly as well as he thought. He'd felt this before, of course, but to experience it now, so profoundly, at the end—Doug was overcome with shame, and a self-pitying anger rose in him: How could he not know this? How could Ellie not tell him something so important?

"I—I'm sorry," Doug said to the pastor. "Please follow me."

The pastor was one of those ageless older people: lineless face, long slate hair. She followed Doug into the living room, where Ellie lay reclined on the rented hospital bed, looking out at a bird feeder that Doug had hung from the rain gutter so they'd have something to watch out the window. But squirrels had figured out how to hang from the rain gutter and eat the birdseed. When this was all over, the first thing Doug planned to do was take that stupid feeder down.

"Thanks for coming," Ellie said to the pastor.

"I'll leave you two alone," Doug said. Then he went to the kitchen and wept.

Give it a year, everyone said. His kids, his sister, his therapist. The first year, you will feel bereft, they said. And he did. Don't do anything drastic, they said. And he didn't.

He got up, went to work, came home, stared at her clothes in the closet, and watched that one-year date like it was a finish line.

But, of course, when the date arrived, nothing changed. Somehow, he thought he would be transformed, or at least that he might feel like being out in the world again, maybe even meeting someone. But Doug found himself indulging the thought—or the fantasy—that, after a year, he might get to see Ellie again.

This, too, was normal, said his counselor. Getting through the funeral and the first year of grief, the bereaved often entertained a subconscious belief that, once the obligations were all met, their loved one would be allowed to return.

It gave Doug no consolation, hearing that his anguish and delusion were so routine.

"Have you been considering self-harm?" the counselor asked.

"I haven't, actually," Doug said. "What would you suggest?"

The counselor didn't even smile. This made Doug miss his wife even more; she would've loved that joke.

In many ways, the second year was even more difficult than the first, as the distance between him and Ellie seemed to grow. He was haunted, too, by the realization he'd had during Ellie's last days, that he had never really known his wife, that the gap between them had always been impossible to bridge, as if what he and Ellie had was a kind of mirage, a temporary detour from the existential horror of being alive and alone. And her decision to see the pastor—what was that? Though he knew it was irrational, he kept imagining that Ellie knew something that he didn't, and that she'd found a secret door to some afterlife that, as a nonbeliever, he would never find. He would lie awake at night and hear his own pleading voice in his head: *Ellie, where are you?*

As the second hard year dragged on, it was suggested by those same people—kids, sister, therapist—that Doug needed a change.

So, he took early retirement, sold the house in Portland, and moved back to Spokane, where he and Ellie had met forty years earlier, and where his son, Aaron, lived. Maybe he could reconnect with old friends from Gonzaga University. Or maybe he could meet new people—

Which is how he ended up at coffee with his sister's friend, the suspiciously blond woman who no doubt had left their only date believing that Doug was a crazed, promiscuous grandfather.

"I wake up every day feeling like I've been left behind," Doug tells his son after the blond disaster. "Like I've missed a train or something. Like there's been a huge mistake."

"You're letting yourself feel that way," Aaron says. He slides a beer across the counter to his father.

"I don't think so." Doug takes a drink. The city feels different, for one thing. His college friends are gone, his favorite restaurants and bars closed. Downtown was once filled with offices and department stores; now it's all condos and coffee shops. Aaron lives in a neighborhood that didn't even exist forty years ago, a strip of train tracks and vacant fields replaced by town houses and wine-tasting rooms.

"You want me to see if I can get them to put the train tracks back in? Come on, Dad." Aaron points to the phone in Doug's hand. "Focus."

Doug sighs and looks back down at the open search page on his iPhone: Best online options for people over sixty. Match. Zoosk. Bumble. eHarmony.

"What are these names? SilverSingles? That one sounds like a slot machine."

"Give it here." Aaron holds out his hand, and Doug recognizes something familiar in his son's expression. Then he remembers: Aaron as a boy, struggling to cut the steak on his plate, shaking the whole table, until Doug finally said, "Give it here"; took the knife; cut his son's meat into small, chewable bites; and slid the plate back.

At the counter, Aaron exudes that same caring impatience as he drums his thumbs on the screen of Doug's iPhone. "All right, I'm setting you up on OkCupid."

"Sure. Because I'm saying, 'Okay, Cupid, I'm ready to date,' or 'Hey, Cupid, just find me someone okay.'"

Aaron hands the phone back. "You really should save this banter for the ladies."

A week before she died, Ellie talked to Astrid the pastor for almost an hour while Doug sat alone in the kitchen. He poured himself a glass of whiskey, stared at it awhile, then poured it down the sink.

Finally, Astrid came out of the living room and told him that Ellie was resting. "It's a difficult time," the pastor said. "A time of transition." He fought the urge to grab her by the shoulders. (*Are you kidding? Transition? It's the goddamn end of the world!*) Instead, he thanked her for coming.

She asked if *he* wanted to talk.

"I don't think so," Doug said, and he showed her out.

He returned to the living room, where the sun was setting and the only light—casting a faint, warm glow—came from a floor lamp that Ellie had taken from her parents' house when her father died. His wife was facing the window with the squirrel feeder, but her eyes were closed, lips pressed together, as if she was concentrating on a problem.

"How was it?" he whispered.

"Nice," she said, without opening her eyes.

He didn't know what else to say, so he asked what he always asked. "How's your pain?"

She opened her eyes and turned on the pillow to face him. "Eighty-six. Got a nice rhythm. Easy to dance to."

He used to think of them as one thing: a *dougandellie*. But, of course, they weren't. Not really. There had always been a Doug. And an Ellie. They had come together for almost forty years, but now they would be apart again.

A sparrow flitted outside the window.

"Can I ask," Doug said, "what are you thinking now?"

"Everything," she said.

.   .   .

Doug's second date in forty years, via OkCupid, is a petite, age-and-hair-appropriate woman named Marcie. They meet outside a craft pizza place near Downriver Golf Course.

This time, the conversation flows. They bemoan the smoke from the August fires and reminisce about the clear blue skies of their childhood summers. Marcie has three adult children, and she smiles and nods at his recent observation about Aaron's impatience over Doug's technological ineptitude.

"So true," she says, and laughs. "They parent us as impatiently as we parented them." It's a nice laugh, unforced, not too high.

"Or maybe I'm just not cut out for online dating," Doug says.

"I think you're doing fine," she says.

What is that feeling? A shiver in his spine, his guts.

Menus come, wine is ordered, then appetizers, then more wine. Doug feels himself relaxing. He looks down at the menu again: the pizzas here are named for streets in the Downriver neighborhood.

He wonders aloud if the pizza names are chosen to reflect the people on those streets—if, say, the folks on Alice Avenue are more likely to be vegetarians than those on Gordon Avenue.

Marcie smiles. "Right. Or this one is for the down-home pulled-pork-and-slaw folks over on Dalton."

They choose two small craft pizzas—a chicken curry and a cauliflower/brussels sprout—then settle into polite, gentle questioning. Retirement, hobbies, travel. This time, when grandchildren come up, Doug simply says, "Not yet, how about you?"

"No, thank God," says Marcie. "I can't imagine learning to date again and being a grandma at the same time." She swirls her wine and seems to get lost watching it in her glass.

But then she looks up suddenly, and says: "Was it hard, losing your wife?" Before he can answer, she shakes her head. "I'm sorry. That was a terrible question."

"No," he says. "It's a fine question. And yeah. It was." *What you can't ever imagine is the distance,* he wants to say. But he's not sure she'll know what that means. *He's* not sure what that means.

She nods, reaches out, and covers his hand with hers. The feeling of her hand on his hand is so intense, Doug is almost relieved when she pulls her hand away. He takes a deep breath through his nose.

She tells him about her divorce then, how she suspected that she and her husband weren't as connected as they had been, but how she imagined that when the kids were gone, they would find each other again. But their youngest went off to college and a week later, her husband left. "You try not to be surprised, but—"

Doug nods. No need to finish that thought.

"It's been a year, and it still feels so raw." Marcie looks down into her wineglass again. "I don't think I've dealt with it very well."

Doug says, "I think you're doing fine."

She smiles at the repeated line, then shakes her head. "I can't even bring myself to use my maiden name."

"Well," Doug says, "this seems as good a time as any." He offers his hand. "Doug Coates. Nice to meet you, Miss—"

After a moment, she smiles, extends her hand, shakes his, and says, "Gearing. Marcie Gearing. Nice to meet you!"

As they shake, Doug feels a different shudder. Their hands separate. "Um, where did you go to high school?"

"Ah, yes," she says, "the classic Spokane question. Surprised it took us this long. Shadle Park. You?"

"I didn't grow up here," he says, distracted. "I moved here for college. My wife did, though."

Yes, his late wife, Ellie, who also went to Shadle Park High School on Spokane's north side, and who would tell you, if she were here, that she had only ever hated one person in her entire life, a cruel girl from high school named Marcie fucking Gearing.

Over the years, Doug repeatedly asked Ellie not to use that word when telling the story of Marcie Gearing and tenth-grade cheerleader camp, but Ellie was incapable of saying "that woman's name" without the profanity in between. And she told the story often. Whenever their kids encountered any social trouble at school, Ellie would inexplicably trot out the tale of Marcie fucking Gearing.

"It's important to always have an archenemy," she would explain to the kids, one of Ellie's occasional moments of insane parenting advice that Doug would counter by shaking his head and mouthing, "No, it's not."

The story went like this: Sophomore year of high school. Cheerleader camp. Chubby nerd Ellie Martin comes back from summer break two inches taller and ten pounds lighter, sans braces—blossomed, one might say—and committed to changing her lowly high school status by trying out for cheerleading.

At camp, the girls are each mentored by a current cheerleader; Ellie's mentor is that pretty paragon of popularity, Marcie fu—

"Ellie," Doug would interrupt as she told the story to eight-year-old Maya and six-year-old Aaron, who were both enrapt.

"Oh, sorry," Ellie would say. Then she'd carefully enunciate each word. "I meant to say, Marcie. *Fucking!* Gearing." Then she'd smile at Doug, who would put his hands up in surrender.

So, back in 1980, Marcie Gearing tells blossoming Ellie to try *this* tumbling run and to hold her pompoms *thusly* and to practice *those* dance moves, and then, on the last day of camp, when the cheerleading mentors introduce their charges to the other cheerleaders, who will vote on the new girls, Marcie Gearing stabs Ellie in the back by standing up and introducing her this way:

"This is Ellie Martin. You might know her as one of the smartest kids in school. And a clarinetist in the marching band. Like I told her, it would be *so neat* to have someone like Ellie on the squad this year."

The first time he had heard the story, Doug looked around, thinking: *Wait, that was it?* Had he missed the cruel part?

"Someone *like Ellie*! Do you seriously not hear that, Doug?"

He did not.

"She was basically saying, *Look, this fat band girl wants to be a cheerleader.*"

"Look—I don't—I mean—" Doug stammered. "Anyway, you would've hated being a cheerleader."

"Of course I would've hated being a cheerleader. Do you think that's the point of the story?"

"Ellie," he said, "you grew into a successful, happy, *beautiful* woman. Who cares what some sixteen-year-old cheerleader said? Why can't you let it go?"

"Let it . . . go?" She stared at him like weevils were crawling out of his eye sockets. "Sometimes I don't think you're human."

"Would you excuse me a moment," Doug says to Marcie Gearing. He stands and walks to the bathroom, where he stares at himself in the mirror. Creased skin around tired eyes. Thin, graying hair. It surprises him, sometimes, this old man's face.

Jesus, what kind of test is this? He likes this woman, really likes her; she is the first person he's connected with since Ellie died. She is pretty and nice and maybe a little fragile, like him. He can still feel the charge from her hand on his.

And yet, of all the people in the world, this is literally the one he cannot date. *Not* okay, Cupid.

What's he supposed to do now? Go back to the table and yell at Marcie fucking Gearing for something she surely doesn't even remember? Sneak out the back door and stick her with the bill? Get Ellie's revenge all these years later?

Or no—perhaps this is another kind of test. He thinks about the pastor, Astrid, and wonders if there *is* a heaven, and the only way he can help his beloved Ellie ascend to paradise is this: here on Earth, to forgive his wife's pointless, lifelong grudge.

Sure. Right.

He can almost hear Ellie's voice in the men's room: "And how do you propose to do that, Doug? By actually *fucking* Marcie fucking Gearing?"

In the bathroom mirror, Doug watches his reflection slap its forehead.

Three days before Ellie died, Doug finally asked: "What did you talk about with that pastor?"

Ellie's eyes opened slowly. She took a deep breath. "My parents. The church. God. Not God. Our kids. You."

"Did she say anything . . . I don't know—"

"Comforting?" Ellie licked her dry, cracked lips. "She did, actually. She said we are the ones who teach babies to be afraid of the dark."

Doug cocked his head, unsure what this meant.

"She said: '*We* put in night-lights. *We* leave lamps on. *We* are the ones who create that fear.' She said: 'Why would babies be afraid of the dark when it is the place they have just come from?'"

In the pizzeria bathroom, Doug comes to a decision. His wife is gone now. Nothing can change that. And sitting out there, waiting for him, is a beautiful, seemingly kind, intelligent woman.

He will go back out there and explain to Marcie why he was gone so long, tell her the reason he reacted so strangely a few minutes ago—that his deceased wife had gone to the same high school as her (without mentioning cheerleader camp), and, hopefully, they will laugh about the coincidence and decide to see one another again.

He takes a deep breath and walks out of the bathroom. "Look, I'm sorry," he says as he settles into his chair. "This is going to sound weird, but—"

"No," Marcie Gearing interrupts him, and now he sees that her eyes are red, that she's been crying. "*I'm* sorry. While you were gone, I . . . I realized—" She covers her mouth. "I'm not ready for this. Forgive me. It's not you. I just— I'm sorry."

Then Marcie Gearing stands, grabs her purse, and rushes out the door. In the thrum of the crowded restaurant, Doug can do nothing but stare at her empty chair.

He sits by himself this way for a while. He looks down at the two half-full wineglasses, then at the tables around him: mostly young families and couples; someone is breaking off pizza crusts for a baby in a high chair, and this nearly ruins him.

But, after a few minutes, a strange sense of calm comes over Doug Coates. Happiness, even.

He hums a laugh, finishes his glass of wine, toasts the empty chair in front of him, and reaches for her glass. He honors the Asian population of D Street by having a few slices of their signature curry-style pizza. The other pizza he has boxed up for lunch tomorrow.

"Is the lady not coming back?" asks the waitress.

"The lady is not," Doug says.

And when the bill comes—ninety-six dollars before tip—Doug smiles and realizes that he cannot wait to tell Aaron about this—his second official date.

No! Aaron will say, and he will smile just like his mother.

Oh yes! Doug will say. *Marcie f-ing Gearing!*

Then Doug will explain how they were having a great time when she suddenly left and stuck him with the bill, and while his delighted son laughs, Doug will think that maybe we never stop loving the people we love, even when they've gone back to the dark from which they came. But maybe, if we're lucky, we get to feel them again, in this case, in the small, shared experience of getting fucked over by Marcie Gearing. And, again, in the warm, familiar laughter of the people we made together.

Allegra Hyde

Mobilization

WE WERE MULTITUDES, we were millions. We lived within dimensions up to fifty feet long, fourteen feet high, but never more than nine feet wide. We were drivers, asphalt-lickers, road-runners, gearheads: the denizens of motorhomes who rolled across the country en masse, a fleet of rubber-soled seekers. We were a city on wheels. A city on the go. A growing city: more motorists joined us each day. Newbies drove shiny RVs off the lot—Class A motorhomes with leather interiors, granite countertops, TVs, bonus sleeper sofas—or they purchased tow-along teardrops. Fifth wheels. Cab-overs. Pop-ups for pickup truck beds. A wealthy actor built a double-decker apartment on a tractor trailer—hot tub on the roof. We let him join, too. We didn't discriminate. We welcomed families of five crammed into campers, as well as heavy metal screamers straying with bandmates from their touring paths. Oddballs joined in custom trollies made from salvaged wood and glue. Whatever works, we said. What mattered was that everyone was always at home, but always away. Gas pedal down, we cracked the code humanity had wrestled with for too many millennia: How to have an adventure yet keep your home close. How to wander the world yet never get lost. If only Odysseus could have taken Penelope and Telemachus with him, could have taken the old lady and the looms, the goats and farmers and the grapevines and Ithaca's gravelly shores, because we did. We brought our Siamese cats and Welsh corgis. One man had a sixty-year-old Greek tortoise that rode in his passenger seat. He let it roam during pit stops; it never got far. We brought our children, cousins, parents, partners, best friends, neighbors— packing together, as condensed as the sardines we ate—everyone headphone-wearing, video game–twitching, knitting, audiobook-listening, steering wheel–gripping. The cramped quarters were worth having the whole country to roam. We furnished our vehicles with macramé. Strings of dried chili peppers. Prayer beads. Great-grandma's ashes sat in an urn on the dashboard. May she rest in peace, we said, forever in motion. We stowed gold bullion in our glove compartments, just in case. Also a couple revolvers. Hydroponic pot plants trembled over speed bumps. Cacti we kept duct-taped to windows. Bicycles, we lashed to the roof. We towed jeeps. Ski-Doos. Kayaks. By Lake Erie, we splashed into the water, kept an eye out for snakes. In Telluride, we made hundreds of snow sculptures—left them to liquefy. Down south, outside El Paso, we lay in the sun and let its rays fry us. There's always room in the desert, we told one another. We meant it. In Quartzsite, Arizona, we purchased gemstones by the armful, installed amethysts by our sinks. Helps with digestion. We pulled into grocery stores, bought out their tuna, pita, eggs, cinnamon, pickles, OJ, Coke, basil, bananas, hot dogs, buns, ribs, batteries, coffee grounds, Band-Aids, beer, Pop-Tarts, gummy bears, Gatorade, iceberg lettuce, salsa, ham slices, sugar-free gum, hand soap, toilet paper.

We moved on.

Sometimes stationary people decried us, jeered at and protested us. Local kids watched wide-eyed from scooters. Local teens shot our flanks with paintball guns. We waved back nonetheless. We tossed candy from our windows in one long parade. We set off fireworks to show our shared patriotism: our love of the country we roamed. We played our radios loud, tuning them to many thousand frequencies, and once in a while to the same station—everybody loved Talking Heads. *Take you there, take you there / We're on a road to nowhere.* We pitied these stationary citizens: stuck, trapped, misguided. We pitied their homes rooted into the earth, the burden of a basement. We pitied the necessities of lawn care. Mailboxes bursting with bills. We pitied their scorn. They don't know what they're missing.

Sometimes they did. A few jeerers always slipped in among our ranks. They rigged up their minivans, followed our trail in the night. Or they made hasty romances—often a glance was enough—and found a seat in a cockpit. Teens stowed away in our storage spaces, emerged tousled-haired and sheepish a hundred miles from home. We never turned them away. We made arrangements, kept going. We flooded Walmart parking lots, NASCAR racetracks, dried-out lake beds. We coated mountaintops like cubed snow. We saturated cities. When we parked, we stretched for miles in every direction—and we parked where we wanted. Who's gonna stop us? We were too numerous to ticket; we always skipped town. Once, we took up the length of every bridge spanning San Francisco Bay. We liked the view, the squawk of gulls. We tried not to litter, but we often couldn't help it. Leaflets, leftovers, stray bits of plastic wrap—they fluttered from our windows. Sometimes our hubcaps detached and rolled away. We'll get new ones later, we told ourselves. Can't stop now.

We scattered seeds, too: the fuzzy inflorescence of Midwestern maiden grass; pinecones from giant sequoias; every kind of acorn. Flush with the miracle of our country's fecundity, we had sex, wildly, on the roofs of our motorhomes, the open plains of Kansas stretching big and balmy in every direction—the moon a voyeur. Afterward, in the night air, we kept driving. We stuck our heads out windows like dogs. We tasted snowflakes. Blackflies. Smog. The sulfuric fumes of a chemical fire, burning to the west.

Motion spared us from disaster. In Oklahoma, we outpaced a tornado. We circumvented riots and "civil unrest." Infectious diseases. Mourning of all kinds. True: some phone calls found us. Your great-aunt passed . . . Even the occasional letter. You owe the U.S. government $29,780 in back taxes . . . We didn't mind—we could out-drive it all. We piped in internet, but not because the news would affect us. A grave tragedy in Rochester, New York, as rescue teams rush to . . . News was a show we tuned in to—tuned out of, just as quick. And anyway, we tried not to read much, lest we get carsick.

True, there were times we broke down; leaks happened; we crashed; but we also got ourselves patched up, inflated, recalibrated, jump-started. We were good at using duct tape. We pooled knowledge, our tools. At rest stops, we intubated fuel lines, wastewater lines; we drank diesel, gasoline, suckled it from gas station pumps, guzzling with greedy abandon because we knew the fuel gave us more miles. We released gray water, black water—chemically sweetened—in an aqueous trade that lubricated our plumbing. We tightened lug nuts. We checked windshield wipers, batteries. We sizzled: liquid and limber.

And then—street signs, construction signs, political signs, lost children signs, personal injury lawyer signs, memorial signs—we whisked past it all. We honked. We whisked past dates, too, dangling lights on our vehicles for holidays—Christmas, Hanukkah, Chinese New Year, Eid al-Fitr, Diwali, Liberalia—though often we got these dates wrong. Time warped, minutes meaningful only in their relation to one place and the next. Women gave birth at sixty mph, on highways stretching straight into the sun, the birth locale changing as we crossed state lines.

I'll call her Texarkana.

We added bumper stickers—line-drawn figures accounting for passengers, phrases for what we wanted to say: Brake for Moose; This Car Climbed Mt. Washington; I'd Rather Be Phishing; USA; NASH; LV; LOL; Not Old, Just a Classic; God

Bless America; COEXIST; Smoke Tires Not Drugs; My Collie Is Smarter Than Your Honor Student—until we filled the backsides of our motorhomes, the text piling on top of itself.

The moon squinted down, a skeptic.

Like we cared—we were fiberglass and steel, plywood and polystyrene. We were a polymer-infused spray when the mood struck, and we waxed the sides of our vehicles. Rainwater beaded. Every droplet demonstrated our invincible ease. During storms, we hydroplaned, skidded—threw our heads back and laughed.

We pissed in restaurants and behind trees.

We forgot stuffed animals at rest stops.

We shoplifted Jolly Ranchers, Crocs, designer sunglasses; we held up the occasional midtier jeweler.

Keep the engines running—

We hurried onward, counting roadkill to keep our minds busy, death as distant as a possum in a mirror.

Children started school with new landscapes out their windows each day.

You're lucky to see the country like this, we told them. *You get to meet people from all over, hear every accent, every perspective. You see every side of a sunset. You know the meaning of a mile, of fresh asphalt and old potholes—*

We had our favorite places, sure, but we never let ourselves stay long. Not-staying kept those places special. Kept them loved.

—Leave while you still want more. Promise to come back, even if you know you never will. Don't let a place hurt you. Don't ever think of slowing down.

We were ephemeral. A current on the tar trails—the interstate webbing connecting the country—our movements a synaptic pulse, the wink and blink of possibility. We were everywhere and nowhere. We went on for generations.

Then one day we heard the gas was gone.

We didn't believe it.

We'd encountered such talk before: theories about peak oil,

unstable supply chains. We didn't think the news applied to us. It was someone else's problem, someone else's life.

Probably a localized issue, we said. These issues usually are.

And anyway, we were in Texas—in the wide-open country between San Antonio and Houston—where the black beaks of pump jacks perched over the earth.

If there's fuel anywhere, it's here.

We pulled off the highway, into a small town with roads that crumbled into dusty paths. Houses had tin roofs. A quiet, closed-door church displayed a sign condemning sinners. Inside the town's gas station, there were bags of salted corn chips. Jerky. Lighters with wolves howling on their sides. No fuel. The clerk shrugged. Told us to try down the road.

We tried down the road.

That town was out of fuel, too.

So was the next one; and the one after that.

A newspaper outlined a disastrous trade embargo. Governments in chaos. A domestic strike. Delayed shipments. Blah blah blah. We took a deep breath.

Fuel could be found—we just had to be strategic.

We pointed ourselves southeast.

The highway stretched long and flat. We tried to coast—to let the wind push us, holding our speedometers steady. We lost a few motorhomes right away—folks with fuel tanks knocking empty. We'll come back for your camper, we said. Climb in. We gripped our steering wheels, willed ourselves onward.

We'd decided on Galveston. Maybe we'd already gone a bit mad. Among us, a hypothesis had circulated, swelled into inevitable reality: they'd have fuel in that island city. We remembered RV hookups flush with gasoline. Potable water. Propane. We recalled driving right onto the beach: the sand firm beneath our tires, the Gulf of Mexico sweeping open like a stage set. Dolphin fins dicing the surf. The island: an easy drive from Houston's energy headquarters—from corporate offices, refineries, chemical

plants. The island, a vacation spot for oil executives and rig workers alike.

Yes, we assured ourselves, *it'll have what we need.*

The sky darkened. We lost more vehicles. *Climb in. Climb in.
Climb in.* Those of us with spare gas canisters sloshed around our
last cups, spreading the remaining fuel like a sacrament.

Nearly nightfall—I-45 ushered us through marshy fields, past
the prickly watch of utility towers. We held our breath as we
crossed the long, low bridge that stretched from the mainland to
the island, our vehicles running on fumes.

Stoic palm trees. Boat dealerships. Chain hotels. Vacation
homes whose windows winked with the fretfulness of lighthouses.

There was no fuel in Galveston, either.

One by one, we ground to a halt. We were stranded.

A few among us—the oddballs, really—had custom electric
rigs, and they went for help, spiriting back over the bridge, their
taillights as bright red as brimstone in the night.

Come back for us, we called.

We'd parked along the shore. A frozen flock, we stared at the
ocean stretching away into darkness. Sea grasses whispered. The
night sky stood tall.

A pause, we told one another. *Temporary.*

Flashlights beamed. Beach chairs were dragged out of vehicles,
unfolded. Cigars smoked skyward. Children Hula-Hooped. Grills
sizzled. AC units were methodically unclogged. Around us: the
wet murmur of the sea.

Above: the moon as bored and unbending as a god.

Rain the next day; the day after. The ocean sloshed, sediment-
filled, turning the color of chocolate milk. Algae on the jetty
rocks: slick as hair, bright green and swaying. Thundery skies.
Skies hysterical, pinched by lightning. Then: a fever-flush of heat.
Our vehicles deadened by stillness. Leaning, exhaling through
leaks. Tires going flaccid. Garbage swirling. Sewage smells. Beach
chairs rusting, sinking into the ground. Bumper stickers peeling.

Flags shredding, sun-fading. Grills gone cold. Our bodies prostrate. Slumped over steering wheels, twin yellow lines racing along the backs of our eyelids. The road right there, waiting.

The others never came back.

Sand, wind-driven, making dunes of our vehicles. Making tombs of our vehicles. Heat as heavy as a fist pummeling the island. More rain. The sea kicked up, frantic—a storm surge rising over the beach, the ocean like a salt blanket: a bedcover pulled above our heads. A demand for dreaming.

Darkness comes quick—sucked down, down into the sea, our vehicles clasp us. Here: algae blooms to toxic proportions, maddened by phosphorus runoff, overwarm waters. The rotting carcasses of fish free-fall in slow motion. Expired zooplankton, phytoplankton: creatures too tiny to see. Bacteria get busy cleaning our skulls, achieve anaerobic ecstasy. The gulf: a gullet. It swallows us, grinds us. Our caravan crushed, axles crunching, fiberglass fraying, cabinet doors already fallen to pieces. Those bones of our motorhomes buried with us. Mud and murk press down on top. Sediment piling, solidifying. The ocean boils, bulges with glacial melt that claws landmasses into muddy plains, stirs atmospheric anomalies into continual tempests.

We are pressed and squeezed beneath all that weight. In our lightless, airless, underwater coffins—down where the moon can't find us—we are fossilized, liquefied, transmogrified. We ooze. The continents creak, make their slow passages. Fault lines find reasons to agitate, tectonic kisses making the whole planet shudder, blush hot, lava throbbing red. Rock steams into the sky. Underneath it all, we are chemicals, superheated; we are millions of years in the making. Time skids along, careless as ever. We wait—to be called up, summoned—to burst to the surface, burned into motion. We are ready.

The O. Henry Prize Winners 2024

The Writers on Their Work

Colin Barrett, "Rain"
What inspired your story?

For a long time I had a couple of lines in what became my first novel, *Wild Houses*. A character comes out of a shop and walks under some recently rained-on trees. She notices the "dark, weighted gleam" of the leaves and the pattern of raindrops on the otherwise dry stretch of pavement protected by the branches. It got cut from the novel because there, it was a piece of nice incidental description but nothing more. Years later, I modified and expanded on those lines to come up with the opening paragraph of "Rain." The Vaughan sisters were, mysteriously, already present, coming out of the store fully formed, laden with shopping. But the story couldn't start until I recovered and recuperated that description of the trees. It wasn't just incidental detailing now. The contrast of light and wet, rain and concrete, and the sisters moving under the tunnel of the branches, making their way toward the fountain where they habitually hunt for coins; there was a poetic weight to these images, a resonance and density. I knew there was something there, something worth writing toward. This is how stories start for me.

Colin Barrett is from Mayo, Ireland. He is the author of the short story collections *Young Skins* and *Homesickness,* and the novel *Wild Houses*.

Emma Binder, "Roy"
What inspired your story?

I have a real, late Uncle Roy whom I never got to know very well while he was alive. But I had heard stories about him eating skinned snakes and trying to run away to the Catskills to live in a hollowed-out tree, like Sam in *My Side of the Mountain*. A photograph also exists of him wearing overalls and a straw hat, holding a raccoon in the air. When I began with those details, the story spilled out easily—I wrote the first draft very quickly at the end of a months-long period of not writing, like the story had been brewing inside me without my knowing. At the same time, I was interested in writing about gender, and what it feels like to be a queer or trans adolescent without identifying language— the alienation of it, but also how joyfully bewildering and liberating it feels when someone finally describes you in a way that feels right. And what it's like to know something about yourself before you feel capable of describing it.

Emma Binder is a writer from Wisconsin and a current Stegner fellow in fiction at Stanford University. They have received fellowships from the Wisconsin Institute for Creative Writing and the Vermont Studio Center, as well as the Gulf Coast Prize in Fiction, the Indiana Review Fiction Prize, and the Tupelo Press Snowbound Chapbook Award. Their work has recently appeared or is forthcoming in *The Kenyon Review, Michigan Quarterly Review, Indiana Review, Gulf Coast, Narrative, Pleiades,* and elsewhere.

Amber Caron, "Didi"
What inspired your story? Why was the short story format the best vehicle for your ideas?

I had three bits of text in my journal that I sensed were in conversation with each other. A man who called his sister, frantic about his daughter's clothes. A character who kept disappearing. And a bit of dialogue: "It's like she's set up mirrors all around her. Like she's constantly watching herself every time she moves." I brought these elements together and just started playing with them, expanding sentences into paragraphs, paragraphs into scenes, and very slowly Didi, Val, and Evan started to take shape as characters. I knew then I had a story, and that the story would orbit around Didi, but it took me many years (and multiple drafts) to realize that Didi's visit, as brief as it was, would change everything for Val and Evan. As for why the short story form, it's less that it was the right vehicle for my ideas—I almost never start a story with an idea—and more that it seemed like the right form for this particular situation. There's an urgency to Didi's arrival, which is only heightened when she disappears, and I suspected that urgency couldn't be sustained over a longer narrative. Once I realized this, the decision to make this a short story was an easy one.

Amber Caron is the author of the story collection *Call Up the Waters* and the recipient of the PEN/Robert J. Dau Short Story Prize for Emerging Writers. Her stories and essays have appeared in *The Threepenny Review, PEN America Best Debut Short Stories, AGNI, Story, Bennington Review, Southwest Review,* and elsewhere. She lives in Logan, Utah, and teaches at Utah State University.

Jai Chakrabarti, "The Import"
What inspired your story?

I wrote this piece amidst the chaotic period of raising a toddler—filled with sleepless nights, moments of joy, power struggles, and a constant feeling of falling behind. For us, as for many parents, the idea of consistent childcare was appealing, a sentiment echoed by my mother, who suggested the radical solution of relocating to India to hire a so-called ayah, at least temporarily. While this was impractical and not something we wanted to do, it sparked my imagination and led to the character of Rupa, who arrives from a village in India to work as an au pair in Brooklyn. As I delved off-page into her past, I was looking to understand what Rupa wants from the arrangement. Even though "The Import" isn't told from her point of view, Rupa's character was always at the center of the story.

Jai Chakrabarti is the author of the novel *A Play for the End of the World,* which won the National Jewish Book Award for Debut Fiction, was a finalist for the Rabindranath Tagore Literary Prize, and was long-listed for the PEN/Faulkner Award. He is also the author of the story collection *A Small Sacrifice for an Enormous Happiness.* His stories have won an O. Henry Prize and a Push-cart Prize, and have been anthologized in *The Best American Short Stories.*

Morris Collins, "The Home Visit"
Why was the short story format the best vehicle for your ideas?

I'm not sure how I knew "The Home Visit" was supposed to be a short story, but when the idea arrived in February 2020, it seemed story shaped and story sized—I had a clear sense of voice, incident, character, and the ways the difficulties in the characters' lives would complicate the situation. And I also knew exactly how it would end. In a larger project, like a novel, this much knowledge might erode my interest in further discovery. But for a story it was a kind of gift and the writing was enjoyable. (These were days, I should mention, where I was already deep into a comic novel about Holocaust survivors, intergenerational trauma, art theft, and the dangers of inherited memory in the early days of the Trump presidency, so I was pretty willing to indulge the distraction.) For about a day I thought I'd turn into a short story writer. The form was full of easy possibility. I wrote notes for five more stories. I jotted some first paragraphs. This was so much simpler than writing novels: all you had to do, in every sentence, was be funny, original, moving, compassionate, idiosyncratic, humane, and beautiful. Then I couldn't get the end to work; the emotions were off and instead of finishing writing "The Home Visit" as a short story, I decided to start it all over again as a play. There are many talents a writer can have and one of those is knowing, it always seems, exactly what they should be writing. This is not a gift I have. So I wrote a full-length play along similar lines. But what do you do with plays? I don't know. I literally don't know what you are supposed to do once you write a play, especially in the early months of the pandemic, when no one was going anywhere, let alone to the theater. My wife and I read it to each other, from inside our panic. Also, by this time we were suffering some problems at home. My wife was sick, my cat was sick, I was bedridden with a nerve injury. Things would get better, but they were still pretty bad. For a while, no one in the apartment could walk more than a few steps. At dinnertime I crawled into the kitchen and tried to prop myself against the stove. This was not bohemian life, but clarity arrived. What was I thinking, writing a play? I went back to the story, and this time the end I wrote was the end I had imagined.

Morris Collins's first novel, *Horse Latitudes,* was published by Dzanc Books. He was awarded a Mass Cultural Council Fellowship in Fiction for his new manuscript, *The Tavern at the End of History.* Other fiction and poetry has appeared in *Gulf Coast, Subtropics, Pleiades, Michigan Quarterly Review,* and *The Florida Review,* among others. He teaches at the College of the Holy Cross and lives outside Boston.

Tom Crewe, "The Room-Service Waiter"
Why was the short story format the best vehicle for your ideas?

One of the famous virtues of the short story is that it allows the writer to combine length and brevity: to range across decades in a paragraph, to boldly mark out the course of a life with a few isolated details, rather than letting it accumulate, slowly-busily, over many chapters. For this reason, it was the perfect vehicle for considering a life that has in fact been rather empty, in which a few isolated details are all that really seem to have mattered. Until the moment at which this story begins, the great event in Charles Bisset's life has been his failed marriage to a woman called Josephine; we meet him as he is reintroduced to a portrait made of him long ago, which has subsequently become an object of great cultural interest (and great financial value). Only the taut expansiveness of the story form could have pulled these two details into such close and vibrating relation, so that they offer the key to Charles's past and to his personality, both of which also manage to be large and small at the same time.

Tom Crewe was born in Middlesbrough, England, in 1989. Since 2015, he has been an editor at the *London Review of Books,* to which he contributes essays on politics, art, history, and fiction. He was named a Granta Best of Young British Novelists in 2023. *The New Life,* his first novel, was published in January 2023 and won the Orwell Prize for Political Fiction, the South Bank Sky Arts Award for Literature, and the Prix du Premier Roman Étranger.

Kate DiCamillo, "The Castle of Rose Tellin"
Did you know how your story would end at its inception?

I never know how any story I tell is going to end. I'm fond of paraphrasing Elmore Leonard, who said something along the lines of: I never know what's going to happen. I write to find out what happens.

I started "The Castle of Rose Tellin" with the words *Sanibel Island, clown car, boxing gloves*. Pretty soon *Chitty Chitty Bang Bang* and Picasso and those little pink shells (my mother called them rose tellins) showed up. It wasn't until I went back and looked at some clips from *Chitty Chitty Bang Bang* and remembered (as Thomas does) that the kids hide from the Child Catcher in a grotto beneath the castle that I started to see how this story might end.

It's pleasing to me to think that stories are castles with great hidden rooms beneath them.

Kate DiCamillo has written more than thirty books for young readers. Her stories have been adapted into movies, stage plays, operas, and puppet shows. She has twice been awarded the Newbery Medal. She lives and works in Minneapolis.

Dave Eggers, "The Honor of Your Presence"
What inspired your story?

A few years ago, I was driving my daughter and her friend Tessa home from a cross-country practice, and we got to talking about graphic design—specifically the designing of invitations to events. Tessa's mom is a designer, and I used to design invitations, so Tessa asked, "Why wouldn't you guys just print a few extra copies and go yourselves?" It was a pretty good question. I'd had the same thought decades ago but had never acted on it.

When Tessa asked the question, we were in the darkest part of the pandemic, and there were no galas, no big parties or fundraisers, and I'd been thinking about whether we'd ever go back to those kinds of events. I heard a lot of people openly advocating for never putting on, or going to, another extravaganza again, given the expense, the trouble, the effort and even waste for such ephemeral moments. And as a part-time homebody, I understand that perspective completely. But then again, every so often a gathering casts a spell, time and timidity are suspended, and people fall in love.

Dave Eggers is the founder of *McSweeney's* and the author of *The Eyes and the Impossible, The Circle,* and *A Hologram for the King,* among other books.

Brad Felver, "Orphans"

Is there anything you would like readers to know about your story?

I wrote "Orphans" as sibling to an earlier story of mine, "Queen Elizabeth." That story had stuck with me, which just happens sometimes. I tend to write long stories, and I tend to get attached. But in this case, it felt acute. The undeniable pull of unfinished business. But I also feared undermining that story by asking too much of it. Move on, I told myself. Don't be lazy. Write something new. So, I did. Then one day in 2021, I was reading some Rick Bass—a sensible way to wait out a pandemic, I've found—and I noticed that he revisited characters from previous stories. He did it so naturally, so confidently, so expertly. Of course he did. In fact, lots of my favorite writers revisited old characters in startling and clever ways: Marilynne Robinson, Paul Harding, Per Petterson, Jim Harrison. None of these stories cheapened the originals. On the contrary. I realize now that I'd been waiting for some permission slip, and this was it. There was more story inside of me, and I needed to get it out. Stop being precious, I thought. Just go write the goddamned thing. So, I let myself write it, and here we are, with my thanks to David Leavitt and Amor Towles. Now, as I write these words on a cold morning in November 2023, I'm procrastinating on the third story in the cycle. And with that, I'm off to go write the goddamned thing.

Brad Felver is a fiction writer, essayist, and teacher of writing. His debut collection of stories, *The Dogs of Detroit,* won the Drue Heinz Literature Prize and was a finalist for the Ohioana Book Award. His stories have appeared widely in magazines such as *One Story, New England Review, Subtropics, Colorado Review,* and many others. "Orphans" is a companion piece to his story "Queen Elizabeth," which was included in *The O. Henry Prize Stories 2018*. He lives in Ohio with his wife and two sons.

Madeline ffitch, "Seeing Through Maps"
What inspired your story?

My story was inspired by the time I was chopping wood at dusk and my cat jumped up on the chopping block and peed. It was chilling. I thought about my friends and neighbors from many traditions who, if they saw an animal act like that, would respect that sign and immediately stop work for the day. On the other hand, I am the inheritor of a Protestant work ethic that can sometimes obscure all the impulses surrounding me. Then I began to think about other animal behaviors, such as a fox pooping while making eye contact with you in a place humans aren't really meant to be. Then I began to think about the appetite so many in the literary world have for causality. Something as recent in the history of storytelling as the advent of Western psychoanalysis has worked its way into many writers' sense of causality in a way that is nearly invisible because it is so complete. I wanted to take the smugness out of causality and instead wonder what makes things happen and what motivates our behavior in an unsettled way. Then I put that together with images and relationships that moved me, and the depth of human inconsistency, self-delusion, and love.

Madeline ffitch is the author of the story collection *Valparaiso, Round the Horn* and the novel *Stay and Fight,* which was a finalist for the PEN/Hemingway Award, the Lambda Literary Award for Lesbian Fiction, and the Washington State Book Award, and was named an Ohio Great Reads from Great Places book for the 2023 National Book Festival. Her work has appeared in *The Paris Review, Granta,* and *Tin House.*

Francisco González, "Serranos"
Is there anything you would like readers to know about your story?

"Serranos" took over a year—and thirty distinct drafts—to reach its final form. The evolving story peaked at fifteen thousand words but settled in the six-thousand-word range. Mostly, its slimming was achieved through the removal of extensive flashbacks, the condensation of dialogue, and the merging of certain characters into a communal voice.

Francisco González is a Wallace Stegner fellow at Stanford University and a Steinbeck fellow at San José State University. His fiction has appeared in *Gulf Coast, McSweeney's Quarterly Concern, The Southern Review, ZYZZYVA, The Best Short Stories 2022: The O. Henry Prize Winners,* and elsewhere. He holds an MFA from Columbia University.

Allegra Goodman, "The Last Grownup"
What inspired your story?

"The Last Grownup" is part of a story cycle about a family. I have written from the point of view of Richard, an attorney going through a divorce. I have also written from the point of view of Richard's young daughter, Lily; his elderly mother, Sylvia; even his aunts, Jeanne and Helen. Here I adopt the perspective of Richard's ex-wife, Debra. Newly divorced, Debra is relieved and at the same time wistful. She is happy that her husband is moving on, and at the same time surprised and somewhat hurt by just how quickly and how joyfully he is starting over. I wanted to do justice to Debra's complicated emotions—and to explore the ambivalence we sometimes feel when hearing other people's good news.

Allegra Goodman's novels include *Sam, The Chalk Artist, The Cookbook Collector, Intuition,* and *Kaaterskill Falls.* She has written two collections of stories, *The Family Markowitz* and *Total Immersion.* She is the winner of the Whiting Award for Fiction and a Radcliffe Fellowship in fiction. Her new novel, *Isola,* will be published in 2025.

Allegra Hyde, "Mobilization"
Did you know how your story would end at its inception?

I knew the ending of "Mobilization" would involve a shift in time—specifically a fast-forward through it. My goal was to use this temporal shift to connect the scope of geologic time with the more recognizable pace of human life that takes place earlier in the story. One of my preoccupations as a writer is finding ways to capture the (sur)reality of the Anthropocene: an epoch defined by many small human decisions, as well as massive planetary changes. In "Mobilization," the vast RV herd that narrates the story ends up stranded in Galveston, Texas, when the world's oil runs out; via the acceleration into the future, we see the RVs and their occupants decay as organic matter and become fossil fuels themselves. If I discovered a surprise upon reaching the end of this story, it was the emotional tenor of ecstatic giddiness. For all the horror of climate change, there is also something awe-inspiring about the inevitability and power of natural processes.

Allegra Hyde is the author of the story collection *The Last Catastrophe,* which was an Editors' Choice selection at *The New York Times*. Her debut novel *Eleutheria* was named a Best Book of 2022 by *The New Yorker* and short-listed for the VCU Cabell First Novelist Award. Her first story collection, *Of This New World,* won the John Simmons Short Fiction Award. She teaches creative writing at Oberlin College.

Caroline Kim, "Hiding Spot"

Do you consider your story to be personal or political?

Both. In fact, for me, this story is about how there really is no division between the two. We're in constant tension between who we are and the context we live in. I find that fascinating. Organically, how we think or act in any given moment is based on who we are as atoms, synapses, hormones, past experiences, etc., interacting within and against a specific environment at a specific time. And, something more, though I don't know what to call it. A hint of magic.

In "Hiding Spot," Mrs. Lee moves through her day, struggling to retain her sense of self as she inhabits constantly changing contexts, all requiring different parts of her to come to the fore, different parts of her identity: Korean, survivor of war, immigrant, mother, woman, human being. And, yet, no one part or identity ever stands alone; they mill about together, comfortably or uncomfortably, depending on the situation. Everything, everywhere, all at once, indeed.

Caroline Kim is the author of a collection of short stories, *The Prince of Mournful Thoughts and Other Stories,* which won the 2020 Drue Heinz Literature Prize, was a finalist for a Northern California Book Award and the Janet Heidinger Kafka Prize, and was long-listed for the PEN/Robert W. Bingham Prize and the Story Prize. Her work has appeared or is forthcoming in publications such as *The Georgia Review, Story, New England Review, The Rumpus, Literary Hub, The Michigan Review,* and *TriQuarterly,* among others.

Juliana Leite, "My Good Friend"
What inspired your story?

I'm interested in stories that gently erase the boundaries between love and friendship, featuring characters who shuffle the two feelings in unexpected ways. This has been the object of my research for some time now, both in art (have you heard about the delightful story of loving friendship between Simone de Beauvoir and her childhood friend Zaza?) and in everyday people's lives. I think it is beautiful to observe the maneuverings around this human experience that is both common and complex, of coming face-to-face with love within a friendship, dealing with the astonishment of this mixture of feelings. Even when friendship drives most of the gestures, as in "My Good Friend," it's interesting to witness how the lexicon of romance ultimately imposes itself and sets the stage for a very particular sense of intimacy, navigating contradictions. It's the lexicon and the shared memory that can calmly confirm it's true; there's also love amongst friends in all its strength.

"My Good Friend" also looks at friendship from a perspective that is very close to my heart: that of the elderly. It seems to me that age can provide a certain benevolent understanding that the border between feelings is just an invention, a social agreement to which the heart doesn't always surrender. It is precisely in the freedom and beauty of ambiguous feelings that the relationship between the two good friends in the story exists, people who have crafted their own unique meaning of loyalty. For these two old folks, friendship is the mountain humans can climb to reach a wider viewpoint on love.

Juliana Leite is a writer of novels and short stories who lives in Brazil.

Zoë Perry's translations of contemporary Brazilian literature have appeared in *The New Yorker, Granta, The Paris Review, The New York Times,* and *The White Review.* Her translation of Ana Paula Maia's novel *Of Cattle and Men* (Charco, 2023) won the inaugural Cercador Prize, and she was awarded a PEN/Heim grant for her translation of *Opisanie świata,* by Veronica Stigger. She was selected for a Banff International Translation Centre residency for her translation of Emilio Fraia's *Sevastopol* (New Directions/Lolli, 2021).

Michele Mari, "The Soccer Balls of Mr. Kurz"
What inspired your story?

A real experience at a summer boarding school, when I was the same age as the protagonists. When we played soccer, the ball would often end up beyond the barrier that separated us from the railway tracks, and it would then stay there waiting to be hit by a train. I took inspiration from that agonizing situation to invent Mr. Kurz, the thief-collector of soccer balls.

Michele Mari, who was born in 1955 in Milan, is one of Italy's most celebrated contemporary writers. He has published over a dozen works of fiction, including the novel *Verdigris* and the short story collection *You, Bleeding Childhood,* both of which were published in English translation by And Other Stories. In addition to fiction, Mari has published collections of poetry, essays, and comics, and he has translated classic works by Herman Melville, George Orwell, John Steinbeck, and H. G. Wells, among other authors. A former professor of Italian literature at the University of Milan, Mari has won numerous literary prizes for his books, including the Bagutta Prize and the Mondello Prize, and his short stories have appeared in *The New Yorker, American Short Fiction,* and elsewhere.

Brian Robert Moore is a literary translator from New York. His translations from the Italian include the novels *A Silence Shared* by Lalla Romano, *Meeting in Positano* by Goliarda Sapienza, and *Verdigris* by Michele Mari, as well as Mari's story collection *You, Bleeding Childhood.* He is the recipient of fellowships and awards from the National Endowment for the Arts, PEN America, and the Santa Maddalena Foundation, among other institutions, and his translations of Michele Mari have received two PEN Translates awards. His shorter translations of prose and poetry have appeared in *The New Yorker, The Nation, n+1, McSweeney's Quarterly Concern,* and elsewhere.

E. K. Ota, "The Paper Artist"
Did you know how your story would end at its inception?

In some ways, I always knew how "The Paper Artist" would end. Before I started writing, for years I had carried around the image of an old man living in Kyoto whose life is altered by the appearance of a young girl. I didn't know the particulars of their relationship, though there was a depth between them that could only come from kinship. What had brought these two together? What contributed to the loneliness that haunted them—the grief that was also somehow limned with wonder? For a long time, I considered these questions, and then one day I sat down to write this story to see if I could come to a place of understanding. So yes, you could say that I wrote the story with the end in mind—the meeting of the old man and the girl—but the image that I started out with was merely an image, the vague outlines of the form before it became flesh. I knew that the two would meet and it would change their lives, but I didn't know what their meeting meant, and so it was exciting to write until the initial vision gave way to revelation.

E. K. Ota was born in Southern California and received her BA from Middlebury College and MFA from Emerson College. She was a 2018 Mass Cultural Council artist fellow and a recipient of the St. Botolph Club Foundation Emerging Artist Award in 2019. Her stories have been published in *Ploughshares, ZYZZYVA,* and *Narrative,* among other journals. Currently, she lives in Japan and is at work on a short story collection.

Robin Romm, "Marital Problems"
Did you know how your story would end at its inception?

I never know how a story will end when I begin it. I rarely know much about the story, actually. I write stories to find out what happens, to work my way through an imagined scenario. I try to amuse and surprise myself, and I hope that, in the end, if I succeed, the reader will have the same experience.

This story actually ended with a different line that more explicitly spelled out the character's final set of feelings, but the *Sewanee Review* editors wisely cut it, allowing for a gentler and more resonant close.

Robin Romm is the author of a memoir, *The Mercy Papers* (a *New York Times* Notable Book), and two story collections, *The Mother*

Garden and *Radical Empathy*. She also spearheaded/edited the essay anthology *Double Bind: Women on Ambition*. Her nonfiction has appeared in *The New York Times Book Review; The New York Times; The Atlantic; O, The Oprah Magazine; Wired;* and *Slate*. She lives in Portland, Oregon, with her family.

Katherine D. Stutzman, "Junior"

What details or characters did you leave on the cutting-room floor?

My process for revising stories often involves writing lots and lots of drafts. Even though each draft may not be very different from the one immediately before or after it, the story has often changed substantially between the first draft and the final one. The earliest drafts of "Junior" contained a lot of backstory about the childhood and young adulthood of Junior's father. I was interested in the way memories and information are lost with the death of a parent, particularly a parent as uncommunicative as Henry Sr.

As I worked, however, that backstory began to fall away. Although the narration remained in third person, the perspective moved closer to Junior with each successive draft. I liked the way the closer perspective emphasized the sense of isolation and confinement. Eventually there was no room in the story for experiences that weren't his or information that he didn't know. Although those details were no longer part of the story, they continued to inform my understanding of the characters and the relationship between Junior and his father.

Katherine D. Stutzman's stories have appeared in *Harvard Review, Ascent,* and *Passages North,* among other journals. Her work has been supported by fellowships from the Virginia Center for the Creative Arts and the Lacawac Sanctuary. She lives in Philadelphia, where she is a proud member of the Backyard Writers Workshop.

Jess Walter, "The Dark"

Did you know how your story would end at its inception?

I almost never know what will happen at the end of a story, but early in the writing process I start to imagine how the ending should *feel*. With "The Dark," I pictured the humor and the grief intersecting, the way tears sometimes give way to laughter. I wanted to reveal that this wasn't a story about Doug getting over his wife's death so much as feeling her presence once more, in this very unlikely way.

Jess Walter is the author of ten books, most recently the 2022 story collection *The Angel of Rome* and the 2020 bestselling novel *The Cold Millions*. Among his other books are *Beautiful Ruins* (2012), a number one *New York Times* bestseller; *The Zero* (2006), a National Book Award finalist; and *Citizen Vince* (2005), winner of the Edgar Award. His books have been published in thirty-four languages, and his stories have appeared three times in *The Best American Short Stories*. He lives in his hometown, Spokane, Washington.

Publisher's Note

A Brief History of the O. Henry Prize

Many readers have come to love the short story through the simple characters, the humor and easy narrative voice, and the compelling plotting in the work of William Sydney Porter (1862–1910), best known as O. Henry. His surprise endings entertain readers, including those back for a second, third, or fourth look. Even now one can say "Gift of the Magi" in conversation about a friendship or marriage, and many people around the world will know they are referring to the generosity and selflessness of love.

O. Henry was a newspaperman, skilled at hiding from his editors at deadline. He spent his childhood in Greensboro, North Carolina; his adolescence in Texas; and his later years in New York City. In between Texas and New York, he was caught embezzling and hid from the law in Honduras, where he coined the phrase "banana republic." On learning his wife was dying, he returned home to her and to their daughter, and subsequently served a three-year prison sentence for bank fraud in Columbus, Ohio. Accounts of the origin of his pen name vary: one story dates from his days in Austin, where he was said to call to the wandering family cat, "Oh! Henry!"; another states that the name was inspired by the captain of the guard at the Ohio State Penitentiary, Orrin

Henry. In 1909, Porter told *The New York Times,* "[A friend] suggested that we get a newspaper and pick a name from the first list of notables that we found in it. In the society columns we found the account of a fashionable ball. . . . We looked down the list and my eye lighted on the name Henry. 'That'll do for a last name,' said I. 'Now for a first name. I want something short.' 'Why don't you use a plain initial letter, then?' asked my friend. 'Good,' said I, 'O is about the easiest letter written, and O it is.'"

Porter had devoted friends, and it's not hard to see why. He was charming and had an attractively gallant attitude. He drank too much and neglected his health, which caused his friends concern. He was often short of money; in a letter to a friend asking for a loan of $15 (his banker was out of town, he wrote), Porter added a postscript: "If it isn't convenient, I'll love you just the same." His banker was unavailable most of Porter's life. His sense of humor was always with him.

Reportedly, Porter's last words were from a popular song: "Turn up the light, for I don't want to go home in the dark."

After his death, O. Henry's stories continued to penetrate twentieth-century popular culture. Marilyn Monroe starred in a film adaptation of "The Cop and the Anthem." The popular western TV series *The Cisco Kid* grew out of "The Caballero's Way." Postage stamps were issued by the Soviets to commemorate O. Henry's one hundredth birthday in 1962 and by the United States in 2012 for his one hundred fiftieth. The most lasting legacy began just eight years after O. Henry's death, in April 1918, when the Twilight Club (founded in 1883 and later known as the Society of Arts and Sciences) held a dinner in his honor at the Hotel McAlpin in New York City. His friends remembered him so enthusiastically that a group of them met at the Biltmore Hotel in December of that year to establish some kind of memorial to him. They decided to award annual prizes in his name for short story writers, and they formed a committee to read the short stories published in a year and a smaller group to pick the winners.

In the words of the first series editor, Blanche Colton Williams (1879–1944), the memorial was intended to "strengthen the art of the short story and to stimulate younger authors."

Doubleday, Page & Company was chosen to publish the first volume, *O. Henry Memorial Award Prize Stories 1919*. In 1927, the society sold all rights to the annual collection to Doubleday, Doran & Company. Doubleday published *The O. Henry Prize Stories,* as it came to be known, in hardcover, and from 1984 to 1996 its subsidiary, Anchor Books, published it simultaneously in paperback. Since 1997, *The O. Henry Prize Stories* was published annually as an Anchor Books paperback. It is now published by Vintage Books as *The Best Short Stories: The O. Henry Prize Winners*.

How the Stories Are Chosen

The guest editor chooses the twenty O. Henry Prize winners from a large pool of stories passed to him by the series editor. Stories published in magazines and online are eligible for inclusion in *The Best Short Stories: The O. Henry Prize Winners*. Stories may be written in English or translated into English. Sections of novels are not considered. Editors are asked to send all fiction they publish and not to nominate individual stories. Stories should not be submitted by agents or writers.

The goal of *The Best Short Stories: The O. Henry Prize Winners* remains to strengthen and add visibility to the art of the short story.

The stories selected were originally published between September 2022 and September 2023.

Afterword

If you read Amor Towles's selection of twenty brilliantly surprising stories in the precise order in which he positioned them, you will realize that he has presented us with a surprise of his own: an arrangement of individual stories that together have something of the momentum, shape, and thematic power of a novel.

He explains:

> I have arranged the twenty stories in two "parts." In the first part, there are ten stories that move roughly through the chronology of life. Starting with stories focused on children, then young adults, young couples, married couples, divorcees, grandparents, and finally widows and widowers—with the attendant issues of each phase of life. The second part repeats the chronology—starting again with children and working through adulthood to widowerhood. By repeating the chronology, the reader will hopefully have that sense of life repeating itself over and over.

Towles has given us a magnificently curated anthology that reflects his unique vision and exquisite taste, showcasing some of the best practitioners of the short story art form working today. As he told us in his introduction, he believes that the element of surprise is what distinguishes the short story from the novel and makes the best short stories indelible. The surprises in these stories are conjured in character revelations and vivid images—a couple driving through snow in a car with a stranger and their cat, a band of RVs in the desert, a canoe drifting on a lake under the stars, a greenhouse full of soccer balls—rather than through the kind of startling plot twists that O. Henry himself was known for.

The methods by which the best stories surprise us have changed a lot since the days when O. Henry was alive and writing his own immensely popular stories. (Perhaps today only Stephen King continues to convincingly pull off short fiction in the tradition of O. Henry's surprise twist endings.) In a recording that was made on an Edison cylinder sometime between 1905 and the writer's death in 1910 and included on the vinyl record *The Golden Age of Opera: Great Personalities, 1888–1940*, O. Henry offered an explanation of his famous technique that seems both misleadingly straightforward and overly modest:

> *This is William Sydney Porter speaking, better known to you, no doubt, as O. Henry. I'm going to let you in on a few of my secrets in writing a short story. The most important thing, at least in my humble opinion, is to use characters you've crossed in your lifetime. Truth is indeed stranger than fiction. All of my stories are actual experiences that I have come across during my travels. My characters are facsimiles of actual people I've known. Most authors spend hours, I'm told even days, laboring over outlines of stories that they have in their minds. But not I. In my way of thinking that's a waste of good time. I just sit down and let my pencil do the rest. Many people ask me how I manage to get that final little twist in my stories. I always tell them that the unusual is the ordinary*

rather than the unexpected. And if you people listening
to me now start thinking about your own lives, I'm sure
you'll discover just as many odd experiences as I've had.
I hope this little talk will be heard long after I'm gone.
I want you all to continue reading my stories then too.
Goodbye, folks.

O. Henry pops onto the recording like a playful ghost. Was he
aware at the time of his impending death? His autobiographical
interview with himself in *The New York Times* in 1905 is equally
puckish and haunting. What strikes me in these transcripts is how
O. Henry never divulges his deepest secret, which only came to
be known after his death: that he had been arrested for embezzle-
ment, fled, and returned to spend more than three years in prison.
Louis Menand suggests in *The New Yorker* that O. Henry's startling endings were inspired by the secret of his own surprising
past, which he kept carefully concealed. Similarly, his claim in
that audio recording that he was merely and simply transcribing
his own ordinary observations and experiences in his stories is a
cover for the ingenious narrative inventiveness with which he reli-
ably entertained millions.

Although we may not read O. Henry's stories as often as we
once did, his spirit of literary surprise lives on in different form
in the honorees of the prize his friends created in his honor. In
the "Writers on Their Work" section, this year's winning writers
offer us peeks into their processes, their inspirations, what Nabo-
kov called "the throbs" of a story. But the true secrets of a writer,
like those of O. Henry, may remain more deeply buried. What
is unusual and surprising in a contemporary short story is more
likely to be the manner of its writing, the spell that it casts upon
the ordinary. *The unusual is the ordinary rather than the unexpected.*
Through these stories, we are allowed glimpses into the minds,
lives, and relationships of ordinary people. We are living in a
moment when it is crucial to be able to imagine the souls of our

fellow human beings, to see past their curated social media perso-
nas, their filtered self-portraits, and their polarized allegiances—to
part the curtains on the fleeting, momentary, miraculous sight of
their secret selves that is essential for empathy and human connection.

Thank you to 2024 O. Henry intern Julia Harrison for her brilliant contribution, enthusiastic commitment, and never-ending
love of short stories. To summer intern Meagan Campbell for her
bright insights and phenomenal taste. To the best readers Marion
Minton, Adachioma Ezeano, Sophie Anderson, Emily Burstein,
Bella Butler, Heather Clay, Caroline Hall, and Lisa Stevenson.
To Louis Menand for his piece in *The New Yorker* and to Mike
Springer for his Open Culture piece about the voice recording
in *The Golden Age of Opera* and reference to the Austin History
Center. To the spectacular team at Vintage Books, Diana Secker
Tesdell, Aja Pollock, Eddie Allen, Kate Hughes, and Anna Noone,
and to Kristen Capano and Diane McKiernan at PRH Audio. To
talented agents Jen Marshall and Dorian Karchmar. To Dan, Gus,
Sam, and Leo Quigley. To the inspired writers of these twenty
mysterious and alluring short stories and to their brilliant magazine and journal editors. To the best editor in town, Amor Towles.

—Jenny Minton Quigley

Publications Submitted

Stories published in magazines and online are eligible for inclusion.

For fiction published online, the publication's contact information and the date of the story's publication should accompany the submission.

Stories will be considered from September 1 to August 31 the following year. Publications received after August 31 will automatically be considered for the next volume of *The Best Short Stories: The O. Henry Prize Winners*.

Please submit PDF files of submissions to jenny@ohenryprize winners.com or send hard copies to Jenny Minton Quigley, c/o The O. Henry Prize Winners, 70 Mohawk Drive, West Hartford, CT 06117.

Able Muse
www.ablemuse.com
www.ablemuse.com/submit-what
 -online
Editor: Alexander Pepple
Quarterly

AGNI
www.agnionline.bu.edu
www.bu.edu/dbin/agni/
Editors: Sven Birkerts and William
 Pierce
Biannual (print)

Alaska Quarterly Review
www.aqreview.org
alaskaquarterlyreview.submittable
.com/submit
Editor: Ronald Spatz
Biannual

Amazon Original Stories
www.amazon.com
Submission by invitation only
Editorial Director: Kjersti
Egerdahl
Twelve annually

American Short Fiction
www.americanshortfiction.org
americanshortfiction.submittable
.com/submit
Editors: Rebecca Markovits and
Adeena Reitberger
Triannual

Antipodes
www.wsupress.wayne.edu/journals
/detail/antipodes-0
digitalcommons.wayne.edu
/antipodes/submission
_guidelines.html
Editor: Brenda Machosky
Biannual

Apalachee Review
www.apalacheereview.org
apalacheereview.org/submissions/
Editor in Chief: Rafael Gamero
Annual

Apogee Journal
www.apogeejournal.org
docs.google.com/forms/d/e/1FAIp
QLSe1abTIw7xgxMoI5W5JM
QDQdyXDNXibAPy3cXBN
Rxb_WH6ksg/viewform
Executive Editor: Alexandra
Watson
Biannual

The Arkansas International
www.arkint.org
acwlp.submittable.com/submit
Editor in Chief: Rebecca Gayle
Howell
Biannual

Arkansas Review
www.arkreview.org
mtribbet@astate.edu
Editor: Marcus Tribbett
Triannual

ArLiJo
www.arlijo.com
ArLiJo@myyahoo.com
Editor in Chief: Robert L. Giron
Twelve to twenty issues a year

Ascent
www.readthebestwriting.com
ascent@cord.edu
Editor: Vincent Reusch

The Asian American Literary Review
www.aalrmag.org
editors@aalrmag.org
Editors in Chief: Lawrence-Minh Bùi Davis and Gerald Maa
Biannual

Aster(ix)
www.asterixjournal.com
Solicited submissions only
Editor in Chief: Angie Cruz
Two or three times per year

The Atlantic
www.theatlantic.com
fiction@theatlantic.com
Editor in Chief: Jeffrey Goldberg
Monthly

Baltimore Review
www.baltimorereview.org
baltimorereview.submittable.com /submit
Senior Editor: Barbara Westwood Diehl
Quarterly

The Bare Life Review
www.barelifereview.org
Not currently accepting submissions
Editor: Nyuol Lueth Tong

Bat City Review
www.batcityreview.org
batcityreview.submittable.com /submit
Managing Editor: Sarah Matthes
Annual

Bellevue Literary Review
www.blreview.org
blreview.org/general-submissions/
Editor in Chief: Danielle Ofri
Biannual

Bennington Review
www.benningtonreview.org
benningtonreview.submittable .com/submit
Editor: Michael Dumanis
Biannual

Black Warrior Review
bwr.ua.edu
bwr.submittable.com/submit
Editor: Samantha Bolf
Biannual

BOMB
www.bombmagazine.org
bombmagazine.submittable.com /submit
Editor in Chief: Betsy Sussler
Quarterly

Booth
booth.butler.edu
booth.submittable.com/submit
Editor: Robert Stapleton
Biannual

Boulevard
www.boulevardmagazine.org
boulevard.submittable.com/submit
Editor: Dusty Freund
Triannual

The Briar Cliff Review
www.bcreview.org
No longer accepting submissions
Editor: Tricia Currans-Sheehan
Annual

Cagibi
www.cagibilit.com
cagibilit.submittable.com/submit
Editors: Sylvie Bertrand and
    Christopher X. Shade
Quarterly

CALYX
www.calyxpress.org
www.calyxpress.org/general
    -submissions/
Editors: Elizabeth Brookbank,
    Marjorie Coffey, Emerson
    Craig, Judith Edelstein, Emily
    Elbom, Carole Kalk, Karah
    Kemmerly, Christine Rhea
Biannual

The Carolina Quarterly
www.thecarolinaquarterly.com
thecarolinaquarterly.submittable
    .com/submit
Editor in Chief: Ellie Rambo
Biannual

Carve
www.carvezine.com
Not currently accepting
    submissions
Publisher: Matthew Limpede
Quarterly

Catamaran
www.catamaranliteraryreader.com
catamaranliteraryreader
    .submittable.com/submit
Editor in Chief: Catherine
    Segurson
Quarterly

Cherry Tree
www.washcoll.edu/learn-by-doing
    /lit-house/cherry-tree/
cherrytree.submittable.com/submit
Editor in Chief: James Allen Hall
Annual

Chestnut Review
chestnutreview.com
chestnutreview.submittable.com
    /submit
Editor in Chief: James Rawlings
Quarterly

Chicago Quarterly Review
www.chicagoquarterlyreview.com
chicagoquarterlyreview
    .submittable.com/submit
Senior Editors: S. Afzal Haider and
    Elizabeth McKenzie
Quarterly

Chicago Review
www.chicagoreview.org
chicagoreview.submittable.com
   /submit
Editors: James Garwood-Cole and
   Clara Nizard
Triannual

Cimarron Review
www.cimarronreview.com
cimarronreview.okstate.edu
   /submission/
Editor: Lisa Lewis
Quarterly

The Cincinnati Review
www.cincinnatireview.com
cincinnatireview.com/submissions/
Managing Editor: Lisa Ampleman
Biannual

Cola Literary Review
www.colaliteraryreview.com
colaliteraryreview.submittable
   .com/submit
Senior Editors: G. E. Butler and
   Jacob Walhout
Annual

Colorado Review
coloradoreview.colostate.edu
   /colorado review
coloradoreview.submittable.com
   /Submit
Editor in Chief: Stephanie
   G'Schwind
Triannual

The Common
www.thecommononline.org
thecommon.submittable.com
   /submit
Editor in Chief: Jennifer Acker
Biannual

Confrontation
www.confrontationmagazine.org
English Department
LIU Post
720 Northern Blvd.
Brookville, NY 11548
Editor in Chief: Jonna G. Semeiks
Biannual

Conjunctions
www.conjunctions.com
conjunctions.submittable.com
   /submit
Editor: Bradford Morrow
Biannual

Copper Nickel
www.copper-nickel.org
coppernickel.submittable.com
   /submit
Editor: Wayne Miller
Biannual

Cream City Review
uwm.edu/creamcityreview
creamcityreview.submittable.com
   /submit
Editor in Chief: Camilla Jiyun
   Nam Lee
Biannual

CutBank
www.cutbankonline.org
cutbank.submittable.com/Submit
Editor in Chief: Jenny Rowe
Biannual

The Dalhousie Review
ojs.library.dal.ca/dalhousiereview
Dalhousie.Review@dal.ca
Editor: Anthony Enns
Triannual

Dappled Things
www.dappledthings.org
dappledthings.submittable.com
   /submit
Editor in Chief: Katy Carl
Quarterly

december
decembermag.org
december.submittable.com/submit
Editor/Publisher: Gianna Jacobson
Biannual

Delmarva Review
www.delmarvareview.org
No submissions accepted for
   2023–2024
Executive Editor: Wilson Wyatt Jr.
Annual

Denver Quarterly
www.du.edu/denverquarterly
denverquarterly.submittable.com
   /submit
Editor: W. Scott Howard
Quarterly

Descant
descant.tcu.edu
descant.submittable.com/submit
Editor in Chief: Matt Pitt
Annual

Dracula Beyond Stoker Magazine
www.draculabeyondstoker.com/
submissions@draculabeyondstoker
   .com
Editor: Tucker Christine
Biannual

The Drift
www.thedriftmag.com
fiction@thedriftmag.com
Editors: Kiara Barrow and Rebecca
   Panovka
Triannual

Driftwood Press
www.driftwoodpress.net
driftwoodpress.submittable.com
   /submit
Editors: James McNulty and Jerrod
   Schwarz
Annual

The Dublin Review
thedublinreview.com
enquiry@thedublinreview.com
Editor: Brendan Barrington
Quarterly

Ecotone
ecotonemagazine.org
ecotone.submittable.com/submit
Editor in Chief: David Gessner
Biannual

Electric Literature
electricliterature.com
editors@electricliterature.com
Executive Director: Halimah
    Marcus; Editor in Chief: Denne
    Michele Norris

Epiphany
epiphanyzine.com
epiphanymagazine.submittable
    .com
Editor in Chief: Noreen Tomassi
Biannual

Epoch
www.epochliterary.com
epoch.submittable.com/submit
Editor: J. Robert Lennon
Biannual

Event
www.eventmagazine.ca
eventmagazine.submittable.com
    /submit
Editor: Shashi Bhat
Triannual

Exile Quarterly
www.exilequarterly.com
exilepublishing.submittable.com
    /submit
Editor in Chief: Barry Callaghan
Quarterly

Fairy Tale Review
www.fairytalereview.com
fairytalereview.submittable.com
    /submit/
Editor: Kate Bernheimer
Annual

Fantasy & Science Fiction
www.sfsite.com/fsf/
fandsf.moksha.io/publication/fsf
Editor: Sheree Renée Thomas
Bimonthly

Fence
fenceportal.org
fence.submittable.com/submit
Editorial Co-directors: Emily
    Wallis Hughes and Jason Zuzga
Biannual

Fiction
www.fictioninc.com
submissions.fictioninc.com/
Editor: Mark Jay Mirsky

Fiction River
fictionriver.com
Not currently accepting
    submissions
Editors: Kristine Kathryn Rusch
    and Dean Wesley Smith
Six times a year

The Fiddlehead
thefiddlehead.ca
thefiddlehead.submittable.com
    /submit
Editor: Sue Sinclair
Quarterly

Five Points
fivepoints.gsu.edu
fivepoints.submittable.com/submit
Editor: Megan Sexton
Biannual

The Florida Review
floridareview.cah.ucf.edu
floridareview.submittable.com
    /submit
Editor and Director: David James
    Poissant
Biannual

Foglifter
foglifterjournal.com
foglifter.submittable.com/submit
Editor in Chief: Michal "MJ"
    Jones
Biannual

Fourteen Hills: The SFSU Review
www.14hills.net
fourteenhills.submittable.com
    /submit
Co-editors in Chief: Michaela
    Chairez and Christopher Jones
Annual

Freeman's
www.freemansbiannual.com
No longer accepting submissions
Editor: John Freeman
Biannual

f(r)iction
frictionlit.org
frictionlit.submittable.com/submit
Editor in Chief: Dani Hedlund
Triannual

Gemini Magazine
gemini-magazine.com
submit@gemini-magazine.com
Editor: David Bright
Four to six issues per year

The Georgia Review
thegeorgiareview.com
thegeorgiareview.submittable.com
    /submit
Director and Editor: Gerald Maa
Quarterly

Gold Man Review
www.goldmanreview.org
goldmanpublishing.submittable
    .com/submit
Editor in Chief: Heather
    Cuthbertson
Annual

Grain
grainmagazine.ca
grainmagazine.submittable.com
    /submit
Interim Editor: Elena Bentley
Quarterly

Granta
granta.com
granta.submittable.com/submit
Editor: Sigrid Rausing
Quarterly (print)

The Greensboro Review
greensbororeview.org
greensbororeview.submittable.com
    /submit
Editor: Terry L. Kennedy
Biannual

Guernica
www.guernicamag.com
guernicamagazine.submittable
    .com/submit
Editor in Chief: Jina Moore
    Ngarambe

**Gulf Coast: A Journal of
    Literature and Fine Arts**
www.gulfcoastmag.org
gulfcoastajournalofliterature
    andfinearts.submittable.com
    /submit
Editor: Rosa Boshier González
Biannual

Harper's Magazine
harpers.org
666 Broadway, 11th Floor
New York, NY 10012
Editor: Christopher Carroll
Monthly

Harpur Palate
harpurpalate.binghamton.edu
harpurpalate.submittable.com
    /submit
Editor in Chief: Hannah Carr-
    Murphy
Biannual

Harvard Review
harvardreview.org
harvardreview.submittable.com
    /submit
Editor: Christina Thompson
Biannual

Hayden's Ferry Review
haydensferryreview.com
hfr.submittable.com/submit
Editor: Susan Nguyen
Biannual

Hobart
www.hobartpulp.com
hobartsubmissions@gmail.com
Founding Editor: Aaron Burch;
    Publisher: Elizabeth Ellen

The Hopkins Review
hopkinsreview.com
thehopkinsreview.submittable
    .com/submit
Editor in Chief: Dora Malech
Quarterly

Hotel Amerika
www.hotelamerika.net
hotelamerika.submittable.com
    /submit
Editor: David Lazar
Annual

The Hudson Review
hudsonreview.com
www.hudsonreview.com
    /submissions/
Editor: Paula Deitz
Quarterly

Hunger Mountain
hungermtn.org
hungermtn.submittable.com
    /submit
Editor in Chief: Adam McOmber
Triannual

The Idaho Review
www.idahoreview.org
theidahoreview.submittable.com
    /submit
Editor in Chief: Anna Caritj
Annual

Image
imagejournal.org
Not currently accepting
    submissions
Editor in Chief: James K. A. Smith
Quarterly

Indiana Review
indianareview.org
indianareview.submittable.com
    /submit
Editor in Chief: Yaerim Gen Kwon
Biannual

Into the Void
intothevoidmagazine.com
intothevoidmagazine.submittable
    .com/submit
Editor: Philip Elliot
Quarterly

The Iowa Review
www.iowareview.org
iowareview.submittable.com
    /submit
Editor: Lynne Nugent
Triannual

Iron Horse Literary Review
www.ironhorsereview.com
ironhorse.submittable.com/submit
Editor: Leslie Jill Patterson
Triannual

Jabberwock Review
www.jabberwock.org.msstate.edu
jabberwockreview.submittable
    .com/submit
Editor: Becky Hagenston
Biannual

The Journal
thejournalmag.org
thejournal.submittable.com/submit
Managing Editor: Isaiah Back-
    Gaal
Four times a year

Joyland
joylandmagazine.com
joylandmagazine.submittable
    .com/submit/89567/joyland
    -submissions
Editor in Chief: Michelle Lyn
    King

The Kenyon Review
kenyonreview.org
thekenyonreview.submittable.com
    /submit
Editor: Nicole Terez Dutton;
    Managing Editor: Jackson Saul
Four times a year

**Lady Churchill's Rosebud
    Wristlet**
www.smallbeerpress.com/lcrw
150 Pleasant Street, #306
Easthampton, MA 01027
Editors: Gavin J. Grant and Kelly
    Link
Biannual

Lake Effect
behrend.psu.edu/school-of
    -humanities-social-sciences
    /lake-effect
lakeeffectaninternationalliterary
    journal.submittable.com/submit
Editors: George Looney and Aimee
    Pogson
Annual

Lalitamba
www.lalitamba.com
lalitamba_magazine@yahoo.com
Editor: Shyam Mukanda
Annual

Literary Hub
www.lithub.com
Not accepting fiction submissions
Editor in Chief: Jonny Diamond

The Literary Review
www.theliteraryreview.org
info@theliteraryreview.org
Editor: Minna Zallman Proctor
Quarterly

LitMag
litmag.com
litmag.submittable.com/submit
Editor: Marc Berley
Annual

Little Patuxent Review
littlepatuxentreview.org
littlepatuxentreview.submittable
    .com/submit
Editor: Chelsea Lemon Fetzer
Biannual

The Louisville Review
www.louisvillereview.org
thelouisvillereviewfleur-de-lispress
    .submittable.com/submit
Managing Editor: Amy Foos
    Kapoor
Biannual

MAKE: A Literary Magazine
www.makemag.com
Not currently accepting
    submissions
Managing Editor: Chamandeep
    Bains
Annual

The Malahat Review
www.malahatreview.ca
malahatreview.submittable.com
    /submit
Editor: Iain Higgins
Quarterly

The Massachusetts Review
www.massreview.org
www.massreviewsubmissions.org/
Executive Editor: Jim Hicks
Quarterly

The Masters Review
mastersreview.com
themastersreview.submittable.com
    /submit
Editor in Chief: Cole Meyer
Annual (print)

McSweeney's Quarterly Concern
www.mcsweeneys.net
mcsweeneysquarterly.submittable
    .com/submit
Founding Editor: Dave Eggers
Quarterly

Meridian
readmeridian.org
meridian.submittable.com/submit
Editor in Chief: Coby-Dillon
    English
Annual

Michigan Quarterly Review
michiganquarterlyreview.com
mqr.submittable.com/submit
Editor: Khaled Mattawa
Quarterly

Mid-American Review
casit.bgsu.edu/midamericanreview/
marsubmissions.bgsu.edu
Editor in Chief: Abigail Cloud
Semiannual

Mississippi Review
sites.usm.edu/mississippi-review/
mississippireview.submittable.com
    /submit
Editor in Chief: Adam Clay
Biannual

The Missouri Review
missourireview.com
submissions.missourireview.com
Editor: Speer Morgan
Quarterly

Mizna
mizna.org/articles/journal
mizna.org/journal/submissions/
Executive and Artistic Director:
    Lana Barkawi
Biannual

Mount Hope
www.mounthopemagazine.com
mounthopemagazine.submittable
    .com/submit
Editor: Edward J. Delaney
Annual (print)

n+1
www.nplusonemag.com
submissions@nplusonemag.com
Senior Editors: Lisa Borst, Tess
    Edmonson, Chad Harbach,
    Charles Petersen, and Sarah
    Resnick
Triannual

Narrative
www.narrativemagazine.com
www.narrativemagazine.com
/submission
Editors: Carol Edgarian and Tom
Jenks
Online content published
continually; print edition
published occasionally

NELLE
www.uab.edu/cas
/englishpublications/nelle
nelle.submittable.com/submit
Editor: Lauren Goodwin Slaughter
Annual

New England Review
www.nereview.com
newenglandreview.submittable
.com/submit
Editor: Carolyn Kuebler
Quarterly

New Letters
www.newletters.org
newlettersmagazine.submittable
.com/submit
Editor in Chief: Christie Hodgen
Biannual

New Ohio Review
newohioreview.org
newohioreview.submittable.com
/submit
Editor: David Wanczyk
Biannual

New Orleans Review
www.neworleansreview.org
neworleansreview.submittable
.com/submit/19686/fiction
-ongoing-submissions
Editor: Lindsay Sproul
Biannual

New Pop Lit
newpoplit.com
newpoplit@gmail.com
Editor in Chief: Karl Wenclas

New South
newsouthjournal.wordpress.com
newsouth.submittable.com/submit
Biannual

The New Yorker
www.newyorker.com
fiction@newyorker.com
Editor: David Remnick
Weekly

Nimrod International Journal
nimrod.utulsa.edu
nimrodjournal.submittable.com
/submit
Editor: Eilis O'Neal
Biannual

Ninth Letter
ninthletter.com
ninthletteronline.submittable.com
/submit
Managing Editor: Liz Harms
Biannual

Noon
noonannual.com
c/o Diane Williams
1392 Madison Avenue, PMB 298
New York, NY 10029
Editor: Diane Williams
Annual

The Normal School
www.thenormalschool.com
normalschooleditors@gmail.com
Editor in Chief: Steven Church
Biannual

North American Review
northamericanreview.org
northamericanreview.submittable
.com/submit
Fiction Editor: Grant Tracey
Triannual

North Carolina Literary Review
nclr.ecu.edu
nclr.submittable.com/submit
Editor: Margaret D. Bauer
Triannual

North Dakota Quarterly
ndquarterly.org
ndquarterly.submittable.com
/submit
Editor: William Caraher
Quarterly

Northern New England Review
franklinpierce.edu/nner
northernnewenglandreview
.submittable.com/submit
Editor: Margot Douaihy
Annual

Notre Dame Review
ndreview.nd.edu
notredamereview.submittable.com
/submit
Fiction Editor: Dionne Bremeyer

The Ocean State Review
oceanstatereview.org
oceanstatereview.submittable.com
/submit
Senior Editor: Charles Kell
Annual

The Offing
theoffingmag.com
theoffingmag.submittable.com
/submit
Editor in Chief: Mimi Wong
Ongoing

One Story
one-story.com
one-story.submittable.com
Executive Editor: Hannah Tinti;
    Editor in Chief: Patrick Ryan
Monthly

Orca
orcalit.com
orcaaliteraryjournal.submittable
  .com/submit
Publishers/Senior Editors: Joe
  Ponepinto and Zachary Kellian
Triannual

Orion
www.orionmagazine.org
Not currently accepting fiction
  submissions
Editor in Chief: Sumanth
  Prabhaker
Bimonthly

Outlook Springs
outlooksprings.com
outlooksprings.submittable.com
  /submit
Editor in Chief: Jeremy John
  Parker
Triannual

Overtime
www.workerswritejournal.com
  /overtime.htm
overtime@workerswritejournal
  .com
Editor: David LaBounty
Triannual

Oxford American
www.oxfordamerican.org
oxfordamerican.submittable.com
  /submit
Editor: Danielle Amir Jackson
Quarterly

The Paris Review
www.theparisreview.org
theparisreview.submittable.com
  /submit
Editor: Emily Stokes
Quarterly

Passages North
www.passagesnorth.com
passagesnorth.submittable.com
  /submit
Editor in Chief: Jennifer A.
  Howard
Annual

Pembroke Magazine
pembrokemagazine.com
pembrokemagazine.submittable
  .com/submit
Editor: Peter Grimes
Annual

The Pinch
www.pinchjournal.com
pinchjournal.submittable.com
  /submit
Editor in Chief: Courtney Miller
  Santo
Biannual

Pleiades
pleiadesmag.com
www.pleiadessubmissions.com
Editor: Jenny Molberg
Biannual

Ploughshares
www.pshares.org
Emerson College
120 Boylston St.
Boston, MA 02116-4624
Editor in Chief: Ladette Randolph
Triannual

Post Road
www.postroadmag.com
postroadmagazine.submittable
    .com/submit
Managing Editor: Chris Boucher
Biannual

Potomac Review
mcblogs.montgomerycollege.edu
    /potomacreview/
potomacreview.submittable.com
    /submit
Editor: Albert Kapikian
Biannual

Prairie Fire
www.prairiefire.ca
Prairie Fire Press Inc.
423–100 Arthur Street
Winnipeg, Manitoba R3B 1H3
Editor: Carolyn Gray
Quarterly

Prairie Schooner
prairieschooner.unl.edu
prairieschooner.submittable.com
    /submit
Editor in Chief: Kwame Dawes
Quarterly

PRISM international
prismmagazine.ca
prisminternational.submittable
    .com/submit
Prose Editor: Natasha Gauthier
Quarterly

A Public Space
apublicspace.org
apublicspacedemo.submittable
    .com/submit
Editor: Brigid Hughes
Quarterly

PULP Literature
pulpliterature.com
docs.google.com/forms/d/e/1FAIp
    QLScGor2WqAXCA1FwKUu2
    gKGcsV88ubFbFyxtx9zsOsecw
    uQnUw/closedform
Editor in Chief: Jennifer Landels
Quarterly

Raritan
raritanquarterly.rutgers.edu
rqr@sas.rutgers.edu
Editor in Chief: Jackson Lears
Quarterly

Redivider
redivider.emerson.edu
redivider.submittable.com/submit
Editor in Chief: Katie Mihalek
Biannual

River Styx
www.riverstyx.org
www.riverstyx.org/pages
    /submissions
Managing Editor: Bryan Castille
Three or four times per year

Room
roommagazine.com
room.submittable.com/submit
Managing Editor: Shristi Uprety
Quarterly

The Rumpus
therumpus.net
therumpus.submittable.com
    /submit
Editor in Chief: Aram Mrjoian

Salamander
salamandermag.org
salamandermag.org/submit/
Editor in Chief: José Angel Araguz
Biannual

Salmagundi
salmagundi.skidmore.edu
Skidmore College
815 N Broadway
Saratoga Springs, NY 12866
Editor in Chief: Robert Boyers
Quarterly

Saranac Review
saranacreview.org
saranacreview.submittable.com
    /submit
Executive Editor: Sara Schaff
Annual

The Saturday Evening Post
www.saturdayeveningpost.com
editors@saturdayeveningpost.com
Editor: Patrick Perry
Six times a year

Short Story Day Africa
shortstorydayafrica.org
info@shortstorydayafrica.org
Executive Editor: Rachel Zadok

The Southampton Review
www.thesouthamptonreview.com
thesouthamptonreview
    .submittable.com/submit
Executive Editor: Lou Ann Walker
Biannual

The South Carolina Review
www.clemson.edu/caah/sites
    /south-carolina-review/index
    .html
thesouthcarolinareview
    .submittable.com/submit
Editor: Keith Morris
Biannual

South Dakota Review
southdakotareview.com
southdakotareview.submittable
    .com/Submit
Editor in Chief: Lee Ann
    Roripaugh
Quarterly

The Southeast Review
www.southeastreview.org
southeastreview.submittable.com
/submit
Editor in Chief: Laura Biagi
Biannual

Southern Humanities Review
www.southernhumanitiesreview
.com
southernhumanitiesreview
.submittable.com/submit
Editors in Chief: Anton DiSclafani
and Rose McLarney
Quarterly

Southern Indiana Review
www.usi.edu/sir
southernindianareview
.submittable.com/submit
Editor: Ron Mitchell
Biannual

The Southern Review
thesouthernreview.org
submissions.thesouthernreview.org
Editors: Jessica Faust and Sacha
Idell
Quarterly

Southwest Review
southwestreview.com
southwestreview.submittable.com
/submit
Editor: Greg Brownderville
Quarterly

St. Anthony Messenger
www.franciscanmedia.org/st
-anthony-messenger/
MagazineEditors@
FranciscanMedia.org
Executive Editors: Christopher
Heffron and Susan Hines-
Brigger
Monthly

The Stinging Fly
stingingfly.org
stingingfly.submittable.com/submit
Publisher: Declan Meade
Biannual

Story
www.storymagazine.org
www.storymagazine.org
/submissions/
Editor: Michael Nye
Triannual

StoryQuarterly
storyquarterly.camden.rutgers.edu
storyquarterly.submittable.com
/submit
Editor: Paul Lisicky
Quarterly

subTerrain
www.subterrain.ca
subterrain.submittable.com/submit
Editor: Brian Kaufman
Triannual

Subtropics
subtropics.english.ufl.edu
subtropics.submittable.com/submit
Editor: David Leavitt
Biannual

The Sun
thesunmagazine.org
thesunmagazine.submittable.com
Editor and Publisher: Rob Bowers
Monthly

Swamp Pink
swamp-pink.cofc.edu
swamppink.submittable.com
    /submit
Fiction Editor: Anthony Varallo
Semi-monthly

Taco Bell Quarterly
tacobellquarterly.org
tacobellquarterly.submittable.com
    /submit
Editor in Chief: M. M. Carrigan
It comes out when we feel like it

Tahoma Literary Review
tahomaliteraryreview.com
tahomaliteraryreview.submittable
    .com/submit
Fiction Editor: Leanne Dunic
Biannual

Third Coast
thirdcoastmagazine.com
thirdcoastmagazine.submittable
    .com/submit
Editor in Chief: Amanda Scott
Biannual

The Threepenny Review
www.threepennyreview.com
www.threepennyreview.com
    /online_submissions/
Editor: Wendy Lesser
Quarterly

Virginia Quarterly Review
www.vqronline.org
virginiaquarterlyreview
    .submittable.com/submit
Editor: Paul Reyes
Quarterly

Washington Square Review
www.washingtonsquarereview.com
washingtonsquare.submittable
    .com/submit
Editor in Chief: Joanna Yas
Biannual

Water-Stone Review
waterstonereview.com
waterstonereview.com/submissions/
Editor: Meghan Maloney-Vinz
Annual

Weber
www.weber.edu/weberjournal
weberjournal@weber.edu
Editor: Michael Wutz
Biannual

West Branch
westbranch.blogs.bucknell.edu
westbranchsubmissions.bucknell
    .edu/
Editor: Joe Scapellato
Triannual

Western Humanities Review
www.westernhumanitiesreview
   .com
whr.submittable.com/submit
Editor: Michael Mejia
Triannual

The White Review
www.thewhitereview.org
www.thewhitereview.org
   /submissions/
Editors: Rosanna Mclaughlin,
   Izabella Scott, Skye Arundhati
   Thomas
Triannual

Willow Springs
www.willowspringsmagazine.org
willowsprings.submittable.com
   /submit
Editor: Polly Buckingham
Biannual

Witness
witness.blackmountaininstitute.org
witnessmagazine.submittable.com
   /submit
Editor in Chief: Xueyi Zhou
Biannual

The Worcester Review
www.theworcesterreview.org
theworcesterreview.submittable
   .com/submit
Editor: Carolyn Oliver
Annual

Workers Write!
www.workerswritejournal.com
info@workerswritejournal.com
Editor: David LaBounty
Annual

World Literature Today
www.worldliteraturetoday.org
worldliteraturetoday.submittable
   .com/submit
Editor in Chief: Daniel Simon
Bimonthly

X-R-A-Y
xraylitmag.com
xray.submittable.com/submit
Editor: Jennifer Greidus

The Yale Review
yalereview.org
theyalereview.submittable.com
   /submit
Editor: Meghan O'Rourke
Quarterly

Yellow Medicine Review
www.yellowmedicinereview.com
editor@yellowmedicinereview.com
Executive Editor: Judy Wilson
Semiannual

Zoetrope: All-Story
www.all-story.com
Not currently accepting
   submissions
Editor: Michael Ray
Quarterly

Zone 3
www.zone3press.com
zone3press.submittable.com
    /submit
Fiction Editor: R. S. Deeren
Biannual

ZYZZYVA
www.zyzzyva.org
57 Post Street, Suite 708
San Francisco, CA 94104
Editor: Oscar Villalon
Triannual

Permissions